This
It m

THE STANFORD LASSES

Isaac Stanford lives in the Yorkshire town of Cottenly with his wife Emily and their three daughters – known locally as the Stanford Lasses. Alice, the eldest, lives for work and chapel, Lizzie is content with her job making umbrellas – until she falls in love – and headstrong Ruth is intent upon marrying a handsome charmer, despite warnings from friends and family. Damaged by a traumatic childhood, Alice struggles to lead a normal life, while war threatens all Lizzie holds dear and Ruth realises she has made a terrible mistake. As time passes, each sister has to confront her greatest challenge...

THE STANFORD LASSES

THE STANFORD LASSES

by

Glenice Crossland

Magna Large Print Books
Long Preston, North Yorkshire,
BD23 4ND, England.

British Library Cataloguing in Publication Data.

Crossland, Glenice
    The Stanford lasses.

    A catalogue record of this book is
    available from the British Library

    ISBN   978-0-7505-2711-8

First published in Great Britain in 2006 by William Heinemann

Published in Large Print 2007 by arrangement with
William Heinemann, one of the publishers in The Random House Group Ltd.

Magna Large Print is an imprint of Library Magna Books Ltd.

Printed and bound in Great Britain by
T.J. (International) Ltd., Cornwall, PL28 8RW

*For my husband, with love and apologies
for all the hours spent with* The Stanford Lasses.
*Also for my son, Peter, for Elizabeth, Joseph, Adele,
Stephen, Liam and Sadie. Love you all.*

With thanks to Georgina Hawtrey-Woore,
without her this book would never have seen
the light of day.

Chapter One

'I'm going to tell our dad on thee, our Lizzie.'

'Don't you dare.' Lizzie brushed her hair vigorously, counting subconsciously with every stroke. '...eighty-eight, eighty-nine...'

Young Ruth paused from straightening the feathers on Lizzie's brown felt hat, to stick out her tongue at Alice. 'Just like you to tell tales,' she said, glaring at her eldest sister.

'I don't tell tales, except when I've good reason to, and when it's for our Lizzie's own good. She'll end up in trouble if she's not careful.'

'No I won't. I only want a bit of fun, that's all. It's only once in a blue moon I ask to stop at Annie's for the night. Our dad wouldn't let me stay to the end otherwise.' Lizzie couldn't help thinking what a sanctimonious old misery their Alice was sometimes.

'You're just jealous,' Ruth said, glowering, 'because nobody ever asks you to go anywhere.'

Alice coloured. 'No I'm not, and if they did, I wouldn't dream of telling lies.'

'I'm not really telling lies.' Lizzie flushed. 'I just said I was going with Annie Hampshire and staying at her house for the night. That's the truth. It's just that her dad won't make us be in by half past nine. Why, it isn't worth going at all if I've to leave at nine. The dancing will only just be starting by then.'

'But tha didn't mention that tha'll be going with George Crossman as well.'

'No, but there again, nobody asked me, so I didn't lie.' Lizzie glared at Alice, becoming more and more exasperated. 'Oh, come on, Alice,' she pleaded. 'It isn't many people from our end of Cottenly who receive an invitation to the Hall, and it is a special occasion. It isn't every day they throw a dinner dance to celebrate a new reservoir.'

'And that's another thing. There'll be all those loud-mouthed contractors there as well, not at all fit company for two innocent girls. Half past nine would be quite late enough.'

Lizzie couldn't help but giggle at hearing herself described as innocent. Not that she had let George do anything really bad, but she wondered what Alice would say if she knew how George made her feel when he kissed her on a Sunday evening on the way home from chapel. Sometimes she even wished he would do something other than kiss her, but George respected her far too much to attempt anything like that.

'I won't be with the contractors, I shall be with George. Besides, Annie knows all the contractors by name. After all, she does work at the Hall – that's why she's been invited.' Lizzie wondered if Alice was jealous because Annie hadn't given her one of the tickets. But no, Alice wasn't interested in that sort of thing. A social at the chapel was much more in her line.

'Annie's sister told me all about working at the Hall,' young Ruth piped up. 'All about the food they serve in silver dishes – hams and salmon, and a pig's head set out on a tray for fancy. She says they can eat all the leftovers and take some home on their days off. I wouldn't mind working somewhere like that, except that poor Annie has to empty thirty po's every morning and she says that when the contractors have been on the beer, they're absolutely full to the brim, sometimes with sick an' all.'

'Ruth, shut up,' Alice demanded, causing Ruth to stick out her tongue once again.

'Anyway, I'm going to bed. I don't want black under my eyes for the big night, and we've to be up at half past five, don't forget.' Lizzie went to the clothes closet for the umpteenth time and peered in, admiring the dress hanging there.

Ruth skipped around the large iron bed and stood beside her. 'Oh, Lizzie, it is lovely. You're going to look beautiful, I know you are.'

Lizzie closed the door reluctantly. She could stand admiring the dress all night. Not that it was completely new – nobody ever had brand new except Alice, and that was only since she was set on in the offices and had begun earning more. But nor did they ever go shabby either – their mother saw to that.

Emily Stanford prided herself on being able to make something out of nothing. An excellent needlewoman, she was often called upon to sew for the people up on the hill: everything from curtains to layettes for expected babies and ball gowns for the spoiled daughters of the business folk and managers from the mills and factories. Most of them lived on the hill overlooking Cottenly and were usually referred to by the townspeople as 'the posh folk'. The majority of ordinary mortals never saw beyond the ornate iron railings and tall poplars surrounding the gardens, but Emily Stanford often had the opportunity to admire the interiors whilst measuring windows, or people, in readiness for curtain or dress making. The ladies of the houses would often pass on cast-off garments to Emily, and it was one of those that had been altered beyond recognition and was now hanging in the closet ready for Lizzie's big night.

Emily accepted that her sewing for the posh folk was a thorn in the side of her husband Isaac, who considered it demeaning for his wife that she had to work. Unfortunately Isaac's income as a plate layer on the railroad to the works in Cottenly didn't quite match the family outgoings, and though at one time Emily had been forbidden to lower herself by offering her services, the opportunity had arisen for her to make use of her talents a few years ago, when Isaac went away to fight. On Isaac's return he found a more dominant Emily, already established and according to her clientele indispensable. With three daughters rapidly approaching womanhood Isaac had accepted the extra income grudgingly, but without much persuasion.

'I'm getting in bed.' Ruth leaped on to the high patchwork-covered bed, dived down below the sheets and snuggled into the centre. She had realised long ago that the middle was the warmest place with Lizzie on one side and Alice on the other, even if it had the disadvantage of being

14

between the pillows. Though tonight, with her hair bound in white cotton curling rags, she was able to manoeuvre them into the gap in such a way that they wouldn't stick into her head quite so much.

'Hurry up, Lizzie, I'm, cold,' she called, and Lizzie pulled down the sheets and followed her into the lumps and bumps of the flock mattress. Ruth smoothed the front of her white starched nightdress so that no creases would dig into her skin when she cuddled up to her sister, and noticed with a shock that her nipples hardened as her hand cupped each in turn. And the swell of her breasts was more obvious, she was sure of it. At last it seemed the long-awaited development was beginning to happen. For a couple of years Ruth's main ambition had been to have breasts like Lizzie, or even Alice, except that Alice's were always tightly encased in concealing black dresses, and so were almost invisible, except to her sisters when they were undressing. Ruth decided that when her breasts did develop she would wear pretty, tailored blouses to make the most of them. She shifted closer to Lizzie and pressed her knees in behind her sister's. 'Come on, our Alice. It's all right for you, but we've to be at work for six.' But Alice was still on her knees beside the bed, deep in prayer.

'I'm going to blow out the candle if you don't hurry,' Lizzie grumbled. 'God knows why your prayers take so long every night.'

Ruth giggled. 'Well, if God doesn't know there's not much point in praying, is there?'

Alice blew out the candle, used the chamber

15

pot from under the bed and joined her sisters beneath the blankets. She smoothed her night-dress and lay straight and stiff on her edge of the bed. Ruth wondered as she did every night how two sisters could be such complete opposites, Lizzie so soft and cuddly and Alice so cold, as though she was afraid of anyone's making the slightest contact with her body. No wonder she was never invited anywhere except the Bible class or the chapel socials. She was too cold and miser-able. Then Ruth suddenly felt mean. Perhaps Alice really did want someone to cuddle her but didn't know how to show it. Reluctantly, she turned over, rearranging her curling rags in the nick between the pillows, and placed her arm round her eldest sister's waist, but Alice still lay there stiff and cold as an icicle. Ruth stuck out her tongue in the darkness, turned back towards Lizzie, placed her cold feet on Alice and drifted into sleep.

Emily normally had the fire well alight by the time Lizzie and Ruth rose for work but today was Friday, the day for blackleading the range. Ruth shivered as she washed at the sink. 'It's not fair,' she moaned. 'Our Alice never has to get up to a cold kitchen. We shall have been on our feet for two hours by the time she opens her eyes.'

'Shut up moaning, our Ruth, and be thankful you've a job to go to.'

Emily poured milk into two cups. She had long since stopped trying to persuade her daughters to take breakfast, not that she blamed them at this unearthly hour. Instead she made certain the pair had a substantial lunch, already wrapped the night before in squares of damp linen.

'Some job,' Ruth muttered in between gulps of the cold milk they were drinking instead of the hot sweet tea they would have had if the fire had been lit. 'Making umbrella frames, day in day out.'

Lizzie took not the slightest notice. She knew the job wasn't exciting, but neither was it heavy; it was more tedious than anything else. In fact once all the girls got together in the mill they quite enjoyed themselves, laughing and singing as they worked, Ruth assembling the ribs and Lizzie lacquering them.

'Trust our Alice to land on her feet.' Ruth was off again.

'Your sister's done well for herself. There's not many would have spent all those hours labouring over a Pitman's home study course. Surely you don't begrudge it to her?' Emily asked as she shook the tin of blacklead on to the brush.

'Oh, no, I don't begrudge it her, but we all know why she's done well. It's because she's a Sunday school teacher and the office manager likes to keep well in with the chapelgoers, that's why.'

'Well, if that's the case you should have gone to chapel more often and then he might have put you a good word in too.'

'No thanks,' Ruth sniffed. 'If it makes one as miserable as our Alice I'd rather be a heathen.'

'That'll do, Ruth,' Emily snapped, though she couldn't argue with her young daughter's comments. Her eldest daughter was a constant worry

17

to Emily. Not that she ever set a step wrong, oh no, it would have been more normal if she had. It was just not natural for a young girl to be so involved in religious activities. Oh, well, she supposed Alice had been influenced by Isaac to some extent. He had always been on at the girls to join the Bible class, to help with Sunday school and read the lesson in chapel, though it was doubtful if he expected to be taken quite so seriously. Even Isaac didn't eat, drink and breathe religion. In fact when he first returned from France, she sometimes wondered whether he still believed in God at all. Where once he would have read a passage from the family Bible each night before retiring, Emily had noticed that the book had remained unopened for many months, except by Alice.

It was only when she questioned him that he revealed the horrors he had witnessed in the trenches, and his doubt that a compassionate God could have allowed them to take place. Then gradually, through Emily, he had relived the nightmare battles he and his comrades had fought, and had finally reached the conclusion that, since he was one of the fortunate few who returned, God must have been guiding him in his fight for survival.

Emily sighed. It was sometimes a strain residing in the same house as two fervent chapelgoers. Not that Isaac wasn't a good man: a kinder, more thoughtful one it would have been difficult to find, but sometimes Emily would have liked to let her hair down, do something frivolous, like making a joke on a Sunday, if she hadn't known that Isaac would be shocked to the core by such behaviour. Poor Isaac. Emily knew it wasn't his fault, any more than it was Alice's. The blame lay at the feet of Isaac's mother if anywhere. It was Grandmother Stanford who had hammered religion into her son's brain, as sure as if she'd used a mallet. Yet was it not Emily herself who was to blame in Alice's case? Should she have allowed her daughter, at the tender age of ten, to become companion to such a cantankerous old woman? Isaac had stressed that it wouldn't be for long: only a matter of weeks. That had been the doctor's opinion when the old woman had lost her legs to gangrene.

Two years, two whole years for a child in the dark, gloomy house with a slowly dying woman. Not that Alice had complained: a little angel, she had been. Reading from the Bible every night, sitting by the four-poster bed with the picture of Grandfather Stanford on the wall at its foot – the picture of Grandfather Stanford in his coffin. Emily cringed with shame, shame that she had not intervened and brought her child home from that house of waiting death. Yet Alice bore her burden bravely. 'I don't mind, our mam. It won't be for long and Grandmother's no bother.' No bother! To a child who should have been laughing, and playing in the sunshine. No wonder Alice was so dour and lacking in warmth. Why, the lass even talked like an old woman.

'Come on, Ruth, we're going to be late.' Lizzie threw her shawl round her shoulders, picked up her lunch and made for the door, her sister hurrying behind her, still grumbling about the cold, dark morning, and the job.

Cottenly was a harsh and cruel place to be venturing out at this time of the morning, especially in January. The wind from the moors whistled and shrieked through the bare tree branches and round the skirts of the sisters as they battled through the darkness. It was a good mile walk and mostly downhill for which they were thankful, except when the narrow cobbled street was iced over and treacherous. Today however there was no sign of freezing and the journey would be made safely and swiftly. The return journey later would be a different matter, when the uphill climb would be torturous after a ten-hour shift, with no more than a couple of short breaks in which to sit themselves down on the mill floor and rest their weary limbs and aching feet.

Today, however, Lizzie's exhaustion would soon be forgotten in the excitement of preparing for the evening ahead. At the moment Ruth seemed to be the more excited of the two.

'Can I do yer hair, Lizzie?' she enquired as she half skipped, half fought against the wind by Lizzie's side. 'How will yer wear it?'

Lizzie shrugged. 'What do you think?'

'I could lend you my mother-of-pearl comb, the one our dad gave me for Christmas.' Ruth turned to peer at her sister through the darkness, 'I could pile your hair high on your head and slip in the comb for fancy. Or leave it long and fasten it in the nape of yer neck.'

'Aye, I think we'll do that. George likes it loose.'

'Oh, Lizzie, what's it like to go out with some-body? A boy, I mean?'

Lizzie smiled in the darkness. 'All right, I sup-pose. Just like going out with a girl,' she teased.

'Except that girlfriends don't kiss each other, like you and George round the back of the chapel.'

'Ruth Stanford, you've been spying on us.'

'I haven't, honest. I found some holly with berries on and was taking it to the grave. I didn't know you were there until it was too late.' Ruth giggled. 'What does it feel like to be kissed? Really kissed, I mean, like George kisses you, for ages and ages?'

'You'll find out soon enough.'

'I doubt it, not if I don't develop!'

Lizzie frowned. 'What do you mean, develop?'

'My chest. If I stay as flat as this nobody'll ever want to kiss me.'

'Don't be daft. You'll fill out all in good time.'

'I doubt it. I'm sure your chest had developed long before you were my age.'

'Well if it had I certainly can't remember,' Lizzie fibbed, to make her sister feel better. 'Besides, you're lovely as you are. With a face like yours no one would even look at your chest.'

'You're just saying that.' Ruth paused. 'Although I think I am developing a bit.'

'I'm sure you are.' The buzzer from the works interrupted the conversation, much to Lizzie's relief. 'Come on, or we'll be late, then we'll have old Charlesworth on our backs.'

The street outside the works was bustling now with scurrying figures, heads bowed against the wind, all heading in the direction of the gates.

'It's enough to waken the dead,' commented Ruth, as the sound of the buzzer grew louder. 'I'm glad we don't live down here. I don't know how the little ones ever get any sleep.'

Lizzie agreed it would be awful to live down here, but for a different reason. The long rows of houses stretched right and left, blackened by the soot and smoke from the mill chimneys, each house a replica of the next. Two up, two down and the stairway up the middle leading to a further curved staircase up to the garret. As the families down here consisted of anything up to thirteen children, the garret was a very necessary part of the dwelling, being large enough to accommodate two double beds – not that many could afford the luxury of beds. The longest row was known as the Twenty Row, for the number of houses it contained. The rest of them, being in close proximity to the fast-flowing river, had been given names like Don View, Little Don Row and Donside. Higher up were the older properties, some of them farmsteads, known as Duncliffe.

Lizzie was always relieved that they lived on the opposite side of the valley which was greener and more fertile. Most of the houses there were no more than thirty years old, and though there were one or two terraces the majority were semi-detached, until Queen Victoria Street wound even higher, leading to where the posh folk lived, in large, detached, gabled properties. Beyond that, the woods and meadows stretched out on to the wild, open Yorkshire moors.

'See you later,' Lizzie said as the sisters parted

company and made for their separate departments, Ruth to the gitting shop where she would use the gits to fix the ribs together, Lizzie to the Japan shop where she would dip the finished articles into the Japanese lacquer and lay them out to dry ready for the ovens and the hardening.

The girls were both clad in long white pinafores to protect their clothing, and before long Lizzie's arms would be lacquered as black as the ribs, as far up as her elbows. She didn't mind the job; what she did mind was the smell of the naphtha used to remove the lacquer which seemed to cling to her body no matter how much she scrubbed herself afterwards. She hoped she could rid herself of the smell tonight – she didn't want everybody knowing she was an umbrella girl.

By the time Isaac Stanford rose from his bed the fire was glowing brightly, after being urged on by the draw-tin, and the kettle was gurgling merrily on the hob. Isaac and Emily would breakfast together on homemade barm cakes and honey, after which he would enjoy a pipeful of tobacco before leaving to join the railway gang and begin work at eight. Alice could normally be heard pottering about in the bedroom above at about the time Isaac left the house. This morning, however, she was downstairs and pouring a cup of tea before Isaac had finished his smoke.

'You're up early,' Emily said.

'Aye.'

'Sit thisen down then, lass, and get thi breakfast,' said Isaac.

'I suppose our Lizzie'll be all worked up about

the dance.'

'Aye, I suppose she will.' Emily wondered if her eldest daughter wished she was going too. 'It's a pity you aren't going with her, lass.'

'Nay, I don't think it'd be in my line. Besides, I doubt if she'd want me watching the goings-on.'

Emily looked puzzled. 'Goings-on? It's only a ball, Alice. I'm sure she and Annie would have liked you to join them.'

'Happen Annie would.'

'What does tha mean, Alice? Thee and our Lizzie haven't had words, have yer?' Isaac frowned.

'No, it's just that seeing as she'll be accompanied by George Crossman, I doubt she'd want me playing chaperon.'

'She's going with Annie,' Emily said. 'Our Lizzie wouldn't lie.'

'Oh, no.' Alice hoped she was doing the right thing. 'I didn't say she wasn't going with Annie, Annie's got the tickets, but George'll be there as well.'

'Well, perhaps that's a good thing,' said Emily, glancing at her husband. 'He'll be able to keep an eye on the pair of them.'

Isaac chewed at his pipe and rocked slowly in his wooden chair. 'George Crossman, you say? Now let's see, isn't that Walter's son? Tha knows, Emily, Walter who married Nellie Sanderson? Didn't they go live over Warrentickle?'

'I remember. A lovely lass was Nellie.'

'Aye, if my memory serves me well they had four, all lads. I can see them now, marching in the Whit Monday procession, as like as four peas in a pod, and just as shining and clean.'

'She always was spotless, was Nellie. They used to come to chapel regularly before they moved. In fact I've seen one of the lads in chapel lately, though I don't know which one.'

'That's George,' Alice mumbled. 'On the lookout for our Lizzie, I expect.'

Isaac wrapped his muffler round his neck and picked up his snap. 'Aye well, our Lizzie could do a lot worse than keep company with a Crossman. Though I should have a word with her, Emily, if I were thee, make sure she knows right from wrong, if tha knows what I mean.'

'She'll be all right. She's a good lass is our Lizzie, in fact they all are. I reckon we're fortunate, Isaac.'

'Aye, well, we've done our best. See thee tonight then, lass.'

'Yes, well, take care with the engines.'

Isaac went out, closing the door behind him.

Emily poured another cup of tea. 'And what was all that about?' She narrowed her eyes as she looked at Alice.

'What? What was all what about?' Alice sounded innocent enough but the flush of colour gave her away.

'Perhaps I was wrong, I hope I was, but I had a feeling you were trying to make trouble for our Lizzie.'

'Nay, Mother, I don't want to make trouble, I want to keep her out of it.'

'How? By stopping her going to the ball with George Crossman?'

Alice almost told her mother about Lizzie's intention to stay out beyond half past nine, but she didn't like the look on her mother's face. 'Well, I just thought our dad should know, that's all.'

'Well, so now he knows.' Emily sighed. 'Our Lizzie's growing up. In fact she is grown up, and so are you, Alice. No doubt you'll be next to find yourself a young man.' Alice shuffled uncomfortably. 'And when you do, I trust you'll know how to conduct yourself just as I trust our Lizzie. I wish you were going with her, lass. You deserve a little fun now and again.'

Alice jumped up and grabbed her coat from the peg behind the door. It was a nice coat, her mother considered, good quality but more suitable for an older woman. Emily sighed. And she was so pretty. Alice had beautiful eyes. Emily watched her put on her hat, grey to match her coat, and pull it down so that her thick dark hair was completely hidden.

'I'll be off then, Mother.' She kissed her mother dutifully on the cheek, but with no sign of affection.

'Aye, don't be late, lass.' Emily knew that Alice would consider it a sin to be even a second late. The girl glanced at the wall clock just as it began to chime the quarter, picked up her gloves and strode purposefully out of the house. Shaking her head sadly, Emily watched her until she disappeared from sight.

'If only our Alice would let herself go a bit, if only she would laugh, she could be the bonniest of the three,' she said to herself, but she had a feeling it would never happen.

26

Alice was sorry now that she had said anything; it had only started her mother on about her needing some fun. She tried to convince herself that she had only mentioned it to protect their Lizzie, but somehow it didn't ring true. She wondered if she was jealous, as Ruth had suggested. Not that she wanted to go to the dinner dance, but Lizzie's suddenly acquiring herself a young man had made her think. After all, Alice was the oldest. She flushed at the thought of Joe Jackson. Not that he had paid her any attention; well, no more than as the girl clerk in the outer office. Except that he had offered to escort her home from the works' Christmas social, and then she had almost snapped the poor man's head in two. 'I'm with my sisters.' Oh, why couldn't she have smiled and thanked him nicely? The truth was that she hadn't taken much notice of him until then. The relationship had been entirely that of supervisor and secretary. From that night, however, Alice had seen Joe in an entirely different light, but by then it was too late.

She waited on the pavement for a trap to pass, the clip-clop of the horse's hooves breaking up her thoughts. At this time the upper management were all turning in for work. Those who had come from Sheffield to make their weekly tour of inspection were travelling by carrier cart; others, immaculate in dark suits and bowler hats, were glancing at heavy gold pocket watches as they walked briskly into the office building. In another hour they would probably have both foremen and factory workers quaking in their clogs, as the weekly assessment was made and wages paid out accordingly. One or two would no doubt have been sacked and others set on. Alice would know the names of the unfortunate ones even before they themselves heard about their dismissal, but being the soul of discretion she never discussed her work with anyone. The truth was that Alice Stanford was a lonely young woman who had built a cage round herself, a cage which could have been made of iron and from which she was finding it impossible to escape.

Wormleighton Hall had once belonged to a wealthy family of the same name, but that was before misfortune and financial ruin made it necessary for the place to be sold. Far from being acquired as a family residence, the Hall had been purchased with the intention of turning it into a profitable business. The state rooms and the marble ballroom remained as they had for generations, but the bedrooms had been refurbished, new bathrooms and heating had been installed and extra staff had been employed. Apart from being run as a residential hotel, the Hall was also hired out for banqueting and as a ballroom. Such was its reputation that gentry from as far away as Leeds and Manchester were eager to flaunt their wealth and outdo their friends by holding their family celebrations at Wormleighton Hall.

Tonight would be an exceptional occasion, as for the first time the working people of Cottenly were to be admitted to the splendid and luxurious establishment. The Hall was surrounded by green parkland and it was said that deer could be seen in the forest beyond. Amongst the attractions for house guests were the grouse and pheasant shoots, and in the hunting season the gentry were invited to join the chase in the hills and moorland surrounding the park.

In the valley below, work on a new reservoir had just begun and would benefit not only Cottenly but also towns and villages further afield. The ball tonight was in honour of everyone concerned in the enterprise: engineers, surveyors and lowly labourers. The girls employed at the Hall had been invited to bring friends, mainly to swell the number of female guests for the pleasure of the menfolk. George Crossman was invited to represent the tyre mill in Cottenly, where he was employed. The dam project would bring business to most of the local firms and the tyre mill's profits were expected to be inflated as the working vehicles needed frequent tyre replacement. The prospect had encouraged the tyre mill to replace its old engine with a new 600-horsepower one. The plant already housed a hammer and a 1250-ton press, and the tyres were rapidly gaining a worldwide reputation. George had managed to acquire an invitation tonight by bribing the fellow concerned with handing out the tickets: he would be walking to work for the next month whilst the bloke concerned rode in style on George's bicycle. It would be well worth the three-mile trek if George could spend a few hours tonight with Lizzie Stanford. According to George, Lizzie was the most beautiful, adorable creature ever to walk Cottenly, and not many in the town would disagree. For some time past George and his brothers had cried off from attending chapel, but once George had caught a glimpse of Lizzie as she and the rest of the umbrella girls came out of the mill for a breath of fresh air at snap time he had suddenly developed religious mania, and couldn't wait for Sunday evening to come round. He had even attended Bible class one Wednesday and been sadly disappointed to find only Alice Stanford amongst the students. His sudden resumption of worship was not entirely necessary, as he could have waited outside the chapel for Lizzie, but he was hoping to be noticed by Isaac Stanford, for to get on the good side of Lizzie's father would be crucial if he meant to ask for Lizzie's hand in marriage. And since he and Lizzie had kissed, out there in the graveyard, marrying Lizzie Stanford was the most important thought to occupy George Crossman's mind.

Lizzie felt like a queen in the midnight blue velvet gown. Emily had added a collar and cuffs of fine white lace and taken in the waist to fit Lizzie's slender frame. Ruth had dressed her hair, which was the colour of sunkissed corn, and she was wearing a neck chain of shimmering silver which Emily had inherited from her mother and also her grandmother's ring. Jewellery was sparse in the Stanford household, but what items Emily owned were shared with her daughters on occasions such as this. Isaac stared, and thought how much Lizzie resembled her mother when he had first courted her.

'Eeh, lass, thar a sight for sore eyes.' He wished he could dress his daughters in such finery all the time. As always, he regretted the fact that Emily was willing to accept charity from the posh folk, but it was worth it on this occasion to see the joy spreading forth from his daughter's countenance.

'I've done our Lizzie's hair,' Ruth informed him proudly.

'Aye, lass, and right pretty it looks too.' He glanced at Alice, the only one who didn't look pleased at Lizzie's appearance. Happen she was wishing she was going with her, though he somehow doubted it.

'What does tha think, Alice? Doesn't our Lizzie look grand?'

'Oh aye, she looks right grand. I just hope she keeps away from those contractors, that's all.'

'She must be civil to them, Alice. They're only human, after all,' Emily said.

'You needn't worry, Mother. I know how to behave, and Annie's brother is fetching us home at–' Lizzie almost let the cat out of the bag, 'when it's time,' she corrected herself.

'You're going to feel the cold, lass,' Emily said, looking out at the dark, frosty night.

'Well, I'm not wearing my coat. It'll only spoil the look of my dress. Besides, it's too short, and it's faded.'

'You can borrow my shawl,' Alice suddenly offered. 'The new one I bought for the social.' Everyone stared at her in silence. She flushed, knowing they were all taken aback at her show of generosity.

'Oh, Alice, I couldn't. It must have cost you the earth ... oh, but it is lovely and warm.'

Alice ran upstairs and brought down the beautiful checked shawl. 'Here, put it round thee.' She suddenly smiled, and looked beautiful. 'Who knows? I might want to borrow thi frock one of these days.' Lizzie threw her arms round her sister. 'Oh, Alice, you can borrow it any time, I promise.'

'Well,' Alice muttered to cover her embarrassment, 'tha'd better not keep Annie waiting.'

Lizzie snuggled into the lovely fringed shawl, picked up a carpet bag containing a nightdress and checked herself in the mirror over the mantelpiece, then hurried off to Annie's a few doors away. Ruth waved as she passed the window and Alice was surprised at how uplifted she was feeling, so much happier than this morning. Why, she almost wished she was going to the do herself. She frowned as she wondered why she couldn't be kind and cheerful all the time, and was disturbed by the memory of how she had snubbed Joe Jackson.

The orchestra could be heard in the stillness of the night as the two girls approached the drive. A carriage ambled past and Lizzie gasped in amazement. 'Gosh, I didn't know the gentry were honouring us with their company.'

'Course they are. There's to be speeches after the meal, just like when it's a do for the nobility.'

Lizzie giggled. 'I hope they don't ramble on too long. I've come to dance, not to listen to speeches.'

Annie put Lizzie in the picture. 'Everyone involved in the reservoir construction will be here. Engineers, financial experts, lawyers, surveyors, labourers, drivers, men from the water works – even the humble chambermaids who look after the upper crust when they stay at the Hall, like me.'

'Oh, Annie, I hope we don't show ourselves up.'

'Why should we? We're as good as that lot any day. They might look all posh in their top hats and tails, but some of 'em have manners worse than pigs. You should see the state of the rooms some of them leave. Too drunk to use the chamber pots, some of 'em are, so they just pee the beds.'

'Oh, Annie, and you have to clean up after them?'

Annie shrugged. 'It's a job, and we have some laughs, I can tell yer.'

They entered the reception area and Annie took Lizzie's shawl.

'Oh!' Lizzie exclaimed. 'I hope it doesn't get lost. It belongs to our Alice.'

'It won't. I'll ask Miss Tudor to take special care of it. She's usually on reception but she's looking after the cloaks tonight.'

Lizzie was mesmerised by the wide, open staircase, lit by a huge crystal chandelier.

'Come on!' Annie grabbed her by the arm and led her into the ballroom. Tables were set round three sides of the room, the other already occupied by the orchestra. Lizzie had never before seen such finery. Flowers had been arranged in huge Grecian urns between the tables and the dance floor, and chandeliers glistened like icicles along the patterned ceiling. An assistant in scarlet livery winked at Annie and bowed.

'Your card, my lady?' he said formally and Annie giggled.

'I'll give yer mi lady tomorrer, Sammy.'

Sammy whispered in Annie's ear, 'Don't eat too much tonight, Annie, then we can have a fuddle tomorrow with what's left.'

Annie laughed and then said seriously, 'Why, I've a good mind to report you to the master, my boy.'

Lizzie chuckled and they handed the tickets to Sammy, who showed the two friends to their places. 'Trust them to put us at the end,' Annie grumbled. 'Oh, Lizzie, you do look lovely. You are lucky having a dress like that – it must have cost a fortune.'

'Aye, when it was new.' Lizzie grimaced. 'I only hope nobody recognises it.'

People were taking their seats at the tables and Annie and Lizzie joined them. 'You see him over there?' Annie said. 'The handsome one with the black, curly hair? He's Irish; five brothers there are, came over specially to work on the dam. There's another of them, the one at the opposite end of the table. I think he's lovely – the one with the black hair, I mean.'

'He's handsome right enough, but you should be careful. I've heard the girls at work – they say the Irish can charm the bloomers off a girl just by opening their mouths.'

'Lizzie Stanford! Whatever would your Alice say if she heard you?' They began to giggle.

'Oh, she's not so bad really, Annie.'

Annie raised her eyebrows. 'Oh? You've changed your tune.'

'Oh, I know, but I sometimes feel sorry for her, like tonight. I could have sworn she'd have liked

34

to be coming with us.'

'Well I for one can't see your Alice letting her hair down and dancing.'

The room had hushed and a dignitary stood at the head of the top table. 'My lords, ladies and gentlemen, may I call on Sir Duncan Batty to say grace.' Everybody rose to their feet and joined in the Amen at the end, then shuffled back on to their chairs with relief as the waiters began to serve the soup.

'Mock turtle,' Annie whispered.

'What?' Lizzie was busy searching for the face of George Crossman, and blushed the colour of the apples in the large bowls of fruit on the table when she suddenly caught him staring and smiling in her direction.

'Mock turtle,' Annie repeated, 'and the next course is to be roast pheasant.'

'I've never had any pheasant,' Lizzie said, trying not to drip soup on to her dress.

'I've only picked the bones I've found among the leftovers.'

Lizzie screwed up her face. 'Oh, Annie, you don't know who left it.'

'Not bothered.' Annie shrugged. 'Like to try anything once.'

The whole menu was delicious and Lizzie felt quite sickly by the time she'd finished, what with the mulled ale, rich with nutmeg, and the York-shire cheesecake. Annie said there would be port wine for the toasts but Lizzie didn't think she could manage that. 'My stomach must think there's been an avalanche,' she said. 'I've eaten enough to last at least a week.'

The speeches seemed to go on for ever. The first speaker went on about how the dam would benefit the works and the surrounding towns and in time would become a place of beauty; the second paid tribute to all and sundry, people on the top table preening themselves at the mention of their name while the occupants of the other tables coughed, fidgeted and scraped their chairs.

'Oh, for Gawd's sake,' Annie whispered, during yet another burst of applause, 'why doesn't somebody shove an apple down his cake hole?'

Lizzie began to giggle, and what with the mulled ale and the port wine found it impossible to stop. Fortunately the speeches ended at that point and the orchestra began to tune up as the guests sighed with relief.

George Crossman couldn't wait to join Lizzie and was by her side even before the tables had been cleared.

'Hello, Lizzie.' He smiled. 'Did you enjoy your meal?'

'Except that I've eaten too much. I hope I don't burst my buttons.'

George grinned. 'That should be interesting.' Lizzie blushed. 'You look beautiful.' She blushed even deeper. 'I never realised how blue your eyes were until tonight.'

Annie grinned at Lizzie, and tapped her foot to the music. George suddenly seemed to notice her. 'You look lovely too, Annie.'

'Oh, thank you, kind sir.' Annie curtsied.

'Would you like to dance, Lizzie?' George asked.

She looked at the dancers on the glistening expanse of marble. It looked very slippery; what if she made a spectacle of herself? But she really did want to dance. 'All right,' she said.

He took hold of her arm and led her on to the dance floor. She hoped she wouldn't feel sick as he twirled her into a polka. However, the thrill of being held close to George soon dispelled all such thoughts and filled her with excitement as they whirled faster and faster to the music. It wasn't until the dance ended that she wondered aloud what had happened to Annie.

George grinned. 'I shouldn't worry about Annie. She seems to be fully occupied.' Indeed, Annie was in intimate conversation with the Irish labourer with the black curly hair, and when the next dance began he whirled her over in the direction of Lizzie and George.

'Oh, I can't do this one.' Lizzie set off for the edge of the floor, but Annie pulled her back.

'Yes you can, I'll show you how. It's fun.'

The ladies were already forming a line opposite the gentlemen for the Sir Roger de Coverly. Lizzie's heart began to pound. Nobody had prepared her for this; she was sure to throw all the dancers into confusion. However, George and Annie set her right by signalling beforehand when she should advance and when she should turn, and soon she had the hang of it and began to relax. After that the night flew by and it seemed impossible when Annie said it was time to go. In fact Charles, Annie's brother, would have been kept waiting twenty minutes already. The Irish labourer was none too pleased when told that

Annie's brother was to chaperon her home, but Annie didn't care. She had had a lovely time and there would be another day. Besides, she didn't want him to think she was all that interested; best to keep him guessing.

Lizzie was a different matter. Her heart was thumping madly and plainly on her sleeve, and George Crossman was delighted. He left with her to collect her shawl and escorted her to where Charles was looking rather put out at being kept waiting. George appeased him by apologising, taking the blame for delaying the girls, even though he'd had no idea of the arrangement.

By the time they reached Annie's house the men had arranged to attend the football match together the following day. Football was not George's favourite pastime, but he had discovered that Isaac Stanford was a staunch spectator and Emily a regular helper with the teas. Lizzie and Ruth would offer to lend a hand and perhaps even Alice if she was still in a generous frame of mind.

Annie and Charles were most discreet when they reached Annie's and supposedly admired the Great Bear and the Milky Way, whilst George held Lizzie closer than ever before and, as Ruth would say, kissed her for ages and ages.

Annie sighed as they crept silently indoors and up the stairs and thought how romantic it was that George and Lizzie should be madly in love. Annie thought she might attend the football match tomorrow too. After all, the Irish labourers often came this way on a Saturday. Annie had no intention of falling in love but there was no harm in a little fun. Then she remembered she would be working late tomorrow, clearing up after the ball. Oh, Gawd. She wondered if it had been worth it, but then she cheered up. Sammy would be working too; he might not be as dashing as the Irish labourer but he was nice, was Sammy. Besides, Sammy wouldn't try to talk her bloomers off. She grinned into the darkness. It had been a lovely night.

The match between the Band of Hope and Banner Saddington's woollen mill was not so much a contest as an afternoon of horseplay. No one was exactly sure of the rules so they changed them to suit themselves, and a hilarious time was enjoyed by all. The afternoon proved an achievement for George Crossman who succeeded in becoming acquainted with Lizzie's parents, which resulted in his being invited to tea on the following day. Alice had surprised them all by not only helping serve the teas, but also being particularly pleasant to George. Lizzie thought – indeed hoped – that perhaps Alice had turned over a new leaf and noticed how beautiful Alice looked when she smiled. Then she went and spoiled it all by giving Ruth the sharp end of her tongue. 'Stop disgracing thiself. You should know better at your age.' All because Ruth had run after the ball and kicked it back to one of the players.

'Leave her be,' Emily said. 'Our Ruth works hard all week, and she's not but a child; she's a right to let steam off on a Saturday.'

This put the scowl back on Alice's face and cast a shadow over Ruth and Emily, but Lizzie and George were enchanted by each other and completely oblivious of any sign of discontent. If Emily had but given the subject a little thought she should have realised that Alice had every right to feel resentful considering she had never been allowed to let off steam, even at ten, let alone Ruth's age. Alice frothed up the square of brown soap and bent her head over the pail of washing-up water in an effort to hide her tears. All around her people were laughing and joking, and outside on the green children were skipping and singing, but all Alice could hear was the voice of Grandmother Stanford. 'Sit up straight. Don't run. God has his eye on thee. Our sins are not set from us, but multiplied around us. Pray for us, child. Has thou learned thy lesson for today? Repent, child, before it is too late.'

Alice lifted up her skirt, dropped the dishcloth and ran, out of the free school and across the green, knowing that if she didn't get away she would begin to scream and if she once started she would be unable to stop.

'What's up with our Alice?' Isaac enquired of Emily.

'Nay, I'm sure I don't know. I only wish I did.' Emily took over the washing up.

Isaac set off for home, worried about his daughter, yet completely unaware of her feelings. Not that he would have thought of her childhood deprivation as anything unusual, having been raised in entirely the same manner himself. Isaac thought a good, strict Christian upbringing never harmed anyone. In fact, in Alice's case he looked on it as a blessing in disguise, Grandmother Stanford having settled her entire fortune on

Alice, in return for her companionship. Oh aye, our Alice'll be well enough off when she comes of age, he had pointed out to Emily. Emily had never questioned Isaac as to whether he thought it was worth it; that would have been admitting her own doubts and her own share of the blame. So Isaac arrived home completely puzzled by Alice's irrational behaviour.

Alice was standing near the window, looking out across the valley, abstractedly flicking dust from the aspidistra with a finely embroidered hanky. Isaac went to stand beside her. 'Well, lass, what's to do?'

Alice glanced at her father's concerned face and forced a smile to her lips. 'I don't know. I think it was the cold – it seemed to seep into my bones. I had to get away from the place, but I'm all right now.' If only she could have explained to her father, told him of the bitterness and resentment that filled her on occasions, but she couldn't hurt her dad. After all, he had suffered the same fate throughout his own childhood, and for longer.

'Aye, it were allus the same in the free school. It freezes folks to the marrow, especially in January. Still, I'm glad you're all right, lass. Tha should have said – I'd have brought you home, instead of running as though the devil himself were after thee.'

Alice smiled again. It wasn't the devil she was running from, it was her memories: memories of the old woman who had stolen her freedom for two whole years.

Isaac stared at his daughter. 'Eeh, lass, tha's

grown to be a beauty and no mistake.'

Alice stood open-mouthed, then she stammered, 'Who, me?'

'Aye, thee.'

Alice felt the tears brimming and then overflowing, to trail over her high, perfectly shaped cheekbones. 'Oh, our dad,' she cried and found herself in Isaac's strong, protective arms, and this time she didn't shrink from him, or stand rigid and unfeeling, but fell against him, seeking his affection, at last the child she should once have been.

'Nay, nay, tha must be sickening for something, lass. It's that freezing schoolroom, it fair gives me the jitters. I'd swear it's bloody haunted.'

Alice was so taken aback at her father's use of the swear word that she stood back, stared at him and burst out laughing. When Emily entered the room she thought the pair were bordering on hysteria.

'What's happened?' she cried. 'Tell me what's wrong?'

Alice couldn't answer, she was laughing so much, but Isaac managed to mutter, 'Nothing's wrong, Emily, we were just having a laugh, letting our hair down a bit like. We all need to do that once in a while.'

Emily didn't say a word, but the thought came to her, 'Aye, and it's not before time, either.' Then she popped the kettle on the fire, the teapot to warm, and set about getting the tea ready.

Chapter Two

Joe Jackson was at one side of the table with Alice, and opposite sat George Crossman with Lizzie. Isaac was a satisfied man. Two of his daughters settled down and courting, both with eligible young men. Well, Joe was not all that young, but there was no doubt that at twenty-nine, nine years Alice's senior, he seemed ideal. Joe was a steady bloke, quiet and sensible; the only criticism Isaac had of Joe was that he wasn't a chapelgoer. Not that Joe had any objection to Alice's attending; in fact he even escorted her to the service and the Bible class in the dark evenings. Besides, it seemed to Isaac that Joe worshipped the ground that Alice walked upon. Another thing Isaac admired was the man's independence. Even though Joe was aware of Alice's forthcoming inheritance he was determined to save until he himself could afford a house, before taking Alice in marriage. He had fought in France, suffered a knee injury and returned to work his way up to a decent job and a steady income. Isaac had no worries on that score. Oh aye, theirs would be a steady partnership, no great passion but a marriage of give and take. For though Joe liked a jug of ale now and then – only one, mind – following the Oddfellows meetings, Alice never objected. Aye, it would be an amicable marriage right enough.

As for Lizzie and George, well, that was a

different kettle of fish altogether. The great passion between those two was there for all to see. The secret smiles, the touches at every opportunity. In fact Isaac thought that the sooner the two of them were wed the better it would be. Unfortunately their financial situation was by no means as sound as Alice and Joe's; the tyre mill's wages were nowhere near as generous. It always seemed a shame that the more physical toil a man put into his work the less he was rewarded. Not that Joe wasn't a clever man – a more studious one it would be hard to find – but all the same it didn't seem quite fair to Isaac.

He studied his youngest daughter, Ruth. Now she was a merry one and no mistake. Couldn't keep still for two minutes together, and a mind just as active. Isaac frowned. He hoped Ruth wouldn't be too flighty. She seemed to favour dressing a bit more frivolous somehow, but no, she was a good girl like the others. He would give Emily her due, she had made a right good job of training the girls. Isaac sucked on his pipe. He would have liked a son but it wasn't to be; no doubt God had His reasons. He shook himself. Any road up, he would soon be father-in-law to two grand lads by the looks of things. He would have to wait and see what fate had in store for young Ruth. So long as she was happy – and young Ruth was certainly that – then Isaac Stanford was a contented man.

Isaac was right, Ruth was a merry one, and not only was she developing nicely but the lads down at the works were beginning to notice. Not one but two of them had asked her to walk on the moor on a Saturday. Up to now she had refused, preferring to go on the monkey run with her friends from the umbrellas. This was a walk from the bottom of Duncliffe across the river and on to the green, and the lads and lasses would troop along in groups of three or four, to the green and back again, giggling and making eyes at anyone of the opposite sex they happened to fancy. Most Saturdays the lads from Warrentickle would join in the promenading, which didn't altogether please the local lads who preferred to keep the girls to themselves. Fist fights were known to have broken out on occasions. Not that anything untoward ever took place – the girls were willing to do little except tease – but it was a way of eyeing them up for the future, and a means of congregating for a talk and a laugh and, if they were lucky, the odd kiss. The fun was increased by the excitement of avoiding being caught on the monkey run, and Ruth knew that if Isaac became aware of his daughter's whereabouts all hell would break loose. All the girls had to embroider the truth slightly, so a plan was devised where each of them would say she was visiting another, one not too well known by her parents, and it was rare for anyone to be found out.

At the moment the monkey run was the highlight of Ruth's week. She and Mary Hampshire would talk of little else as they assembled umbrella frames from Monday to Saturday and it was obvious that Lizzie was bound to find out. Lizzie had only once joined the monkey run, before George Crossman came to occupy her thoughts night and day, but she was worried about Ruth, particularly as an unsavoury bunch of lads were on the prowl around Cottenly, some of whom had arrived in the town to work on the dam, and others who had begun travelling up from Sheffield now the new branch line was in operation. Lizzie had a few words of warning for Ruth and was disturbed when her sister disregarded her advice. The closeness between the sisters had somehow evaporated now that George was on the scene.

As it happened it wasn't a newcomer who captured Ruth's interest, but the son of a local family. Walter Wray was employed in the wire mill down at the works and could be quite charming when it was to his advantage, like the night he first met Ruth Stanford. They met as they were both crossing the bridge, Ruth with Mary and another girl she had known from school.

'Nice night,' Walter commented, addressing himself pointedly to Ruth. She thought he was very manly with his broad shoulders and hairy arms showing beneath his rolled-up shirt sleeves. 'Lovely for a walk.' He grinned.

'Yes.' Ruth blushed. 'We're walking along to the green.'

'Mind if I join yer?' he asked. Mary giggled; she was always giggling.

'All right.' Ruth shrugged. She didn't mind as long as she and her friends stayed together.

Walter moved over to walk beside her and slid his arm round her waist. She felt the colour rise into her cheeks. It was ever so exciting being with him, even if the others were trailing behind. She could smell the manly scent of him, a kind of sweet, clean smell. She glanced up at him. He had the thickest brown hair she had ever seen, and the longest lashes. He caught her staring and grinned, tightening his arm round her narrow waist.

'Do you live round here?' Mary enquired.

'Aye, up on't Duncliffe.'

'Oh! Do you live on a farm then?' Ruth said, trying to work out which one. She could see all the way up to Duncliffe from her bedroom window.

'No, the row just round the corner from the bottom.'

'Oh.' Ruth felt let down. The farms always looked so quaint, even though they were on the wrong side of the hill.

'You live up Queen Victoria Street, don't yer?' Walter said.

'How do you know?'

'Oh, I've had my eye on you for some time. I make it in me way to find out the whereabouts of a girl if I like the look of her.'

'Oh,' said Mary, 'so how many have yer got on yer list then?'

'Oh, I don't know, but I can tell yer you're not on it.' Ruth thought that was unkind of him. 'Can't yer friends go somewhere else?' he said to her.

'No,' she answered swiftly, 'we came together, we stay together.'

Mary had taken the huff. 'It's growing dark,' she said. 'I think it's time we were going. If I'm late me mother won't let me out again.'

'Nobody's keeping you,' Walter said.

'Right then, we'll be off,' said Ruth.

'No, I didn't mean you.' Walter looked uncomfortable. 'I'll see yer home. I don't even know yer name yet.'

'Then you'd better find it the same way you found my address.' Ruth removed Walter's arm and set off back along the track towards the bridge with her two friends laughing beside her.

'That told him straight,' Mary said.

'Well, he shouldn't have insulted you like that.' Ruth paused. 'Oh, but don't you think he's handsome?'

'I don't like him.' The quiet girl spoke for the first time.

'Neither do I,' Mary agreed.

'Oh, we just started off on the wrong foot, that's all. After all it must have been embarrassing for him, with three of us trailing after him.'

'We weren't, it's him who trailed after us. Anyway I still don't like him.'

Ruth didn't answer. She had liked the feel of his arm round her waist. She turned to see if he was still following but he had disappeared in the direction of the Rag. The Rag stood on the main street between the pawnshop and Miss Fiddler's sweet-shop, and it was said the public house would have closed without the pawnshop and the pawnshop wouldn't have kept open but for the Rag. Her father had never set foot in either place, as far as Ruth knew, and she hoped Walter Wray wasn't a frequent visitor either, because she liked him, she liked him a lot, and she couldn't wait for next Saturday and the monkey run.

Isaac was happy to give his consent when George asked if he might marry Lizzie; in fact he thought it was long overdue the way they were carrying on. Not that he suspected George of having taken advantage of his daughter, but all the same he reckoned they'd be better off wed.

Lizzie looked a picture in a cream dress gathered at the hips and a large-brimmed hat to match, without a piece of second-hand material in sight. Isaac had been emphatic that no daughter of his was to be wed in anybody else's cast-offs, and true to his word he had arranged an outing for the whole family in order to purchase anything anyone might need for the wedding. It had been a lovely surprise when he had suggested the trip, not just to Sheffield, but a whole day excursion to Buxton by train.

'Our Lizzie's leaving the family home,' he said, 'which is as it should be now she's found herself a husband. Still, it might be the last chance I get to take my family out, all five of us together. So we'll make a round tour of it, kill two birds with one stone, do some shopping and enjoy the scenery whilst we're at it.'

They had set off early one Saturday morning, after leaving the key with Mrs Barrington next door, in order that she might keep an eye on the house and pop a bit of coal on the fire to keep it aired.

The girls were highly excited by the time they changed trains at Sheffield. Isaac pointed out places of interest on the way, and after a forty-minute journey the family arrived at Buxton. Isaac advised them to breathe deeply of the pure

Derbyshire air in what he described as the highest town in the British Isles.

'Just imagine that.' Ruth was awestricken as they stood in the beautiful Pavilion Gardens. 'Here we all are at the top of our country.' She and her sisters were impatient to make for the shops, so Isaac handed over a pouch of money to his wife and settled himself down to wait for them.

'If I'm not here when tha gets back, lass, I shall have taken mesen off to look at the baths and the pump room.' He guessed he would have time to go to Matlock and back, now that Emily had been let loose at the shops with a bit of brass, and he was proved right. The four of them were fascinated by the exclusive shops, not rowdy like the ones in Sheffield, but select and quiet. Emily realised why when she noted the prices, obviously set for people like the posh folk on the hill. However, Isaac had brought them and he was paying so she bought all that was necessary before they made their way back to Isaac in the gardens.

The train back to Sheffield was late, and by the time they reached the city their intended connection had already left. 'We're not going to let a little thing like that spoil a lovely day,' Isaac said. 'We'll go and have summat to eat, pie and peas or summat, and catch the last train.'

'Oh, our dad,' Ruth exclaimed, 'that's the one they say all the drunkards go on after a night out.'

'Be that as it may, we shall enjoy our trip no matter what.'

Then Isaac led them to a little restaurant, and

it wasn't until they arrived home and realised Mrs Barrington had long since retired to her bed and they were locked out that Ruth stopped giggling.

'Tha'll have to get down't cellar grate, Ruth lass, and let us in,' Isaac insisted.

'Oh, I can't, Dad, not in my best clothes!'

'Take thi frock off then. I'll turn me back and no one else'll see thee at this time of night.' It was the others who were laughing now, fit to burst, as Ruth took off her dress and slithered down into the cellar to go and open the door.

'Oh, it has been a lovely day, our dad,' Lizzie said, and knew she would remember it for the rest of her life.

'Aye well, lass, as I said, it might be the last one we have all together.' Lizzie smiled, but almost wished she was staying single, rather than having to leave this lovely, caring family.

The actual wedding day dawned with a sky as blue and clear as Lizzie's eyes. 'The sun shines on the righteous,' Isaac said as he and Lizzie left the house for the short walk to the chapel. The small chapel yard was filled to overflowing with friends, workmates and puny, ragged children from the Twenty Row and Donside. Isaac was well prepared with a pocket full of pennies which he scattered for the eager children.

'Eeh, lass,' he said to Lizzie, 'I bet there isn't a Congregationalist in Cottenly or Warrentickle who hasn't turned out to see thee and George wed.' Then he turned serious as he said, 'I know he's a good lad, Lizzie, but tha knows it's not too late to change thi mind if thar not sure. When tha comes back out of't chapel tha'll have made thi bed and tha'll have to lie on it. There'll be no turning back then.'

'I don't want to change my mind. I love George, for better or worse. I shan't have any regrets.'

Isaac grinned. 'Then we'd best not keep him waiting any longer. Let's get it over with.' He tucked his daughter's arm through his and led her into the small, sparsely furnished chapel and towards the smiling faces of George, Emily, Ruth and even Alice.

'Aye well,' he said to himself, 'that's one of my little lasses grown up and leaving the nest. I only hope she's as good a wife to George as her mother's been to me.'

By the time Alice followed Lizzie into wedlock, Lizzie was already carrying her second child, and contented as the day was long. The circumstances this time were different altogether. For one thing, whereas Lizzie and George had begun married life in a neat but small rented house almost at the bottom of Queen Victoria Street, the end one in a row of six, Joe had saved a substantial deposit and was purchasing a semi-detached villa with a small secluded garden overlooking the green. Even the wedding reception was a more exclusive affair. Lizzie's had taken place in the chapel lecture room, but Joe had booked a private room at the Rag Inn. He had also hired a photographer to take pictures of them all, standing to attention like a row of penguins. Alice's costume had been bought from an exclusive Sheffield shop and though it had cost far more than the material Emily had used to make Lizzie's dress, and though Alice looked smart as a mannequin, Isaac couldn't help but compare her cold, dark beauty to the soft, warm loveliness of Lizzie on her day. He wished now he had thought of a photographer; he must remember that when it was Ruth's turn.

Isaac frowned as he looked across at Ruth, pretty as a picture in one of Emily's creations, and his gaze wandered to where Walter Wray was paying attention to another young lady, one of the girls from Alice's office he shouldn't wonder. There was something about Walter Isaac couldn't take to. Oh, he was keen enough on Ruth, he supposed, but Isaac wondered if he was keen on a few others too, as well as his daughter. Besides, he seemed to spend far too much time here, down in the tap room, but what with young Ruth thinking he was some kind of Greek god Isaac was at a loss as to what to do about the situation. He just hoped the lass would come to her senses sooner or later.

When the reception was over Ruth made her way home with Isaac and Emily. She was feeling miserable, not only because Walter had been paying too much attention to one of Alice's friends but because he had also consumed an enormous amount of ale and seemed to turn sarcastic by the end of the night. However, when Ruth had accused him of showing her up, he had become all lovey-dovey again and apologised, looking at her in a put-upon way. 'I'm sorry,' he said. 'It's just that your sisters are both wed and going off to their marriage beds, and I can't even get close enough to you for a kiss and a cuddle. We could go outside for a breath of air.'

'I can't,' Ruth had insisted. 'Our dad's never taken his eyes off me all night.'

'He doesn't trust me, that's why.' Ruth had blushed, knowing that was true. In fact nobody at all seemed to approve of Walter. Lizzie thought he was too gushing to be genuine and Alice had given her a talking to about his drinking too much. 'Tha'll never have a nice home if tha marries Walter Wray, he'll fritter every penny away. And another thing,' Alice had stressed, 'he has too much time off work. Too many hangovers I shouldn't wonder.' The awful thing was that Ruth knew they were right and yet she was besotted with Walter. He only had to look at her with those large, brown eyes and she was lost. Besides, he was more fun to be with than anyone else she knew. She realised, though, that Walter was now playing for sympathy. 'Your family will never accept me, just because I haven't as much money as Joe Jackson, and I don't go to chapel like George Crossman.'

'Oh, Walter, how can I convince you that it isn't you personally? It's just your drinking, that's all.'

'And don't yer see why I drink so much, Ruth Stanford? It's because I love yer and want to be with you so much it hurts, so I drink to take my mind off yer.'

'Oh, Walter,' Ruth muttered helplessly.

'It'll be different when we're wed, you'll see.'

Ruth's eyes shone. 'Is that a proposal then?'

'Aye, it is that, and the sooner the better.'

'But we'll have to wait a few years, Walter, until I'm a bit older.'

'I'll wait, but I'm going to marry you, I'm determined.'

That was another thing Ruth couldn't resist about Walter; he was so forceful, and she admired that in a man. She went over the conversation in her mind as they climbed the hill.

'You're quiet, Ruth. Is something the matter?' Emily asked.

Ruth sighed. 'Not really, it's just that it won't be the same now without our Alice.'

'Aye, we're all going to miss her,' Emily said. 'But she's got a good man in Joe. He'll look after her, we can count on that.'

'It isn't the same, though. It was awful without our Lizzie, and now it'll be even quieter on my own.'

'Eeh, but young Harry's a credit to our Lizzie,' Isaac mused. 'He'll liven the house up when he gets another year or two on his back.'

'Oh, he's a lovely bairn all right, and the image of George.' Emily hoped Lizzie's next confinement would go as smoothly as her first and would be the last for a while. She blushed as she found herself wondering how Alice would cope with the intimacies of marriage. Emily had never worried about Lizzie on that score, but Alice was different. Oh, well. Joe seemed to approve of Alice the way she was and that was all that mattered.

Alice had worried for some time about her wedding night. Unlike Lizzie and the umbrella girls, she had never giggled and discussed the subject of sex, but no doubt Joe would know how to carry on and she would do her duty by him, however painful it might be. It was with some trepidation that she donned her lovely new silk nightdress and brushed out her hair. She sat before the dressing table mirror and began to plait her thick, dark tresses, then changed her mind. Joe had never seen her with her hair loose and it looked lovely against the pastel pink of the nightgown. She pulled down the bedclothes and climbed in between the pristine whiteness of the brand new sheets, and lay waiting, her heartbeat quickening as she heard Joe's feet on the stairs. The candle flickered with the draught as he opened the door, sending shadows rising and falling on the newly papered wall. Joe stood gazing at Alice, transfixed by the sight of her, transformed by her hair falling in waves about her face. He had always thought her attractive in a severe sort of way, but now he recognised her as a startlingly beautiful woman.

Joe took off his jacket and trousers, fumbling as the latter became entangled by his shoes. He kicked them off, embarrassed by his state of undress, but Alice didn't flinch. She watched him, mentally preparing herself for the ordeal to come. Joe walked round the bed and climbed in beside her, and only then did he remove his long underpants and kick them down the bed. He moved closer to Alice and thrilled at the warm silkiness of her gown. He drew her towards him and threaded his fingers through her hair. Her fragrance began to arouse him, a mixture of lavender and roses

56

which had trimmed the prayer book she had carried in chapel.

'Oh, Alice,' he murmured, 'I love you, lass.'

'And I love thee, Joe,' she answered.

He touched her breast gently and felt the heaviness in his hand and the stiffness of her nipple. He moved his hand downwards and felt the softness of her pubic hair through the flimsy silk of her gown. Gently, he caressed her until he felt the moistness enrich his fingers. Alice was soft now, relaxed and yet alert, eager for the ache in her body to be resolved. She moved her hips upward, pressing herself towards the hand which was giving her such intense pleasure, and, slowly, she moved her own hand down and placed it over Joe's rigid erection.

'Oh, God,' Alice muttered and moved her body closer. Joe sensed his wife's eagerness and slowly entered her. He heard her cry out momentarily and then they were moving as one, slowly at first and then faster, then slowing again and deeper until they reached a mind-shattering climax and she cried out again as pleasure, painful in its intensity, overwhelmed her.

'Are you all right, Alice?'

'Never better, Joe.' Then for the first time in her life Alice moved from her own side of the bed and snuggled closer to her bedmate.

Ruth was filled with excitement. Walter was meeting her after work and taking her to the music hall in Sheffield. Walter was always arranging treats and even Mary Hampshire was jealous, but she still insisted she didn't like Ruth's young man.

'If he's so eager to marry you, why isn't he saving his money for a house?' She always had to spoil things, Ruth thought.

'Because he likes me to have a good time,' she retorted, but deep down she knew her friend was right.

'Well, have a good time then.' Mary smiled, not wanting to be a spoilsport but concerned for her friend.

Mary wasn't the only one worried about Ruth. Emily had tried to convince her daughter that she could do better. 'You're a lovely lass, Ruth. Why, you could have the pick of all the boys and yet you choose one like Walter Wray.'

'You're all against him. No wonder he likes a drink – it's because he's sensitive to your rejection. Once we're married he'll be different, just you see.'

'I hope I never see the day when you marry Walter Wray.' Emily frowned. She knew Ruth was about to cry again – these conversations always ended with tears – but Emily still hoped to talk her daughter out of the planned wedding.

Isaac had even gone as far as to forbid Ruth to see the man, but she had refused to eat and changed so much from her usual carefree self that Emily had advised him to unbend a little. By way of compromise he had instead pleaded with his daughter not to rush into marriage and Ruth had agreed. But now another problem had arisen: the longer Walter was being made to wait, the more insistent he was becoming as regards his and Ruth's making love. When they stood now in the ginnel halfway up the hill to kiss goodnight, it was proving difficult for Ruth to stop his hands from roaming to places they shouldn't. It wouldn't have been so bad if the feelings taking place in her body hadn't made her want him to do things she knew would shame her.

The music hall proved to be the most exciting entertainment Ruth had ever seen. Walter urged her to join in the singing, and the acts all turned out to be first class. Afterwards, though, he spoiled her whole evening by insisting on their calling at a public house. Luckily they didn't have time for more than one drink before leaving for the station, for Ruth's upbringing didn't allow her to frequent such places as the Black Swan without feeling guilty. Besides, the women slouched at the tables were not the type Ruth wished to be seen in the company of. She had heard of such creatures and was now seeing them at first hand. She found herself wondering if Walter had ever become acquainted with such people and felt slightly sick at the thought of it. She left half the drink he had purchased for her and hurried out as soon as he had finished, but not before she had seen one of the crudely made up women rush over and gulp down her unfinished wine. She shuddered and was relieved to be on her way home. Walter snuggled her towards him and pulled her into the ginnel and Ruth felt a flood of desire wash over her at his closeness. He removed the hatpin and then her brown, feather-trimmed hat so that he could run his fingers through the fair silkiness of her long hair. 'Oh, Ruth love, I'm telling you I can't wait much longer. I'm a normal, virile man and enough is enough.'

Ruth kissed him into silence, which only inflamed him even more. He started to undo the buttons of her fitted jacket, and then the miniature buttons of her white, frilled blouse. 'No.' She stilled his hand. 'I've got to go, it's late.' Walter pushed her hand away roughly and continued with the buttons. Ruth found her hat in the darkness and disentangled herself from Walter's grasp. She experienced the urge to assist him and remove the blouse and knew if she didn't leave him now it would be too late to resist. 'I'm sorry, Walter, I really am.'

'Aye well, come on then, I'll take you home, but next time...' He followed her as she hurried up the hill. 'How about tomorrow, if the weather holds out, shall we go up the moor?'

'Yes, we'll take a picnic.'

'Two o'clock, then. Don't be late.'

But Ruth didn't answer. She was hurrying towards the house. Walter Wray kicked a stone and cursed. What was it about the girl? It wasn't in his nature to become so involved: safety in numbers had always been his motto, until she came along. The trouble was she was so bloody desirable. Of all the girls he had ever known he was willing to marry this one if it was the only way to have her, and it looked as though it was.

He set off towards the river. There was one thing for sure, he couldn't wait much longer, so it seemed like he'd better start looking for a house. It wouldn't be in the same league as the one her sister lived in – she would just have to be thankful for a roof over her head. Besides, she should think herself lucky if she got him. He grinned in the darkness. What was it his father called him? The lousiest bugger ever to walk Cottenly, not fit to wipe the little Stanford lass's arse. Aye well, maybe he was right. All the same, he would have her. He was determined on that.

The sun beat down on the dusty lane as Ruth and Walter walked hand in hand up the hill and out towards the open moor. They crossed over a stile and took a short cut over Dolan's Fields before leaving civilisation behind. 'I'm sure there'll be a storm before the day's out. It's abnormally hot,' Ruth said.

'Aye, it's a scorcher all right. We'll make for Windy Caves and find some shelter from the sun – we can't have you burning that peachy, soft skin.'

Ruth flushed, and he placed his arm round her shoulder and squeezed her upper arm, sending a flood of desire through her veins.

'I know where there's a house to let.'

Walter watched Ruth's reaction to his words and wasn't disappointed. Her eyes shone as she enquired, 'Oh, Walter, where?'

'Don't get excited, it's not among the posh folk, so don't go getting big ideas.'

'I didn't expect it to be, but do tell me where, Walter.'

'In Wire Mill Place.' He watched Ruth's face fall. 'Oh, I know it's not the best of places but home is what you make it, that's what I always say.'

The wire mill was situated between the coke ovens at the filthiest end of the works and the tyre mill, and Wire Mill Place was wedged between its stark black walls and the deepest part of the river, where it gushed down the hill before levelling out.

'Oh, Walter, it would be awful living there. It never sees any sunlight and gets all the smoke and fumes from the coke ovens.'

'Oh well, if you're going to be particular, it looks like we won't be fixing a wedding after all.'

'I didn't say I wouldn't live there, I was just a little disappointed, that's all.'

'Aye well, I'm sorry I can't compete with other members of yer family, but as it's all I can manage it's either take what I can offer or start looking for a rich husband.' He switched on his put-upon look and continued, 'I don't blame you if you do. I know I'm not good enough for somebody like you. I don't deserve yer.'

He looked so sorry for himself that Ruth threw her arms round his neck and kissed him. 'I don't want a rich husband, I want you, Walter, and I don't mind where we live as long as I'm with you.'

Walter placed the picnic basket amongst the heather and pulled Ruth down into the bracken. 'Right then.' He grinned. 'I'll arrange to pick up the key tomorrow.' He lifted Ruth's skirt and trailed his fingers up the length of her stocking, but she stilled his hand before it reached its goal. A curse almost sprang to his lips but he controlled his tongue. He would bide his time. She would soon belong to him and by God he would show her who was boss then and no mistake.

And all the time Ruth was thinking that he

could have afforded somewhere better than Wire Mill Place if only he would keep away from the Rag. But he would change once they were married, she was sure he would. Then they settled down to enjoy their picnic.

It was still stiflingly hot and Lizzie knew her confinement was imminent. She went to the door where George was sitting on the step bouncing little Harry between his legs and touched her husband on the shoulder.

'George, can you fetch Old Mother Buttercup?'

'Why, lass, has yer time come?' He jumped to his feet, lifting the infant as he did so, and rushed off down the street without waiting for her reply. George had never known Old Mother's real name; come to that neither did anybody else as far as he knew. She lived in a two up, two down cottage in a patch of garden which was once river bank, until she had adopted it, bit by bit, over the years. Now it contained almost every herb and flower under the sun, each of which was a cure for something or other, according to Old Mother. At present the garden was a blaze of colour, with dazzling golden buttercups and pale primroses vying with tall, fragrant lilies and white lilac for the attention of large fluffy bumblebees and pale, fragile butterflies. George trod his way through a bed of lavender and feverfew and knocked at the battered old door.

'Are you in, Old Mother?' he called and shifted Harry on to his other arm.

'Aah, lad, I'm in. Is it thee, George?'

'Yes. Lizzie says can you come?'

'Aah, lad, I were expectin' you some time today. I could tell by't way she were bottoming't house yesterday that her time was near. You be away back and I'll not be many minutes before I'm following on.'

George looked anxious and would have liked to tell her to get a move on, but instead he rushed across the garden and back to Lizzie.

'What are you doing?' He stood in the doorway unable to believe his eyes.

'Just cleaning the window bottom. I can't keep pace with the flies what with the heat.'

'Lizzie, you should be in bed. I'll clean the windows if it's so important.'

'Nay, George, Old Mother'll not approve of me lying there in idleness. You know how she had me traipsing round the bedroom on my hands and knees last time.'

'But, Lizzie, you're sweating like a bull. You should be resting, saving yer strength for later.'

'Of course I'm sweating.' Lizzie cringed as another pain clutched her body. 'It must be eighty outside, at least.'

Old Mother hobbled into the room on her bent, rheumaticky legs. 'Well, lass, are yer nearly ready? Have you had a show?' She looked at George standing by the door. 'Can you make yourself useful, George lad, get some water boiling on't fire or summat?'

'Boiler's full. I saw to that just in case. It'll be boiling by now, what with fire roaring away, and on a day like this as well.'

'Open't window then, lad, and let some air in, not that there's much to let in today. It's fair stifling; a storm brewing if you axe me. Come on then, lass, upstairs with yer and let's have a look at yer bits and pieces.' George blushed and was relieved when the two made their way up the narrow, steep stairs.

In less than an hour George heard the cry of a new baby and rushed fit to break his neck up the stairs. Lizzie was sitting up in bed, her face as red as the baby Old Mother was sponging down in a blue and white flowered wash bowl, but much more beautiful, George thought. He never had considered newborn babies to be very appealing; more like skinned rabbits, he considered. 'Are you all right, Lizzie?' he asked softly.

'Fine, George. Oh, and isn't she beautiful?'

'She? A girl then.' He grinned and kissed Lizzie tenderly.

'Aah, a girl, and she's a right bonny little blighter at that.' Old Mother handed the baby to George, so tightly wrapped he wondered how she could breathe.

'And Lizzie, is she all right?' he asked the old woman. Old Mother was hobbling towards the stairs and George followed her closely.

'What? Lizzie all right? Made for child-bearing if you axe me. Just as easy as laying an egg. Course, the raspberry leaf tea I gave her accounts for that. There'll be another on the way in six months, and another three or four after that.'

George looked stunned. Old Mother Buttercup was well known for her predictions and more often than not she was right. Old Mother's face had clouded. 'What's wrong, Old Mother?' George enquired, but the look had disappeared, and she grinned a wide, toothless grin.

'Naught wrong, lad, just the hotness making me thirsty.' Her eyes were roaming to the sideboard on which a decanter of elderberry wine was displayed.

George grinned. 'Aye well, I dare say we could all do with a drink, and I don't mean water, we have a birth to celebrate.' He poured the rich dark liquid into two glasses. Old Mother took a sip and smacked her lips together.

'A drop of the good stuff, this. Remind me next time you come to my place and I'll give you a sup of my elderflower. Naught can beat that if you axe me.' She finished her wine and wrapped her shawl round her shoulders. George marvelled at how quickly she had cooled down, and how she could bear the layer upon layer of thick, dark garments. 'I'll be away, then.' She hobbled to the door, pausing to stroke Harry's little fair head. 'Sleeping like Rip Van Winkle. Oh for the sleep of an innocent babbie, no regrets of the past to bother about and no worriting about what the future's going to bring. Best time of our life if you axe me, and not a one of us can remember it.' She grinned her cavernous grin and hobbled out into the hot sunshine.

'What do I owe you?' George called after her.

'Not a dicky bird, lad, but you could name the new babby after me. I should like that, having no kith or kin of my own.'

George was stunned. 'But I don't know your name.'

'Olive.' Old Mother paused. 'She'll be a dark-haired beauty, that one.' She laughed. 'Not like

Old Mother, you'll be thinking, eh? Aye, but I was once, many moons ago, a right beauty. Aye, Olive'll suit her, just you see.'

George didn't know what Lizzie would say about that. He took the stairs two at a time. 'Lizzie, are you awake, love?'

'Oh, yes, George. I want to see little Harry's face when he's introduced to his sister.'

'Lizzie, what do you think about Olive for a name?'

'Olive! Well, it isn't what I would have chosen. I thought about Annie, after Annie Hampshire.'

'It's Old Mother's name. She wants us to call our daughter after her.'

Lizzie looked down at the baby. 'Olive! Well I don't see why not, if it makes an old woman happy. Besides, we might need her assistance again sometime, we never know.'

'At least another three or four times, according to Old Mother.'

Lizzie's mouth fell open, then she burst into laughter. 'George Crossman, I think you're making that up.'

'No, Lizzie, it's the truth. That's what Old Mother said.'

'Then we'd better have separate beds,' she said, but there was laughter behind her words. The passion Isaac had seen between the two was still there, as strong as ever. If ever a marriage had been made to measure it was this one.

'If that's what you want, Lizzie,' George muttered.

'Don't you dare even think about it,' Lizzie warned. 'Now fetch our Harry up to see his

67

sister, and then come and lie beside me for a while, before you go break the news to her grandparents.' The thought of George in a separate bed was unthinkable. Besides, Lizzie didn't mind having babies, so long as she could feed and clothe them, and bring them up in a house of love. No, she didn't mind at all ... but half a dozen? She wasn't sure about that.

Ruth hadn't mentioned to anyone about going to look at a house. She knew there would only be another argument and she hated unpleasantness. Nevertheless, if it came to siding with one or the other, Walter would have to come before family.

Walter unlocked the door with the huge rusty key and then the stench met them, almost overwhelming Ruth with nausea. She recognised the stink of uncleaned drains and urine, but there were other sweet, sickly smells she had never before encountered. The bare flagged floor was coated with grease and mouse droppings, and the previous tenants had left a large, square table in the centre of the room, on which huge black blowflies had become glued to the spills and stickiness of dried on food. The unplastered walls had at one time been lime-washed but it had peeled off with the damp and the bricks were fluffy with mould and dry rot.

'Oh, Walter, we can't possibly live here.' Ruth was close to tears.

'It'll be all right once it's cleaned.'

'But I wouldn't know where to start. Look at the fireplace, it's red with rust.' She walked to the slimy stone sink and examined the set pot in the corner. 'It stinks like old cabbage water, and look at that! It's disgusting.' *That* was an old iron saucepan which still contained the remains of some ancient stew, which had congealed into green mould. Ruth suddenly burst into tears. 'I'll never get the place clean. It isn't fit for pigs.'

'My mother'll help, and our Mable,' Walter volunteered. Ruth knew poor, frail little Mrs Wray would help. She was kindness itself to Ruth, and was relieved that her son had found himself a lovely girl after all his philanderings. Mr Wray on the other hand had already warned Ruth Stanford to have nothing whatsoever to do with his son.

'Tha'll regret the day tha ever set eyes on him, lass. He'll never change, not even for a grand lass such as thiself. Send him packing before it's too late.'

'Well?' Walter broke into her thoughts. 'Do yer marry me or don't yer?'

'Oh, Walter, of course I want to marry you. It's just this place. I imagined we would begin our marriage in somewhere better than this.'

'Somewhere like your Alice's, I suppose. Well, that's it then. We'd better call it a day.'

Ruth couldn't bear it when she upset Walter. 'No,' she said defiantly, 'we'll look upstairs whilst we're here.'

The stairs were dark and narrow; come to think of it, the whole house was dark. The first bedroom looked out on to the walls of the wire mill, and she strode across the top of the stairs into the other one, looking for something, anything, to be optimistic about.

'There you are, you see, it's much pleasanter at this side. We can see the river and the other side of the valley – well, a little way up at least.'

'So we'll take it?' Walter asked, impatient to be out of the filth and stench.

'Well, if it's the only way we can be married, yes.'

Walter grinned and lifted her up by the waist, twirling her round in a circle. 'So we'll arrange the wedding, then. Nothing elaborate, mind.'

'No, nothing elaborate.' Ruth had the feeling her parents would want as quiet a do as possible. Her stomach churned as she realised she would have to tell them about this place, and tell them as soon as possible. In fact, tonight.

Alice sent George off to work after reassuring him that Lizzie would be well cared for. Her own house was kept permanently clean and sparkling and could be left for a couple of weeks without any noticeable neglect. Indeed, Alice was delighted to have something to occupy her days whilst Joe was at the office and had brushed aside her mother's offer to look after Lizzie. If the truth were told, Emily wasn't feeling at all herself, what with the worry of Ruth foremost in her mind, and though she usually found the slightest excuse to have little Harry to spoil she didn't think she could cope with a lively toddler for the moment, and was very relieved at Alice's offer to take over.

The nappies had been boiled and dolly-blued and were dazzling in their brightness as they blew in the breeze, on the piece of spare ground at the side of the house. Lizzie was lucky in that respect,

Alice thought as she finished pegging out. George had fenced off the grassy triangle so that little Harry had a place to play, unlike other houses in the row. In fact George had done wonders with the little place and it was warm and comfortable and just as spick and span as her own more spacious residence.

Alice frowned as she thought of the place young Ruth was to live in. No wonder Emily was in such a highly strung state. She knew Lizzie would have to be told the news and that Ruth herself wouldn't wish to be the bearer of such tidings. She swilled the doorstep and flags outside with water from the washtub and scrubbed them clean with the yard brush, leaving the tub turned upside down to dry in the sun, then she caught little Harry up in her arms, just in time to prevent him from sitting down in the water. He chuckled as if to say, 'You only just caught me that time,' and his aunt cuddled him close and stroked the baby-blond hair.

She went to check on the new baby in the pram – a gift from Joe and herself when Harry had been born – but little Olive was contentedly sleeping. Isaac said the baby was the image of Alice herself as an infant and she certainly had the same dark hair. Alice wondered what it would be like to bear a child. She had missed the last month's bleeding and sometimes found herself in a state of panic as she thought she might already be carrying. One part of her thought it would be wonderful to be the mother of a child like Harry; the other wondered if she would find the burden too great. Could she give a child the love and complete devotion necessary for its well-being, or would the cold, unbending side of her manage to escape from the deep, dark recess of her mind where she mostly managed to keep it hidden away and prevent her giving an infant the love it needed?

She squeezed Harry and he squealed with delight. 'What nonsense am I thinking now?' she said to the gurgling child. 'I'm a normal, warm, loving woman. Haven't I proved it with thi uncle Joe? The nightmare years are behind me, Harry Crossman, and if I bear a child as bonny as thee I'll make thi uncle Joe the proudest man in Cottenly.'

'Baby,' Harry said, pointing to the pram. 'Mam.' He pointed to the house and laughed at the sound of his own voice and Alice laughed with him. It had taken her a long time to learn how to smile, let alone laugh; it had taken a loving man to teach her.

'I've some news for thee, Lizzie. I might as well tell thee before somebody else does. Don't let it upset thee, though God knows it's upset every-one else in the family.'

'What is it, Alice? What's wrong?'

Alice came straight out with it. 'Our Ruth's getting wed to Walter Wray.'

'Oh, no! I hoped she'd come to her senses sooner or later.' Lizzie rocked the new baby vigorously in an effort to bring up its wind.

'But that's not the worst of it. They're to live down Wire Mill Place.'

Lizzie's mouth dropped open, then she stammered, 'But she can't, Alice. Wire Mill Place is

72

nothing but a slum.'

'I know that, our Ruth knows that, but it's the place Walter Wray's taking her to and tha knows how infatuated she is with that awful man.'

'Oh, Alice, we must do something. She can't live there. Our mam will be so upset.'

'Upset isn't the word I'd use, Lizzie – deranged is more how I'd describe her. The last thing I heard she was refusing to go to the wedding.'

'No! She can't do that, not her own daughter's wedding.'

'I don't know. Our dad was doing all he could to talk her round but without much success. Besides, he's just as distressed by the whole thing as she is.'

'I'm sure he is, but knowing our mam she'll not only have the anxiety of her marrying someone like him but she'll also worry about what folk will think of a daughter of hers living in such a place.'

'I knew no good would come to our Ruth when she ceased going to chapel and began meeting him instead. Tha can't turn thi back on God without repercussions, we all know that.'

'Oh, Alice, how can it be anything to do with religion? George stopped going to chapel before he met me, and Joe doesn't go either. Are you telling me he's not a good man?'

Alice flushed. It was a thorn in her side Joe's not being one thing or the other, but she couldn't deny he was a good man, without doubt one of the kindest and most thoughtful people she had ever had the good fortune to meet. 'Aye well,' she said, 'Joe's different. He doesn't booze all the money away as soon as he gets it, and never once has he tried to turn me away from my religion.'

Lizzie placed the sleeping baby in the cot beside the bed and tried to imagine how a house in Wire Mill Place could ever be made habitable, but all she could see were dirty, ragged children sitting forlornly on bare bottoms, too dejected to even play. 'The children have rickets down there, Alice. I've seen them.'

'Is there any wonder? The sun never reaches them, and I've heard tell the walls inside are bare brick, and they drink out of jam jars.'

'What can we do?' Lizzie was close to tears.

'I could offer her money to do the place up, make it decent, but it would look as if I approved of her marrying him. Oh, Lizzie, what does she see in him?'

'Well, that's easily answered. You must admit he's a handsome-looking lad, Alice.'

'But our Ruth's not daft, she's probably the brightest of the three of us. Surely she can see beyond the smarmy smile and the broad shoulders.'

'She's in love, Alice, or at least she thinks she is. She might come to her senses later but right now she's besotted with Walter Wray, and love does funny things to a person, makes you blind to their faults.'

Alice sniffed. 'By the time she does open her eyes it'll be too late.'

'Oh, God,' Lizzie said. 'You don't think she's marrying him because she's–'

Alice interrupted. 'Expecting? No. Our dad asked her straight out. Seems he hasn't touched her that way.' She blushed deep red at the mention

74

of such a subject.

'Well, we can't accuse him of that, then.' Lizzie's head jerked as she heard Harry stirring in the room across the landing. 'That's our Harry awake,' she said.

'Tha must have better ears than me,' Alice said as she moved away from the bed. 'I'll go and fetch him.'

'Don't worry.' Lizzie laughed. 'It only takes a baby to develop your hearing. Your turn'll come.'

Alice stopped in her tracks. She would have given anything to confide in her sister about her possible pregnancy, but it wasn't something she could talk about, even to Lizzie. Besides, when she was sure, Joe would be the first to know.

She delivered a sleepy Harry into his mother's care, then went down to make the tea. Spotting movement outside, she called back up the stairs, 'It looks like you've got a visitor. Old Mother Buttercup is on her way.' Memories of childhood came back to her, the happy part of childhood, before Grandmother Stanford's time. 'Can tha remember, Lizzie?' she called. 'When we thought she were a witch, and wouldn't go near the cottage in case she bewitched us?'

'Yes.' Lizzie laughed. 'And we waited outside until she popped out and then peeped in her window, looking for her broomstick.'

'Aye,' Alice called. 'Maybe she'll put a spell on Walter Wray and make him disappear.' They were still laughing when Old Mother hobbled in at the door.

'It gets steeper, if you axe me.' She flopped in a kitchen chair and set her basket on the table.

'Aye, it's a rare pull up that hill,' Alice agreed. 'I'm just making a fresh pot. Perhaps that'll revive thee.'

'I won't say no, though a pot of good strong peppermint tay would do us more good on a day like this. Remind me to bring some up next time I call.'

Alice poured the tea into three cups and Old Mother rambled on about the various advantages of peppermint, camomile and other kinds of teas, some of which Alice had never heard of. Then Old Mother lifted the cloth from over her basket. 'There's summat here for Lizzie. Give her four drops a day in a drink of summat.'

'What is it for?' Alice eyed it with suspicion.

'Just summat to get her strength back. She'll need her strength with two little babbies to see to.'

'But what is it?' Alice examined the tiny green bottle.

'Just an infusion of flowers: clematis, mimulus, impatiens.'

'But our Lizzie's perfectly all right.'

'Aye, and we'll try to keep her that way. What with an upset in the family, she'll need her nerves calming. It takes a toll on the nerves having a babby if you axe me.'

Alice almost retorted that nobody was asking her, and wondered how she knew about the upset in the family, which could only be the worry about Ruth. Instead she drank her tea and let Old Mother chatter on. 'Do you want to see our Lizzie? I'll take thee up,' she asked when the visitor showed no sign of moving.

'Aye, and the babby.' Old Mother struggled to her feet and followed Alice up the steep stairs.

'I thought you were never coming up, Old Mother.' Lizzie smiled.

'I came as soon as somebody axed me.' She looked at Alice closely. 'Still, we have to make allowances. How's the babby?'

'Wonderful. Lovely. Don't you think she's like our Alice?'

Old Mother removed the bonnet from round the doll-sized face. 'Aye, she's a little beauty all right. Set some hearts aflame when she grows up if you axe me.' She touched Harry under the chin. 'And you're a grand little chappy an' all.'

'Baby, bye byes.'

Old Mother chortled with delight. 'Aye, the babby's gone to bye byes. He's going to be a clever one, just you mark my words this day.' She suddenly stood up from the chair by the bed and hobbled to the door. 'I'll be off then, and don't forget the drops, will you?' Alice shook her head, and the old woman turned and looked at her closely. 'Raspberry leaf, that's the one you'll be needing. Remind me to bring some up next time I call.' Then she hobbled down the stairs and out the door.

Lizzie didn't say a word, but could tell by the blush on Alice's cheeks that another of Old Mother's predictions was about to come true.

'Tha must attend the wedding, Emily. Our Ruth'll never forgive thee otherwise.' Isaac's face was chalk white and seemed to have aged ten years in the last month.

'There shouldn't be any wedding. You could refuse to give permission. She's under age.' Emily's hand was trembling as she lifted the iron from the hob over the fire.

'I've threatened that, tha knows I have, but she's a determined lass. Told me in no uncertain terms that if I don't agree, she'll simply go and live with Walter out of wedlock. Surely tha doesn't want to be a party to that, because I know I don't.' Isaac sighed. 'No, lass, there'll have to be a wedding and if tha won't attend it then I shall have to take my lass to chapel on my own.'

Emily knew Isaac was right. Alice had been up at the house all morning trying to persuade her to show some interest in the wedding, if not for Ruth's sake, then for Isaac's.

'Our dad doesn't know what to do for the best. Thee and our Ruth'll make him ill between the two of you, can't you see that, our mam?'

Emily had begun to weep. 'And what about me? Doesn't it matter that the whole affair is worrying me to death? What kind of marriage will it be, Alice? Married to a wastrel and a drunkard. You know as well as I do that that's what he is.'

'Well, according to our Lizzie he is trying to turn over a new leaf. Nobody's seen him in the Rag for a couple of weeks now and Joe says he's even done overtime.'

'Oh aye, and why is that? So he doesn't have to help our Ruth fettle out that pigsty, I shouldn't wonder.'

'Well, I don't know about that, but Mrs Wray and Mable have been working like horses alongside our Ruth. It isn't half as bad now the walls

78

have been scraped and whitewashed, and I've scrubbed all the floors and Walter's cleaned out the closet across the yard.'

Emily spat on the iron and pressed furiously on the shirt collar.

'Tha could at least go and look at the place, our mam, or make her up some curtains.'

Alice had gone on and on until Emily knew she was beaten. 'Very well, but it's for your sakes, mind, and our Ruth mustn't come crying to me when it's too late.'

'Tha must learn to be more forgiving and tolerant,' Isaac had said. 'It isn't Christian to hold grudges.'

'Oh, and I suppose Walter Wray is a good Christian, the way he's against our Ruth going to chapel?'

'Nay, lass, tha can't blame him for that. If she wanted to attend neither Walter nor anybody else'd stop her. I reckon she's never been as keen on the chapel as our Alice.'

Emily couldn't argue with that, and it was of some consolation that by all accounts Walter Wray was attempting to change.

If Emily had but known, Walter's reformation was merely a flash in the pan, and though he had resisted visiting the Rag the overtime money was already spent on one of the obscenely painted women Ruth had hurried away from in disgust on the night of the visit to the Empire. And all the time Ruth was attempting to transform the hovel in Wire Mill Place into some semblance of a decent home in which to begin married life.

79

Alice was filling out round the hips and had let out the waistbands on her black dresses and skirts. Joe had hinted that she would look prettier in blue or even grey, but it was as though his wife was afraid of looking attractive. Sometimes he found it hard to believe that the profile Alice presented to the world by day could belong to the same woman who greeted Joe in his bed. If he had but realised it, Alice had been conditioned by Grandmother Stanford into believing that vanity was the most deadly of sins, but nothing, not even the memory of Grandfather Stanford's cold, dead face gazing from his coffin, could silence the murmur of tenderness which rose in a crescendo of passion each time she and Joe came together between the sheets. Now she was to present Joe with the ultimate prize and could wait no longer to give him the news.

She shared out the meat and potato pie she had made for supper and seated herself opposite her husband. She wished she didn't feel so embarrassed as she attempted to tell him. 'Does tha think I'm putting on weight, Joe?' Her face began to burn and she gulped down a drink of water from the crystal tumbler.

'You look fine to me, Alice.'

'I shall put on a lot more before I've done, Joe.' Joe paused, his fork in the air, and noticed the blush on his wife's face. Alice knew the only way was to blurt it out. 'I'm carrying thi child, Joe, to be born in February.'

The fork and the chair both fell with a clatter as Joe jumped up and reached for his wife. 'Oh, Alice, how long have you known? You should have told me, and there you've been, scrubbing out for your Ruth. You must take care, lass.'

'Don't talk daft, Joe. Our Lizzie's worked right up to the day, even the hour, and had no trouble at all.'

'But you must take care all the same, lass. We want no complications. Have you seen a doctor?'

Alice laughed. 'What for? I'm not badly, I don't need any doctor. I shall send for Old Mother Buttercup when my time comes. She did well for our Lizzie.'

'You'll what?' The glare Joe threw at her caused Alice to break into laughter again.

'I said I'll–'

'I heard what you said, and you'll do no such thing. What with her potions and concoctions it's a miracle Old Mother hasn't poisoned somebody before today.'

'Oh, Joe, I shan't be taking any concoctions. She'll see me through the birthing, that's all.' She placed her arms round Joe's waist and pulled him towards her. 'And don't start thi fussing. I'm not an invalid. I'm beginning to wish I hadn't told thee.' Joe kissed her, first on the forehead, and then, tilting her chin upward, a long hungry kiss until the longing began and she felt the hardness of him through her dress. 'The tatie pie's going cold.' She pulled away. 'We'd best eat.' She picked up the toppled chair. 'And another thing, I'd like to know where tha learned to kiss in such a manner.'

'Now that'd be telling.' He grinned. 'Let's get the tatie pie down us and then you can give me a few more lessons.'

'Joe Jackson, it's still daylight and there's thee talking about making love.'

'Well it's you who started it. You asked me if you've put on any weight. I can't tell with that frock on so I'd best take it off.' Alice ate her pie without answering, but he couldn't help noticing how her eyes sparkled.

When Joe had married Alice he had thought companionship was all he craved. He had never been one for chasing the lasses, though there had been a girl before France. The lovemaking on that occasion had left a lot to be desired and he had decided he could do without a repeat performance, but by God Alice had changed his mind. The passion between them had transformed Joe's whole existence, and now he was to be a father to top it all. And by gum – he finished his pie – she was a bloody good cook too. He grinned across the table, 'Alice Jackson, did I ever tell you how much I love you?'

'I'd rather tha showed me,' she said, and led the way up the stairs.

Once Emily was persuaded to attend the wedding she pursued the preparations wholeheartedly. She wasn't happy with the arrangement but if she was to be present she would make sure her daughter was given a good send-off. Beyond that she would not interfere.

Isaac footed the bill as usual, relieved that this would be the last do he would be responsible for. Ruth resembled a princess in the powder-blue dress, made up by Emily in the very latest style, and Isaac wished once again that he had hired a photographer. Unfortunately, that had been the last thing on his mind, and now it was too late. When Ruth smiled up at him as they entered the chapel he experienced a strong desire to hold her in his arms and protect her from the life he knew was to follow, to prevent her wasting her grace and beauty on the likes of Walter Wray. But Ruth smiled radiantly at Walter, and nobody could deny he made a handsome groom in his dark suit and stiff-collared shirt. Only Walter's own father noticed the way his eyes roamed over the figure of Mary Hampshire as she took her place beside her best friend for the ceremony.

Nevertheless Walter behaved impeccably throughout the reception, probably because no drinks were allowed in the lecture room, and because this was the night Walter had been waiting for, when Ruth Stanford would become his own personal possession. Emily had the feeling that both families were putting on a brave face for Ruth's sake and was relieved when the guests began to drift away. Only Lizzie and George seemed to be genuinely happy as they showed off their offspring with pride. It was as if nothing would be allowed to penetrate the circle of contentment they had formed around their family. It was only when her daughter had left for her new home that Emily finally gave way to the tears which had threatened all day, and nobody, not even Isaac, tried to comfort her. They were all just as dejected as she was.

'Well, it's all over, lass,' Isaac remarked, merely for something to say.

'No, Isaac, you're wrong,' she replied. 'It's only

just beginning.' Then they walked home together, silent in the darkness.

Initially Emily wondered if she had been wrong to condemn Walter. She had to admit Ruth seemed blissfully happy, despite the deprivation in which she lived. The family had rallied round and done the best they could with the house, and though it was by no means ideal Ruth kept the place as clean as possible considering the dust and soot which seemed to settle on everything from clothes to walls and windows. Alice had insisted on spending some of their grandmother's money on a bed, a table and some chairs, which Ruth had refused at first, pointing out that her sister had earned every penny by putting up with the miserable old woman. Walter, however, said it would be throwing the kindness in her sister's face if she didn't accept. Ruth would have had more admiration for her husband had he followed the example of George, who had refused a similar offer when he had married Lizzie. Nevertheless, the furniture was gratefully received.

It was only after a couple of months, when he began gradually drifting back to the Rag, that Emily knew her original doubts were justified. Walter knew he had a prize in Ruth. Not only was she a worker when it came to running a home, but she had knocked him for six when it came to making love. She had a figure more desirable than any he had seen and he had to admit he had set eyes on a few. The love Ruth felt for her husband made her responsive in every way and it was only when she began complaining about the amount of money he was spending in the Rag that he began to regret his responsibilities.

'Stop nagging, woman. I won't be told what to do with my own money.'

Ruth would retaliate by turning away from him. 'I'll not make love when you smell like a brewery,' she said. At first he would merely grunt and turn over to sleep off the booze, but then suddenly he began to show another side, a side only his parents had witnessed and they preferred to forget. The first time he came home in a rage brought on by the beer Ruth chose to ignore him, put on her hat and coat and went on a visit to Lizzie's. By the time she returned Walter had gone to bed, but not before he had thrown the dinner Ruth had prepared for him at the newly whitened wall, shattering the plate into a dozen pieces. Ruth had cleaned up the mess, and for the first time acknowledged that Walter wasn't quite the man she had expected.

Chapter Three

Alice's child was born on Shrove Tuesday. A fine son, who Old Mother said was the biggest babby she had ever delivered. Old Mother stayed with Alice throughout the two-day labour and for the two days following, alongside Emily, who feared for her daughter after a long and arduous confinement. Joe was all for fetching a doctor when Alice's temperature suddenly rose. 'She needs medical care,' he told Emily, but his mother-in-law had every faith in Old Mother who had supervised all three of her own daughters' births.

'She's in good hands, Joe. Old Mother will see her through, better than any doctor,' Emily consoled him as she rocked her new grandson in his wooden cradle.

Alice was in the cold stage of fever, brought on by weakness, according to Old Mother. Her nails were blue and her trembling alarmed Joe, who was torn between going for Dr Swinbourne and staying by his wife's side. The chamber pot was continually being taken to be emptied by Emily, as Alice was violently sick. Old Mother felt Alice's pulse as her face became more shrivelled and her eyes more sunken. She left the bedside only once, and when she returned proceeded to administer a tea to her patient, little by little.

'What is it?' Joe demanded.

'Naught but sage and senna,' Old Mother answered. Gradually the colour returned to Alice's skin, and once more the old woman felt for her pulse. 'That's better,' she said.

'I don't feel better.' Alice's voice was weak. 'I feel as if I've been pummelled all over.' Old Mother bathed her head with vinegar water. 'I need a drink.' Emily reached for the glass on the window ledge.

'Not yet if she doesn't want to be sick again! Well, maybe just a little drop of watter,' Old Mother allowed. Emily let her daughter sip a little of the liquid. Alice couldn't rest, throwing off the sheets and writhing about the bed. 'Let's see thi tongue, my dear.' Alice was too restless to comply. Old Mother opened her patient's mouth to reveal a thick, yellow-coated organ. 'What a sight.'

'What's happening? Is she worse?' Joe enquired anxiously.

'No worse, no better. Give her time, lad. She'll be sweating before the day's out. Go get tea ready for her mother, it must be teatime.'

Emily worried about the baby. 'I can't put him to her breast and he won't take cow's milk.' Her words were drowned by the infant's lusty cry.

'What about Lizzie? If you axe me she'll have enough milk to feed a dozen.'

Emily laid the crying child in his cradle. 'I'll fetch her,' she said.

By the time the baby was fed and sleeping, Alice's skin looked softer and more natural, her pulse was almost normal and her breathing easier, and a fine film of sweat coated her brow. Old Mother left the sickbed once more.

'What is it?' Joe left his task of washing the dishes immediately Old Mother entered the kitchen.

'Naught that can't be put right.' She brought out another mysterious bag from the large pocket in her pinafore. 'Have you a jug? And some boiling watter?'

'What are you making?' Lizzie asked.

'Naught but spearmint and pumpkin seeds, the finest thing for her if you axe me.'

Joe looked dubious but Emily had every faith in Old Mother's remedies.

'Get yerself to bed, lad. She'll be as right as rain in a day or so. Weak as a kitten, but right as rain,' the old woman said.

'I'll take the baby and keep him until our Alice can care for him. By the way, what's he to be called?' Lizzie asked.

'Joseph. It's Alice's choice.' Joe gazed down fondly at the child.

'He's a grand baby.' Lizzie cuddled the child and wrapped him snugly in a hand-crocheted shawl. She knew Alice's son would be dressed in nothing but the finest garments, but she felt no envy. George provided for her and their family as well as he was able and Lizzie wouldn't have exchanged her lot for anyone's, not even Alice's.

Old Mother had settled once more in the bedside chair. 'It's you who should be in bed,' Joe told her. 'You must be all in. I don't think you've slept for four days or nights. Besides, I'd like to lie beside Alice, if I may.'

'Lie beside her, lad. The closeness'll comfort her if she wakes, but I'll stay where I am. I'll sleep with one eye open, so I'll know if I'm needed.'

88

She let out a cackle of laughter, showing a wide, open gap where her teeth had once been. 'I'll be keeping my eye on thee, Joe, so don't be going misbehaving yerself when the lamp's turned low.' Despite Joe's anxiety he couldn't help but smile at Old Mother's attempt to cheer him up.

Once Emily knew her daughter would recover she went home to Isaac, who was waiting worriedly for his wife's return. 'How is she, lass?'

'Old Mother says she's going to be fine.'

'Thank God,' Isaac breathed.

'I think it's Old Mother we should be thanking, Isaac.'

'Aye, maybe,' Isaac agreed, 'but the way I've prayed this last few days I think God may have had something to do with it, so we'll thank Him just the same.'

Emily kissed her husband gently. 'Let's get to bed, Isaac,' she said. 'I've missed you these last few days.'

'I've missed thee and all, Emily. I don't know what I'd do without thee, lass.'

'Oh, I dare say you'd manage, and maybe you'd get a bit of peace and quiet.' Emily smiled. Isaac put out the lamp and climbed the stairs, Emily ahead of him, to the bed they'd been sharing for nigh on twenty-five years, and God willing they would share for another twenty-five.

The general strike came and passed, supported wholeheartedly by Isaac. As a member of the Railway Workers' Union he had expected the militancy to precipitate strike action long before it did. Now it seemed the fire of the working classes

89

had burned itself out. There was very little to see for the hardship, of which the miners suffered the most with eight times as many striking days as other trade unionists. In Cottenly it was the industrial giants who complained the loudest, whilst the lower workers, who were ill prepared for financial loss and terrified that they would not be reinstated, knew all they could do was stand with the majority. Nevertheless a sigh of relief was heard in most households when the strike finally ended. Lizzie Crossman, heeding her father's advice, had prepared herself for any loss of income by finding a cleaning job at one of the houses belonging to the posh folk.

Desiree Rubeck was the wife of a travelling man, known to the likes of Lizzie as the tallyman. Mr Rubeck was a well-known visitor to many of the households in Cottenly and Warrentickle, where he had called on George's mother every Saturday morning for many years. During that time the family had bought everything from linoleum to sideboards from him, and wedding suits to prams. Goods would be paid for at a shilling in the pound, per week, and the family would gather excitedly to see what he had to offer over a pot of tea and a slice of Mrs Crossman's fruit cake. Lizzie was relieved when the strike came to think she had always resisted the temptation to put things on the book, following Emily's sound advice to do without anything that couldn't be paid for. Even so, she was grateful to the Rubecks for offering her the two mornings' work a week. Unfortunately Mrs Rubeck was nowhere near as nice a person as her husband

and George didn't much care to have his wife scrubbing floors on her hands and knees whilst the mistress of the house was dolling herself up and acting all la-di-da, as he put it, for her afternoon callers. As a matter of fact Lizzie wasn't too keen either. The tall windows had to be cleaned, the range in the kitchen blackleaded, the bellows and fender scoured until they shone and the carpet squares taken out on to the line and beaten. Any outside work had to be done first, before any neighbouring posh folk condescended to leave their beds, as it wouldn't do for Lizzie to be seen by them in her pinafore and her worn down shoes. But Mrs Rubeck grudgingly handed over her wages each Tuesday and Friday and the strike was weathered without any mounting debts. Afterwards Lizzie wondered how she could leave without seeming ungrateful, and was thankful when the problem was solved by her becoming pregnant again. On the day she told Mrs Rubeck, she was feeling nauseous and looked as bad as she felt.

'I won't be coming any more,' she said, 'unless you want me to stay another week until you find a replacement.' She sighed. 'I'm pregnant again, and not feeling too well this time.'

'No wonder. How many is that?'

'This'll be the third,' Lizzie answered proudly.

'Oh, well. I suppose it's only to be expected from you people who don't know any better.'

Lizzie could feel the heat in her cheeks. 'What do you mean by "you people"?' she asked.

The woman looked embarrassed by the question. 'Well,' she said, 'I don't suppose there's

91

much for the lower classes to do with themselves except breed like animals.'

Lizzie had just finished scrubbing the flagged floor and had dried it as thoroughly as she could. The bucket of dirty water stood by her side waiting to be emptied. She looked up at the woman's smarmy face and was tempted to remind her that it was the lower classes who were keeping her in luxurious idleness. Her eyes travelled down the immaculate white lace-trimmed blouse, the ankle-length poplin skirt and shiny black shoes, then she picked up the bucket of grey, sludgy water and flung it across the almost dry kitchen floor. Mrs Rubeck's eyes widened and she spluttered as she searched for words that wouldn't somehow form.

Lizzie walked to the door. She felt terribly sick but exhilarated by her action. She turned to her ex-employer. 'Being of the working class, like you said, I can't be expected to know any better.' She walked out of the house, leaving Mrs Rubeck standing, gaping at the flooded floor, the hem of her skirt dripping with dirty water. She paddled towards the door, intending to call Lizzie back, even to plead with the girl to clear up the mess. She was just in time to see Lizzie, who could contain her morning sickness not a moment longer, vomit her elevenses all over the newly whitened step.

Lizzie felt better by the time she arrived home, and better still as she and Emily laughed and agreed it was well worth the forfeiture of her morning's pay just to think of Mrs Rubeck attempting to clean up the kitchen.

Winnie Armitage watched Walter Wray go off to the Rag at opening time, knowing he should have been at work. Still, it was nothing unusual for him to knock a shift out once or twice a week. The Lord only knew how he hadn't been sacked before now, or how young Ruth put up with the obnoxious sod.

Winnie had been born in Wire Mill Place, was used to the grime, but because her house was not actually joined on to the others was quite content. According to Emily, Mrs Wray, and everybody else who knew her, Winnie was a grand woman. The reasons for these opinions varied. Walter's mother said she had no edge on her and considered everybody, even the unfortunates in her immediate neighbourhood, to be every bit as good as she was. Emily knew that she had not only nursed both her parents through long illnesses, but had also married a man who was suffering from a disabling lung complaint, although he had a heart every bit as large as Winnie's.

Winnie could see Ruth hanging out the coloureds on the clothes line. No doubt the house would be cluttered with the whites, steaming and drying on the rack over the fire, the clothes horse and everywhere else she could find to hang the never-ending laundry she did for the posh folk. None of it could be hung out no matter how suitable the weather, because of the soot from the works chimneys.

Winnie called out to Ruth. 'Are yer popping over, lass? I'm just about to mash.'

'Thanks. Just give me time to change the twins

– I won't be five minutes.' Winnie nodded and went in to brew the tea. She lifted a date and rhubarb pie from the oven and moved another one from the top shelf to take its place. Then she riddled the fire to make it draw better and tested the large bowl of rising dough in the hearth. Ruth popped her head round the door, a baby in each arm.

'Come in and close the door gently, lass.'

'Mmm! Something smells good.'

'Aye. You must take a pie with yer when yer go.'

'Oh, I couldn't. You're always giving me something. I never go home empty-handed, yet I never give you anything in return.'

'Well, nor would I expect owt. With a bugger like him, love, you've all on to feed yerselves.' Ruth blushed but didn't deny it. Mrs Armitage had no time for Walter and Ruth knew it. Come to think of it, Walter knew it too. Mrs Armitage had been shown the door by him on numerous occasions, and one time a frying pan had followed, missing her by inches, but it hadn't stopped her from standing up for Ruth and even threatening him with a huge butcher's cleaver if he didn't leave his wife alone. Ruth had no doubt she would have used it, too, if he hadn't staggered up the stairs to his bed.

Winnie took little Sadie from Ruth and they sat to the table, each with a blonde, rosy-cheeked baby on her lap.

'Who's a little cheeky face then?' Winnie assumed the special high-pitched voice she reserved for baby talk, which always made Ruth cringe as she talked of such things as bow-wows, chuck-

chucks and puff-puffs. Yet Ruth wouldn't have said anything to hurt the good woman's feelings for the world.

'Is your Billy at school then?' Winnie asked.

'Oh, yes. Nothing would keep him away.'

'Aye, he's a good lad, your Billy. A pity his father isn't as conscientious. I suppose he had another skinful last night.'

'Oh, I hope he didn't keep you all awake, Mrs Armitage. You must have heard him come home – I should think everyone in the Place did.'

'Never mind, lass. As long as he was singing I wasn't bothered. It's when he comes home cursing that worries me. Why don't yer leave him, lass?'

Ruth gave a cynical smile. 'What, with three kids? Where would I go?'

'Back home. I know for a fact yer father would take yer in.'

'Oh yes, our dad would, and since you mention it our mam would too. But just imagine what it would be like. She would never stop saying "I told you so". She never lets me forget it even now. Oh, no, I couldn't stand it. Besides, it wouldn't be fair to lumber her with three youngsters at her age.'

'Well, yer mother does have a point, love. She begged yer not to marry him.'

'I know that, but it only makes me more determined.'

'Well, I'd rather you than me. Where's he got the money from this time?'

Ruth swallowed hard before replying, as though a lump was choking her. 'He's been to the pawnshop again. The canteen of Sheffield cutlery the

95

girls at work bought me for a wedding present.' Ruth began to sob. 'Oh, Mrs Armitage, what can I do?'

'Nay, lass, I'll be buggered if I know, apart from getting old Buttercup to give yer summat to poison him with.'

Ruth couldn't help smiling through her tears. Mrs Armitage always made her feel better.

'Here, hold her a minute.' Winnie placed Sadie on Ruth's other knee. 'I'll just have to knock back me dough, love.' She emptied the dough on to the floured board, floured her hands and proceeded to knead the bread dough, the muscles in her arms flexing as hard as any man's as she did so. Then she formed it into flat cakes and placed them on a baking tray, blackened with use over the years. 'I'll bring yer round a couple when they come out of the oven,' she promised.

'Oh no, I couldn't,' Ruth said. 'Besides, I already have some bread. I got my laundry money yesterday, and I always make sure I spend it on bread and a pot of jam before anything else.'

'Bloody bread and jam, and breast-feeding two bairns. No wonder yer all skin and bone. Yer need some good stew down yer, your Billy as well. As for that bugger, I should think he'd have room for nowt in his belly except the ale.'

Ruth rose to her feet. 'Look, our Frankie has dropped off. I'll go put him in the pram and get some ironing done while I have the chance.'

'Aye, all right, lass. And see if you can put yer feet up a bit. They look right swelled to me.'

'Oh, don't worry about me. I might get low sometimes, but physically I'm as fit as a fiddle.'

'Aye, well, you'll need to be with three bairns. And think on, keep yer legs crossed or he'll get yer another right quick.'

'Not while I'm breast-feeding, I hope. Our Lizzie says I won't catch on as long as I'm feeding.'

'Not in every case, lass. You can't depend on it. Besides, it hasn't stopped your Lizzie, has it? How many has she now?'

'Five, and another on the way and none of them seem to bother her.'

'But she's a good man in George.'

'Yes, one of the best, and so has our Alice.'

'Oh, don't mention Joe Jackson to me. I shall never forget the kindness he showed to my Albert when he was in hospital. Couldn't do enough to help, and he was only a young man at the time. Oh, I know they were both in the Oddfellows, but apart from coming on their behalf he helped in so many ways. I'll never forget and nobody mon say a wrong word to me about Joe Jackson or they'll have me to deal with.'

Ruth chuckled. 'And if Winnie Armitage starts to deal with them they'd better watch out.' She was still smiling as she set off for home.

''Ere, hang on. I'll come with yer and carry the pie.'

'Oh, Mrs Armitage, I don't know what I'd do without you. You're like a second mother to me.'

'Aye well, you know where I am if you need me, love.'

'I do, and it helps, thanks.'

They lifted the washing on the lines as they wended their way across the yard. 'This lot's dry.

I'll pop the pie on the table and then I'll bring it in for yer. If I fold it carefully yer might get away without ironing some of it.'

'Oh, I iron the lot. I couldn't bear to think they weren't ironed.'

Winnie smiled. 'Yer'll learn, lass, as yer get older. What the eye doesn't see, the heart doesn't grieve over.' Then she began to gather in the washing before it became too dry to be ironable.

Ruth placed the babies one at each end of the pram. Soon they'd be too big and have to be put to bed in the afternoon. She stood the flat iron on the hob and folded a blanket across the table with an upturned enamel dish to stand the iron on. What a life – nothing but drudgery day in day out. If only the house would stay clean once it was done, but every day the whole place had to be gone over again. It wasn't too bad whilst the twins were babies, but Ruth was dreading the toddling stage when it would be impossible to leave the door open in case one of them wandered off towards the river. She glanced in the pram. Oh, but they were beautiful, worth all the work, and Ruth was so proud when she wheeled them over to Lizzie's or to see Alice on the green. People would stand and admire them. In fact the only one who didn't seem proud was their own father. Some times he didn't seem to remember they were there at all, except when they would cry and he would bawl at them fit to waken the dead. Even Billy could not arouse Walter's interest. He would bring pictures home after a drawing lesson at school, or a paper with all the sums correct and a *V Good* to prove his ability, and Walter would merely grunt and push the child aside. At first Ruth would cover up for her husband with the excuse that he had been working and was tired, but Billy was too intelligent to be hoodwinked and soon realised his father wasn't interested in him, his mother, or anything at all except the beer.

Ruth's stomach turned a somersault as she heard Walter's feet on the cobbles outside the door. She prayed to God that he would be in a reasonable frame of mind as she hurriedly cleared away the ironing from the table and replaced it with a cloth. He didn't like it if his dinner wasn't ready to be served on his arrival. She brought a cottage pie from the oven. He would complain about the lack of meat but that couldn't be helped.

Walter threw his jacket over the pram handle, causing Frankie to stir. Luckily he settled down again and Ruth breathed a sigh of relief. Surely it wasn't natural to live in fear of one's husband.

'What's this?' he asked, sitting to the table.

'Cottage pie,' she answered brightly. 'And there's rhubarb and date to follow.'

'Is this all there is?' he asked, stabbing the potato topping with his fork. 'No greens?'

'No. In fact you're lucky to have that. Our Billy and me have had nothing except a potato in its skin.'

'Our Billy's not a grown man, nor is he working.'

'Neither are you most of the time.' Ruth knew she had made a mistake the minute the words left her tongue. The knife and fork few across the table in Ruth's direction and Walter sprang to his feet, undoing his belt as he approached her. She grabbed the iron from the hearth, holding it out in front of her. 'Don't you touch me, Walter Wray, or I'll mark you with the iron and that's a promise.'

His raised arm lowered reluctantly and he backed away. 'One of these days I'll smash that pretty face in, just you wait.'

'And one of these days I'll swing for you, Walter Wray, I bloody will.' Ruth felt ashamed as the swear word slipped out. 'Now, eat your dinner, or our Billy'll eat it and enjoy it.'

'Oh aye, that'd suit yer, wouldn't it, little Billy getting the meat and me the taties.'

'We could all have the meat if you'd go to work and bring home some money instead of handing it over the Rag bar. Don't you know you're a laughing stock? Don't you know they're laughing at you for keeping the landlord's money rolling in?' Before Walter could retaliate Ruth grabbed the pram and hurried it out of the door as her husband staggered once more to his feet. Fortunately his gait was unsteady and his wife was too quick for him. With a bit of luck he would go to bed; with an extra bit of luck he might fall from the top to the bottom of the stairs.

Ruth prayed for forgiveness for her thoughts as she wheeled the twins over the cobbles towards the bridge. She would meet Billy out of school and take the kids to see their grandparents. Emily would like that and she needn't know that the visit was a means of escaping, from the man Ruth had long since ceased to love. Now never a day went by when she didn't regret marrying Walter Wray, the idle, drunken bully everybody except herself had recognised. Ruth held her shoulders back and her head high as she climbed Queen Victoria Street. She knew one thing for sure: Walter Wray would never wear her down, no matter what he did. She had her children to consider. Three lovely children, and no one except Mrs Armitage would ever know the humiliation she was forced to suffer for their sakes.

When Emily opened the door she was greeted with her daughter's radiant smile and nobody, not even her own mother, would have guessed at the ache in Ruth Wray's heart.

Although Harry Crossman tried not to be, he couldn't help thinking he was his Grandad Stanford's favourite. Not that he was treated any differently from the rest of the grandchildren. Every Saturday morning his cousin Joseph, Olive and himself would take the others down to Miss Fiddler's sweetshop, each with a penny given to them by Grandad Stanford, and there they would stand, noses pressed against the window as they decided what to spend the money on. Sometimes they would choose a twist of marry-me-quick or a liquorice shoelace. Then Olive would take Bessie, Jimmy and Mary back home where they would share out the sweets and then go out to play in the garden George had developed by the side of the house. It had been walled in so that the children could play in safety, giving Lizzie peace of mind.

Afterwards Harry, Joseph and sometimes Billy – if he wasn't out collecting wood in the self-constructed old barrow – would go along to the green to play football. Grandad Stanford or Grandad Wray would come along sometimes and watch their games, and though Billy was more agile and had a stronger left foot Grandad would never praise one against the other. Oh no, there was never any favouritism expressed. It was on a Tuesday that the special closeness between Harry and Isaac came to the fore. That was the night of the penny library down by the smithy, and Harry would accompany his grandfather to spend sometimes a full hour, browsing and discussing in a whisper the many delights upon the shelves.

Harry loved the atmosphere of the penny library: the fusty, dusty smell of the books; the calm and quiet as they examined the wealth of wisdom and wonder within the pages. Isaac would recommend the ones he had read and they would choose three, sometimes four, to borrow until the following week. Then they would saunter home, discussing all manner of things, from trains to motor cars, Isaac's anxiety about a man called Hitler being appointed Chancellor of Germany and problems close to home, here in Yorkshire.

'Fill thy head with knowledge, lad, and it'll never be wasted.' Isaac would advise his grandson on all manner of things and Harry would nod his head solemnly, and dream that one day he would go to college or university where he could absorb even more knowledge. He knew his hopes were probably in vain for theirs was a poor family, albeit a happy one, and he suspected he would never realise his ambition. If he had been in Joseph's shoes, money would have been forthcoming, but

Joseph had no such scholarly leanings; all Joseph talked about were motors and engines. His cousin Billy on the other hand wanted the outdoor life of a farmer but knew he would have no alternative but to enter the steel works as soon as they would employ him. So Harry cast aside his dream of a decent education and thanked God he wasn't in Billy's shoes, for Billy wasn't only poor where money was concerned, he had never had a loving father's support. And although Joseph Jackson would never want for anything, Harry considered being an only child must be an absolute tragedy. So he absorbed the knowledge from the library and enjoyed the close companionship he shared with his grandfather, at the same time considering himself luckier than either of his cousins, especially as he believed himself to be his grandad's favourite. He did sometimes wonder, though, how many more babies would be born before his parents decided enough was enough. Not that he didn't like having brothers and sisters, but money was scarce and the younger girls were beginning to complain about always having to wear hand-me-downs.

It wasn't only Harry whose thoughts were on limiting the family. Lizzie hoped that when the expected baby was born it would be the last. The trouble was she seemed to catch on when George as much as looked at her. George talked about a kind of rubber thing which would prevent her becoming pregnant but never seemed to do anything about it until it was too late. Perhaps Old Mother would know what to do. She would ask her when she came to deliver the child. In the meantime Lizzie went serenely about her duties, delighted now that George had done out the loft and added a ladder for the boys to climb. With a double bed manoeuvred up there, the girls had a room of their own and there was more privacy for George and herself.

Ernest Crossman was born on a beautiful summer's day. Afterwards Lizzie said to Old Mother, 'I hope I don't have another in a hurry.'

Old Mother looked at her. 'No, lass, this'll be the last. I told yer there'd be a half a dozen babbies and that's the lot.'

'But how can I be sure? I don't want to risk it and I love George, Old Mother. I can't deny him his comfort and I wouldn't wish to.' Lizzie blushed but Old Mother just grinned her toothless smile.

'What you need, lass, is a sponge if you axe me.'

'A sponge! What kind of sponge?'

'A sponge soaked in vinegar and put inside yer.'

'Will that prevent me becoming pregnant again?'

'It might and it might not, but it'll be better than naught, and wont do any harm.' Old Mother rocked little Ernest in her arms. 'Not that you will need it. This little man'll be the last.'

'Oh, I hope you're right, but then you usually are. Where and how you became so wise, that's what I'd like to find out.'

'That's what they'd all like to find out, but I shan't be telling anybody till I'm good and ready.'

Lizzie knew that would be the last word on the subject and resigned herself to taking it easy for a few days. Emily would no doubt be down to spoil her, and Alice. She wondered how Alice had avoided becoming pregnant again but it wasn't a subject she could approach her sister about. She would try the sponge all the same.

She put the baby to her breast, experiencing once again the feeling of satisfaction in feeding her child. She would miss this fulfilment which only a mother could know, but it was time to call it a day. Half a dozen mouths to feed were enough for anyone these days. She would mention to Ruth about the sponge, before Walter Wray decided to increase his family, a family he neither cherished nor supported. She sighed contentedly. Oh, she did love George. He would be pleased about the sponge, she knew he would.

She called to Olive, who was no doubt clearing up downstairs, 'You can bring them up to see the baby now, Olive love.' The stampede up the stairs caused the bed to shake and then they shyly entered the room, Olive carrying Mary in her arms.

'Are you all right, Mam?'

'I'm fine, love. Come and look at the baby,' Lizzie invited. They crept silently round the bed and peeped one at a time at their new brother. 'Is it a boy baby?' Jimmy enquired.

'Yes. We're to call him Ernest.'

'Good. We've got enough girls.'

'We've got enough lads an' all,' Bessie said. 'Besides, I don't like Ernest for a name. I want him to be called Edward.'

'Then he shall be. He'll be called Ernest Edward, specially for you.' Lizzie knew Bessie was usually the jealous one and hoped to avoid any animosity between the children.

Bessie's eyes lit up and she snuggled down on the bed close to Lizzie. 'Can I hold him?'

'Yes, each of you can hold him in turn, if you're careful not to drop him.'

'Or squeeze him,' Olive added, ever the little mother. Oh, but Old Mother had been right: her eldest daughter was turning into a beauty. Lizzie looked from one to the other. They were all beautiful, even the boys. She was so fortunate. When she went to chapel to be churched she would say a prayer, a special prayer, thanking God for her fortune. But she still hoped little Ernest Edward would be the last.

Joseph tapped on Lizzie's door and entered. Nobody ever waited outside Auntie Lizzie's; it was home to any child who knew any of the Crossmans and sometimes Joseph wondered how everybody fitted in. The large table was usually set for some meal or other and in between meals a neighbour, a friend or one of the many Crossman relatives would more often than not be perched up to it for a gossip and a cup of tea. It wasn't a bit like Joseph's house, where the red plush table cover with its tassels to the floor was hastily replaced after every meal and the vase of flowers set in the centre. Joseph definitely preferred Auntie Lizzie's, where nobody was ever bored, or reprimanded for not wiping their feet. Not that he didn't appreciate his home and his mother and father who loved him dearly, but Auntie Lizzie's was a happy house.

'Come on in, Joseph,' she called as he opened the door. 'Sit yerself down, my love.'

'I'm not staying, Auntie. Mam sent me to see if you feel like going on a picnic. She says we can paddle if we go up Warrentickle way.' He edged a bit closer to the table where a game of happy families was in progress. 'It's shallower up there.'

'Oh, can we, Mam?'

'Let's, Mam, please.'

'Can I swim?'

Joseph laughed as his cousins bombarded Auntie Lizzie for an answer.

'Well, I don't see why not. Providing you're good,' she added, welcoming the chance to bribe them into behaving.

'Right, then. I'm to go and ask Auntie Ruth if they're coming as well.' He hoped Uncle Walter was at work; he didn't fancy a mouthful of cursing from him. 'Are yer coming with me, Harry?' he asked hopefully.

'OK.' Harry closed the book he was reading rather reluctantly, and tucked it under his arm in case he got a chance to read it on the way.

'What time are we going?' Olive asked and wondered what they could take to eat. There wasn't much of anything, it being the day before pay day. It would probably be bread and jam, or lard. She would help her mother to make the sandwiches.

'We're setting off at three. Mam says we'll meet by the bridge, oh and not to bother about food, she's packing enough for us all.'

Olive noticed the relief on her mother's face. The little ones were skipping with excitement. Jimmy found a ball and a battered old cricket bat and started to practise batting.

'Stop it, don't be so daft,' Olive chided. 'You nearly knocked the ornaments off the dresser.'

'Go and wash your faces, all of you, or we shan't go,' Lizzie threatened, and they began pushing each other to get to the sink. 'There isn't a water shortage,' she called. 'And don't forget to use the soap.' She set about raking the fire. If she popped some scrubbed potatoes in the oven now, they'd just about be done for George on his arrival home from work. She frowned at the meagre fare and wished there was some meat, but there was plenty of good grist bread to go with them, and one thing about George, he never complained. She changed Ernest's nappy, coating him liberally with baby powder, before cuddling him and laying him in his pram.

Joseph and Harry kicked at a stone all the way to Ruth's. Joseph hated Wire Mill Place and felt sorry for Billy, especially when the lads at school belittled him for living there. Once Billy couldn't go to school for a week because the bugs had come through from next door and covered them all with huge, red bites. Auntie Ruth had kept him away until they had disappeared rather than let him be bullied. Then she had sprinkled DDT all round the skirting boards in an effort to be rid of the horrible, brown, bloodsucking pests.

'I hope he's not in,' Harry said. 'I don't like him, especially when he's drunk.'

'I don't like him when he's sober either,' Joseph agreed. 'He's a pig.'

Harry laughed. 'Don't let yer mother hear you say that.'

'I don't care if she does. In fact she can't stand

him either.'

Ruth for a change had brought a chair outside and was watching the twins playing in a pile of soil Billy had loosened for them to dig in with a spoon. Some of the little ones from next door had joined them, one wearing nothing but a grey-looking vest and the other, a pretty, curly-headed little girl, looking as though she'd never been in a bath since the day she was born. Harry wrinkled his nose at the strong smell of urine. Ruth welcomed the invitation to get away and hurriedly set about washing the little ones with a flannel and brushing their hair. Nobody could accuse Auntie Ruth of not keeping them all clean. Joseph had heard his mother praising her for the way she coped against the filth and grime of their surroundings many a time.

'Where's our Billy?' Joseph popped his head round the door in search of his cousin.

'Over at Mr Baraclough's, shovelling in the coal. They had a delivery this morning.' She frowned at the thought of her son doing the back-aching work of an adult. 'He should be back any minute.'

'So he'll be coming with us then?'

'Oh, yes. I wouldn't go without him.'

'Goody.' Joseph liked his cousin, who was always optimistic and joking. Billy never let anything get him down. 'We can have a better game if there's more of us.'

Harry thought he would prefer to find a quiet place under the trees and read his book but knew he would be called a spoilsport if he suggested such a thing. 'I should think he'll be too hot and exhausted if he's just got the coal in,' he said.

'Oh, not our Billy. He's strong as a horse,' Joseph said, causing Ruth to smile proudly. 'Right then, we'll be off. Mam says to meet by the bridge at three. Oh, and she'll bring enough food for everybody.'

Ruth felt relief wash over her. Sometimes she wondered what she'd do without Alice, and to think she'd considered her selfish at one time. But that was before she'd met Joe. She supposed it was love that had changed her sister, just as it had changed herself – made her hard and bitter in a way. But then, it hadn't been love which had changed her. It was only when the love had turned to hatred that she had changed, and only towards him; she would never change towards her children. She would be a loving mother to her children and not even Walter Wray would change that. She hoped Billy would be back in time; if not they would follow on later. She wondered anxiously what Walter would say if he arrived home before they returned. He never came straight home without calling at the Rag, so it was unlikely that he would, but if he did she would just have to bear the consequences. She had made a pot of tripe and onions which would only need warming. He could pop it in the oven if she wasn't back; it wouldn't hurt him for once. All the same she couldn't help worrying as she cleaned the twins' down-at-heel shoes, worrying too about what to do when their feet outgrew them, which would happen in the next few weeks. She combed her hair in the mirror, cracked by a pint pot thrown at it in one of Walter's rages. Examining her reflection, she thought it was a miracle she wasn't grey and lined with all the worrying she did, but no, although she wasn't at all vain Ruth knew her skin was soft and unblemished and her hair still as glossy as ever – both due no doubt to the concoctions Old Mother brought with her on every visit, such as rose and myrtle water, and oil of almonds. Ruth would repay her by doing the old lady's washing free of charge. She worried about Old Mother, who had startled her on one of her weekly calls by turning all dizzy and almost fainting. The old woman had laughed it off and blamed the heat but Ruth knew it was something more than that. 'Hot weather and old age don't mix,' she had laughed after the dizzy spell had passed. Ruth wondered how old she actually was but hadn't liked to ask. 'What I need is a drop of summat to buck me up.' Old Mother's eyes had searched the kitchen, but she knew without being told that if any spirits had been available she'd have been welcome to them. Come to think of it, any spirits would have been downed by Walter Wray before they ever reached Wire Mill Place.

Ruth had mentioned Old Mother's queer turn to Lizzie, who had given Olive the task of calling every day after school to see if Old Mother was in need of any assistance. Olive had accepted the job eagerly. She had always been fascinated by the tiny cottage with the mysterious odours and the row upon row of earthenware pots, each containing oils and spices. The low, beamed ceiling was almost hidden by bundles of herbs hanging to dry. Old Mother would explain to Olive what each of them could be used for and then she would totter out into the garden along the river bank and show her young namesake where to find them growing. Olive was so interested, she had saved her Saturday pennies and bought a notebook in which she could enter a description or a sketch of each plant and a list of things it could be used for. One day she had heard Auntie Lucy Crossman complaining about a weakness of the bladder and recommended she take a spoonful of dried parsley every morning. After a week Auntie Lucy had thanked Olive and laughingly told her the chamber pot had been allowed to cool down at last.

Old Mother liked nothing better than to sit on the settle beside the fire chatting to Olive about the old days. Gradually the past was being pieced together like a jigsaw, and Old Mother was letting slip things which no one else in Cottenly knew about. Olive now realised that Old Mother was not as poverty-stricken as everybody thought. Her real name was Olive Burlington and her father had been an educated man and a pharmacist. Mr Burlington had employed a governess to assist with his daughter's education, and then to his dismay she had suddenly fallen deeply and passionately in love. Unfortunately a child had been conceived and the lover had tragically died of typhoid before the wedding day arrived. Olive Burlington had lost not only her lover and her stillborn child but her family too, when her shamed father had disowned his only daughter. Olive was still waiting to hear what happened next, but no more information had been disclosed as yet, and the girl never asked. Neither did she tell anyone about Old Mother's stories.

Somehow it made her feel closer to the old lady.

Billy arrived back in time for the picnic, his body covered in coal dust and sweat, which had washed clean bits on his cheeks as it had trickled from his forehead, and soaked his thick, wavy hair.

'Oh, Billy, you could do with a bath, love,' Ruth told him anxiously. Billy grinned, found an old towel and a block of brown carbolic soap and announced himself ready for the picnic. 'I'll have a bath in the river,' he said. 'It'll cool me down. I can wash me shirt while I'm at it. It'll soon dry in the sun.'

'Come on then.' Ruth smiled. 'Let's not keep the others waiting.'

'Nic nic.' Frankie liked new words. 'Nic nic.'

Sadie gazed at her brother with large, solemn eyes. She was the only one of the three who looked like her father, but fortunately her temperament was as placid as Walter's was violent. 'Sadie, nic nic.' She always repeated everything her brother said or did and it was uncanny how, if one of them had a pain, the other one would be out of sorts until the other was well again.

'Picnic,' Ruth corrected. 'Come on, into the pushchair. Your turn first, Sadie. You can help me push, Frankie, and change over halfway.' The pushchair was Ruth's pride and joy, given to her by Annie Hampshire, who had made up her mind that she and Sammy would have no more babies. Annie had had her fun with one or two boys, including the Irish contractors, but Sammy had always been there on the sidelines and it was

113

to him Annie turned when she decided she was ready to settle down. Mary said they were the ideal couple and an adorable little girl had made their happiness complete. Mary on the other hand was still fancy free and Ruth couldn't help envying her best friend her freedom and the fashionable clothes she always wore. However, Mary, who spent her evenings out dancing or at the cinema over in Warrentickle, passed on any unwanted garments to her and was always buying something or other for the children, brushing aside Ruth's protests by declaring that nobody would ever accuse her of neglecting her god-children. Today Ruth was wearing one of Mary's blouses and felt no shame at doing so. In fact she knew she looked lovely in the pink cotton with the puffed sleeves and the Peter Pan collar.

It was lovely on the river bank, away from the town. Tiny streams trickled into the river proper, and it was near one of these that the picnic spot had been chosen, so that the little ones could paddle in safety and the older ones practise swimming, with Joseph supervising and showing off his breaststroke, taught to him by his father on holiday in Scarborough last year.

'Oh, it is lovely to get away from the smoke and get some fresh air into our lungs.' Ruth breathed deeply and stretched out on the grass slope, lifting up her skirt so the air could cool her legs.

'By but it's hot though,' Alice said, fanning herself with a frond of bracken.

'No wonder, with that dress on,' Lizzie admonished her. 'Haven't you got any summer ones?'

Alice coloured. 'I'm right enough. I'm not one

for flouncy, flowery things.'

'Well no, but you'd be much cooler in something cotton. I'll bet you're wearing corsets as well.'

Alice changed the subject. 'Look at that butterfly over there. Right by thi side, our Ruth.'

Ruth turned her head and the red admiral took flight. 'I wish I was a butterfly,' Ruth mused out loud, 'flitting about amongst the moonpennies and the clover, away from the muck and the washing and ironing.'

'I'm afraid tha made a life of drudgery for thiself, the day tha got wed, lass, there'll be no escaping. Though I've told thee often enough if he ill treats thee, tha must come to us.'

'No, Alice. Thanks for the offer, but I won't run away.'

'But you've only one life, Ruth love.' Lizzie frowned. 'You can't waste it being miserable.'

'Something will turn up.' Ruth smiled and chewed on a blade of grass. 'I have faith in Mother Buttercup. She's usually right.'

'Why? What did she say?'

'It was the day she delivered the twins.' Ruth assumed the voice Old Mother used. '"Their father'll not live to see them growed." That's what she said.'

The three women watched the frolicking children in silence. The drone of a bumblebee and a blackbird's song vied with each other against the flapping ripples of the flowing river. Suddenly the sound of a horse's hooves echoed from the path along the top of the bank.

'Mam, mam, it's the ragman. Can we go and

meet him?' little Jimmy called.

'Well, so long as you don't make a nuisance of yerselves, I suppose so,' Lizzie answered. The youngsters, bare-footed and wearing nothing except pants, or in Bessie's case with her frock tucked down her knickers, ran hell for leather along the bridleway, shrieking and laughing. When they returned they were riding either on the cart or astride the docile grey horse, held securely by Jack Dolan's capable arms.

'Afternoon, ladies,' he called as they drew level. 'It's OK for some, nothing to do but lie in the sun. Though I must say, the sight of three pretty things like yerselves brightens up the day for the likes of us working men.'

'Flattery'll get yer nowhere, Jack Dolan,' Alice called, but she was laughing all the same.

'Oh well, that's a shame, but there was no harm in trying.' He lifted the youngsters down and produced a bag of jelly babies, handing them round the little ones and counting out some for the older ones.

'Let's see, how many of you are there al-together?'

'Nine,' Bessie answered, 'not counting Ernest Edward because he's too little.'

'Good Lord, it's like the Sunday school outing.' Jack laughed.

'You're only jealous, Jack Dolan,' Ruth chided. 'It's time you had a couple of yer own by now.'

'I need a woman first, lass.' Jack laughed again. 'And as all the best-looking lasses are spoken for it looks like I shall have to remain a poor, lonely bachelor.' The crestfallen look he put on his face caused the sisters to moan in sympathy, before they all burst into laughter. Then the man slapped the horse's rump and continued his journey. 'So long, ladies. Be seeing yer.'

'I wouldn't mind a roll in his haystack,' Ruth commented after he was out of earshot.

Alice looked shocked. 'Ruth Stanford, thar a married woman and don't thee forget it. Besides, I'd have thought tha'd have had enough of men.'

'I'm Ruth Wray, not Ruth Stanford, more's the pity, and you're right, I don't care if I never sleep with another man ever again.'

'Well, I'd certainly miss sleeping with George. Well, not sleeping, exactly – it's what we do before we go to sleep that I'd miss.' Lizzie blushed as she realised what she'd said, in front of Alice as well.

Alice's face was redder than her own. 'Aye, I must agree with thee. I'd miss sharing my bed with Joe.'

'Alice?' Lizzie's eyes were twinkling. 'Are you and I talking about the same thing?'

'I reckon so. I can't think of owt else a husband and wife would do before they go to sleep.' She grinned. 'Unless it's reading in bed.'

Lizzie sighed. 'Oh, it is good to be with you both, talking like this. We should get together more often.'

Only Ruth looked troubled. 'I'd better be getting back,' she muttered. 'Besides, the bloody midges are biting something shocking.'

'If tha doesn't pull thi frock down, they'll be biting up thi bloomers,' Alice warned, and even Ruth laughed.

'It's been a lovely picnic. Thanks for bringing

117

the food, Alice. It was really good.'

'There's still some sandwiches left. Take them home – they'll only be thrown to the ducks otherwise, and I think they've had enough today. They'll be sinking if the kids have their way.'

It was turning dusk as they wended their way along the bridlepath, tired and well fed, and happy that tonight the kids wouldn't need to be coaxed into being washed. They were all spotlessly clean, except little Ernest Edward, who was sleeping soundly, full of good, fresh Warrentickle air, and, as Old Mother had once said, without a thought in his head to worry about.

Ruth knew she would pay the price for her afternoon out when she saw that the door was open and Walter was already home.

'Oh, God,' she muttered to herself and Billy glanced anxiously at her.

'Well! And where do you think you've been?' Walter wasn't shouting, which meant he must be sober, but the quiet tone of his voice sent shivers down Ruth's spine.

'We've been on a picnic up the river, haven't we, Billy love?'

'Oh aye, you and who else?'

'Our Lizzie and Alice and the kids.'

'And I suppose they'll have let their husbands come home after a hard day's work to an empty house and no dinner ready.'

'Yes, I expect they will, except that your dinner was ready and only needed warming.'

'Then it wasn't ready, was it?'

'It would have been if you'd have come home at

your usual time. What's happened, has the Rag burned down or something?'

Walter reached over suddenly and grabbed hold of his wife's blouse front, pulling her forward so that a couple of buttons flew across the room.

'Don't tear my blouse, please, Walter.' Ruth decided to try being nice to him. Difficult as it was.

'Oh, and who bought it then, this blouse of yours? Some man, eh?' He grabbed her cheek, pinching it between his fingers. 'You don't get tarted up like that to go out with yer sisters and their kids.'

'Where else would I get dressed up for? I never go out.' She pulled away from him and managed to get the table between them. 'You never take me anywhere. And don't you dare accuse me of having a fellow, though not many would blame me if I had.'

Walter circled the table suddenly and the back of his hand suddenly smashed into his wife's face, knocking her backwards with its force. Ruth didn't cry out. She wouldn't give him the satisfaction, or let the children see she was hurt.

'Don't, Dad. Don't hit me mam. Look, I've got some money here. You can have it, if yer don't hit me mam again.' Billy threw a handful of small change on to the table.

'Oh aye, and I suppose she gave you money instead of putting a decent meal on the table.' Walter gathered up the money, wondering if it would be enough to pay for a pint. The only reason he was home early was because he had been refused any more beer on the slate by the landlord's wife.

Billy stood close to his mother with a protective arm round her. 'She didn't. I earned it. I got the coal in for Mr Baraclough, and he gave it me.'

'Aye, well, it's about time you started earning yer keep.' He looked at Ruth, who was as white as a sheet, except for the blood oozing from her cut lip. He pulled out a handkerchief and handed it to her before skulking out of the kitchen and along towards the pub.

'Oh, Mam.' Billy got a chair and helped his mother towards it. Then he fetched a flannel and dabbed at her face. The twins began to cry, as though they were frightened to do so whilst their father was in the room. 'Shall I fetch Mrs Armitage?'

'No, Billy,' Ruth answered shakily. 'I shall be all right. But you shouldn't have given him your money. You worked hard for it, and now it'll be wasted on ale.'

'I didn't want him to hit you again. I know I shouldn't have given it him. It was for you.' He began to sob. 'Oh, Mam, I hate him. I wish he were dead.'

'Don't say that, love.'

'I do, though.' Ruth hugged him close and they rocked together, oblivious of the twins who had found the remains of the picnic and were consoling themselves by gobbling a sandwich each. 'I do. I wish he would bugger off and never come back.'

'Billy, I'll have none of that language in this house.' But she hugged her son tighter. 'I know, though,' she said, and to herself she whispered, 'And you're not the only one, son. So do I.'

Old Mother was uneasy. She didn't usually turn out after dusk, although sometimes she would sit on her doorstep and think of the old days, but tonight she wrapped a shawl round her shoulders and ambled down to Wire Mill Place, where she tapped lightly on the door, knowing the twins would be asleep and loath to wake them.

'Are you in?' she called as she pressed the sneck and opened the door slightly.

Ruth was sitting at the table with her head resting on her folded arms. She hastily changed position, trying to conceal her anguish.

'Old Mother, what's wrong? Are you all right?'

'I'm all right. It's you who's summat wrong if you axe me.' She lifted Ruth's chin and examined her swollen cheek and cut lip. 'It's a blessing he hasn't knocked top off yer beauty spot. They can be funny things if disturbed.'

Ruth cringed. 'Beauty spot? Is that what you'd call it? It's exactly like the one on the end of Walter's you know what, and there's nothing beautiful about that.'

'He wants a horsewhip taking to him if you axe me.' Ruth tried to smile but it hurt too much. 'And locking up in the madhouse and never let out,' the old woman added. 'I'll hop along home and fetch some tincture of arnica. It's the best thing for bathing bruises if you axe me. I'll not be long before I'm back.'

Ruth didn't argue. She was too dispirited, and already dreading her husband's return. She knew

121

he would either be filled with remorse and insist on making love – her face slipped at the expression but soon slipped back as the pain shot about her jaw – or he would be spoiling for another fight. She wondered how much more she could endure.

Old Mother was busy bathing Ruth's face when Walter Wray entered the kitchen. The old woman ignored him and so did Ruth.

'What's going on here, then? A bloody hospital now, is it?'

The old woman carried on and Ruth found the pain easing already beneath the gentle hands.

'Who sent for the old witch then?' When nobody answered he came round the table to confront the pair. 'Are yer deaf or summat? I happen to be talking to you.'

'Please, Walter, I've had enough for one day. Why don't you go to bed? I'll be up as soon as I've packed your snap for morning.'

'I'll go when I'm ready and I'll not go at all while the old hag's here.' Old Mother never batted an eyelid and continued her work, making a poultice now to leave with her patient. Walter's temper was rising to boiling point and he suddenly grabbed at Old Mother's head.

'Let go of my hair,' Old Mother said in her posh voice, the voice that had once been her normal one many years ago, before she had adopted the broad Yorkshire dialect of the locals. Walter yanked harder at the lank, grey tresses.

'Let go of her now,' Ruth demanded. She picked up the scissors Old Mother had been using to cut the linen. 'Or I'll kill you.' Walter smirked and Ruth gripped the scissors firmly, the blades pointing towards her husband. He let go of the handful of hair and lunged for them. Unfortunately Ruth plunged them towards him at the same time and the sharp, slim points dug deep into his cheek. Ruth recoiled as she realised the instrument had found its mark. Walter's face paled as he touched the wound and his fingers came away covered in warm, flowing blood.

Old Mother lifted the dripping flannel, wrung it almost dry and pressed it firmly against his cheek. 'Well, are yer satisfied?' she asked the trembling man. 'Yer should be now the lass has got even. An eye for an eye, and it might have been an eye. Another inch higher and it would have been.' Ruth shivered at the thought, but Old Mother continued, 'Should have been yer throat if you axe me.'

Walter never uttered a word. His face was ashen and Ruth thought he might faint. 'Oh, God,' she thought, 'and there we were wishing he were dead.'

Old Mother laughed as she poured more boiling water into the basin, knowing how it would smart when she pressed the hot flannel once again on to the wound. 'Where's the big, strong man now then, the one who beats a helpless woman?' Walter trembled, still not saying a word. 'Looks like he's a coward if you axe me, a coward and a bully. Oh aye, it ought to have been yer throat she cut, and no one would grieve, no one at all.' She finally set down the flannel. 'I reckon yer'll do.' She went to empty the bloody water down the low, stone sink.

'I'll be going up then,' Walter said tremulously. He looked from one to the other but nobody answered. Then he made towards the stairs, feeling at the wound gingerly and wondering what the men at work would say, especially if any of them saw Ruth's swollen face. Bloody hell, she might have blinded him. Never once did he feel any sympathy for his wife. Old Mother was right as usual. Walter Wray was a coward and a bully, and now, with his scarred face, even his looks were less than perfect.

Chapter Four

When the schoolmaster came to Lizzie's they were just about to sit down to tea. Olive opened the door and then slunk away upstairs, thinking he had called about her absenteeism. Olive thought school a waste of time and though she was bright as a button, and well above average when it came to lessons, she much preferred learning from Grandma Burlington, as she now called her old friend. So, remembering the afternoons she had played truant to spend them amongst the herbs and mysteries at Old Mother's cottage, she sneaked away seeped in guilt.

As it happened, the visit was nothing at all to do with Olive. The schoolmaster was here to talk about Harry.

'I've just made the tea. Would you like a cup?' Lizzie wasn't at all sure how to treat a guest as important as Mr Jones.

'No, I won't be long about my business. My wife will have a meal ready. Thank you all the same.'

'Well, sit down anyway. Mr Crossman will be home any time now.' Lizzie didn't like to ask what he meant by business. She hoped her children hadn't been misbehaving. If any of them had it would ten to one be Jimmy, who was always up to some mischief or other.

'You will be wondering why I am here, Mrs

Crossman. I'm sure you will be most proud when I tell you that your son Harry has been offered a place at grammar school. Unfortunately, he has refused to even discuss the subject. Simply says that he doesn't wish to accept.'

Harry's face was scarlet as he found himself being stared at by everybody in the room. Lizzie gazed at her son with pride. 'I don't think that's the case, Mr Jones,' she said. 'But I'm proud of my son for using that as an excuse. The trouble is, we simply could not afford to send him, and Harry would realise that.'

'But surely Harry must be given the opportunity. He has a remarkable capacity for knowledge. It would be sacrilege for his education to be neglected.'

'Be that as it may, Mr Jones, we have five other children besides Harry. It would be even more sacrilegious for them to go hungry in order to pay for books and uniforms. Nobody is more sorry than I am, but it can't be done. My children are wearing hand-me-downs as it is. My husband works like a slave, he does not drink or smoke and not a penny is wasted on frivolities. So it would be impossible to economise in order for my son to have fancy blazers and scarlet ties, not to mention leather satchels and sports equipment.'

'But you will regret your decision, I know you will. Harry could rise to great heights given the opportunity.'

'Regrets do not enter into it. It is the purse strings that will not stretch to meet the costs. I'm sorry, Mr Jones. It isn't our fault my son cannot attend grammar school, but the fault of the authorities who require the pupils to wear special uniforms and purchase their own equipment.' Lizzie was on her soapbox. 'It is one way of making sure poor children are denied the chance to make good, Mr Jones. One way of giving only the children of the wealthy the opportunity to rise to great heights, as you so aptly put it.'

'But won't you at least consider ways and means?'

'The only ways and means lies with the authorities, as I have just said, and you know as well as I do that their consideration will be for the rich, as always. And now, Mr Jones, if you don't wish to take tea with us perhaps you won't mind if I feed my family, which is the main priority in our humble abode.'

Mr Jones rose to his feet, fidgeting with his trilby as he made for the door. Lizzie suddenly felt sorry for the man. 'It was kind of you to come. I know you have my son's welfare at heart, but it really can't be done. You do understand?'

'Yes, I do see. It is an unfair society in which we live, Mrs Crossman, when children are deprived of an education because of their class.'

'Unfair! I don't think that's the word I would use, Mr Jones, more like disgraceful. But I have every faith in my son, and I'm sure that even without a place at grammar school he will still rise to great heights.'

'I hope so, Mrs Crossman. I sincerely hope so.'

By the time George arrived home Lizzie had recovered from her outburst and was serving out the thick brown hash.

127

'Dad, Dad, Old Jonesy has been, here to our house.' Bessie couldn't wait to report on the visit. 'And you ought to have heard our mam.'

'What's all this about, Lizzie?' George frowned anxiously.

'It's our Harry. He's passed for the grammar,' Lizzie announced proudly.

'And I don't want to go, so Mr Jones came to persuade me. But he couldn't.' Harry tried to hide his disappointment, but without much success.

'Harry, that's the best news I've ever been given. I'm right proud to be your father.' Harry's face lit up. 'Not just at the news of you gaining a place – I'm proud of the courage with which you've refused, Harry.' George looked close to tears. 'We all know you wanted to go, son – you'd be a fool not to. But you've accepted your disappointment like a man, a brave man, and that's why I'm so proud of you.' George coughed to cover his emotion.

Harry grinned. 'Oh, Dad, I don't really want to go. I wouldn't have any mates there, and I'd look a right sissy in a red and black neb cap.'

'Well, let's get our teas then.' Lizzie smiled.

'You ought to have heard our mam. She didn't half tell Old Jonesy. And she used big words an' all.'

'And I was right proud of you, Mam.' Harry added his thoughts to Bessie's.

The meal was eaten amongst much laughter, but the hearts of Lizzie, George and Harry were heavy with disappointment that the grammar school place would be given to some other less deserving child.

'We should help the lad,' Isaac said when he heard.

'How can we help?' Emily knew her husband was thinking about financial assistance; she also knew it couldn't be done.

'We could pay for his requirements. I know we aren't rolling in money, but we aren't paupers either.'

'Oh, yes, we could. We could buy him a uniform and whatever he requires to begin at the new school. But what of next year, and the year after? And the year after that? What happens when he outgrows his shoes? What about books, games kit and other essentials?'

Isaac frowned. Emily knew how disappointed he was, almost as disappointed as her eldest grandson. She noticed with a shock that her husband seemed suddenly to have aged. He looked smaller somehow, and greyer. She also realised that had it been any other grandchild than Harry, his disappointment wouldn't have been quite so acute. 'And another thing,' she said. 'What if the others prove to have the same ability? Are you going to fork out for them too?'

Isaac emptied his pipe, tapping it irritatingly on the fire grate. 'But I feel responsible, Emily.' He sighed. 'I thought I was doing the right thing encouraging him in his learning. Cramming as much knowledge as I could into his young head. Doesn't tha understand how bad I feel, lass, now it's all going to be wasted?'

'Nay, Isaac, it's you who always insisted that education is never wasted, and I'm sure you're right. Our Harry will make something of himself, with or without the grammar school.'

'But I would really like him to go, lass.'

'So would I. I'd like them all to go, but it can't be done. Oh, I know he's your favourite – no, don't deny it, he is. But I'm not going to allow you to make more of one than the others. Besides, George wouldn't allow it. He's an independent man and wouldn't feel right, having someone else paying out for his son.'

'Aye, Emily, I suppose thar right, but, oh, I do feel bad that the lad can't be given the advantage. It's what I'd have wanted for my own son if I'd had one.'

'Yes, and that's the trouble, isn't it? We didn't have one, and our Harry's been put in place of one. But he isn't ours, Isaac, and much as we love him he's still George's. So shall we let the subject drop?'

'Aye, I suppose so. But I can't help thinking we should spend some of our savings on such an important matter.'

'And I can't help thinking you should spend it on yerself. You work hard, Isaac, and aren't over-paid, as you well know. We're not getting any younger and nobody knows what the future might bring. We'll need a little comfort and security in our old age. So now we'll change the subject, if you please, and for goodness' sake stop tapping, will you?' It was unusual for Emily to become irritated and Isaac suddenly realised his wife was just as disappointed as he was, but more fair-minded, he supposed.

'Oh, lass, I don't know where I'd be without a

wife like thee, one who's sensible at times like these.'

Emily blushed and concentrated on threading her needle. 'Is that supposed to be a compliment, Isaac Stanford, sensible?'

'And lovely besides, for someone with ten grandchilder.'

Emily laughed. 'And that's another back-handed compliment.'

'Well I never was one for fancy talk, but tha knows what I feel for thee all the same, doesn't tha, lass?'

Emily smiled and looked lovingly at the man on the opposite side of the hearth. 'Yes, Isaac, I know,' she said. But then he began tapping his pipe on the chair arm and she knew he was still disturbed. It was all the fault of that toffee-nosed headmaster Mr Jones, who couldn't begin to comprehend the difference between the haves and the have nots, and for all his fancy education didn't have the common sense to know when to keep his big mouth closed. She jabbed the needle aggressively through the material belonging to one of the posh folks, and for once resented the work she was doing for them.

The subject of Harry's education was not only a topic of discussion for his grandparents, but also for his Auntie Alice and Uncle Joe.

'What does tha think, Joe? Should we offer George financial help so that young Harry can attend the grammar?'

'You know I'd be willing, Alice, but I doubt if George will accept.'

'Aye, I've considered that possibility, but does tha think we should offer?' Alice bit her lip. 'Or does tha think he'd be offended?'

'Make the offer by all means. They can always say no.'

Alice sighed with relief. Spending Grandmother Stanford's legacy on herself always galled her somehow, mainly because she was reminded of the misery she had suffered in order to receive it, but using it for the benefit of her sisters always gave her a pleasurable feeling. Unfortunately, Lizzie and George were the most independent couple she had ever come across and she doubted they would accept, even for something as important as Harry's education. She settled down on the sofa with her Bible. It amused Joe that she should still read a few verses every night. 'I shouldn't think you need open the pages, lass. You must know it off by heart from cover to cover by now.'

'Aye, some of it. It just gives me a warm feeling, reading a little before I go to bed, that's all. Tha should try it sometimes.'

'Nay, lass, I do whatever good I can in the world. I don't reckon I need Bible-bashing as well.'

Alice smiled and closed the book. 'I reckon that's right, Joe. Thar a good man, and I know there's many who go to chapel who could learn a bit about kindness from thee. All the same I feel better in myself if I read a few words before I go to bed. It might not make me any better, but it pleasures me a little.'

'Aye, well, I'll take my pleasure in bed, if you

please. Shall we be going up, lass?'

'Ready when you are.' Alice turned out the lamp. She considered spending some of her money on having electricity installed. She would wait and see what Lizzie said first about young Harry, although she was already certain what the answer would be. She checked the door Joe had already locked. As always, she glanced into her son's bedroom. It was a pity Joseph didn't have the same inclination for learning as his cousin, but all Joseph's brain seemed to focus on was anything mechanical. Still, he was rapidly becoming known as the lad who could make summat outa nowt, according to Joe. Alice looked lovingly at the mound beneath the eiderdown and felt a sadness that Joseph still remained an only child. Even so, Alice knew she was a fortunate woman and counted her blessings as she joined her husband. Besides, there was some pleasuring to be done and Alice was more than eager for it to begin. Who knew, tonight might be the night she would conceive the second child she so longed for.

George declined the offer, but with grateful thanks. He pointed out that this would be a valuable lesson on life for Harry. It would make him realise that if money was short there were some things that one just had to do without. Joe admired his brother-in-law's principles and told him so; he also promised that when the time came he would do his utmost to find Harry a situation in the works where he could better himself. George appreciated the offer and said he was sure his son would do well in whatever situation he was fortunate enough to find. So there was nothing else for it but for Harry to accept he would be attending the senior school with all his pals, except of course the chosen few who would be starting at grammar school, most of whom were less talented than Harry but had wealthier parents. Harry knew however that he wasn't the only boy to be denied a place for financial reasons, and, as his father said, nothing could change the fact that he had passed. It was small consolation, but Harry accepted it with good heart and soon settled down happily in the senior section, consuming as much knowledge as the teachers could offer him, and a whole lot more from Grandfather Stanford.

Olive however continued to miss lessons whenever possible and became more and more knowledgeable about Grandma Burlington's herbal remedies. She already knew what she would do when she left school. Grandma Burlington had advised her to become an umbrella girl like her mam, but only because her mam needed the money Olive could earn. The rest of the time she would be a herbalist, and when Grandma Burlington had taught her all she could, Olive would sell her cures and potions on the market. There was money to be made, Old Mother told her. Oh yes, she would be an umbrella girl, but not for long, she was certain about that. Old Mother knew there was money to be made for it had been necessary for her to make it. After her father had shown Olive Burlington the door she had been destitute. With only a bag of clothing she had scoured the countryside around Bakewell for a place to earn a living and birth her child. She had walked for weeks, sleeping in hedgerows and any shelter available, covering villages such as Carver and Grindleford. She had found work at a house in Hathersage for a few weeks, until her child began to show and then she was on the road again. Olive had been a beauty. In fact, when she looked at young Olive Crossman it caused a pain in her heart to see herself over again.

Old Mother had covered the miles to Bamford and the bleak hills of the Pennines and had finally come to rest in Cottenly, where her child had been born, a girl as dark and pretty as her mother but cold and lifeless, a stillborn babe, helped into the world by a feeble old woman here in this very cottage, only to be laid to rest the next morning in the churchyard on the hill. The frail old woman had been glad of Olive Burlington's company. Almost crippled by rheumatism, she had cried out in pain in the mornings, until her old bones had become accustomed to the movement of each new day. Olive had massaged her limbs with extract of smartweed, dressed her, administered beef tea and kept her as comfortable as possible in the circumstances.

In return, the old woman had signed over to Olive the deeds of the cottage and the small piece of land surrounding it. Because neighbours had seen a complete stranger come into the old woman's life and end up owning all her possessions Olive was said to have bewitched her. Yet it hadn't prevented those same neighbours from seeking Olive's help when any disease reared its ugly head, and though she soon became known as Old Witch Buttercup it was accepted that she was a white, kind, healing witch for all that. So here she had stayed, handing out remedies, administering advice, delivering babies and laying out the dead.

At first she had taken a basket of potions to Cottenly market, some for cooking, some for beautifying the posh folk and some, more importantly, for healing. Gradually her customers had begun calling at the cottage and it had become unnecessary for her to stand in the market any more. With the passage of time the title of Old Witch had been changed to Old Mother, but she had remained a lonely woman until the day she had delivered Olive Crossman into the world. Her second sight had told her that here was a child to replace the one she had lost, and she had once again been proved right. Olive Crossman devoured knowledge as fast as Old Mother could deliver it, and now, when Old Mother knew her end was drawing nigh, she decided it was time to put her affairs in order. Though it wouldn't do for the young girl to know it, there wasn't much belonging to Old Mother that wouldn't belong to Olive when she had moved on to the next world. But before that day came there was more work to do, more teaching, more notes to be written in Olive's notebook, and something told Old Mother there wasn't much time to lose, not much time at all. She wasn't afraid to meet her maker; she knew she would be reunited with the child she had lost, and its father who had gone before her.

She was afraid, however, of going before Olive had learned all her secrets. So instead of going to school Olive visited Grandma Burlington, in the cottage which would one day be hers.

Whether the sponge was responsible or not Lizzie had conceived no more children after Ernest Edward, and now with all her children at school her lot was far easier than it had been. Joe Jackson had kept his word and asked around on Harry's behalf when the time had come for the lad to leave school, and a position had been found for him, not in the works, but in the town hall where there would be every opportunity for promotion in the years to come. Old Mother's premonition that Harry would be a clever one had proved correct and Isaac had dreams of his grandson's one day going into politics, a subject which interested Harry every bit as much as his grandfather. The only obstacle standing in Harry's way was the threat of war, which Isaac could see hanging like a shadow over Europe. Emily would wave any such morbid talk aside, preferring to ignore what Isaac said was as plain as the nose on his face.

'Even if there is a war, I can't see it affecting Cottenly,' Emily said, and Isaac knew that his wife would be happier kept in ignorance than worrying about something before it happened. But Isaac knew it would start soon if the events in Austria and Germany were anything to go by.

Though Harry's earnings weren't colossal, they eased Lizzie's worries a little and provided a few small luxuries for the children. One of these was the Saturday trip to the pictures in the new picture palace which had been built at the far end of town, financed by the local business folk, and was proving a popular night out for adults and children alike. Olive was already besotted with Charles Farrell and Janet Gaynor, but George insisted that Charlie Chaplin was still the best, even without the talking. Despite the arguments for and against their favourite actors, the Saturday trip proved to be the highlight of the week. On one occasion George offered to stay at home and let Ruth and the children go instead, but despite his offering to foot the bill Ruth daren't accept, dreading her husband's displeasure on learning about the outing.

'It just isn't normal, her being afraid of her husband. I don't know how she stands it,' Lizzie said to George.

'She's no option, lass, that's why she stands it, but he'll get his just deserts one of these days, you wait and see.'

'Aye, but when?'

Ruth couldn't help wondering what would happen if there should be a war, which her father said was likely. She wondered if Walter would go. 'Oh, God, forgive me for hoping,' she prayed. She couldn't stand it much longer: the drinking; the beatings, mostly with the leather belt; and most of all, the sex. In fact he had been all for it lately, and some of the things he demanded of her were unnatural, repulsive acts, which hurt her for days after. Up to now the sponge seemed to have worked, although she thought it more likely that it was the way she usually managed to put him off in the middle of the month, which according to Old Mother was the most dangerous time. How long she could keep him at bay on those days she was afraid to think. Now the twins were at school she found she could relax a little and look forward to the time when they were a little older and she could find some kind of work which would bring in a bit of extra money. She was sick of the poverty, of not knowing where the next meal was coming from, of having no coal for the fire. That was the worst thing, for if there was no fire there was no hot water and no laundry could be done. She had lost one or two of the posh folk's washing orders only last week, when Walter had been on a drunken binge for three days and she had not been able to pay the coal man. If she could avoid any more babies, there was a chance that in a few years she might escape from this living hell, and if there was a war, and Walter had to go, it might even happen sooner.

Ruth knew it was wicked even to think such thoughts, for if Walter had to go the good men would have to go too: George for instance, and Sammy. Oh, no, she mustn't even contemplate such a thing. Best to look to the future, for if Old Mother was right and he wouldn't see the twins grow up she wouldn't have many more years to wait. Unfortunately, even one year with a husband like hers was a year too many.

Ruth's dream came to an end the following month when Walter forced her to submit against her will to what amounted to no less than rape. He had not got up for work on that day, had risen from his bed at about eleven o'clock, just as Ruth was standing on the kitchen chair hanging the whites on a line at the back of the table. He walked behind her and slid his hand up beneath his wife's skirt. 'Oh, God,' Ruth silently prayed, 'please don't let him do anything, not today.' She suddenly remembered with horror that she was not protected by her sponge.

Walter's hand had reached its goal, the long, jagged nails he used to keep so neat cutting into the soft flesh.

'I have to get on, Walter,' she coaxed, 'or the water in the tub'll be cold.'

'Bugger the bloody water.' He lifted Ruth down and pulled her to him, the whiskers on his unshaven face scraping her chin as he kissed her forcefully. She could feel the bulge in his trousers. Perhaps if she appeared to be eager, she could satisfy him without going all the way. She undid his buttons and took his erect penis in her hand. 'Come here, Walter,' she whispered. 'I feel like touching you, stroking you, like this.'

Walter's eyes gleamed at Ruth's enthusiasm, but as she rubbed him harder, and faster, he suddenly realised her intention. He turned her round, bent her over the table and threw her skirt over her head, pulling violently at her undergarments until her buttocks were bare. The shape of their rounded smoothness and her white thighs inflamed him. He thrust his hard, throbbing manhood between Ruth's legs until it found its way into the warm softness. She kept herself taut, aiming to prevent its entry, but he held her down, almost suffocating beneath her skirts, pressing her on to the hard table top, until her breasts were bruising under the pressure. On and on he went, until ecstasy took over and he could no longer prevent the shuddering climax. Ruth knew, even then, that she had conceived another child. If she had ever believed in prayer, her faith was destroyed at that moment. A loving God would never have allowed an innocent child to be conceived out of violation such as this.

Walter buttoned up his trousers and went out of the house, to brag to his cronies at the Rag about what he had just done to his wife, until even his fellow drinkers were repulsed by his boasting. Ruth carried on with the washing, bent over the rubbing board, her tears falling like raindrops into the soap suds, but not until she had scrubbed herself red raw inside and out in an attempt to remove every seed of Walter Wray's from her body.

Exactly nine months later Margaret Wray was born. A perfect little girl, delivered by Old Mother with no fuss whatever, whilst Walter Wray drank away his wages at the Rag.

Despite the bitter winter weather Ruth was on her hands and knees scrubbing the doorstep, even though little Margaret was only two weeks old. 'I don't know. If I did this doorstep a dozen times a day it wouldn't look any better,' she muttered, but it was Saturday and she liked everything done for the weekend. Suddenly, she heard Mrs Armitage calling her.

'Ruth, Ruth lass, your Frankie's fallen in the river again.'

'Oh no! Is he all right?'

'Don't worry, love. The rag and bone man fished him out. Lucky he was passing when he was.'

'Where is he?' Ruth wiped her hands on her pinafore and set off across the Place.

'Don't worry, he's bringing him home. Our Florrie has just run on and told me.'

Ruth relaxed a little.

'You ought to put a fence up at the bottom of the yard, otherwise he's going to drown himself one of these days. You know how deep it is just here.'

'But we can't fence the whole river off. Besides, he hasn't fallen in just here this time, has he?'

'No, but he has before. And when the baby starts running about there'll be her to watch as well.'

'I know, I know. How do you think I went on when the twins were toddling? But you just try telling him that. It takes me all my time to get a stone of flour out of him, let alone a bloody fence.'

Mrs Armitage shook her head sadly. 'Eeh, love, you have changed. I never heard either you or your sisters use a single swear word until you married him, not that you haven't got cause. Still, you should have known what he was like when you got hitched to him.'

'Oh! If anybody else tells me what I already know I shall–'

Fortunately Winnie Armitage was spared hearing what Ruth would do by the sound of a horse's hooves on the cobbles. 'Here they come now, the ragman with your Frankie.'

'He wants his backside tanning,' Ruth threatened, but was so relieved to see her son all in one piece that she took him in her arms and hugged him instead.

'Oh, love, you look like a drowned rat. You're going to end up with pneumonia. How many times have I told you to keep away from the river? I ought to tan yer backside. Come and get yer clothes off. I'll have to wrap you in a towel – I've washed your other pair of trousers.' Suiting the action to the word, she rubbed vigorously at her son. 'Oh, I don't know how to thank you, Mr Dolan. I'll make you a pot of tea. I'm sorry I've no dry clothes to lend you.'

'I'm reight enough, love; don't worry about me. I've plenty of clothes on't cart, if I could just fetch some in and change into them.'

'Yes, of course you can.' Ruth hoped Walter wouldn't come home yet and find out what had happened.

'Eeh, it was lucky I happened to be passing. He was just about to go under for the second time when I reached him. Not that I'm a strong swimmer, mind, and I can't say I wasn't scared when I realised how deep the watter was. I should put a barrier fence up at its deepest and teach the kids how to swim an' all if I were their dad.'

Ruth sighed deeply. 'Yes, I expect you would, but you don't happen to be their dad.'

Jack Dolan looked uncomfortable. 'Aye, well, I'll just fetch some dry things in then.' He went out to his cart and Ruth found a frayed towel.

'Is there somewhere I can get changed?' Jack

143

Dolan had returned with an armful of clothing. Ruth handed him the towel and opened the door at the bottom of the stairs.

'Through there. Nobody'll disturb you. Then you must have a drink of tea to warm you up. I'm sorry I can't offer you anything stronger.'

'A pot of tea'll do fine. I'm not much of a drinker anyway, especially when I'm working. I like to look respectable when I go to the fancy houses where the well-off folk live.' He laughed. 'I wouldn't like to offend me best source of supply by looking like a drunkard.' He went to change his wet things, closing the door behind him.

'Oh, Frankie.' Ruth sighed. 'I don't know what I'm going to do with you. I'd better get you upstairs and in bed before your dad gets home. Let's hope nobody sees him and mentions what's happened or you'll be in for another hiding when he comes in.' She glanced at the clock anxiously.

'Don't let him hit me, Mam. Don't let him take his belt off to me.'

Jack Dolan came back with a bundle of wet things. 'We might as well chuck these away – they only came off't cart in't first place. There's no point in wearing anything decent on't cart – if I don't end up picking up fleas, I only end up stinking of t'owd horse.'

'I could dry them out for the next time you come round.'

'Nay, love, don't bother.'

'Well, if you're sure you don't want them I could dry them out for our Billy. He'd be glad of them to go to school in.' Ruth coloured, embar-

144

rassed now at almost begging.

'Do what you like with 'em, love, and look after that little lad of yours.' He took a gulp of tea. 'He's a plucky little devil – he didn't even cry.' Jack finished his tea. 'So long then. I'll be off on me rounds. Not that I do much on a Saturday, and not much to do in the fields either at this time of year, except for the livestock.'

'Well, then, thanks ever so much.' Ruth pushed Frankie forward. 'Thank Mr Dolan, Frankie.'

'Thank you, Mr Dolan.'

'You're welcome, son. And keep away from the watter, right?'

'Ta-ra, mister.' Frankie grinned, and then hurried upstairs to be out of the way if his father heard about the incident.

Walter Wray had been in Sheffield since finishing his shift. He had picked up a woman in the Mucky Duck and gone back to her place until after dark. It was when he called at the Rag on his way home that he heard of his son's ordeal. Ruth's stomach turned a dozen cartwheels when she realised Walter had heard what had happened.

'I reckon you've had a visitor?'

'Yes.' Ruth tried to keep her voice steady. 'The rag and bone man brought our Frankie home. He slipped in the water.'

'It's coming to something when a man can't go to work without his wife having a man in the house.'

'Don't talk silly, Walter. I hardly know the man.'

'What difference does that make? Paid yer well,

145

did he?'

'What do you mean, paid me well? What do you think I am, one of the whores you like to keep company with?'

'Well, I always said a woman's got a gold mine between her legs. If you're going to let 'em dig in it you might as well accept payment.' Billy walked in at that moment and looked from one to the other, wondering what had set him off this time. 'Did you know your mother's taken to entertaining men while I'm out?' Billy looked at Ruth.

'He doesn't know what he's talking about, Billy. Take no notice.' The baby began to cry and Ruth lifted her from the pram and cuddled her.

'And who does she belong to, I wonder? Oh aye, it's all coming out now, isn't it? We'd better get to the bottom of this. Where's our Frankie?'

'In bed, of course.'

'Oh! Sent him out of the way, I suppose, so you could entertain yer fancy man.'

'Our Frankie was here the whole time. And how dare you accuse me of whoring, and with the baby only a fortnight old? What do you think I am?'

'Fetch our Frankie.'

Billy hurried upstairs and came down with his brother cowering behind him, still wrapped in a blanket against the bitter cold.

'Well! What's all this about you being in the river?'

'I'm sorry, Dad.'

'Take off the blanket.' Walter undid the buckle of his belt. 'Bend over.'

Frankie's face was as white as the washing on

the line above his head, but he turned and bent over the chair back, trembling like a leaf in a storm. Walter brought the belt down across the small boy's back twice before his mother intervened. 'Stop it! That's enough.'

'Oh, eager for your turn, are yer?' He grabbed his wife, still with little Margaret in her arms, and turned her over with such force that she almost dropped the crying infant. He lifted the belt and brought it down over her shoulders, cutting into her cheek with its metal buckle.

Billy could take no more. He grabbed the knife from his pocket, the knife Uncle Joe had bought him to encourage him in his hobby of whittling wood. It was Billy's most treasured possession; he had never had anything of his own before. He opened the blade. 'Leave her alone or I'll kill you.'

Walter Wray laughed coarsely. 'You and who else?' he taunted. He lifted the belt again, and as it lashed once more against his wife's back Billy stabbed hard with the knife into the arm wielding the leather strap. Walter's face paled as he dropped the belt and surveyed his upper arm. His coat sleeve and his probing fingers were soaking with blood. He reeled at the sight of it and almost fell to the ground. Billy still held the knife gripped tightly in his hand, ready for his father to come at him in retaliation, but Walter turned and staggered through the middle door and up the stairs, unsteady less from drunkenness than from shock at being the victim of violence for a change. He could be heard ranting: 'Just you wait. I'll kill the bleeding lot of yer, just

147

you see.'

'Get our Sadie,' Ruth demanded. She found Frankie's trousers, which were almost dry, and helped the trembling child into them. Billy came back into the room with Sadie. The little girl had heard the commotion and went to stand, crying, in front of the fire.

'Come on, get dressed, love.' Ruth helped her gently into her clothes. 'Get yer coats on,' she said to the boys, but Billy, unable to contain his emotions any longer, had already gone out into the bitterly cold night, so that he could allow the tears to flow in the darkness, where nobody could see.

'Where are we going, Mam?' Sadie enquired through her sobs.

'Ssh.' Ruth held a finger to her lips. 'We don't want him to know.'

'Are we running away?' Frankie asked, still shaken, but excited now that something unusual was happening. 'Has our Billy killed him?'

'No, love, he hasn't killed him.'

'I wish he had. I wish he would bleed to death, do you, Sadie?'

'Yes.' Sadie agreed as usual with anything her brother suggested.

Ruth wrapped the baby warmly in her pram, which had long ago seen better days, and opened the door.

'Come on,' she said, and turned down the lamp. Forlornly, the little family ventured into the night.

'Are you ready for going up, lass?' Joe Jackson

said. 'It's getting late.'

'Aye, Joe, I won't be a minute,' Alice said. 'I've nearly finished.'

'What yer reading this time, lass?'

'My favourite.'

'Not again! You must know the parable of the good Samaritan off by heart. Don't you ever get fed up of reading the Bible?'

'Never.'

'Why don't yer read something a bit more cheerful for a change?'

'I get more than enough cheer out of the Good Book, thanks, without needing a change.'

'It seems a bit sanctimonious if you want my opinion.'

'Nobody's asking for thi opinion.'

'Aye well, if yer've nearly finished, I'll be locking up.'

The peaceful atmosphere of the living room was suddenly shattered by a loud knocking on the door.

'Who the hell can that be on a perishing night like this?' Joe mumbled.

'I'll bet it's our Ruth again. Nobody else'd be out at this time of night, only somebody who were desperate.'

Joseph's voice could be heard from his bedroom. 'What's up, Mam? Is me Uncle Walter having blue 'uns again?'

'Go back to sleep, lad. It's nigh on eleven,' Joe called as he opened the door. 'Come on in, lass. Don't stand there shivering on the step like that.'

Ruth lifted little Margaret out of the pram and pushed the twins in before her. Alice's heart missed a beat at the sight of the pathetic little group standing by the door.

'Come on, Sadie love, and you, Frankie, up to the fire. It's a wonder you haven't got hot aches in yer fingers and toes.' Joe went towards Ruth. 'Give us hold of the baby, lass.'

'Oh, Ruth love, what's he done this time? He's not been hitting thee again, has he?' Alice said. 'Come here and sit near the fire. Let's have a look at thee.' She examined the red welt on one side of Ruth's neck, where the buckle from the belt had cut deep. 'Eeh, lass, he's made a right mess of thee this time. I'll get a bowl and some iodine.' Alice went through to the kitchen and came back with a bottle of iodine and some cotton wool. Then she returned to the kitchen for some hot water from the kettle. Ruth squirmed as the iodine touched the wound.

'Oh, Alice, he's like a madman. He's beaten our Frankie – you'd better see to his back first. God knows what would have happened if our Billy hadn't turned on him. Oh, Joe, our Billy's stabbed him in the arm with his penknife. There's blood all over the place.'

Young Joseph didn't like to think he was missing anything. 'Can I come down, Mam? I might as well with all the racket going on. I'll never get to sleep.'

'No yer can't,' Joe shouted back. 'Get yer head under the bedclothes and shut up.' He turned to Ruth and asked softly, 'What started him off this time, lass?'

'He came home from the Rag, ranting and raving about me having a man in the house. I told him it was only Jack Dolan getting dried after saving our Frankie from drowning. Then he said if I had started entertaining men in the house I might as well start charging them for the privilege, said I was sitting on a gold mine. He meant it, Alice, he really did.' Ruth broke off in sobs.

'Eeh, lass, it'd be the drink that was talking.' Alice went to the kitchen. 'I'll make a pot of tea. Has tha eaten owt?'

'Eaten owt? That's a laugh! I've had all on to feed the kids, what with my laundry money paying for a bag of coal.'

'But it's the day after pay day, lass. Surely tha's some food in the house? He should have been paid.'

'Oh, he'll have been paid all right, and taken it straight to the Rag. I doubt there'll be much left of it, and if there is I shan't be seeing it. I can't take much more of it, Alice. You don't know what he's like.'

'We all know what he's like. I'll swing for him one of these days, I swear I will.'

'Don't say that, Joe,' Alice said. 'He deserves his come-uppance and he'll get it one of these days, but it'll be God who gives it to him, not thee.'

Ruth began crying again. 'God!' she spluttered. 'Don't talk to me about God! If there is such a one, which I very much doubt, He's a queer way of looking after us.'

Alice backed away from her sister, a look of horror on her face. 'Eeh, Ruth, our grandmother would turn in her grave if she could hear thee talking like that. And after the way our dad's brought thee up to go to chapel and all. With all the

151

scripture exams tha got through tha should know that God meant us to suffer in this world to reap our rewards in the next.'

'Then it's a bloody cruel way of carrying on,' Joe answered, 'that's all I can say.'

'And all I can say is we'll have less of the swearing.'

Joe lifted the twins, one in each arm. 'Come on, me bairns, yer almost asleep on yer feet. Let's get yer undressed and take a look at that back of yours, Frankie.'

The little boy forced his eyes open. 'It's all right, Uncle Joe, and I'm not tired. I've had a ride on the ragman's cart. I like the ragman. I like him better than me dad. Why didn't yer marry the ragman instead of me dad, Mam? I–'

Joe interrupted him swiftly. 'Come on, let's have yer up to bed. Sadie love, you can go in our bed. Yer mam and Auntie Alice won't be long before they join yer. We'll manage for one night with me on the couch.'

He carried the little ones up the stairs, and Joseph groaned. 'Oh no! Not again. I always get nits when they come in my bed.'

'Well, he's coming in whether yer like it or not, so yer'll just have to sleep with yer head out of bed, won't yer.' Joe set off down the stairs. 'And be quiet or yer'll get more than nits.' He reached the bottom and heard Joseph's voice following him.

'It's not fair.'

'What was that?'

'Nothing, Dad.'

Joe came into the living room. 'Cheeky young

bugger. He's getting spoiled is our Joseph.'

'No, he's a good lad, Joe.' Ruth sighed. 'And he's right about the nits. I feel right shamed. There's only Mrs Armitage who seems to bother down the Place. I no sooner get rid of them than one of them picks them up again. I can't stop them playing with the other kids – it isn't their fault, poor little mites. It's nothing but a slum down there. I wish I'd never set eyes on the house. "It'll put us on," he said, "until we get something better." That's a laugh.' But she didn't laugh. She cried as though her heart would break.

'Tha should never have married him, lass. Our mam told thee no good would come of marrying a heathen.'

'Oh, don't start yer preaching again, Alice. Your Ruth knows she made a mistake without you rubbing it in. Besides, they're not all perfect that goes to chapel. Bloody self-righteous hypocrites some of 'em are. Where's our Billy, then?'

'I don't know. He ran outside. He'll be frightened to death, I shouldn't wonder. He could be anywhere.'

'I'll go find him.'

Alice looked alarmed. 'Be careful, Joe!'

'Don't worry, lass. A woman and child may be no match for yon monster, but this time he's gone too far. By the time I've done with him he won't hit yer again, lass; not for a while, any road. Let me get my belt off and he's due for a dose of his own medicine.'

Old Mother knew she wouldn't be on this earth for many more days. In fact the dizziness and drowsiness of the last few hours had caused her to drift off to a faraway place. She had seen a vision, an angel with outstretched hands and the face of her long lost sweetheart. If only she could float away into the welcoming arms and leave this exhausting world behind her. If only there was not something holding her back. Old Mother was confused. Her affairs were all in order. Olive had been taught all there was to know and was well prepared for her old friend's death. 'Don't grieve for me, little one,' the girl had been told. 'I'll be going to a far better place than this, if you axe me.' But there was something she must do, and regretfully she had returned to her old, worn body. She dozed fitfully, uneasy about something but not knowing what. Oh well, she supposed she would find out sooner or later. She hoped it would be sooner, for she was tired, and ready for Heaven. The wall clock chimed twelve and she slept at last.

Joe slithered and slipped on the iced-over cobbles as he made his way to Wire Mill Place. He could make out a figure sitting hunched on Mrs Armitage's doorstep. 'Billy lad, is that you?'

'Hmm.'

'Hitch up and let me sit beside yer. By gum, this doorstep's cold. Are yer all right?'

'I think so. I slipped flat on me back when I ran out and banged me head. I went all dizzy, but I'm all right.'

'Where's yer dad?'

'He's not me dad. He's an animal.'

'Nay, lad, it's the beer that makes him like that.'

154

'No it isn't. He's always the same. He doesn't love any of us, not even the little ones. I spent all day last Saturday down in the wood, trying to find enough branches to make a fence, to stop the twins going down by the water. Then the first thing Sunday morning he chopped them all up for firewood. He won't even buy a bag of coal. Sometimes me mam can't even light a fire to heat the water to do the washing, let alone keep the little 'uns warm.' Billy began to sob as though his heart would break.

'Don't fret yerself, lad.' Joe put an arm round his nephew in an effort to comfort him, but Billy carried on.

'Every penny he earns he takes to the Rag, that's when he bothers to go to work at all, and there was me mam, working right up to the day our Margaret was born, and again a few days after. It's like a washhouse, with the tub and mangle out all the time. She washes for all them idle lot up in the big houses, and for next to nowt. Why did she marry him, Uncle Joe?'

'Nay, lad, I'll be buggered if I know. Perhaps she were just rebelling against yer grandad. Chapel three times on a Sunday, Bible classes during the week. She never did take to all that religion like yer Auntie Alice did. I suppose she was looking for something more exciting. Besides, yer dad put on a good side at first – took her to the theatre and that. And he was handsome, nobody could deny that. But I never thought she would up and marry him. I don't think yer grandma has ever got over it. They say love is blind, but it was a right eye-opener when she found out what he was

155

really like.'

'She wouldn't have a rag to her back if it wasn't for me Auntie Alice and Auntie Mary Hampshire. Our Sadie even had to go to school with her toes sticking out of the hole in her shoe last week. Everybody laughed except the teacher, who gave her another pair. They were two sizes too big, but better than nowt. No wonder she's got chilblains.'

'You should have told me. I'd have bought her a pair of shoes, you know I would.'

'Me mam didn't want you to know, she was too ashamed. It's his fault. I wish he was dead.'

'Nay, lad, don't turn all bitter. He's not worth it.'

'He hit me mam when she had our Margaret in her arms. He almost hit her too.'

'Where is he, lad?'

'In the closet. To be sick I expect, filthy pig.'

Billy had no sooner got the words out than the creak of the closet door reached their ears.

'He's coming out. Don't let him see me.' Billy moved closer to Joe.

'Stop yer trembling, lad. He won't see yer. He'll be too drunk, and if he does he'll have me to deal with.'

Then the sound of Walter Wray's boots seemed to change direction and instead of walking towards the house the footsteps clattered and slithered in the direction of the river. Suddenly there was a cry, followed by a huge splash.

Billy started to his feet, but Joe's hand on his shoulder restrained him. 'What's up, lad?' he said. 'Sit yerself down.'

'I thought I heard–'

Joe interrupted his nephew swiftly. 'I heard nothing, lad.'

Billy seemed flummoxed. 'Perhaps it were a rat in the river.'

'Aye, perhaps it were. There're some bloody big rats around here.'

Billy looked confused, then seemed to brighten. 'Uncle Joe,' he said, 'what'll happen if me dad doesn't come back? What'll they think happened to him?'

'They'll put two and two together, lad. There'll be plenty of witnesses from the Rag to say he was drunk. They'll realise he went to the closet, slipped on the ice and ended up in the river. It's a pity he didn't buy a bag of coal instead of burning the fencing. Especially with nobody hearing owt.'

Billy's sense of elation suddenly changed to anxiety. 'What'll me mam do for money, though?'

'Well seeing as she's never been used to having any off yer dad, I can't see her being much worse off. Yer Aunt Alice and me'll help out until you can leave school. It won't be long, and if you're man enough to protect yer mother I reckon you're man enough to tackle a man's job.'

'Do yer think I'd get one? A decent job, I mean?'

'I'm sure you would. I'm not personnel officer for nought, yer know. Yer dad'd have been sacked long ago if it hadn't been for me.' Joe rose stiffly to his feet. 'Well, I don't know about you but my bum's gone numb. We'd best be getting home. The women'll be wondering what's become of us.'

'Uncle Joe, just in case it really was a rat I heard, can I sleep at your house tonight? Just in case.'

Joe forced a laugh for his nephew's sake. 'It were a rat all right, Billy. A bloody great big one that couldn't swim at that. And with the river being at its highest at this time of the year, nobody would have had a cat in hell's chance of getting him out in the darkness. So don't start letting yer conscience prick. Yer can sleep at our house just the same, then first thing tomorrow we'll set about getting a fence put up. I mean, we don't want anyone slipping and ending up in the river, do we?'

'Eeh, Uncle Joe, I don't know what we'd do without you and me Aunt Alice.'

'And God, lad, never forget God. He works in the most mysterious ways, according to yer Aunt Alice. Do yer know, lad, it isn't often I agree with her but after tonight I must admit she's probably right. Come on. What we need is a drop of brandy to warm us up.'

'No thanks, Uncle Joe. I've made up my mind, there's going to be no more drinking in our family.'

'Aye, lad, you've got some sense. A cup of summat hot'll do us a lot more good. Besides, it'll not start yer Aunt Alice off nagging either. Still, she's a good woman, Billy.'

'I know, Uncle Joe, and you're a good man.'

It was not quite light when the first morning worshippers on their way to the Catholic church sighted the body of Walter Wray. It had been swept half a mile down the river before becoming wedged amongst the branches of low-hanging trees on the bank. It was a grotesque sight, icicles having formed on the hair and shoulders, and both the man and his wife were in shock when they reported the find. The young constable needed no identification of the body. Walter Wray was a well-known character around Cottenly and had been dumped in a cell on numerous occasions for disorderly behaviour. After the body had been taken to the mortuary, he and the sergeant made their way to Wire Mill Place.

'If there is one part of my job I hate it's this,' Sergeant Reynolds admitted as they prepared themselves to break the news to Walter Wray's wife. Though neither of the men mentioned the fact, they both knew that on this occasion the news would not be met with the usual hysteria, but they fixed an appropriate expression on their faces nevertheless as they knocked on the door, helmets in hand. Before they had time to knock again the Place was crowded with neighbours, some on the pretext of visiting lavatories, others sweeping the yard for the first time in months – any excuse to get an eyeful of what was going on. Only Mrs Armitage was genuinely alarmed and hurried across to Ruth's. Receiving no response, Sergeant Reynolds tried the door and made his way inside. 'Looks like they're still in bed,' he said as they made their way across the kitchen. 'He obviously went across the yard, slipped on the ice and ended up in the river, hence the unlocked door.'

Winnie Armitage followed the two men into the

house. 'What's he done now?' she enquired. 'Beat the lass up again, has he? The rotten swine.'

The young constable silenced the woman by asking, 'Does she usually stay in bed this late?'

'Who, Ruth Wray? You must be joking. She'd have had the baby fed, the others ready for Sunday school and the nappies on the boil by now.'

The sergeant went to the bottom of the stairs and was just about to call her name when he noticed the bloodstains on the bare wooden stairs. 'What do yer make of this, lad?' he asked the young constable. 'It seems it isn't an open and shut case after all.' He turned to Winnie. 'Did you happen to hear or see anything unusual last night?'

'Unusual! Nowt short of murder'd be unusual in this house, and it'd have been done long ago if the bugger'd belonged to me. But no, for owt I know he were out all day. Apart from the little lad falling in the river I don't know as owt unusual happened.' Winnie frowned. 'But she was afraid of Walter finding out and belting the bairn.'

'Thank you. Do you know where Mrs Wray might be at the moment?'

'Well! She could be at either of her sisters', or her parents' ... but no, it would take a lot for her to worry them. A thoughtful lass is Ruth Wray. One of the best, and with a bugger like him to deal with. If it had been me I'd have swung for him long since.'

'Yes, so you keep telling us. Will you keep an eye on the house, Mrs er...'

'Armitage.'

'Only wherever they've gone, the door has been left unlocked.'

160

'Well it would be. She'd have no call to lock it seeing as the lass has nowt worth pinching.'

Sergeant Reynolds led the way out and closed the door behind them. 'Ask the nosy parkers if they heard anything. It doesn't look like they'd miss much.'

The woman next door to Ruth was not only filthy and covered in bug bites but also a little bit slow on the uptake. Nevertheless she made no bones about the fact that Walter Wray had beaten his wife and youngest son and the other son had threatened to kill him. 'The walls are very thin, you see,' she said, 'so we can't 'elp overhearing.'

'What time would that be, madam?'

'About closing time. Aye, that's when it was – 'e walked 'ome wi' my Herbert. It were just after.'

'Thank you.' The sergeant turned to his colleague. 'See what time he left the Rag, and what condition he was in, though I think we can guess.'

He would have guessed wrong on this occasion. Both the landlord and his wife swore Walter Wray had not entered the pub all day until almost closing time, and although he had downed three pints, one after the other, three pints were nothing compared to his normal intake and he wasn't as drunk as the night before. 'Of course, he could have been drinking somewhere else during the day, but it's my guess he had been with a woman. He often went down town and frequented the pick-up places. Your lot should be closing them places down, that's what I say.'

'That would be easier said than done,' the constable pointed out. 'While ever there are men willing to pay for their services, there will always be women willing to oblige.'

'I'd like to know where the blood came from,' Sergeant Reynolds said. 'I think another look at the corpse wouldn't go amiss.'

'It could belong to the wife, sir, or child.'

'It could. But if it didn't somebody knows where it did come from, by what the woman next door heard.'

'She looks less than a full shilling to me, sir.'

'Aye, too gormless to make things up. Come on, lad, we've work to do. Why is it always Sunday when something like this happens?'

'Murders don't happen very often in Cottenly, sir. In fact I can't ever remember another one.'

'Who mentioned murder? The evidence shows that Walter Wray slipped on the ice whilst visiting the lavatory and fell into the river. But not quite so likely now that we know he wasn't in a drunken condition. First we must find Mrs Wray.'

'And her son, sir.'

'Aye, and her son.'

Joe, Joseph and Billy were just leaving the house when the police arrived at Green Villa.

'What is it, sergeant?' Joe looked concerned.

The sergeant knew and respected Joe Jackson. 'I think you'd better come back inside, Mr Jackson. We're looking for Mrs Ruth Wray. Does she happen to be here?'

'She is. And I'm afraid she will remain here for the time being. She was beaten by her husband last night, along with her son, and came to us for protection. I think it's him you should be looking for.'

'We've found him.' The sergeant glanced at Billy. 'Is this your son, Mr Jackson?'

'No, this one's my lad. This is Billy Wray, my nephew.'

Ruth and Alice were pottering in the kitchen with the twins, unable to concentrate on the normal household duties. Their faces paled at the appearance of the constabulary.

'Mrs Wray, will you be seated, please? I'm afraid I have to tell you your husband Walter Wray has been found dead.'

Ruth's hands covered her face and she gasped at the news. 'Oh, God, what's happened?'

'We have reason to believe he may have slipped on the ice outside the lavatory and fallen in the river. After the recent bad weather you will realise how fast the water is flowing and unless he was an extremely strong swimmer he would find it impossible to escape the deluge.'

'He couldn't swim,' Ruth stammered. 'He beat our Frankie only yesterday for falling in. Oh, God, it could have been my bairn who drowned.' Ruth burst into tears, not for the loss of her husband but at the thought of Frankie drowning.

'I got the wood to put a fence up but he burnt it. If he'd let me put it up he wouldn't have drowned,' Billy said bitterly.

'When did you last see your father, Billy?' the sergeant asked. Billy paled but Joe nodded for him to speak out. 'Last night about half past ten. He had just hit me mam and our Frankie. Look at me mam's neck. Show him, Mam.' Billy looked close to tears.

'It's all right, Billy. We need to ask you a few

questions, that's all.' Sergeant Reynolds would have given anything to spare the young lad having to relive the ordeal, but duty had to be done. 'What happened then?'

'He ... he went to bed. He was shouting that he would kill us all.'

'I was frightened. I didn't want to be killed,' Sadie said.

'I'm sure you didn't, sweetheart.' The young constable lifted Sadie up into his arms and her large, solemn, brown eyes gazed into his.

Frankie spoke up. 'I wanted him to be killed. We wished he was dead, didn't we, Sadie?'

'Yes.' Sadie was still gazing at the constable, unsure whether she liked him or not. Then she decided he was certainly better than her dad.

'So you didn't see him after he went to bed? And you, Mrs Wray, did you go to bed?'

'No. I dressed the children and got out of the house as quickly as we could. We stayed here last night.'

'Is he really dead? Really, really dead?' Frankie asked.

'Yes, son, I'm afraid so.'

'What do I do now?' Ruth looked bewilderedly from one to the other.

'We'll let you know when you can arrange the funeral, love. After the post-mortem, of course. I'm sorry to be the bearer of such bad news. If there's anything I can do...'

'No, thank you, sergeant. I'll see to things and let his parents and sister know. Oh, Joe, his poor mother and father! I must go to them at once.' Ruth knew there was no love lost between the old couple and the son who had treated them so badly, but he was their only son after all.

'I'll come with you, lass,' Joe said.

'And I'll go let our mam and dad know.' Alice knew what her mother's reaction would be: one of immense relief. She was ashamed that she should be feeling a similar emotion herself. And her a good Christian woman at that.

Sergeant Reynolds broke into their varied thoughts by clearing his throat. 'And you, lad,' he said to Billy, 'you'll have to come with us, son. Just a few questions, that's all. Nothing to worry about.' He hoped he was speaking the truth, for the lad's sake, as well as his mother's.

Joe placed a reassuring hand on his nephew's shoulder. 'Don't be alarmed, lad. I'll be with yer as soon as I've taken yer mother to yer grandma's.'

Billy nodded, close to tears. 'I'll be all right,' he said, then followed the two policemen out of the door.

Old Mother thought her young friend had forsaken her. All day Sunday she waited for Olive, but the girl never came. It was Monday morning before she turned up in a tearful state, and Old Mother found it impossible to console her.

'It's our Billy,' she managed to explain. 'He's been taken to the police station. Uncle Walter's dead and Auntie Ruth can't stop crying. Me mam says she'll be having a breakdown, what with the new baby only just born, and our Billy arrested.'

Old Mother rallied as best she could and made a pot of camomile tea. 'Get this down yer and take a deep breath, count to seven and breathe

165

out again. There, that's the way.'

Olive found herself calming down and gradually the story was told.

'And you say young Billy stabbed his father with a knife?'

'Yes, in the arm. With the knife Uncle Joe bought him for Christmas. He bought our Harry one exactly the same.'

'And are you saying he killed the drunken brute?'

'I don't know. Auntie Ruth's all confused. I think they've found some blood and want to know where it came from. Even though he was found drowned in the river.'

'What's he done with the knife?' Old Mother needed to know all the details as a plan formed in her mind. She knew now why she had come back from the brink of death. She prayed her strength would not desert her until she had carried her plan through.

'Uncle Joe's got rid of it. He's warned our Billy to keep quiet about its existence. Because he didn't hurt him all that much. It was a super ... super something, but I've forgot.'

'Aye, I know, lass, a superficial wound, and you say he fell in the river?'

'Yes, and Uncle Joe says if they know our Billy took the knife to him, they might think he pushed him in the river.'

'Aye, maybe they would. Can you get hold of Harry's knife?'

'I think so. It'll be in his drawer. But he's got nothing to do with it.'

'Go get it and hurry, and don't tell a soul.'

Olive ran all the way home. She would do anything to save Billy. Although he was younger, he
was her hero. Not only did he protect her from
some of the girls from the posh houses, who
sometimes bullied her, but he knew where many
of the rare herbs grew in the wood towards
Warrentickle and would gather them for her
when he went with his barrow for firewood.

When she came back with the knife Grandma
Burlington had written a note and sunk back into
her bed. She looked ever so poorly, Olive
thought. 'Take this to the police station and tell
the one in charge – Mr Reynolds, I think it'll be
– to come at once.'

Olive hurried away, her heart racing wildly,
hoping she wouldn't see anyone she knew from
the umbrella mill. She was supposed to be ill; in
fact she had been feeling too ill to go to work in
the morning. Fortunately she met no one of
importance.

'What's this all about?' Sergeant Reynolds
looked flummoxed as he read the note.

'I don't know, but she says it's urgent.'

'Well, we'd better see what she wants, I
suppose. Let's be on our way.'

The young constable was left in charge, much
to his relief. He was always a bit dubious about
Mother Buttercup.

'Well, Miss Burlington?' The sergeant had
almost addressed her as Mother Buttercup.
'What can I do for you?'

'I expect you'll have to arrest me,' Old Mother
answered, 'but I'm not saying I'm sorry cause
I'm not.' She sighed deeply. 'I ought to have done

it years since if you axe me.'

'Done what?' The sergeant perched on the bed and thought how ill the poor old dear looked.

'Stabbed him. That filthy beast, that Walter Wray.' She motioned for Olive to leave them, not wanting the young girl to hear the rest.

Sergeant Reynolds almost laughed but thought better of it. 'You stabbed Walter Wray! How?'

'With me knife. The one I use for cutting me herbs.'

'Where is it, the knife?'

'Over there, in me drawer. And I'll not tell yer why I did it so don't axe me.' She knew he would.

The sergeant went to the drawer in the table and found the knife, surprised to see that it was of the type said to have been used for the crime. 'But we need to know why, Mother Buttercup.' She didn't pick him up as he let the name slip out, as she had on so many other occasions.

'I can't talk about it. It's too disgusting if you axe me.'

'You can to me. I won't be disgusted, I promise. Just tell me what happened from the beginning.'

'He came looking for Ruth, thought she'd come to me, but she hadn't. When she wasn't here he said if he couldn't have her he'd have me. I axed him to go but he came closer, and all't time he was undoing his trousers.' Sergeant Reynolds found his mouth dropping open as he listened. 'And then he exposed himself, the filthy devil.'

'Exposed himself? To a woman of your age. I can't believe that.'

'Believe it or not it's true. Great ugly thing he had. Besides, I can prove it.'

'Prove it! How?'

Old Mother beckoned him closer and hoped her memory wasn't playing tricks as she remembered the night she had mentioned Ruth Wray's beauty spot. 'Right on the end of it he's got a big, brown mole. Well, either that or it was a beetle. Me eyes aren't as good as they used to be.'

'You're telling me that Walter Wray has a mole on his...' He stopped, too embarrassed to say any more.

'On his willie,' Old Mother whispered. 'So I stabbed him. Then he ran away, went home as I thought. I didn't know I'd killed him. But I'm not sorry, only that I didn't chop it off.'

'You didn't kill Walter Wray, Miss Buttercup. He drowned in the river.'

'So aren't yer going to lock me up then, for stabbing him?'

'Oh, I don't think so. I think anyone would have done the same in the situation you were in. Nay, my old love, I don't think you'll be hearing any more about it. But I thank you for solving the puzzle.'

'Will yer take a glass of elderberry wine before you go?'

'Not whilst I'm on duty, but I might call in later and have a drop.'

Old Mother flopped back on to the pillow when he had gone, and knew if he came back later he would be too late. She had carried out her last good deed. Old Mother prayed for God's forgiveness for the lie she had told, but was in no doubt that one lie against all the good she had done in her life would balance the scales of judgement in

169

her favour. Now with relief she could give herself up to the weakness which was gradually defeating her. She sighed a deep sigh of contentment. Soon she would be with her lover and her child, and this time there would be no turning back. She saw the light coming towards her, more brilliant than the brightest sun. She held out her hands in welcome and was carried away, leaving her cottage for the last time.

When Olive came to tell Grandma Burlington that Billy had been released she found her old friend smiling as though something was amusing her, but no one would ever know what, for Old Mother was far away, at peace with the angels, never to return.

Olive knew what she must do. Grandma Burlington had told her. She was to look in the black tin box in the bedroom, where Old Mother hadn't slept for months. She found the box and the envelope, on which was written *Last Will and Testament.* Her hands shook as she saw the box was half full of bank notes, five pounds and one pounds. There was also a book for the Yorkshire Bank. Olive locked the box carefully and carried it down the narrow, winding stairs. Then she left the cottage and locked the door.

She ran all the way home and gave the door key to her mother, leaving Lizzie to arrange for the old lady's laying out. Then she delivered the tin box to the tall, gabled house in the main street, with the brass plate on the door displaying the name of the solicitor. Her heart was almost bursting, since she had run the whole way, and she was relieved when the door wasn't opened immediately, giving her time to regain her composure.

The woman who bade Olive to enter resembled a wizened-up prune, especially as she was dressed in brownish purple from top to toe, but she seemed kind and invited Olive to be seated and indicated a high-backed leather-upholstered chair. Then she left her and entered another room with a *Private* sign on the door.

Olive wondered if she had been forgotten and coughed a few times to remind them she was there. After what seemed an age she was asked to follow the prune woman into the private room.

The solicitor was the tallest, thinnest man Olive had ever met, and the only one she had ever seen wearing gold rings. She couldn't help staring when he walked round the desk and shook her hand.

'How do you do, Miss Crossman? I trust you are well?'

'Oh yes, I'm very well, thank you,' Olive replied.

'Allow me to offer my condolences on the death of Miss Burlington.' Olive didn't know what to say to that so remained silent. 'Are you aware that Miss Burlington was quite wealthy?'

'Not until today, when I opened her box and saw all the money.'

'Then it is all the more to your credit that you saw to the old lady's needs without any expectation of gain.' The man opened the will form and studied it silently and at length, and Olive thought that if he went any thinner he would be just a skeleton.

'And now, I am happy to say that you are a

wealthy young lady.'

Olive didn't answer.

'Did you know that Miss Burlington had bequeathed her cottage to you?'

Olive wasn't sure what bequeathed meant and wished she had paid more attention during English lessons at school.

'You are now the owner of Miss Burlington's cottage, as well as a very large sum of money. No doubt you are unaware that Miss Burlington's father, after many years of estrangement, had a change of heart, discovered the whereabouts of his daughter and bequeathed his estate to her. Miss Burlington, however, chose to invest her inheritance, except for a large amount which she has donated to charitable causes over the years. Oh, there are some formalities to be negotiated, but I think I can safely say that within a month everything will be in order.'

Olive was speechless, as she suddenly realised what the solicitor was explaining.

'Miss Burlington requires your father to be nominated as your trustee, until you come of age. Does that seem agreeable to you?'

Olive suddenly found her tongue. 'Does that mean the money is mine? All the money in the box?'

'Oh, my dear, much more than that. And the cottage can be rented, to bring in further income, until you wish to take possession of it in the future. Of course it could be sold if you wanted.'

Olive was shocked at the suggestion that anyone else should ever occupy Grandma Burlington's home.

'Oh yes, Miss Crossman, I can safely say that before the month is out you will be an extremely wealthy young lady.'

'And can I give some to my mam and dad, and my brothers and sisters?'

'Well, we shall have to discuss that with your father. I dare say an amount can be made available for your immediate requirements. Though I advise you to accept Miss Burlington's wishes and let your father handle your affairs until you reach the age of responsibility.'

Olive's mind was in a whirl. She was rich, or so the thin man said.

'So I will make a further appointment for you in due course. In the meantime, may I be the first to congratulate you on your good fortune and to say how much Miss Burlington valued your friendship.'

Olive suddenly became aware that he was discussing Grandma Burlington in the past tense. The hectic events of the day had prevented it from penetrating that her old friend was dead. Now she could feel the tears welling and her throat filling as she realised she would never see her again. Then, to her horror, Olive burst into tears, right there with the thin man watching her. He came round the desk and offered her an immaculate white handkerchief and rang a bell so that the prune woman came fussing in with a tray on which she carried a coffee pot and two tiny cups. Olive had never tasted coffee and wasn't sure she liked it, but it smelled lovely, and when she was handed a plate of chocolate biscuits the tears disappeared as if by magic. Just fancy, she thought, she could eat chocolate biscuits every day from now on if she wished. She smiled her most ravishing smile at the thin man, and he wished, oh, how he wished, that he was at least twenty years younger.

Olive Crossman's tears flowed profusely as Old Mother was laid to rest beside her child in the churchyard on the hill. The funeral procession was one of the largest ever to be seen in Cottenly and amongst the followers were many with reason to be grateful to Olive Burlington, either for their safe delivery into the world, or for her healing and advice whilst in it. Most mourners shed tears as they laid flowers along the grass verge of the churchyard path and everyone agreed that Olive Burlington would be sadly missed. It was all in vast contrast to the small gathering at the grave of Walter Wray. Only the family and one or two workmates and drinking pals from the Rag bothered to attend the ceremony and Ruth was saddened that her husband had commanded so little respect from the townspeople. Nevertheless, she strove to remember the man she had first known, the handsome, outgoing man who had courted her in her youth. Yet even for him she found she could shed no tears. The compassion she felt was for his elderly parents and sister, for after all Walter had been of their own flesh and blood. Ruth vowed that they would receive more comfort from their grandchildren than they had ever received from their son, who had brought them nothing but shame over the years.

She wondered what she would do now that Walter was no longer bringing home a wage, for though he had given her very little the rent had been deducted from his pay every Friday and she knew it would be within the firm's rights to insist she vacate the house now that he had gone. She pinned her hopes on the management's being of a compassionate frame of mind when she went – as she must – to appeal for the tenancy to be signed over to her. She must stress that her son was hoping to join the firm as soon as he was allowed to leave school and had already been offered a position. Even so, Ruth was apprehensive as she waited for the interview with the manager on the day following the funeral.

Mr Hubert Hancock was a red-faced, stocky man who seemed to have difficulty prising his body from the chair to shake her by the hand. He had heard all about the woman's impoverished lifestyle and the brute of a husband she had had to deal with. He had sent a wreath, not out of respect for an employee but as a small token of consolation for his widow. Mr Hancock was a hardened individual who demanded sweat, and sometimes blood, from his workers. But fortunately, where a pretty woman was concerned, he was soft as a pound of putty.

'Well, Mrs Wray, do sit down.' He indicated a chair opposite his where he could admire her at close range.

'Thank you, sir.'

'May I offer you my condolences at this tragic time?'

'Thank you, sir.'

'I suppose you've come for your husband's out-standing wages.' He opened a drawer and took out a wage packet which he placed on the desk.

'Oh, no, sir. I didn't know he had any money due to him. No, sir, I'm here to ask you for the tenancy of the house. I won't fall behind with the rent and I'll keep the place clean – you can inspect it if you wish. Only if you decide to evict us I don't know what will become of us, the children and me.' Ruth hadn't intended to cry but suddenly the worry of it all became more than she could bear, what with her beating, Billy's arrest and the funeral. It had all been bottled up inside her and now she could no longer control its release.

'Oh, my dear Mrs Wray.' Hubert Hancock never could abide to see a woman in tears, especially a lovely, feminine creature like Ruth Wray. He hurried towards her, went down on his knees and spread his arms round her. He couldn't help but compare her warm softness with the stiff, corseted figure of his wife. Ruth's breasts, heavy and swollen with milk, were only inches away from him. It was almost more than he could bear. He dabbed at her cheeks with an initialled hanky, devouring the beauty of her large, sorrowful eyes, and the lips which seemed to be inviting his own to caress them. He withdrew hastily, ashamed of the desire rising within him. 'My dear Mrs Wray, please don't distress yourself. It grieves me to see a woman cry.'

'I'm sorry. It is unforgivable of me to behave in such a manner.' Ruth managed a weak smile. 'You are very kind, Mr Hancock, sir.'

'Not at all. Now I'm sure we can arrange a transfer of tenancy, particularly as your son will be joining our firm in the near future.'

Ruth was lost for words. She stared at the man with large, unbelieving eyes. 'You mean we can stay in the house?'

'Yes.'

'Oh, sir, you won't regret your kindness, I'm sure. Our Billy's ever such a good worker, I promise.' She rose to her feet.

'No, I'm sure I won't regret it.' Mr Hancock took her hand in his, a fat, sweaty hand, but Ruth shook it warmly. 'Don't go without the pay packet. I'm sorry it's not more, but Mr Wray had been absent from work for two days the week before he died, you understand.'

'I know.' Ruth blushed and then thought how mean it was to stop two days' wages from a dead man. But she had the house and, to Ruth, a roof over the heads of her children was all that mattered. She would worry about the rent money later. 'I'm so grateful, Mr Hancock, sir.'

'You're more than welcome, Mrs Wray. Good afternoon.'

'Good afternoon, and thanks again.' She almost skipped out of the office but knew he was watching her as she walked across the yard and out of the gates. She realised it was her slim figure and decent looks which had appealed to his better nature and wondered why she felt so uneasy. She told herself she was imagining things, but remained unconvinced as she hurried back to Wire Mill Place. Suddenly, however, she experienced a feeling of freedom, for the first time since moving

177

into Wire Mill Place. Freedom from fear, freedom to laugh, to sing and look pretty, freedom from the jealousy and brutality that had filled the house since the day she had been fool enough to marry Walter Wray.

Chapter Five

For the first time ever, as far as Lizzie could remember, Olive was causing mayhem in the house, with her sulks and tantrums. She would start as soon as she rose in the morning and as soon as she arrived home in the evening. Not that it was for her own benefit that she was nagging away at George. All she wanted was to be allowed to spend some of her inheritance on other people. First of all she wished to buy her mother a lovely new dress she had seen in Caroline Swann's window. Then she decided her brothers and sisters should all have a bicycle like their Joseph's. It was only when she began going on about having her beautiful long dark tresses cut and permed in a hideous new style like one of the girls from the mill that George put his foot down.

'Look, Olive, you would never have had the money at all if it hadn't been for Old Mother, and now you are not even respecting her wishes. Do you think that's fair?'

'Grandma Burlington wouldn't mind me buying a few things.'

'Oh yes she would. The inheritance is for your future. She deliberately requested that I should take care of your interests until I think you're responsible enough to handle them, and the way you're acting at present you're not in the least responsible.' Olive coloured at his words. 'Look,

179

love, if Old Mother could see you now, do you think she'd be pleased by your tantrums, or that you were going against her wishes?' Olive said nothing but George could see her lip trembling. 'Do you know what I think, Olive love?' She looked at her father questioningly. 'I believe Old Mother can see you now. I don't think you go away just because your body isn't here any more. I think Old Mother will be watching over you, guiding you, until you're a little bit older at least. So why don't you prove you're worthy of her money? The money she worked hard for all those years. Surely you don't wish to squander it all away? It wouldn't be fair. I think she meant you to carry on in the way she had taught you, but not just yet. You're fourteen, love. Give it a year or two, and then we'll invest in your future. In the meantime, sell your scents and potions to the girls at work, anywhere you like, see how well they go, and I promise you, if you still wish it, in two years' time I'll have some of the money released to set you up with a stall, not in Cottenly but in Sheffield market, where you'll be inside, protected from the weather.'

Olive's face radiated happiness and her eyes glistened, 'Oh, Dad! Do you really mean it? A stall in Castle Market?'

'I mean it. So now, can we have a bit of peace and quiet? And let me tell you a secret.' Olive listened eagerly. 'They are all having a bike for Christmas. I've already arranged it, out of the rise I was given on my promotion. I've been paying so much a week into the savings club, but don't you be letting on.'

Olive giggled. 'I won't, Dad, honest. Oh, and Dad, I won't mention the money again.' She wrapped her arms round his neck, happy that they were friends again, because she did love her dad, and he was right about Grandma Burlington being here. Olive could sense her, especially when she went to the cottage where she was busy making packets of pot pourri and mixed herbs. She had also almost perfected a cough mixture which Grandma Burlington had started to concoct before she died. Sometimes Olive would be unsure how much ginger or lemon to add to the mixture and it would come to her out of the blue, just as if her old friend was whispering in her ear. She knew help would always be at hand, as long as there was work to do, and she was determined never to let Old Mother down. She would be a herbalist – maybe part time at present, but as soon as she was sixteen she would be a full-time one on a stall in Castle Market. Her dad had promised.

Alice and Joe proved to be worth their weight in gold to Ruth after the funeral. Joe arranged for her to receive the widow's pension of ten shillings, as well as five shillings for Billy and three shillings for the others. Alice also promised to care for little Margaret if Ruth wished to find employment, rather than take in washing. She also visited the pawnshop and retrieved the canteen of cutlery and other bits and pieces pawned by Walter. Ruth shed more tears at the kindness of her friends and family than she had shed on the death of her husband, and she actually felt a sense of guilt at the relief she experienced now she was free of his

181

fearsome presence. Even the children seemed more relaxed, and Ruth endeavoured to make up for the unhappiness of the past years. Mrs Armitage kept an eye on her and presented her with a sum of money she had collected from neighbours and members of the chapel, and another sum donated by the girls from the umbrella mill where Ruth had once been employed. 'No point in buying flowers, yer can't eat them,' she told Ruth, reducing her once more to tears as she realised some of the contributing neighbours were probably even poorer than herself.

'Come on, lass, there's nowt to cry about. You've a future ahead of yer, four lovely kids, and things can only get better.'

'I know. I'm not miserable – it's the kindness that makes me cry, folks I never thought would care. I know I'm daft but I can't help it.'

'Perhaps yer don't feel miserable, but all the same yer need something to buck yer up.'

'Oh, I've got a tonic. Our Olive's made me up a potion, one that won't hurt the baby when I'm feeding her.'

'I don't mean summat like that to buck yer up. I mean a change. So get on yer best bib and tucker and we're off out.'

'I can't, unless it's somewhere I can take the children.'

'Oh yes yer can. Our Florrie's promised to look after them. You and me are going to the pictures, and I'll not stand here arguing so don't start. We'll go to the first house so be ready by five.'

The visit to the cinema did prove to be a tonic. Ruth laughed at the antics of Will Hay and swooned over Charles Boyer, surprised she could even consider fancying another man after her past experiences. Only the newsreel depressed her as she realised her father's prediction seemed to be looming closer. 'Do you really think there'll be another war?' she asked her friend as they nibbled chips out of newspaper on their way home.

'Sure to be, according to my Albert. Thank God he'll be too old to be called up this time. Besides, I doubt they'd have him with his chest.'

'Isn't it any better?' Ruth frowned. Albert Armitage could be heard coughing all over Wire Mill Place when he was at his worst.

'No. I doubt it'll ever get any better. There's not much can be done about dust on't lungs. Bloody brickworks. I always said they'd be the death of 'im and I wasn't far wrong. I'll tell you what, though, that inhalant stuff Old Mother gave him doesn't 'alf fetch some stuff up. Poor old girl.'

'Oh, I don't know. She told me she was ready to go. But she'll be missed and no mistake.' Ruth chuckled, relaxed for the first time in weeks. 'Our Olive's determined to carry on where Old Mother left off. She's down there every night after work. Got a good little business going already, selling skin creams to the umbrella girls.'

'Well nobody could be a better advert for beauty ointment. I don't think a bonnier lass ever walked Cottenly. Your Lizzie'll 'ave to watch her when the lads start sniffing around.'

Ruth laughed. 'They'll have a job to get near her if our Billy's anything to do with it. He watches her like a hawk.'

'Aye well, I'll take my Albert his piece a fish.

183

Tell our Florrie to come straight home or hers'll be cold.'

'I won't keep her,' Ruth answered. 'Oh, and thanks for the treat. It's really done me good. I feel better already.'

'Me too. My Albert's not one for the flicks – gets too many black looks when he gets a coughing fit. And as for our Florrie, well she'd rather go with the lasses, or on the back row with the lads. Not as much fun going on yer own.'

'Well, thanks anyway.'

'Goodnight, lass. The kids'll be wanting their chips.'

'Goodnight, and thanks again.' Ruth made her way across the yard. Funny – the place didn't look half as bad as it used to. Then she realised that it hadn't been the Place that was bad but the man she had lived with who had made it so. But that was all behind her now. She may be poor, but as Mrs Armitage had said things could only get better, and she could feel they were doing so already.

Ruth was on her hands and knees whitening the step when she heard the boots on the cobbles. She turned round as the rag and bone man approached her.

'Hello, scrubbing again?' He smiled.

'Aye. It's not much of a place but I like to keep it clean.'

'Er, I'm sorry about the accident. Your husband, I mean.'

'Thanks.' Ruth emptied the bucket over the flags and scrubbed it in with the yard brush. 'Would you like a cup of tea?'

'If it isn't too much trouble, I just called to see if the little lad was all reight after his soaking. I didn't like calling before, what with your husband's accident and that. I see yer managed to get a fence up after all.'

'Aye, our Billy and Joe put it up.'

'They made a decent job of it.'

'Aye. He's a good man is our Alice's Joe.'

'One of the best.'

'You know him, then?'

'I used to work for the firm. He was always well respected. That was before I took over from me grandfather.'

'What about your father? Wasn't he interested in the rag and bone business, or had he enough with the farm?'

'He died.'

'Oh, I'm sorry.'

'It's all reight. I can't remember anything about him. I was a bairn at the time.'

'What made you leave the works? It can't be much fun trudging the streets in all weathers, fishing kids out of rivers and things.' Ruth laughed nervously as she poured tea into two cups.

'Oh, I like the open-air life, especially in summer. Besides, I'm me own boss, just like me grandfather before me. And there's money to be made – not a lot, but I'm not without a bob or two. Besides, I love the farm. I could never let that go – it's in me blood, all that rich, fertile land.'

'Aye, it's lovely up there. We used to play in your fields when we were little.' Ruth's face clouded momentarily as she remembered that her last visit had been with Walter on the picnic.

'Why not bring the kids up one day? They could run around to their hearts' content, and no danger of them falling in any watter or owt.' Jack grinned.

'I couldn't.'

'Why not? Me mother'd be there. She hardly ever goes out.'

'It wouldn't be right, not with Walter hardly cold.'

'By what I can gather you're a lot better off without him. You look ten times happier than last time I was here.'

'Yes, but even so, what would people think?'

'Be buggered to what folks think.'

'Well, maybe after a little while.'

'I'll look forward to that then. Don't leave it too long – it's nearly time for the lambing, and the little 'uns'd like that. They'd enjoy seeing the lambs.'

Frankie suddenly burst in with the energy of a hurricane.

'Hello,' Jack Dolan said. 'You're getting to be a big lad.'

'Where's yer horse?'

'In't field at home.'

Frankie's mouth drooped. 'Why didn't yer bring him?'

'I thought I'd take an hour off and come to see yer mam.'

'Why?'

Jack looked embarrassed. 'Well, I just wanted to see yer were all all reight.'

Frankie suddenly brightened considerably. 'Me dad's not,' he said. 'He's dead, thank goodness.' He suddenly had a brainwave. 'Mam, can the ragman be our new dad?'

Ruth wished the floor would open up and swallow her. 'Don't be so silly. Go out to play. Go on, go and find our Sadie.' Frankie ran out with all the energy with which he'd entered and Jack Dolan grinned. 'Sorry about that,' Ruth apologised. 'I never know what he's going to come out with next.'

'Nay, don't be sorry. Perhaps it's not such a bad idea about them having a new dad. I mean, it can't be easy bringing up four kids on yer own.'

'It's a damn sight easier than bringing them up with someone like their father to contend with.'

'Aye, well, we're not all like him, so don't dismiss the idea without giving it a second thought.'

'I won't. Here, get your tea before it goes cold.'

Jack looked thoughtful. 'Yer don't mind me calling, then?'

'No, I don't mind you calling.' Ruth quite liked Jack Dolan. He was nice to talk to.

'Perhaps we could go to chapel together then, on Sunday. Surely nobody could see owt wrong with that.'

Ruth laughed. 'I shouldn't be too sure about that. But yes, I'll go to chapel with you. I reckon it's about time I started going again, if only to set the kids a good example. Besides, I should go and thank the minister for organising the collection. I was very grateful and I haven't thanked him yet.'

Jack beamed. 'I'll see you on Sunday, then. By, but it's a good cup of tea, lass.'

Ruth smiled and assumed Jack's broad Yorkshire accent. 'Aye, lad, it is that.'

187

Hubert Hancock broke into a sweat every time he thought of Ruth Wray. He couldn't forget her softness and femininity or the way he had held her close and breathed in her womanly scent. Hubert was a fool where women were concerned. The trouble was he wasn't the sort whom women found attractive, and the only way he could enjoy their company was to dig deep into his pocket. Not that he actually paid for the favours of prostitutes; he was more subtle than that. An invitation to dinner at one of the top class hotels over in Derbyshire, a few bottles of expensive wine and a double room for the night was all it needed to tempt a woman into his bed. The bored wives of his business associates were the easiest prey, especially on the weekends when their husbands chose to join a shooting party or golfing weekend at Wormleighton Hall. But he had yet to come across one with even half the beauty of Ruth Wray. He knew he was playing with fire by calling on her, particularly if his visit was discovered by his wife Sophie. Yet he had the perfect excuse. It was most unusual for a tied property to be rented out to a tenant not employed by the works and he could always say he was checking on the condition of the house, or delivering a new rent book. The manager had weighed up the pros and cons for a week now and could no longer resist setting eyes on the young widow. Discreet enquiries had informed him that three of her children were of school age, so he straightened his tie, flattened what remained of his hair, which wasn't much, and set off early in the afternoon, banking on her being alone in the house.

Winnie Armitage frowned as she saw the well-dressed man approach Ruth's door. She had always been relieved that their own home was owned by a private landlord rather than tied to the works. There was something about Hubert Hancock that made Winnie's flesh crawl.

Ruth had just finished feeding Margaret when she answered the tap on the door, still fastening the buttons of her blouse.

'Good afternoon, Mrs Wray. I hope I'm not inconveniencing you, but I thought it my duty to call and check on your health, particularly after the distress on your visit to my office.'

Ruth was flustered at the sight of the man standing on her doorstep. 'Oh, Mr Hancock, sir, won't you come in?' Her heartbeat quickened as she worried that he might have changed his mind about the tenancy. 'It's kind of you to enquire but I'm really quite recovered, thank you.' She stood aside to let him in and he sidled round the table and lowered his heavy weight on to a chair by the fire.

'Can I offer you a cup of tea? I'm sorry that's all I have in the house.'

'No, don't trouble yourself on my account. I've just eaten lunch.'

Ruth sent up a silent prayer: 'O God, please let him go.' The prayer went unanswered.

'I take it the house is to your satisfaction? No complaints to be reported?' He knew she wouldn't dare complain, even if the house was falling down around her.

'No. Oh, no, everything's fine.' She made an

189

effort to smile. 'The rent's been paid. My brother-in-law paid a month's in advance.'

'Quite, quite.' He settled himself more comfortably, conspicuous in the shabby surroundings. 'It's a heavy burden you have on your shoulders, my dear. A young woman on your own – my heart reaches out to you.' Ruth smiled weakly, remaining silent. 'If there is any way I can be of assistance, any way at all, you must let me help.'

'You're very kind, but I have a good family. My father's always on hand if I need anything.'

'But a father can't provide everything.' His fat cheeks quivered and glowed a florid scarlet. 'For instance, affection such as a man can provide to a lonely woman, a most attractive woman I might add.'

Ruth's face was burning. 'I've only just buried my husband, Mr Hancock, sir. I'm still too shocked to think about such things.'

'Quite, quite. No need to rush, so long as you know I'm here if needed.'

Winnie Armitage thought Ruth's visitor had been there long enough. She picked up a pie that was fortunately cool enough to carry and marched across the Place. She knocked smartly on the door and entered. The scene before her told her she had been right to intrude. The man was obviously settled for the duration and the gleam in the small, close-set eyes mirrored the thoughts on his mind.

'Oh, I didn't know you had a visitor. Just thought I'd better remind you about your appointment at the clinic, lest you'd forgotten.' Winnie turned to the man with an air of conspiracy. 'She's not herself, you see. Can't remember the slightest thing at the moment.' She turned to Ruth, winking as she did so. 'I'll see to the baby whilst you get ready.'

Ruth tried not to show her relief. 'I had forgotten, Mr Hancock, sir, if you'll excuse me.' She went to the door and held it ajar. 'It was good of you to call, but really there's no need to worry on my account.'

The man had no option but to leave, his anger simmering inside him and almost reaching boiling point when Winnie Armitage said, 'Remember me to your wife. We went to school together, you know. Tell her Winnie Stedman was asking about her.' He flounced across the Place, wondering what he was doing visiting such a devil of a spot. And that bloody woman; it would be just like her to bump into his wife and mention where she had seen him. Nevertheless, he would come again. Ruth Wray was worth the risk. If he could only get his hands on her his wife could go to hell for all he cared, and he would get his hands on her no matter what.

'Oh, thank God you turned up when you did.' Ruth flopped into a chair.

'He didn't get his filthy hands on you, did he, lass?'

'No. Oh, no, but Mrs Armitage, what do I do now? He's bound to turn up again and you won't always be there to rescue me.'

'He's nothing but a filthy old sod. I've heard about him and his dirty weekends. And there's old Sophie, all prim and proper. Not two pennies to rub together had her family when they were all small. But she'd make a dozen of him any day.

191

Lovely friendly lass she was.'

'But what happens now? If I spurn his advances he'll evict me, I know he will, and then what will I do?'

Winnie frowned. 'I don't know, lass, but we'll think of something, so don't worry yerself.'

But Ruth couldn't help but worry. In fact she wondered if there would ever be an end to all the worry. Still, she had Sunday to look forward to, even if it was only a visit to chapel.

Music drifted round the small, sparsely furnished chapel, which meant that members of the congregation could have a good old gossip without making themselves conspicuous.

'I see Agnes Boothroyd's got a new hat,' the woman next to Mrs Armitage whispered.

'Aye, and you know what they say, red hat and no knickers,' Winnie joked.

'That wouldn't surprise me, either. That Horace Holroyd doesn't spend all that time at their house for nothing.'

Winnie looked shocked at such a suggestion. 'Mr Holroyd and his wife were friends of the Boothroyds for years. They've been right good to him since she died.'

'Oh, I'll bet she's been good to him all right. Funny 'ow he always turns up when her old man's just gone on't afternoon shift over at pit.' The woman's voice rose with excitement. 'She gets washed and changed every day before he arrives. Dolled up like a dog's dinner she is, you ought to see her.'

'She gets washed and changed every day. She

always did like to keep herself nice. There wasn't a smarter-looking lass walked Cottenly than Agnes in her heyday, nor a pleasanter. What's more, yer never get her talking about folks, or letting her imagination run riot like some I could mention.'

The already assembled congregation turned to see what the commotion was about as Ruth and her children shuffled their way into the pew behind Winnie, with Jack Dolan as escort.

'Mam, I don't want to sit next to our Frankie. He sings all the wrong words and then people stare at us,' Sadie whispered.

'I don't want to sit next to her either, Mam. Can I sit next to the ragman?'

'It's Mr Dolan, Frankie. I've told you umpteen times.'

Jack didn't mind. 'It's all right. I am a rag and bone man after all.'

The woman next to Winnie looked as if her eyes might pop out of their sockets at any moment. 'Eeh, just look who's walked in with Ruth Wray, as brazen as brass, and her old man not yet cold.'

'Oh, I think you're wrong there. He were bound to be cold after being covered in ice in't river all night.'

The woman whispered louder in her frustration. 'Yer know very well what I mean. Walking into't chapel with him. I don't know how she dares.'

'Well, I don't know what there is to be scared of in't chapel, except mucky-minded scandal-mongers like some I could mention.'

The woman ignored the insult. 'I heard tell the other day that that rag 'n' bone man were sniffing around before her old man copped his clogs.' She put her hands together as if praying, muttering, 'God rest his soul.'

Winnie Armitage had heard enough and her voice rose as high as her temper. 'God won't rest his soul if He's any sense. The lass is well rid of a bugger like him and everyone knows it, including you.'

The minister, who was about to begin the service, hurried down from the pulpit. 'Ladies, ladies, may I remind you we are in a place of worship? Either watch your language or leave the premises. I'm particularly surprised at you, Mrs Armitage.'

'Eeh, I am sorry. I don't know what came over me except that I was driven to it. May God forgive me all the same.'

Sadie pulled at her mother's coat. 'Mam, did you hear Mrs Armitage swearing?' she asked.

'Yes, Sadie, we all heard what she said, and we all know why she said it.'

The minister had never known anything like it.

He mopped his perspiring brow and hurriedly started the service. 'We will begin today with hymn number 373, "God Moves In A Mysterious Way His Wonders To Perform".'

Billy couldn't believe it. The very words his Uncle Joe had used on the night his dad had died. He looked across the aisle and caught his uncle's eye and neither of them could stifle a giggle. Alice glared at Billy and nudged her husband, 'Joe, shut up and remember where thee are.'

Suddenly, in the hush between the introduction and the music beginning, a loud bang echoed through the hall, and: 'You did that on purpose, Winnie Armitage. You dropped that book on my foot on purpose.'

'Eeh, you know I would never do a thing like that.'

Everybody in the place began to laugh, except Alice. 'My grandmother would be turning in her grave if she was here.' She had been so pleased to see Ruth taking to the chapel again, but now she wondered if it was a good idea after all. Joe, who was only here because it was the anniversary of the opening of the chapel, thought it was time the place was livened up a bit, and decided he might even come more often if there was summat to laugh at. Billy found hymn 373 in the hymn book and glanced at his mother, who was sharing her book with Mr Dolan, then began to sing, completely happy for the first time in his young life.

Hubert Hancock, crafty as always, casually mentioned Winnie to his wife.

'Oh, by the way, dear, I was taking a breath of air after my lunch when I happened to meet an old friend of yours. Not of our class at all, but she seemed to think highly of you, sent her regards.'

'Oh!' Sophie was absorbed in her *Woman's Companion*. 'Who would that be then?'

'A Winnie Stedman, I believe she said.'

Sophie came to life. 'Winnie Stedman? Why, I haven't seen her to speak to for years. We were good friends, Winnie and I, in our youth.' She fell silent as she reminisced. 'Oh, yes,' she remarked after a while, 'we were poor but they were happy days.'

Her husband frowned. He didn't like being reminded that his wife originated from the meanest part of town. 'So you haven't kept in touch, then?'

Sophie smiled. 'Oh, no. I can't remember when I last spoke to her.' So that was all right then, he thought with relief. 'No,' she went on, 'the only time I see Winnie is when I'm under the dryer in the hairdressers. She's usually passing the shop on the way to chapel. I expect it's a meeting of the Sisterhood.'

Hubert Hancock pricked up his ears. If the woman was at the chapel she would be unable to intrude on Ruth Wray's privacy. All he had to do now was take notice which was Sophie's hair day. Then he would seek his pleasure without any hindrance.

He didn't have long to wait. Two days later Sophie's hair was so stiff and rippled, it resembled a washing board. He knew now which day to pay another visit to Wire Mill Place. He felt a tremor in his loins as he anticipated being alone with such a ravishing creature. Young, too, and he guessed she was intelligent enough to realise she would have to give up one or the other, her body or her home. He had her in a corner and there would be no escaping this time.

Harry Crossman enjoyed working for the council. He also enjoyed the evening classes he attended two nights a week, one for business studies and the other for economics. The classes had initially been the idea of Grandfather Stanford and were encouraged by his superiors at the town hall.

Harry found his work varied and interesting and was at present assisting with the preparation of buildings for when the expected war commenced. Harry had been shocked as he read his instructions to read the word *when* instead of *if*. Although he was sworn to secrecy about some of his work, he confided in Isaac about other things, knowing that whatever he told his grandfather would be kept confidential. The latest news came as no surprise to Isaac, who had seen it coming for months. The only consolation he could think of was that his grandsons were all too young to be conscripted yet. He prayed that it would all be over by the time they came of age. There was no way he could see this one lasting as long as the Spanish war, which was thankfully over at last. Harry on the other hand was disappointed that he wouldn't be able to broaden his experience and see the world.

'Keep on with thi studying, lad,' Isaac advised him. 'When thar old enough tha can do the country far more good by putting up for't council than by fighting any war.'

So Harry carried on with his studying, cramming his brain with as many facts and figures as could be absorbed, and though the war was imminent the vitality of youth prevented him from worrying about it. In fact he found the prospect most exciting, and was sorry when his grandfather said it would be all over and done with almost before it began.

By Whitsuntide Ruth decided that she was fond enough of Jack Dolan to accept his invitation to visit the farm.

The children had joined in the procession of witness in the morning, each dressed to the best of Ruth's ability considering her financial state. Sadie and Margaret were wearing pretty dresses, made specially for the occasion by Emily, and Billy, for the first time ever, was wearing shoes instead of clogs. His Grandfather Wray had taken his grandson to Sheffield and bought him a suit with long trousers and Ruth couldn't help shedding a few tears at the sight of her son in his first grown-up clothes. Frankie – who couldn't usually care less what he wore – had been given a suit his cousin Joseph had long since outgrown. Because Alice bought nothing but the best for her son, the suit was as perfect as the day it had been purchased. An argument had taken place as to why Billy could have long trousers when Frankie had to make do with short. The argument had remained unresolved when Mr Armitage had come across to see them all dressed in their finery and given them each a shilling to put in the pockets of their new clothes.

Jack and Ruth had joined the rest of the family to watch the walk, except for Alice who was of course marching along with the children in her role as Sunday school teacher. The walk ended on the green where the singing was to take place. Afterwards the children were given lunch at Sunday school whilst all the grown-ups were invited to Emily's for a cold, makeshift dinner. As usual the spread was excellent and was soon devoured amongst much jollity. Ruth was touched by the enthusiasm Jack showed at the get-together. 'You

198

don't know how lucky you are having a family all around you,' he remarked.

'Haven't you any family, then, except your mother?' Ruth enquired.

'No, lass, none at all. But I'd like one.'

Ruth blushed, knowing the friendship was changing course, to a more serious relationship. She was determined not to jump in at the deep end, but the feelings she had for Jack were making it difficult to resist his advances. Not that the latter were of an improper nature, but sometimes Ruth found herself hoping they soon would be.

In the afternoon the children joined Ruth and Jack, and instead of taking part in the sports on the green they set off through the woods towards the moors, on the edge of which stood Dolan's Farm. Apart from where the sun filtered through the trees the woods were dark and mysterious and filled with the fragrance of bluebells. The twins ran this way and that, carrying on a game of hide and seek along the way, and Billy searched the undergrowth for ground ivy or any other plant which would be of use to Olive. He must remember to look for ribwort when he reached the farm, which Olive would dry immediately before the leaves had a chance to turn black.

As they wheeled Margaret along in the pram Jack took the opportunity to place his hand over Ruth's, a touch which sent shimmers of desire through them both. Jack twisted the wedding ring on Ruth's finger. 'I'd like to replace that with a new one,' he said thickly. 'One which would be ours, not yours.' He moved his hand and circled her waist, turning her towards him and kissing her. 'I love yer, Ruth. Will yer marry me, lass?'

'Well,' Ruth mumbled, 'it's a bit sudden. We haven't known each other long.'

Jack smiled. 'I've known you Stanford lasses as long as I can remember, and I've loved you since you first moved into't Place.'

'I didn't know you'd even noticed me.'

'Oh, aye, but you were married.'

'Let me think it over, Jack.'

'But not for too long. I'm almost forty. Don't let's waste time, lass.'

'Oh, no, we mustn't, not when we're almost in our dotage.' Ruth laughed.

'Well, no, I know we're not old, but I want to be with you now.'

'But there's your mother. You couldn't leave her to come and live with us.'

'Oh, lass! You don't think I'd expect you to go on living in a dump like't Place? Besides, the farm's my livelihood and I couldn't leave it.'

'But your mother might not want us there, especially with four children. It'd be too much to ask of her.'

'But the farm's mine, Ruth, and what's mine is yours from now on.'

'Well, we'll see, but only after you've discussed it with your mother.'

Jack knew his mother would grumble, but she grumbled about everything. It had become a habit with her. Well, if she didn't like it she would just have to lump it. Besides, she was always telling him he should be married, and if he didn't marry Ruth Stanford he would never marry at all. He couldn't think of her as Ruth Wray; the three had always been known as the Stanford lasses, though it had been the eldest two he had known in his youth. Now there was only Ruth, as far as he was concerned, and if she would have him he would make her his wife.

They crossed the meadow where the first-born lambs were frolicking beside the ewes. The twins knelt to run their fingers through the warm, tightly curled fleece, Frankie lost for words for a change and fascinated by the lambs' antics.

'Oh, Mam,' Sadie whispered, 'can I hold one?'

'Aye, but not that one!' Jack walked away from the path and picked up a slightly older lamb, bringing it back and placing it in Sadie's arms.

'Can I hold it next?' Frankie asked. He noticed Ruth and added, 'Please, Mr Dolan?' before his mother had time to remind him.

Jack gave one to Frankie. 'These two are twins like you and Sadie,' he told the wide-eyed boy.

Billy was more interested in the ancient tractor he could see in the next field. 'You can start it up if yer like,' Jack said, 'but first come in and meet me mother.'

'I met her once,' Ruth told him. 'But I was only a girl; she was talking to my mother after chapel. She won't remember me, though.'

'Oh, I think she does. Or at least she knows your Alice.'

'Well she would, if she goes to chapel. Our Alice might as well have lived there in her youth.'

'My mother doesn't go to chapel much these days. I couldn't even persuade her to come and watch the procession, though I couldn't have kept her away at one time.'

Ruth frowned. The prospect of starting married life with a mother-in-law who never went out didn't sound too promising.

The kitchen door was open, and the smell of newly baked bread wafted out to mingle with the fragrance of lilac from a shrub in the yard. They picked their way through a brood of clucking hens, one of which spread its wings and landed with a flurry in Margaret's pram. The twins began to squeal with laughter and Mrs Dolan came out to see what all the noise was about. She picked up a yard brush and shooed away the excited birds.

'Don't mind them lot,' she said. 'Bring yerselves in and sit yerselves down at table. Tea's ready.'

'This is Ruth, Mother,' Jack announced. 'This is Billy, Sadie and Frankie, and the one almost smothered in feathers is Margaret.'

Ruth held out her hand. 'How do you do, Mrs Dolan? I hope you are well.'

'I could be better, but mustn't grumble, there's plenty a lot worse. Nice to meet yer, but I'm thinking I've met yer before.'

'At chapel,' Ruth reminded her.

The table was set as if for royalty with a beautiful willow-patterned service. There were plates piled high with sandwiches, as well as scones and a dish of red jam, a chocolate cake, and a jelly which had been turned out on to a tray.

'Cor, look at that, Sadie,' Frankie whispered. 'It looks like a castle. I wonder how they made it?'

Jack laughed. 'Magic,' he said.

Mrs Dolan poured out the tea. 'Help yerselves,'

she ordered. 'We don't stand on ceremony here.'

The sandwiches soon disappeared and the jelly was dished out into the willow-patterned dishes. A large jug of cream was brought in from the pantry and poured over the dessert. 'Straight from the cows,' Mrs Dolan announced. 'The first one to see the rickety bridge in the bottom can have some more.'

The children gobbled up the jelly and cream. Ruth would have liked to remind them of their manners but Mrs Dolan was really to blame so she let it go.

'I can see the bridge,' Frankie cried.

'And I can see a lovely lady with a fan,' Sadie said.

'Well then, I expect you'll both be entitled to some more.' There was nothing the good lady enjoyed more than seeing a child eating well, and as she knew Billy would consider himself too old for silly games she plopped another spoonful on to his dish without mentioning it. She was enjoying being able to entertain again. It reminded her of happier days in her youth, but that was before– She shied away from the memories, not allowing them to escape from the recess of her mind where they were locked away.

'That was delicious,' Ruth said. 'Especially the scones. I can never get them to be all soft in the middle. They usually turn out more like biscuits.'

'Aye, well, I expect I've had a lot more practice at my age.'

Jack left his mother and Ruth clearing the table and took the twins and Billy on a tour of the farm. Frankie wanted to see the horse and pigs,

Billy the machinery and Sadie the lambs again.

Mrs Dolan weighed Ruth up. She supposed she was pleasant enough and got on with the dish washing without any fuss, but the prospect of sharing her kitchen with another woman filled her with alarm. The rows between her and Jack over the past weeks had seemed never-ending, and when they did end it was always with the same words, always spoken softly: 'If she'll have me, Mother, I'm going to marry her. If you don't want her here I can always sell the farm, get yer a place of yer own and go and live with Ruth, or you can stay here on yer own.' He knew she would never contemplate leaving the farm, which her father had worked all his life and her grandfather before him. Neither could she run the place without him, nor would she want to. Her son was all she had; he was a good lad, allus had been. Come to think of it, he was right to want to marry. Who would carry on the place when he had gone otherwise? But a widow with four childer. She shuddered at the thought of it.

She stacked the crockery carefully on the dresser. 'Our Jack has a mind to marry you then?'

Ruth stopped what she was doing and turned to the woman. 'Yes, though it's a bit soon to my way of thinking,' she said.

'Yer'll not find a better or kinder man.'

'Oh, I know. It isn't that,' Ruth insisted. 'It's just that I haven't known him long, and it's a lot to take on, four children who aren't his. He might regret it.'

'He's made up his mind, and once he has neither you nor me nor the man in the moon'll change it.'

'But it's your home.' Ruth searched for the right words. 'How do you feel about another woman trespassing, so to speak?'

'Nay, it's not my home. Our Jack's worked his guts out for the place, and what good would I be if he left? Neither use nor ornament.'

'Well, what do you think I should do? Should I accept or not?'

'Do yer love him?'

Ruth was astounded by the question and even more astounded when she answered without even needing to think about it. 'Yes, I love him.'

'Then marry him, lass. For he'll never rest, now he's made up his mind, until yer do.'

Ruth felt a weight drop from her, the weight of the past fifteen years. She smiled at the other woman who was too busy to notice, broddling the fire which didn't need attending to at all. 'Then I'll marry him,' she said. 'That's if you want me to.'

'Yer'll need some new beds for the young 'uns, and it'll be a way for 'em to go to school, specially in't winter.'

'They'll love it. After the place we're living in at present it'll seem like Heaven. And our Billy'll soon be leaving school, and working.'

'There'll be plenty of work here, I shouldn't wonder.'

'I...' Ruth was suddenly overcome by shyness. 'I'll try not to intrude on your privacy. It's your home, not mine. You must remember that, Mrs Dolan.'

'Oh, I dare say I shall be glad of a bit of intru-

205

sion. It's time I put me feet up and had a bit of a rest. I'm not getting any younger.'

It was only when the twins came flying in like a hurricane that Ruth wondered how she would manage to keep the children, especially the baby, quiet enough for Jack's mother to have a bit of a rest. However, her mind was made up. If Jack loved her as she loved him she would marry him, and cross any bridges later. And she had no doubts about his loving her, none whatsoever.

Billy couldn't believe they were to live at the farm and could hardly contain his impatience, but his mother insisted on waiting a decent number of weeks and the wedding was arranged for the beginning of July. Jack was determined Ruth would have a memorable wedding and had given her a sum of money to be spent on new clothes for herself and the family. She had gone to Sheffield with Emily one day when the children were at school and Alice was minding the baby, and had bought a length of cornflower blue crêpe de Chine for seven and six a yard, a pattern, buttons and thread from Cole Brothers, along with a remnant of white satin from which her mother would make a pretty bridesmaid's dress for Sadie. They also bought shirts and shoes for the boys, before treating themselves to lunch in a nice little restaurant in Change Alley. Afterwards Emily purchased a new hat which when worn tilted to one side made her look quite flirtatious. They laughed a lot, and browsed around the market where they ate cockles and mussels served on tiny plates. Emily couldn't help comparing her excitement about this wedding to the distress she had felt on the occasion of her daughter's first marriage. This time everyone was happy to welcome Jack Dolan into the heart of the family.

Hubert Hancock could restrain himself no longer. What with board meetings and one obstacle after the other it was some weeks now since his visit to Mrs Wray's. He straightened his tie, greased his hair and combed it over his bald patch before setting off along the river bank to Wire Mill Place. He kept a lookout in case anyone familiar should see him but the coast was clear. He was relieved to see no sign of Winnie Stedman as he tapped on the young widow's door.

'Oh, my dear Mrs Wray, so good to see you looking so much better.' He wasn't exaggerating. The woman was positively blooming.

Ruth stepped back in shock at the sight of the man on her doorstep, but he moved smartly into the house before she could close the door.

'I just stopped by in case there were any repairs which have been overlooked, any improvements to be made?'

Ruth was tempted to say the place needed rebuilding if it was to be improved but thought better of it. 'No, everything's fine, thank you,' she replied. She waited by the door, holding it open, but ignoring her he managed to seat himself comfortably by the fireplace.

'I wouldn't say no to a cup of tea,' he drawled.

Ruth prayed silently, 'Please, God, let me be rid of him,' but the man remained in his place, his small, beady eyes drinking in every line of Ruth's body, the high, swollen breasts, the narrow waist and the way the print dress fitted perfectly over her soft, rounded hips. She wished she didn't need to pass him but the kettle was on the hob. She bent to pour the boiling water into the teapot and felt his hand linger on her buttock. He chuckled.

'Whoops,' he said, 'I thought you were about to overbalance.'

'No.' She moved his hand forcefully. 'I'm quite steady, thank you.' Her face was burning with indignation, which only made her more attractive to the man.

'Oh, yes, you certainly look much better. In fact you're absolutely ravishing, and I could make you even more ravishing if you'd let me, my dear. A pretty new dress, silk stockings, satin underwear.' He licked his lips and stood up, placing his hands on Ruth's waist, turning her to face him. Suddenly his fat, slobbery mouth was over hers, his flabby body pressed into her. She struggled frantically to free herself, wondering how best to reject his advances. She knew the house was no longer important and would have been tempted to pick up the nearest heavy object as a weapon, but Billy's promised job was still at stake. Though Joe decided whom to employ she knew his decision could be overturned, and would be, should she spurn the manager's advances. Far better to keep within his good books until Billy was settled in his job.

'Mr Hancock,' she chided with as much flirtatiousness as she could muster, 'what are you doing? And my husband only just buried.' She wagged a finger at him. 'We mustn't lose our patience now, must we? After all, we've all the time in the world, but we must show a little respect. Now, drink your tea before it gets cold.'

Hubert Hancock fought against the burning desire within him. He mustn't spoil his chances with this beautiful creature. He flopped down in his chair, attempting to regain his composure. 'I do beg your pardon, my dear, it's just that you're the most charming woman I have ever come across. You understand, I'm sure.'

'But what of your wife? Surely you wouldn't wish to be unfaithful to her!'

The question was unexpected and he stammered as he searched for words. 'Um, I, er, no, I have no wish to hurt her, but what the eye doesn't see the heart doesn't grieve over, as the saying goes. Besides, she doesn't seem to mind me enjoying a life of my own.' He didn't want to discuss Sophie. That wasn't what he was here for.

'Really?' Ruth gasped in amazement. 'Then she must be a very understanding woman. Now I'm afraid I really must ask you to go, before my expected visitor arrives. We mustn't let anyone know you've been here, must we?'

'No. Oh, no, we mustn't spoil things for another time.' He fiddled with his braces, which held his trousers high up beneath his armpits. 'There will be another time, my dear?'

Ruth smiled coquettishly as she held the door ajar. 'Goodbye, Mr Hancock,' she said.

'Call me Hubert. Till a fortnight today, then.' He cursed silently at having to wait another two weeks owing to prior engagements.

Ruth's eyes widened as he dared to arrange

another visit. Well at least now she knew when to expect him. She frowned as she wondered what could be done to discourage the repulsive man. 'But what if someone finds you here? Surely you won't wish to risk such a thing.'

He wouldn't be dissuaded so easily. 'Then we must be prepared, my dear. I shall simply say' – he paused as if considering what he would say – 'I shall say I have come about the position being offered to your son.'

Ruth didn't reply. She held open the door and stiffened as she thought he was about to kiss her again. She stepped outside where he knew he would be seen if he attempted to come close to her. 'Goodbye, Mr Hancock.' She stressed the Mr. 'I do think you should consider your wife's feelings.'

Hubert Hancock merely smiled and hurried away towards the works yard. However, Ruth's words had made him uneasy. This was the first time he had risked womanising here in Cottenly and he knew all hell would break loose if he should be found out. Though he was departmental manager he still had to answer to the upper management, all of whom were members of the chapel. In fact it had been Sophie's connection with the chapel that was responsible for his promotion to his present position. Any hint of scandal on his part would be disastrous. Sophie turned a blind eye to many of his carryings-on away from home but he dreaded to think what might happen should he embarrass his wife in her own back yard, so to speak. He hurried back to the office, glancing furtively about until he reached the safety of his desk.

Ruth was torn between turning to Jack for assistance in dealing with Hubert Hancock or handling
the situation herself. She was sure Jack would lose
his temper and probably land himself in trouble
by using violence towards the man. That would
mean the end of Billy's job prospects without a
doubt, but what was the alternative? When Winnie
returned from her Sisterhood meeting she was
dismayed to learn of her young friend's dilemma,
not to mention the man's visit during her
absence. The two women decided to handle the
problem of Hubert Hancock without Jack's in-
volvement and Winnie eventually thought of a
possible solution.

Oblivious of Ruth's problem, Jack Dolan was
doing his utmost to involve his mother in arrange-
ments for the wedding. He had tried persuading
her to buy a new outfit from Caroline Swann's
and she had compromised by buying one from
the Co-op on account of the divi. 'Well, how do I
look?' she asked as she tried on the coat and hat,
the first she had bought in years.

'Very smart.' Jack grinned. It was true, his
mother did look smart. Her figure was lithe, probably because she was never still, though he wished
she would smile more often, and he thought blue
would have been more appropriate than the dismal brown which she seemed to wear day in and
day out. Nevertheless she had made the effort.
Jack frowned as he wondered how she would
react to Ruth's permanent presence in the
kitchen, and he knew Ruth was wondering how

211

best to deal with the situation. She had considered leaving the cooking to Mrs Dolan but thought the elder woman might find the job too much with an extra four mouths to feed, not counting the baby who was not yet fully weaned.

'Do as yer like, lass,' Jack had said. 'The house will be yours once we're married, and choose how you try I can't see it suiting.'

'Then I shall have to try and suit. I couldn't bear to live in an atmosphere of unpleasantness, and after all it will be us who are intruding. Oh, Jack, I hope it will all work out.'

Jack simply waved her doubts aside. 'We shall be together. That'll make it all reight.' As usual they had ended the discussion in one of the close embraces which were becoming increasingly more passionate and harder to resist. The feelings Jack awakened in Ruth were different entirely from any Walter had ever aroused in her, even in the early days, probably because this time there was a tenderness about Jack that had always been lacking in her husband. When he held her close all doubts about the future disappeared and she knew any problems would be halved when she shared them with Jack, and share them she would. She frowned as she remembered the problem of Hubert Hancock. She vowed it was the last secret she would ever keep from the man she loved so dearly.

Winnie Armitage looked over the top of the net curtain which was hung across the salon window. She could see a couple of women with perming equipment attached to their heads and another under the dryer, and she recognised the drying head as that of Sophie Hancock. Good, she had timed it perfectly. She walked along the High Street and back again, then just as the hairdresser was lifting the hood from Sophie's head she opened the door and entered the shop. The stench of perming lotion filled her nostrils as she walked to the reception desk and feigned surprise as she glanced at Sophie.

'Well, if it isn't Sophie. Well, what a surprise. I'll bet you don't remember me, but I'd have known you anywhere. You haven't changed one bit.'

Sophie smiled and recalled her husband's meeting with Winnie a few weeks ago. 'Neither have you, Winnie, though we're neither of us getting any younger, unfortunately.'

'Oh, we're only as old as we feel, Sophie. But when I think about the good old days they seem a million years away.'

'But they were the good days,' Sophie answered, for despite the easier living she now enjoyed she looked back on her early days with sincere fondness.

Winnie made an appointment for a set in readiness for Ruth's wedding, and stood watching the hairdresser take out the metal clips from Sophie's hair. 'I'll tell you what, Sophie, I've a picture at home of the whole class. Standard three, I think it was. You could pop along and look at it over a cup of tea. Unfortunately I'm due at the chapel this afternoon but I'll tell you what, I'll give it a miss next time and you must come along to our house. We'll have a good old chinwag about the good old days.'

Sophie was delighted to be remembered by her old school chum and even more delighted to be accepted as a friend instead of being thought too la-di-da to congregate with the lower townsfolk. She didn't hesitate to accept Winnie's invitation. 'I'd be delighted.' She wondered what Hubert would say and decided not to tell him. He much preferred mixing with the toffee-nosed lot from the various clubs he attended.

'Good.' Winnie smiled. 'Number one Wire Mill Place.'

Sophie cringed at the sound of Winnie's address but no doubt the place would be spotless, knowing Winnie, and even if it wasn't Sophie didn't mind a bit of honest muck. After all, where would she have been today without the workers of the wire mill? She patted her hair into place, put on her hat and paid for her shampoo and set. Then she left with her old friend.

'I'll see you next week at two then.' Winnie knew old Hancock wouldn't arrive until after that.

'I'll look forward to that,' Sophie said, and the women each went their separate ways, both of them smiling in anticipation.

Ruth was both dubious and nervous about the plan. Winnie said nothing could go wrong, providing Ruth left the door unlocked and remembered not to encourage the man in any way. Even so, the morning proved nerve-racking as Ruth waited for Hubert Hancock's promised visit. She jumped when the knock fell on the door shortly after she had seen the man's wife arrive at Winnie's.

'My dear,' he enthused. 'You look as beautiful as ever.' He was through the door almost before Ruth had opened it.

'I really don't think you should be here,' she warned.

'I should find it most difficult to keep away.' He rolled his fat body round the table and wedged himself in the chair. Ruth picked up the baby from her pram and cuddled her close. 'A lovely child,' he said, 'but we mustn't spoil her, must we?' Ruth hugged her closer. 'Why don't we put her back in the pram and make ourselves comfortable?'

'She'll only cry. She's teething,' Ruth answered. She wished Mrs Armitage would hurry and put her plan into action.

Across the Place, Winnie was enjoying herself, anticipating the expression on the man's fat, flabby face when he saw Sophie. She thought it was about time. 'I'll tell you what, Sophie, I'll take you to meet a friend of mine, a lovely woman, a widow with four young children, about to marry again. She'd love to meet you, I know. You can have a look at her wedding dress. Her mother's a fine needlewoman, sews for a lot of the houses in your area. I'm sure if you needed any sewing doing she'd be happy to oblige.'

Sophie Hancock was always interested in fine needlecraft and followed her friend over the yard to Ruth Wray's. She wondered how anyone could be expected to put up with such dark, dismal buildings, and knew her husband had the power to insist on the places being modernised, if only he had been blessed with a little compassion for the less fortunate.

Winnie opened the door wide, making sure Sophie was in a position to witness the spectacle of young Ruth, cowering near the door with little Margaret in her arms. The girl looked frightened as Hubert Hancock loomed towards her. At the sight of his wife the lecherous grin changed dramatically to a look of bewilderment, but it was nothing compared to the expression on Sophie's face. Winnie thought the woman would surely explode as she realised what her husband was up to. Having rehearsed the scene over and over, Winnie finally played her part. 'Oh, I say, what a coincidence. I didn't know he was here again. Are you all right, love?' she asked Ruth anxiously.

'Again?' Sophie spat out the questions, one after the other. 'Have you been here before? What for? Why aren't you in the office?'

Ruth moved closer to Winnie's side, a smile of relief lighting her lovely face. Hubert Hancock spluttered as he searched for an explanation.

'I, er, I came to offer her son employment. When he's ready, that is.'

'What, twice?' His wife showed her disbelief openly.

'Yes, er, I mean no. Last time it was to offer Mrs Wray the tenancy, as a widow of one of our past employees.'

Sophie had regained her composure. She would wait until he came home tonight before giving him what for. But by God, he wouldn't know what had hit him by the time she had done with him. 'So will you continue to live here after your marriage, my dear?' she asked. Ruth watched the fat face turn even more scarlet.

'Married? I didn't know there was anyone... I mean I didn't know there was to be a wedding. That will obviously change things. We can't allow the tenancy to be passed to someone not employed by the firm, you understand.'

'Oh, I'm sure she understands,' his wife said. 'And as for your son, my dear,' she turned to Ruth, 'you do realise he will be paid a mere pittance until he is eighteen, whilst doing the work of a man?' Hubert Hancock almost choked as he glowered at his interfering wife.

'No, I won't expect to live here after my marriage.' Ruth smiled. 'But as my son will be in need of employment, and as Mr Hancock has kindly offered our Billy a job, no doubt he'll be pleased to accept, and I can promise he'll work as hard as any man.'

'Well, good luck to the boy then. I'm sure he'll need it.' Sophie shot a look of venom at her husband, 'Well? You've promised the boy a job, what are you waiting for?'

Hubert Hancock hesitated not a moment longer. He wondered what his wife was doing in Wire Mill Place but he didn't stop to find out. He nodded curtly at the ladies and hurried out and along the cobbles in the direction of the works.

'And now,' Sophie smiled, 'perhaps I can take a look at your wedding dress.'

Ruth wondered what a nice woman like Sophie was doing saddled with an awful man like Hubert Hancock, and strangely enough Sophie was asking herself exactly the same question.

Chapter Six

'Can I just say a few words if you've all finished eating?' Isaac tapped the side of his glass with a spoon. 'I'd just like to say what a pleasure it is for us all to be here together on the auspicious occasion of our Ruth and Jack's wedding.'

'Can I have some cake, Mam?' Frankie's voice rang out above the mutters of 'Hear! hear!'

'In a minute, love, give us a chance to cut it. Grandad hasn't finished speaking yet.'

'I'd like to offer a toast to the happiness of our Ruth and Jack.'

'To Ruth and Jack.'

'Can I have some toast?' Frankie was ignored.

'Come on, Jack! Give us a few words, lad.'

Jack Dolan wasn't one for being in the limelight and he could feel his face burning as he rose to his feet, but Ruth squeezed his hand in encouragement. He began by clearing his throat. 'Unaccustomed as I am to making wedding speeches, especially my own—'

'I should hope so an' all,' Joe said to much laughter.

'I should just like to say a few words, first of all to you, Alice, for this lovely spread you've laid on for us today.'

'Nay, lad, it were thee who supplied poultry.'

'Aye, but it's you who cooked it, and a grand job you made of it too.' He paused and looked round

218

the room. 'Next I'd like to thank Billy for giving his mam away, and to reassure him I shall look after her to the best of my ability and welcome them all warmly into their new home. Next I'd like to thank Sadie for being the prettiest bridesmaid ever to walk into Cottenly chapel.' Sadie covered her face with her napkin and giggled. 'Oh, and Mrs Armitage, for looking after Margaret whilst we got through the ceremony, and for being such a good friend to Ruth when she needed one. I know she's going to miss her a lot.'

'Eeh, it was a pleasure, I'm sure.' Winnie wiped her eyes as the tears brimmed over and ran down her cheeks.

'What about me?' Frankie didn't like being left out.

'Don't worry, Frankie, I haven't forgotten you. If you hadn't fallen in the river in the first place I'd never have got talking to yer mam. Not that I hadn't noticed her, knelt down scrubbing the doorstep every week. I used to time it specially so I could have a good look at her. In fact I fell for her backside long before I saw her face.'

Ruth thumped her new husband. 'You cheeky devil.'

'Well, our Ruth always did have the cleanest doorstep in the Place.' Emily smiled, then she coloured as she noticed a grimace on Ruth's face. 'That's apart from Winnie's, of course,' she added hastily.

'Sometimes I wonder if that's the reason she consented to marry a rag and bone man,' Jack joked, 'so that she'd never be short of a donkey stone.'

The assembled guests laughed as Jack proposed further toasts, before sitting down with relief that the ordeal was over.

'Aye well, I'm sure we've all had our minds set at rest, now our Ruth's taken to going to't chapel again,' Alice remarked. 'Grandmother Stanford'll be able to rest peacefully in her grave from now on.'

'Let's not bring your grandmother into it today, Alice,' Emily said. 'After all, it is supposed to be a happy occasion.'

Joe reached for the bottle. 'Come on, let's all have another glass of sherry. After all it's not every day we have a wedding in the family.'

'Aye, well, I don't suppose it'll do any harm for once.' Alice looked towards the minister, who was helping himself. 'Besides, it doesn't look as though't parson objects. He's almost emptied that bottle of elderberry wine.'

Mrs Dolan sniffed. 'Naught but hypocrites the lot of 'em,' she muttered. 'Preaching one thing and practising another.'

Joe glanced at the clergyman and grinned. The man was in a world of his own, oblivious of everything except the bottle and glass in front of him. 'Here you are, Mrs Dolan.' He offered her a glass of sherry. 'Or would you prefer port? Or a bottle of Nut Brown?'

'No, thanks,' she said. 'I don't hold with all this drinking.'

'Nay, Mother! The Lord knows, none of us drink all that much, but after all it is a wedding.'

'Aye, and that's another thing I don't hold with either. Marry in haste and repent at leisure, that's what they say, and you two seem to be in too much of a hurry.'

'Aye well, only time'll tell about that.' Jack leaned towards Ruth and gave her a kiss, which caused a cheer to rise amongst the guests.

Joe carried on round the room. 'Come on, Billy lad, a drop of sherry won't hurt yer. After all, it isn't every day a lad acquires a good man for a father.'

'That makes two good men in the family then, counting you, Uncle Joe.' Then Billy suddenly remembered. 'Then there's me Uncle George, and me grandad,' he added. Joe smiled at him, the shared secret foremost in both their minds.

George Crossman had by now seated himself at the piano, the latest piece of furniture to be purchased by Alice, who was driving Joe mad by practising every evening. He wouldn't have cared, but her repertoire seemed to consist of nothing but hymns. Still, it was something his wife had always wanted and she spent little enough on herself usually. So Joe was content to retire to the front room with Joseph, the wireless, and the Meccano set. 'That's right, George,' he called, 'let's have some music and a bit of a sing-song. Or are we going to sit here like tripe all night?'

Before George could begin, Frankie's voice rang out. 'Can I 'ave some cake?'

The room filled with laughter as Jack said, 'Oh, come on, lass, let's cut the cake and put the little fellow out of his misery.'

Ruth removed the tiny pair of silver shoes and white doves from the beautifully iced cake and turned to Mary Hampshire. 'Oh, it's such a shame to cut it, Mary. You've decorated it better than any expert.' The cake was a wedding present from Ruth's friend, who blushed a deep red at the compliment. 'And don't you go making yourself sick,' she warned Frankie as she handed him the first slice. 'Not on my wedding night.'

Suddenly the sound of breaking glass caused a stir as the minister toppled off his stool. 'Oh, look, Dad.' Joseph thought it was hilarious. 'The parson's got drunk. It's me mam's homemade wine. He won't half have a thick head in the morning, and with Sunday service as well.'

George decided it was time to strike up on the piano and before long everyone in the room joined in the good old family sing-song, even Alice and Mrs Dolan.

Although Ruth and Jack had made love until the early hours, Ruth was awake before it was quite daylight. The unfamiliar sounds caused her to wonder at first where she could be: the scurryings of creatures she hoped were birds and not vermin in the loft above them; the cock crowing in the yard below. Then Jack changed his position and moved closer, gathering her body into his own, and she remembered she was in her marriage bed, with a husband who loved her, and whom she adored in return. She slipped out of bed and into her clothes, and prayed the baby would stay asleep, at least until her mother-in-law was awake. Then she crept silently downstairs, filled the boiler, raked out the flues with the cowl rake and emptied the ash pan. Finally she set the fire, which was soon well ablaze.

By the time Jack came downstairs she had sliced some bacon from the side hanging on a hook in the low, beamed ceiling, and it was sizzling away appetizingly in the huge iron frying pan.

'What are yer doing up at this unearthly hour?' he asked, planting a kiss on her cheek and brushing a spot of soot from the tip of her nose. 'And on yer honeymoon an' all.'

'I'm a farmer's wife now.' She grinned. 'How do you like your eggs? Crisp round the edges?'

'However they turn out. Two, please.'

Ruth cut a few slices of bread and brewed the tea. 'What about your mother? Would she like a cup, or will she still be asleep?'

Jack chuckled. 'Asleep? My mother? She'll have been awake this past two hours at least. Normally she'd have fed the hens and the pigs by now.'

'So, shall I take her a cup or not?' Ruth looked flummoxed. The truth was she didn't know what the routine of a farmhouse consisted of.

'You can, but I doubt if she'll thank you for it.' Jack emptied his enormous pint pot and slapped the remainder of his bacon between two slices of bread. 'I'll be off then. Sam'll be ready to loaden the milk in ten minutes.'

Sam must have been seventy if he was a day, though with the ruddy complexion of an outdoor man he looked no more than sixty. Jack said he could depend on Sam completely and had left him in charge the previous day knowing everything would be done to his satisfaction. Not only did he deliver the milk to the posh part of Cotenly, he also helped out in the fields and accompanied Jack to the cattle market at Warrentickle

223

every Thursday. Jack said Sam was an expert when it came to buying new stock. One day Mrs Dolan had told Ruth that when her father was alive Sam had followed him about like a shadow, assisting the farmer even as a five-year-old boy. 'We were almost brought up together,' she had explained to Ruth. 'Funny thing was, he wouldn't be took on full time, didn't want to be tied, or so he said.'

'So what did he do for a job then?' Ruth had enquired.

'Chimney sweeping mainly. Took over when his old man died. Regular round. Still, he always seemed happiest when he was out on the land; built the far chicken house all on his own. Thinks world of our Jack, he does, but he likes to be free, or so he says. A free spirit like the birds. A bit perculiar to my way of thinking, but a good man all't same.'

Ruth poured another cup of tea and climbed the stairs, carrying it carefully so as not to spill any in the saucer. She tapped on her mother-in-law's door and opened it an inch. 'Mrs Dolan, are you awake?' she whispered.

'Aye. I suppose it's time I were up.'

'Oh, no, I haven't come to get you up. I've brought you a cup of tea.'

'Aye, well, I'm not one for tea in bed, but seeing as you've brought it I dare say I'd better sup it.'

'I just wondered, what do I do first? I'm not used to the livestock but if you tell me what to do I can learn.'

'Nay, you'll have enough on in the kitchen with four bairns. And I reckon seeing as it's Sunday we can give some of't housework a miss for once. Though I reckon floor'll need scrubbing in't kitchen all't same, what with mucky feet and poultry in and out all day.'

'Right then, I'll do that as soon as I get the children off to Sunday school.'

'Aye, and I'll be getting up. Hens'll be thinking their throats have been cut if I don't feed 'em.'

'Shall I put your breakfast on, then? Bacon and eggs?'

'Nay, I can't stomach owt greasy first thing in a morning. A boiled egg's what I normally have.'

'Hard or soft?'

'Medium.'

Ruth left the woman to finish her tea and went to prepare her breakfast. And to begin her first day's apprenticeship on the way to becoming a useful farmer's wife.

Ruth's days were now following a familiar routine, and as she stood in the kitchen gazing out at the sunrise she thought she would never become accustomed to the glorious view from this side of the house. The colours changed continuously from purple to rose-pink, orange and then gold, and as the hues spread over the landscape the fields, and even the rooftops down in the town, resembled an artist's painted canvas. In the evening another masterpiece would be worked, but then it would be on the opposite side of the sprawling old house and the colours would spread above the vast open moors, gold, purple and then navy blue, dotted like a pin cushion with twinkling stars.

She had fed the hens and gathered the eggs, and already the washing was blowing merrily in the early morning breeze. Jack lectured her daily about leaving her bed at such an unearthly hour, but the truth was, Ruth was too happy to waste her days lying in bed and wouldn't wish to miss this quiet period of solitude, before the children awoke. She stood at the open door and watched a blackbird in the lilac bush as it broke into song. Sometimes a cock pheasant rested on the wall and a grey squirrel was a regular visitor. She could never remember a period in her life when she was so at peace with the world. The twins were well fed and happy as the day was long, passing the school holidays familiarising themselves with the animals, playing in the Dutch barn on rainy days and amongst the gentle giants in the cow house. The dairy herd had all been given names, along with the lambs. Baby Margaret was thriving and rosy-cheeked as a full blown poppy. And at last, Billy resembled a carefree young boy, instead of a worried little man. The lad was constantly at Jack's side, whether working the fields, milking, or out on the rounds. He could hardly wait until the time he would be permitted to leave school and begin work.

Ruth hadn't realised how much Jack managed to achieve in a day. Not only was the farm fully productive but the rag and bone side was thriving. His cart was the main form of transport for any removals or deliveries in both Cottenly and War-rentickle. What he would have done without Sam she couldn't imagine. Now he was considering the purchase of a motor lorry so that the haulage side could be developed. Up to now the tractor had been the only mechanical vehicle the farm owned. Jack said he must look to the future now he was a family man. He had already dismissed the idea of Billy's going to work at the mill.

'There's more than enough work on the land for the two of us, as well as Sam,' he pointed out, and for once Mrs Dolan had agreed. She had suggested long ago that the arable land on the edge of the moor should be turned over and used for crops, but Jack had never managed to find the time.

Ruth frowned as she thought of her mother-in-law. She didn't exactly make the newcomers feel unwelcome, but nothing seemed to please her. Ruth had asked Jack if she was unhappy about their being here but it seemed she had never been one to smile very much. In some ways she reminded Ruth of the way Alice had been before marrying Joe. Mrs Dolan could be heard now, pottering about as she dressed herself. Ruth warmed the teapot and placed a newly laid egg in the pan. By the time the elderly woman entered the kitchen, her breakfast was ready.

'Shall I toast your bread or not?' asked Ruth, reaching for the three-pronged toasting fork.

'No, thanks. I don't feel worth a row of pins this morning.'

'Are you poorly?' Ruth asked anxiously.

'Nowt that a good night's sleep wouldn't cure, if only I could get one, what wi' bedsprings creaking, babbies crying 'alf the night and one thing and't other.'

'I didn't know you could hear us. I'll have a

word with Jack.'

'Nay, I'm not blaming 'im. Our Jack's never been one for womanising – not till he was led on, that is. Some women 'ave no shame.'

'Shame! I'm not ashamed. I'm sorry if we've embarrassed you, but we've done nothing to be ashamed of. We are married, after all. And as for the baby crying, it's the first time she's woken in the night since we moved here, and that's only because she's teething again.' Ruth felt her face burning nevertheless.

'I never had a woken night wi' our Jack, not that I can remember.'

'I don't see as how you would remember, seeing as it's going on forty years ago. Well, if you don't want any toast, I'll fetch the washing in. It's drying quicker than I can peg it out.' Ruth went towards the door, picking up the clothes basket on the way.

'Aye, I'll give credit where it's due – you're good at getting up in the mornings to say how you spend the nights romping about, and yer know how to do a good clean wash an' all.'

Despite Ruth's embarrassment she couldn't help laughing. 'I ought to,' she said, 'I've had enough practice. They'll be missing me up at big houses.'

'Aye, I dare say they will. Still, if I never wash another thing, I've done my share of work in my day. Twenty-four piddle pots I had to empty up at lodging house, and all for drunken devils who'd been on a night's boozing.'

'It were bad enough clearing up after one drunkard,' Ruth replied, relieved to have the subject changed.

'Aye, well, I'm not saying some men aren't driven to it.'

Ruth could contain her anger no longer. 'Oh! I'm going to get the washing in.' The old panelled door almost swung from its hinges as she slammed it after her and went out into the yard.

The house was silent except for the creaks and groans normally heard in a house as old as Mooredge Farm, and the occasional hoot of a barn owl. The clock struck eleven, the signal for Ruth and Jack to retire for the night. The army of cats had been sent out into the yard and Shep the dog was sprawled across the pegged rug, as close to the fire as he could possibly get without scorching his hair.

'Are you ready?' Ruth yawned. 'I don't know how you manage to keep your eyes open with the amount of work you get through during a day.'

Jack grinned. 'Oh, I never did need a lot of shut-eye. As my grandad used to say, "Bed's a place to die in, not to live in."'

Ruth laughed. 'Well, I'm ready even if you're not.' She lit the candle and waited for the flame to settle. Jack rose to his feet, raked down the fire and turned out the lamp as Ruth led the way upstairs. He was out of his clothes and into bed before Ruth was half undressed.

'Don't put that nightgown on, love,' he said. 'It'll only be taken off again in a minute. Besides, I want to look at yer.'

Ruth blushed. 'I don't know why, a woman who's borne four kids.'

'Nobody'd ever guess,' Jack said. 'You've got

the body of a young girl. I don't know how you've managed it, but you have.'

'Plenty of hard work, love, that's how.'

Jack frowned. 'I know. Don't think I haven't noticed. It's a slave-driving house and my mother hasn't pulled her weight since you came. She seems to have handed over all the work to you.'

Ruth hopped into bed, cringing as the bed groaned. 'Well, she's no spring chicken. Besides, two women in one kitchen isn't easy. And I'm not complaining about the house, it's a lovely place. In fact I've never been happier.' Ruth stiffened as Jack moved towards her. 'Be careful, love. She's been moaning about the bedsprings.'

'She hasn't! Why, the old bugger. I'll give her something to moan about.' Jack deliberately made the bed creak louder than ever, and though they both started off by laughing the laughter quickly died down as they began to make love. Soon they were carried away by a passion so fierce and over-whelming that both the bedsprings and Mrs Dolan were forgotten. It was only as they relaxed in each other's arms afterwards that Ruth remembered.

'Now you've done it,' she said. 'I don't know how I'm going to face her in the morning. It's all right for you, out in the fields all day – you don't have to face her until teatime. Besides, she blames me, not you.'

'Well, it was your fault as far as I can see, looking so damned sexy, you're enough to turn a corpse on.' Then as Ruth grabbed him between the legs he let out a howl of laughter. 'No, seriously, love, take no notice. If the truth be known

230

she's as happy as a pig in muck having summat to moan about. Besides, I happen to know she loves having you all here.'

'Well she could have fooled me.'

'It's true. I heard she's been bragging to a friend in the Co-op about how well behaved her grandchildren are.'

'I can't believe that.'

'It's true, and she's right an' all. They're a credit to you, the lot of 'em.'

'Well, if that's the case, she must be changing her tune. She upset our Sadie only last week by saying she wouldn't get round her by calling her Grandma.'

'Oh, she doesn't think before she opens her mouth. She always was tactless.'

'Well! I didn't think she'd accepted them at all. She was only grumbling this morning about the baby crying. Still, it must be a strain; I mean, she isn't getting any younger.'

'Don't let her deceive yer – she's more energy than I have. Mind you, that's only to be expected with a wife who's never satisfied.'

'Oh, and who is it who urges me on in the first place? Mind you, I'm not complaining.' Ruth kissed her husband in the darkness, then enquired thoughtfully, 'Was she always so full of misery, your mother?'

'Always! Sometimes I wonder how she ever got me. In fact when I was a little lad I used to wonder sometimes if I'd ever had a father at all.'

'Perhaps it was your father's death that changed her. What was he like?'

'I wish I knew. She never talks about him, just

shuts up like a clam if I mention 'im. I never understood how she could carry on being so miserable all those years. That was until I met you. Now I understand what it must be like to lose the one you love.' He kissed Ruth long and deep, stirring her again so that she pressed herself against him until he became aroused once more. 'I love yer so much, lass, I don't think I'd ever get over it if I lost you.'

'Oh, Jack, I love you just the same. I never knew it was possible to feel like this.'

'Come 'ere then and show me.' Jack moved over her and the bed groaned.

Ruth giggled. 'I might as well be in for a pound as a penny.' Then she arched her body, sliding herself further on to her husband.

Chapter Seven

Emily and Isaac were enjoying the usual Sunday gossip in the chapel yard. Emily loved this quiet time when Lizzie, George and Alice would saunter with them amongst the flower-bedecked graves and discuss any family happenings which had occurred during the week.

'I thought our Ruth might have put in an appearance,' Alice said.

'Oh, you know our Ruth.' Lizzie smiled. 'She's so busy I doubt she'll even realise it's Sunday.'

'Still, I thought she'd try and make it sometimes,' Alice said.

'Never mind.' Emily sorted out the dead flowers on the Stanford family grave. 'So long as she's happy that's the main thing. At least I can rest content in my bed now she has Jack to take care of her.'

'Oh, she's happy all right.' Lizzie grinned. 'She's blooming like George's prize dahlias.' At the mention of his pride and joy George began to describe the various blooms to Isaac, which ones had done well and which not so well. Lizzie, who had heard it all before, rolled her eyes upwards.

'Pop in while you're passing and I'll give you a bunch.' George was always happy to show off his flowers and the silver cup he had just been awarded at the local show. They sauntered out through the gate and towards the green, a handsome group in their Sunday finery.

'What's up with Joe?' Alice suddenly asked. Her husband was hurrying towards them, a frown on his usually smiling countenance. Alice quickened her stride. 'What is it, Joe? Is something up with our Joseph?'

'No, nor with me. It's just been announced the country's at war, lass. It's been on the wireless.'

The group stopped abruptly in their tracks. Emily began to cry and Lizzie caught her mother in her arms, attempting to console her.

'Nay, lass, it's no use thee crying. It's not as if it wasn't expected. I told thee it would happen sooner or later,' Isaac pointed out.

'Oh, we all know you told us.' Emily sniffed impatiently. 'We've heard nothing else from you except Poland and the emergency powers act. But that doesn't make the news any easier to bear.'

'Come on, Mam, I'll make some tea.' Alice attempted to take her mother's hand.

'No, love, we'd best be getting home. I've a bit of sirloin in the oven, and I mustn't let it burn. There isn't much of it to start with, and if it shrivels any smaller we shan't find it.'

'Oh, our mam!' Alice looked shocked. 'How can you think of dinner when the country's at war?'

'Nay, love, no good'll come of starving ourselves. We shall need all our strength in the coming years,' Isaac said.

'Years? Oh, our dad, surely it won't go on for years.' Lizzie could only think of George and Harry, and the family, and hope it would all be over before any of them were needed, or in Harry's case were old enough to enlist.

'I hope not, love, I sincerely hope not.' But the tone of Isaac's voice didn't send out much confidence, and filled the group with a sense of foreboding, for they all knew that Isaac's predictions were not usually far wrong. So it was with heavy hearts that the family separated to wend their various ways home, George's prize-winning dahlias for once forgotten.

Emily frowned as she climbed Queen Victoria Street at her husband's side. If it wasn't one worry it was another. First it had been Alice, then Ruth, and just when it seemed she could enjoy peace of mind this had to happen. She placed her arm covertly inside her husband's. At least this time Isaac wouldn't be leaving her. She couldn't have borne that. The house was silent enough without her daughters, but to be without Isaac didn't bear thinking about. Suddenly Emily became aware of people out in the street: wives in pinafores discussing the news, men who would normally have been sitting comfortably reading the Sunday papers, or down at the Rag enjoying a quick predinner pint, but were instead crouched down on the white-edged doorsteps, sharing their views on what changes were to come. Children dressed in Sunday best were chattering excitedly about what to expect, some of them hoping for the school to be blown to smithereens, preferably with Old Jonesy in it, and hopefully before tomorrow morning.

'Has tha heard the news, Isaac?' Len Barrington called as Isaac unlocked his front door.

'Aye, Len, I've heard.'

'Tha were reight all along. Tha said it'd happen before't year were out.'

'Aye, it's a rum do. Still, we must all pull together. There'll be summat we can do to help, I expect.'

'Aah, though we've done our share. It'll be up to't young 'uns this time.'

'Aye,' Isaac agreed sadly, 'it'll be up to the young 'uns, more's the pity. Does tha know, Len, I really feel my age this morning.' Emily thought he looked it too.

'Me an' all,' Len replied. 'It isn't a nice feeling knowing we're nowt but a pair of old has-beens.'

'Oh, for Heaven's sake,' his wife called. 'Be thankful they won't be calling you up, the pair of yer. And come and get yer dinner, afore it goes cold.'

A game of soldiers was in progress and a small boy threw himself on the pavement and proceeded to shoot Isaac. 'You're dead, Mr Stanford. I killed yer,' he called excitedly. 'I'm going to be a soldier when I grow up.'

'Nay, lad, I hope it's all over by then,' Isaac answered.

The boy's mother came out and dragged her son indoors. 'Look at yer, and in yer Sunday trousers. You're not fit to be seen.' She gave her son a sharp slap on the bare leg before closing the door on the pair of them. Isaac prayed fervently to the God he tried so hard to keep faith with. He prayed right there on the doorstep that his family be protected from the war. He prayed for all his family, but it was Harry who was foremost in his heart. For Isaac knew deep down that it would be Harry, the grandson dearest to him, who would be the one to go to war, and it would be no game of soldiers, but the real thing. He went in to carve the Sunday joint but it stuck in his throat and threatened to choke him.

'I reckon I've overcooked the meat after all.' Emily put down her knife and fork. 'Leave it, Isaac, it's too tough to be digestible.'

'Aye, lass, it is a bit on the tough side.'

They both knew the meat was perfectly cooked, but neither of them was hungry. The declaration of war had killed their appetites. Emily washed the dishes in silence.

Alice had been feeling low, even before the news. After yet another false alarm she wasn't pregnant after all. It broke her heart to see Lizzie's large and happy family, and Ruth's baby tore at her heart-strings every time she smiled at her aunt. Joe reckoned he was quite satisfied with an only son, but Alice knew he was disappointed at her inability to conceive a second child. She thought how ironical it was that her sisters – who could ill afford their offspring – should be blessed with fertility whilst she, so comfortably off, seemed unable to provide a brother or sister for her son. Now, after so many false alarms, she had plucked up courage to see a doctor, a specialist at Jessop's Hospital. Her heart beat wildly as she waited in the cubicle, a thin cotton gown protecting her modesty. She dreaded revealing her body to a stranger, the first person – apart from Joe – ever to see her private parts. But it had to be done.

'Mrs Jackson, the doctor will see you now.' The efficient but unsmiling nurse led her through into the consulting room. 'Lie on the bed,' she ordered.

Alice could have died of shame when the doctor bent her knees and opened her legs wide. She concentrated on the ceiling and jumped as the cold metal instrument entered her body.

'So, you would like another child?'

'More than anything,' Alice whispered.

'You've been trying for many years, I gather.'

'Yes, doctor.'

'And you didn't have an easy time with your first child.'

'Not really.'

'Hmm! Just as I suspected. A tilted womb.'

'Is that serious?'

'No, no nothing that can't be rectified, though it will entail surgery.'

'And after the surgery, will I be able to conceive?' Alice began to relax and feel optimistic.

'Technically, yes, though there is no guarantee that you will become pregnant. However, without surgery it's highly unlikely that you will ever bear another child.'

'When can you operate?'

'The sooner the better. At your age I don't think you should delay. Of course, the decision is yours.'

'I've already decided. I want the operation.'

'Good! I shall arrange surgery as soon as possible. You may get dressed. You will be notified.' The doctor had already disappeared by the time Alice had climbed down from the bed and followed the nurse back to the cubicle.

'As soon as you're dressed, you may go.'

Alice thanked her, relieved that the examination was at an end.

The letter came a few weeks later, whilst Joe was at work. She waited until they were settled down for the evening, she to read an article on William Blake, Joe to write a speech for the Oddfellows.

'I'm going in hospital, Joe. I'm to be operated on, next Monday.'

'Operated on?' Joe looked startled. 'What for? What's wrong, lass?'

'Nothing to be alarmed about. I've a tilted womb. I'm to have it straightened, that's all.'

'Are you in pain, Alice? Why haven't you mentioned it?'

'No, except for a bit of backache I haven't any pain. It's just stopping me from catching on.' She blushed. 'With a bairn, I mean.'

'But that doesn't matter, Alice. We have our Joseph. I thought yer were content. I won't have yer going through surgery when you aren't badly.'

'No, Joe, I'm not content. When I look at our little Margaret, my arms ache to carry her home. Wouldn't tha like a daughter, Joe?'

'Aye, obviously I would, but don't build up hopes, lass. I love yer and I would hate you to get all excited and then have them dashed. If it wasn't successful you would be so disappointed.'

'I'm disappointed already. Anyway, it's all arranged. I'll need thee to sign the consent form, being my next of kin.'

Joe came to sit beside her. 'Oh, Alice, I shall worry about yer. I don't know that you should go through with it, but I do admire yer for thinking about it.'

'I'm not thinking about it, Joe. I've already thought, and now I'm just waiting.'

'Alice Jackson, I'm married to a lovely, brave woman, and I love yer.'

Alice's eyes sparkled. 'And I love thee, Joe Jackson.'

He drew her towards him and kissed her warmly. Just then the door opened and Joseph rushed in, his hands and face smeared with grease.

'What the hell have you been up to now?' Joe moved swiftly away from his wife.

'Mending a motor bike. It needed a new grommet, but it's OK now. We've been a ride up to our Billy's.'

'I've told thee about riding that pillion. I won't have it,' Alice warned, terrified that something might happen to her only son.

'It's OK, Mam, he doesn't speed. Oh, Dad, I can't wait to get one of my own.'

'Well, I'm afraid you'll just have to wait, lad. You'll need to save up before you can afford one.' Joe knew the lad would probably get one as soon as he was old enough, but it didn't do to let him know that. He had to learn that money had to be worked for.

'I don't know why you don't buy a car, Dad. Uncle Jack is on about buying a lorry.'

'A car's not much use in wartime. Petrol'll be spoken for in a few months. I shouldn't be surprised if it isn't rationed.'

'I'm going to be an ambulance driver. Our Harry says there'll be a demand for them when the air raids begin.'

'There'll be no air raids in Cottenly.' Alice sounded confident.

'Our Harry says there could be with the works, and especially with the reservoir.'

'Our Harry doesn't know what he's talking about.'

Joe looked at his father but decided to keep silent. After all, what did women know about war? They should concentrate on washing and ironing, and washing-up and babies and things. If he had but known, that was exactly what his mother was concentrating on, but before a baby could come about she had an operation to go through, and, though she would never admit it, Alice Jackson was scared stiff.

Joseph didn't miss his mother too much. In fact he couldn't wait to escape each teatime from the works and his new job. He would pedal away on his bicycle up to the farm, where he was to stay until his mother came out of hospital. He had been alarmed at first to think she was ill, but after his dad had explained that it was just a routine thing he had made up his mind to enjoy himself. Joseph hated the works. All he had done up to now was to act as errand boy, fetching and carrying: tools from the store, letters to the offices. What he had set his heart on was a job in the motor room, but his dad said that would come later, after he had proved himself. It had come as quite a shock to realise that his dad – who was in charge of personnel – would not be seen to hand out any special treatment to his son. So the farm was a respite from the job that Joseph privately considered dead boring, and not only did Jack gain an extra pair of willing hands but he was quite happy to give his newly acquired nephew a few lessons on driving the tractor. Not that the lessons were really necessary – the lad proved to be a natural when it came to anything mechanical. Ruth wondered what Alice would have said had she seen her son driving across the potato field, every bit as competent as old Sam, who had never quite taken to modern contraptions and preferred the security of a horse and cart.

Lizzie was happy to fuss around Joe, popping a bit of dinner on a plate and seeing that it was nicely warming in the oven on his return from work. Then he would hurriedly wash and change and catch the bus into town, so that he would be the first through the door of the hospital and into the ward for the half-hour's visiting allowed twice during the week and a whole hour at the weekend.

It was while he was waiting for the bus that he caught a glimpse of Hubert Hancock. He couldn't help but be flummoxed by the man's attitude. For the past couple of months the man had glared a look as sharp as a dagger at Joe whenever they had come into contact, and even now the man's face had turned almost purple as he had crossed the street without so much as a nod to his colleague. Not that Joe was particularly bothered. He had never really cared for the man, who always seemed too smarmy for Joe's taste, but there had never been any friction between them and Joe was puzzled as to what had caused the ill feeling.

The truth was that the very sight of Joe reminded Hubert Hancock of the way Ruth Wray had escaped his advances. He had never believed that Sophie's arrival in Wire Mill Place hadn't been a well-planned scheme cooked up between Winnie Stedman and the widow. Now her brother-in-law reminded him once again of the trouble they had landed him in on that fateful afternoon. He cringed now as he recalled his return from the office to face the wrath of his wife. Sophie had slapped a plate of egg on toast on the table without speaking a word. Hubert, who normally had a far more substantial dish than this merely as an appetiser, had eyed the snack with disgust and hoped for a nice slice of rump steak or halibut to follow. However, Hubert had been served all he was going to get, and on this occasion he knew better than to complain. He had grudgingly devoured the undercooked egg and overcooked toast, little realising that this was a sample of what would be his normal fare from now on. Worse, however, was to follow, when Sophie had moved her clothing and herself to a separate bedroom and turned the key in the lock behind her. Though her husband had enjoyed the titillation of extra-marital affairs on numerous occasions he had used discretion until now, and while Sophie had harboured her suspicions she had never been sure. Now, however, she had been deeply humiliated in front of her old friend, and as her husband's selfish and pathetic attempts at lovemaking had never given his wife the slightest satisfaction it was without any qualms that she decided to withdraw her wifely duties once and for all.

The problem for Hubert was that he was finding it difficult to tempt any of his past fancy women into accompanying him on his dirty weekends, and though he pondered on why this was so it never occurred to him that women might possibly be repulsed by his fat flab and his self-centred attitude. So, as Hubert lay each night in his lonely bed, suffering from either hunger or indigestion, he dreamed of the soft, slender body of Ruth Wray, and vowed that some day he would make her pay for his embarrassment and rejection. No matter how long it took, he would seek his revenge.

Alice was sitting up in bed as pretty as a picture in her pink lacy bedjacket. She was impatient now to be home, and had been stunned when the mass of padding had been removed from inside her, padding she hadn't known was there. She was also exasperated to learn that she must stay in bed for two whole weeks. Joe kissed her and enquired how she was feeling.

'Fine,' she said. 'I don't know what I'm doing here, propped up in bed like an invalid.'

'You may feel fine, but I wonder if we've done the right thing, lass. After the time you had with our Joseph I don't know that we should be considering having another.'

'Well, we've never bothered for all those years,' Alice pointed out. 'I could have got caught at any time the way we've carried on.' She blushed as she realised what she'd said.

'I know.' Joe frowned. 'It just never occurred to me that we could have another. I thought somehow, with all the difficulty with our Joseph, that there wouldn't be any more.'

'Well, tha were right, Joe, but all that's changed now. There'll be nowt to prevent me from conceiving from now on.' Alice's eyes glistened and her face glowed with optimism.

'I don't know, lass. I thought I was about to lose you after our Joseph. And there'll be no Old Mother to care for you this time.'

Alice grinned, 'Why, what an old turncoat! Tha never wanted her to care for me in the first place.'

Joe squeezed her hand between his. 'Aye, I know, but she did well for you, Alice, I admit that. But what if you have the same bother again?'

Alice brushed aside Joe's worries. 'I won't. It's never as bad with the second, and, oh, I do want another child, Joe. Our Joseph's growing away from us now he's working. Besides, it might be a little lass next time.'

'Hey, don't build up, lass. You have to get over the operation first, and even then we can't be sure you'll catch on.'

'No, but I'll tell thee something, Joe, if I don't, it won't be for the lack of trying, will it?'

Joe laughed. Alice never ceased to amaze him. Anyone looking at her would never believe how passionate she could be. He kissed her tenderly. 'No, lass, it won't be for the lack of trying. But not for a while. We've to get you back on yer feet first.'

'Aye, Joe, but we'll make up for lost time once I'm better. In fact I feel better already. I might even eat a few of those grapes tha's brought me.'

'I'm thinking it should be me eating grapes. It

sounds as though I'll be needing me strength building up.'

Alice giggled. 'Here, then. We'll share 'em between us.' But the visiting time ended then with the jingling of the bell. Joe was last out of the ward, reluctant to leave the wife he was missing so badly.

Isaac was feeling happier and more useful than he had for years as he set off with Len Barrington for the British Hall and the meeting of the Local Defence Volunteers. As an old soldier he had been put in charge and was enjoying himself immensely. He had even been persuaded to call in at the Rag with the rest of the lads after the last training session, and though he had drunk no more than half of shandy he had joined in the lively gossip and gone home in a more cheerful frame of mind than Emily could ever remember. The next morning he had seemed embarrassed about having gone into a place he had so often frowned upon in the past. 'What will folk think, Emily? Me, a chapelgoer, frequenting a public house?'

Emily had laughed at his unease. 'Nobody'll think anything. In fact I reckon you should have gone out and socialised years ago. Anyway, you seemed quite cheerful when you came home.'

'Aye, well, they're a lively lot, and none of them supped more than a couple.'

'Well then, what are you worrying about?'

'So tha won't mind if I call again, then? Just for a bit of stimulating conversation like?'

Emily had smiled as she spread honey on

Isaac's bread. 'Of course I won't mind. It'll do you a world of good.' A damn sight more good than reading the Bible, she had thought. Isaac had cleaned out the bowl of his pipe and looked quite pleased with himself. It would be a change being able to discuss such things as who had won the darts match, and how the landlord had a parrot which mimicked George Formby. In the past he had felt rather left out of the railway gang's conversation.

'What's on the agenda for tonight then, Isaac?' Len enquired.

'I'm to demonstrate how to use a stirrup pump,' Isaac said.

'That'll not tek long then.'

'No, I shouldn't think so.'

'We might 'ave time for a pint, then. Will tha be joining us for one?'

'Aye, I don't see why not.' Isaac tried to sound casual, as if it were a regular occurrence. 'Though only one, mind.' After all, it was his duty to mix with his comrades, develop a culture of closeness. A vision of his mother suddenly came to mind, frowning and stony-faced. He dismissed it as suddenly as it had risen.

'It's a grand neet,' Len remarked.

'Aye,' Isaac replied, 'a right grand neet.' He looked up at the clear starry sky and wondered how long it would be before it was filled with fighter planes. 'We shall be ready for 'em when they come,' he said.

Len looked at his friend. 'Who? What tha talking about?'

'Oh, I was just thinking out loud.'

'Tha knows what they say – it's first sign when tha starts talking to thisen.' Len chuckled.

Isaac grinned. 'Tha might be right at that.' They passed Lizzie's house at the bottom of Queen Victoria Street. He wondered if Harry was at home. The lad was already talking about joining up. The air force he was interested in. He must have a talk with him, persuade him to change his mind. After all, there were many responsible jobs for civil servants to do without dashing off to fight. But Isaac knew deep inside that he could talk from now to kingdom come and his grandson wouldn't listen. His name might be Crossman, but he was a true Stanford, a chip off the old block, and like his grandfather he would go to war. Isaac wouldn't have wanted it any other way. All the same, he would arrange that talk. It would give him the opportunity to spend some time with his grandson, for time was a scarce commodity in war, and must not be wasted.

Olive polished the heavy and ancient furniture with vinegar water. She loved Saturdays, when she would spend the afternoon cleaning Buttercup Cottage. Afterwards she would experiment with herbs and spices in the solitude of her cosy kitchen. With the cough syrup perfected and already in demand she was now concentrating on a perfume, consisting of herbs such as rosemary, mint, thyme and lavender. As usual she was finding it difficult to assess exactly the right amount of the main ingredient, which was to remain a secret from everyone except Billy from whom

Olive had no secrets. When the perfume was perfected it would be coloured a delicate shade of blue, by adding cyanin obtained from cornflowers, but according to Olive that would be in the far distant future. In the meantime her weekends were spent working on her new project.

Tonight, however, she was to attend a war savings campaign meeting, where suggestions would be put forward and discussed, with a film show to follow. Olive had been persuaded to attend by the umbrella girls, though umbrellas had been set aside for the duration of the war and the mill turned over to the production of cartridge clips. The girls had welcomed the change and production was soaring as they sang, or listened to the wireless which had been brought in to keep up the workers' spirits. Olive had also joined a first-aid class, where she had been praised – much to her embarrassment – for her patience and nursing manner by the officer in charge.

The truth was that Olive was enjoying life to the full, and only one cloud was casting a shadow over her busy and carefree existence: the fact that her father, at the age of thirty-nine, had been called up under the military training act. Her mother was distraught and no amount of reassurance could comfort her. George was relieved now the decision had been taken out of his hands. He had known all along that he would volunteer in the end and the only thing holding him back had been Lizzie and the children. He had dreaded breaking the news to her, and had been relieved when conscription was extended to all men between eighteen and forty-one.

The children had reacted in various ways to the news. Harry had shaken his father by the hand, assured him how proud he was, and promised to join up himself on his eighteenth birthday. Little Ernest Edward had cried, not because he understood what was happening, but because his mother was crying. Jimmy thought everything about the war was exciting, and because he knew he could get away with fewer reprimands with George out of the way he privately welcomed the news. Bessie, usually the most robust and easy-going of the Crossman brood, had taken it the hardest. She seemed to think the father she idolised was deserting his family, and because she was sharp as a needle she knew from listening to people like her grandfather that war was a dreadful thing, so for three days she withdrew into herself, ate very little and worried a lot. It was little Mary whom George dreaded parting from the most. Mary was the timid and frail member of the family. She had suffered every childhood illness which had done the rounds of Cottenly, and never seemed to recover from one before contracting another. Alice and Joe had taken her with them on their annual holiday, and even changed their resort from Scarborough to Southport because of the air, but little Mary was still underweight and pallid on her return. So it was with a heavy heart that George contemplated his departure and wished the bloodiness of war could be ended and his family back to their usual harmonious state.

Olive knew she would miss her father, but in her calm manner accepted his call to duty. She couldn't help wondering what would happen to her inheritance, but hadn't the heart to mention it. She no longer thought about the stall in Castle Market. The war had put paid to such schemes, and she knew she was trapped in the works for the duration. The only alternative would be to volunteer at the hospital in Sheffield, and Olive had already decided that was the course she would take. She had discussed her plan with Billy, who thought she would be highly suited to the healing profession. Of course in Billy's eyes Olive could do no wrong: from the day she had promised to marry him at the tender age of five he had been her willing slave. And though they laughed now at his proposal, their friendship was still as strong as ever, not romantic in nature but of the most loyal and faithful kind. Sometimes Olive experienced a feeling of guilt, for though she loved her brothers and sisters and indeed her other cousins she could never bring herself to confide her innermost thoughts and dreams to anyone except Billy.

She locked the door with the large iron key and placed it in the hidey-hole in the wall, wondering what to wear for the film show. Not that she was over-interested in fashion, but she liked to look her best whenever possible, having no intention of resembling her Aunt Alice, who seemed to prefer dressing like a cross between a nun and a Quaker with her black dresses and severely coiled hair. Olive couldn't help but compare her lovely mother and fascinating Auntie Ruth to the dismal, unfashionable Aunt Alice. She suddenly felt ashamed as she remembered the times her aunt had come to the rescue when the family was in need of assistance. The toys at Christmas; new shoes for Harry's interview at the town hall. The offer of help so he could attend grammar school. The times Mary had been looked after whilst recuperating from her many illnesses. Why, Aunt Alice had even offered to adopt Mary as her own, in order to give her the best possible chance in life. The offer had almost caused friction between the two families as Lizzie had taken it as an insinuation that they were unable to care for Mary in a right and proper manner. Aunt Alice was a good and generous woman and Olive hoped she herself would be of the same strong character, but the way she dressed certainly left a lot to be desired. Still, Uncle Joe seemed to adore her. Perhaps she was different beneath the sombre garments. Olive blushed at her thoughts, which were filling her head more and more of late. Especially whenever she came into contact with Tom Baraclough.

The first time she ever set eyes on him was when she was called upon to practise her first aid. Attempting to follow instructions and administer artificial respiration, she had turned Tom on his stomach with his head on one side. Then came the embarrassing part of the exercise, when she had to kneel astride her patient and place her hands just above his waist. Olive's dress had not been designed for such manoeuvres and had ridden up above her knees so that the tops of her stockings were in full view. As she had swung back and forth forcing the air from his lungs and allowing it to re-enter, she was sure Tom must be receiving an eyeful of her lithe young limbs. That everyone else

252

in the room was witnessing her predicament hadn't occurred to her. It was Tom alone, and the contact of her body against his, which disturbed her. The smell of fresh, clean sweat on his shirt and the muscles which seemed to ripple between her manipulating fingers were enough to turn her cheeks to flame and her limbs to jelly.

After that Olive had taken care never to volunteer unless she was suitably dressed, which brought her back to what to wear tonight, bearing in mind that Tom Baraclough would be present. She decided on her best costume and a broderie anglaise blouse which Grandma Stanford had made her. Joseph had giggled as he mentioned he could see her flesh through the holes, but she had noticed he couldn't take his eyes off her. Perhaps Tom would find her attractive too. Olive sang to herself as she climbed the hill home and only became dispirited as she arrived and remembered her father's approaching departure. The house didn't seem the same any more; only Jimmy acted in his normal manner, and though his practical jokes and over-activity usually drove the household mad, Olive welcomed his good humour. As they sat down to tea, Olive thought the place would have resembled a morgue without Jimmy's chatter.

'Can I go to the pictures, Mam?' he asked.

'No,' Lizzie answered, and Olive thought her mother hadn't really been listening.

'But Mam, everybody else is going.'

'Another time,' Lizzie said, hoping to silence him so she could sink back into her pool of self-pity. Olive frowned. It wasn't like her mother to be like this.

'Oh, Mam,' she said, 'I wish you'd cheer up. It'll only make Dad miserable if he leaves you in this frame of mind.'

Lizzie burst into tears. That was happening a lot at present. At the sight of her tears Ernest Edward and little Mary began wailing too.

'Come on, Mam, I didn't mean to upset you, but we should try to be brave for Dad's sake. He must feel bad enough as it is without us making it worse.'

Lizzie dabbed her eyes. The sobs seemed to come from way down inside her. Harry looked up from one of the books he read through every meal. 'Our Olive's right, you know. We should let him see how proud we are, and give him a good send-off.'

'That's right,' Olive said. 'Let him remember us as a happy family, not a load of miseries.'

Lizzie looked at her daughter and then from one to the other of her children. The anxious faces gazed back at her and suddenly she felt ashamed. 'You're right,' she said. 'We are a happy family. We always have been, and we shall be again when your father returns.'

George came through the door at that second. 'Well, that's the last of the beetroots. I suppose that's the last the garden'll see for a year or two.' He handed the bucket to Lizzie, half full of large, perfect beetroot globes.

'Oh no it isn't. Our Harry and me'll be growing them next year. Of course I expect you'll be home by then anyway.' Lizzie smiled.

Olive winked at her mother in approval. 'And

the dahlias?' she asked.

'Aye, and the dahlias,' Lizzie said. 'And now, for Heaven's sake can we all sit down and eat our teas in peace.'

'Can I go to't pictures then?' Jimmy enquired, adding 'please' to be on the safe side.

'Oh, I suppose so.' Lizzie even grinned and the atmosphere changed instantly. Their mother was once more her lovely, normal self.

Chapter Eight

It was a strange Christmas. Emily had trimmed the tree with cut out stars and bells, painted and covered in glitter by little Mary and Bessie on one of their Saturday visits. She had hung paper chains in the front room and made a special effort for the Christmas Day family gathering. George's leave had coincided with the holiday, for which they were all thankful. But all the same, an uneasy atmosphere pervaded the party. Young Jimmy insisted on being told all the details of his father's life as a soldier and was disappointed that no one had been shot yet, or blown to smithereens. Little Mary refused to be separated from George, lest he should leave again and next time fail to come back, whilst Bessie plied him with endless cups of tea and stood like a faithful servant by his chair. The atmosphere did lighten towards the evening when games like blind man's buff, charades and a good old-fashioned sing-song began to progress. Isaac gave everyone quite a shock by producing a case of Nut Brown ale from the cellar, the first time as far as Emily could remember that any alcohol – except for medical purposes – had ever been allowed in the house.

'Well, as I won it in a raffle I couldn't very well refuse it. I mean, thar not supposed to give thi luck away, or so the saying goes.' Ruth teased her father about joining a raffle so that they could all get drunk, but it was good-natured teasing and everybody except Alice was pleased at the change in Isaac. All in all it was a grand do, as Ruth remarked when the family took their leave, with the children hugging brand new dolls and games. Little Margaret chewed at a teddy bear's ear as Jack carried her through the wood and across the fields, led by Billy with a new, slitted torch.

'It's the bestest Christmas I've ever had,' remarked Frankie, as he struggled with the compendium which wouldn't quite fit under his arm.

'Me too,' Sadie said. 'Will we stay with my new daddy for ever?'

'Of course.' Ruth was taken aback by the question.

'And our old daddy won't ever come back, will he?' the little girl asked anxiously.

'Course he won't. How can he when he's dead?' Frankie sounded disgusted. 'How can girls be so dopey?'

'I'm glad, because I love my new daddy.'

Jack almost choked on the lump in his throat, but he managed to mutter, 'That's the nicest thing anybody's ever said to me, love. The best Christmas present I could have wished for.'

'I love yer as well.' Frankie, not to be outdone, forced the words out of his mouth.

'Cor blimey,' Billy said. 'Is it the Christmas spirit that's making everybody so soppy?' Then he added, 'Why don't we just say we're the happiest family in Cottenly and have done with it.'

'Tell you what,' Ruth suggested, 'seeing as we're all so happy, why don't we sing as we go?'

257

'That's a good idea,' Jack said. 'And if we sing loud enough, Grandma and Sam might hear us and join in as well.'

Mrs Dolan had refused Emily's invitation to join the party, insisting that the family was quite big enough without outsiders shoving in. However, Jack had explained that old Sam had always joined the Dolans for Christmas Day and would continue to do so for as long as he lived. Actually the pair had enjoyed the peace, the roast goose and the wireless, and best of all each other's company. Nevertheless, Mrs Dolan was pleased to hear the sound of voices approaching. Though she was loath to admit it, she would miss the lot of them now she had grown accustomed to their being there. She smiled at Sam on the other side of the fire. 'Sounds like Christmas, Sam.' Then she closed her eyes and drank in the sound of childish voices singing 'Oh Little Town Of Bethlehem' echoing across the yard. She rose to her feet and met them at the door. 'Bring yerselves in,' she said, 'sit yerselves down and let's all join in. Jack, bring out the bottle of sherry and let's all celebrate Christ's birthday.'

Ruth stared at her mother-in-law, then took off Margaret's siren suit and carried the sleeping child up to her cot. By the time she came down the others were tucking into huge slices of Christmas cake.

'Right then, what shall we sing?' Mrs Dolan enquired.

'"Away In A Manger",' Sadie said. And they did. The old farmhouse was filled with song, with stories of the old days, and laughter. It's like a miracle, Jack thought, a bloody miracle. Still, it was Christmas and Christmas was a time for miracles.

Alice was disappointed when she hadn't conceived after a few months, but her health was back to normal and she decided to find something to occupy her days instead of sitting about moping. Olive had already involved her in the war effort fund-raising and Alice had taken over the book-keeping for the local volunteers' committee. Then out of the blue came the news that evacuees would be arriving in the West Riding from London.

'What does tha think, Joe?' she asked excitedly. 'We could take two or even three, it's up to thee.'

Joe wasn't too keen on the house being invaded by a trio of rowdy children, but thought it was an ideal way of taking Alice's mind off her inability to have another child of her own. 'Maybe two,' he compromised.

So it was arranged, though Joseph didn't like the idea at all. 'I'm not having them in my room,' he grumbled.

'Of course they won't be in thi room. The spare room is all ready and waiting to be occupied.' She didn't add that it should have been a brother or sister who was to occupy it. 'Anyway,' she said, 'I thought tha'd be happy, seeing as all thi spare time is spent up at our Ruth's or amongst our Lizzie's lot.'

'But that's because of our Billy and our Harry. These'll be babies most likely – crying, screaming babies.' Alice almost told him that was what she was hoping for, but thought better of it. After all, Joseph had been used to having his own way for a long time. She wondered if she was being fair. But after all, if the evacuees were sent, she hadn't any option.

As it happened, the children who arrived at Alice's were not babies, but a skinny little lad with a freckled face and carrot-coloured hair and his sister who was even more freckled and ginger. There they stood at the gate with a small, battered suitcase between them, and a gas mask over their shoulders. The little girl, although five years old, looked small for her age and ready to burst into tears at any moment. Her brother, two years her senior clung hold of her hand as though someone was about to separate them. He didn't like the look of Mrs Jackson at all, in her severe black dress with her tightly coiled hair. Then she smiled and held out her hands. 'Hello,' she whispered, 'I'm Mrs Jackson, but it might be better if you call me Auntie Alice. Shall we go in the house and find summat to eat?' She took one grubby hand in each of her own and led them up the path towards the door.

'We've got to bring our case. Our mam will belt us one if we lose it.'

Alice cringed at the thought of them being hurt. 'It'll be all right. Nobody'll take it.' But the little girl looked so worried that Alice hurried back and brought the case in with them. Then she took off the little girl's pixie hat and coat and retied the ribbon on the bottom of one of her plaits. 'Now then, what about some hash and pancakes to warm us all up?'

'I don't like hash. I only like beans and chips.' The little girl finally let go of the tears that had been threatening all the way from London.

'There, there, there's no need to cry. Chips and beans it shall be.' Alice lifted Jennifer up on to her knee and cuddled her close.

'I want my mammy,' the little girl cried. Her brother moved close and stood with his elbows on the chair arm.

'Don't cry, Jenny. You know my mam couldn't come wiv us so there's no use crying.'

Alice's heart went out to the small boy, trying so hard to be brave. She gathered him up to her and hugged them one in each arm. 'Look,' she said, 'I know you want your mam and your mam wants you too, but because she loves you she let you come to Yorkshire so you'll be safe. It'll make her sad if she thinks you're unhappy, so shall we get a pen and paper and write her a letter? Tell her you've arrived safely and that she's no need to worry?' Alice spoke slowly and tried to curb her accent so as not to sound strange to the little ones. Jennifer wiped her face with her sleeve, leaving a patch of white slime on the faded navy blue jersey. Alice delved up her cuff, found a hanky and ordered her to blow her nose. 'Now,' she said, 'let's find some paper. Who wants to write first?'

'I can't write.' Worried, Jennifer began to sob again.

'Well, I'll just have to help you then. What shall we say?'

'Say I want to go home. Tell my mammy to fetch me.'

Brian seemed more cheerful as he gazed round

261

the room. It was a nice house, much cleaner than theirs, and it smelled better. 'No,' he decided. 'I don't want to go home. Just say you've got a garden and a pianner.'

Alice smiled, relieved that at least the little boy was taking an interest in his new surroundings. 'Do you want to have a go on the piano?' she asked.

Brian's grey-blue eyes lit up. 'What, me? Play a pianner?'

'Yes. I'll show you how, if you like.'

Jennifer suddenly realised she might be missing out if she didn't speak up. 'Me as well?' She searched Alice's eyes hopefully.

'Aye, we'll all have a go. But you'll have to wait – if I'm to start cooking chips and beans it'll take longer than hash and pancakes.'

'I don't mind hash and pancakes.' Brian decided he'd eat anything if it meant he could play a piano.

'I don't mind vem eiver,' Jennifer said, 'Well, just this once.'

Alice gave her a squeeze. 'Right then, I'll just switch on the gas and it'll be ready in two ticks.'

She made a show of tossing the pancakes high in the air, enjoying the admiration on the faces of her new family. Then she set the piled-up plates in front of them. 'There,' she said, when the plates were emptied and cleared away, 'you didn't do too bad to say you didn't like hash, did you?'

'I like yours. My mam's is all turnip and no meat,' Brian volunteered.

'And it's all watery, instead of fick like yours,' Jennifer added.

'Right then, who wants to play first?' Alice opened the piano lid.

'Me.' The voices came in unison. She lifted them both up on to the green velvet stool and proceeded with their first music lesson. Tomorrow she would begin teaching them some simple tunes, but today she allowed them to tinkle about on the keys, happier than she had felt for years.

When the letter was finally written to Mrs Smith, in London, it was short and to the point.

Dear mam, we like it ere. We ave a pianner, a garden and a field to play in wiv goalposts. We ave a auntie alice and a uncle joe and josef oo as a train set and lets us play wiv it if were careful.

love brian and jenny

Mrs Smith read the letter hurriedly between applying her lipstick and sipping at her glass of gin and was easily consoled by the postscript from Alice.

Dear Mrs Smith, the children are settling in happily. They were dreadfully upset at first but we are all doing our best to keep them occupied. Please don't worry about them – the country air is doing them good.

I'm sure it won't be long before they are back home.

Yours sincerely, Alice Jackson

But please God don't let it be too soon, Alice thought as she stamped the envelope. Then she asked for God's forgiveness as she thought about

263

George, away from his family, and the loneliness of Lizzie and her children. She thought of Mrs Smith, not only with her husband away in the war, but also without her children. And with London in the thick of persistent bombing and a million homes already destroyed, how could anyone wish for such carnage to be prolonged? Still, she might as well make the most of it whilst they were here.

She sat them both in the long, white enamel bath, enjoying the wonder in their eyes. Aye, she would make the most of it whilst it lasted.

Ruth had never been busier, or happier. She could see the truck arriving with the land girls; soon they would be at work in the fields. The farm had been expanded to almost twice its size now the extra acres towards the moors were being worked. She set out breakfasts for the children and Sam, and couldn't help feeling slightly resentful at the thought of Mrs Dolan still lying in bed with so much to be done.

'Come and get your breakfasts,' she called. Billy was back in the yard, unloading the empty churns. 'Come on, Billy, it'll be cold.' The twins clattered downstairs and perched at the table. 'Hurry up.' Ruth sliced the tops off their boiled eggs. 'It's almost time you were off to school.'

'I've got stomachache. I'd better not go today,' Frankie moaned.

'No wonder, with all the blackberries you ate yesterday. I warned you what would happen.' She cut a slice of toast into soldiers and placed them on each of the twins' plates. 'Anyway, if you've got a stomachache you won't want to go to the concert tonight.'

'The concert?' they both piped up together.

'Yes, the concert. Dad says he'll take us, but if Frankie has a stomachache he won't feel like going. Never mind – he can stay and keep Grandma company.'

'It's gone off. Are yer ready, Sadie? Can we take our pennies to the concert, Mam? The ones Grandad Stanford gives us on a Saturday?'

'Yes, if you've saved them, though I don't know what there'll be to spend them on. Perhaps ice cream or crisps, if you're lucky.' Ruth caught hold of Frankie before he could escape and checked to see if his neck was clean. 'Go on then, off you go, and watch where you're putting your feet across the fields. Don't go trailing cow muck into school. Come here and give us a kiss, then go say ta-ra to your grandma. It's funny her not being up by this time. And don't shout or you'll wake our Margaret.'

Sadie walked to the bottom of the stairs and called up to her grandma. Ruth rolled her eyes upwards in exasperation. She might as well talk to a stone wall. She could hear her mother-in-law answer, 'Ta-ra, love.'

'Ta-ta, Grandma,' Frankie called even louder. 'Do yer want to come to the concert with us?'

The voice answered softly, 'Nay, love, I'm too old for shows. Ta-ta, love – go on now or you'll be late.'

Ruth watched the children dodge between the hens and ducks and cross the yard to the gate. She waved until they were almost at the first stile and then prepared her mother-in-law a cup of tea. She knocked at the door of Mrs Dolan's bedroom, thinking it strange that she wasn't up and about by this time. 'Ma! Are you all right?'

'Aye, lass. I shall be up in a minute.'

Ruth opened the door and entered the room. It was a beautiful room, with the best view in the whole house in Ruth's opinion, and furnished with pieces which would raise a small fortune in any antique rooms in the country. 'What's the matter? Are you poorly?'

'I had a funny turn when I tried to get up, that's all.'

'Shall I fetch the doctor?' Ruth couldn't help being concerned at the sight of the woman's pallid face.

'Nay, lass, I shall be all right. I've had a lot on me mind lately and there's nowt meks yer badly as much as worrying.'

'What are you worrying about? Is it since we've come? I hope we haven't upset you. It's just that the kids are so much happier up here and so much healthier I've all on to keep them quiet.'

Martha Dolan heaved herself up and sipped her tea. 'Nay, lass, it's not you lot, it's just that you've made me realise how wrong I've been, all these years, not telling our Jack about his father. We could 'ave been happy like you lot if I hadn't been so full of guilt all these years. Seeing a family as happy as yours made me realise what I've been missing. I might even 'ave married again if I hadn't been so wrapped up in meself. All these years wasted in bitterness and guilt.'

Ruth gazed at her mother-in-law in astonishment. 'I don't know what you're talking about. Guilt? Nobody can accuse you of not being a good mother. Why, Jack thinks the world of you – in fact I don't think he'd have married me if I hadn't agreed to move up here.' Ruth knew that wasn't true, but hoped to lift Martha out of the misery which seemed to be encloaking her. 'Look, I'll fetch another cup of tea up, and then you can tell me all about what's bothering you. That's if you want to.'

Ruth hurried across the creaking floor, leaving the older woman nibbling at her fingernails and muttering to herself, 'Eeh, I don't know if I'm doing the right thing. Perhaps I ought to keep it to meself.'

The bed groaned as Ruth sat down on the edge of it and placed the hot milky tea in Martha's trembling hand. She took a sip from her own cup and looked questioningly at her mother-in-law. 'Well, are you going to tell me what this is all about?'

'Eeh, I've never told a living soul all these years. And I don't know if I'm doing right by telling you now. It's just that I can't go to me grave without easing me conscience. I daresn't go to chapel nowadays. As soon as I set eyes on't parson I feel that guilty. I can't put up with it any longer. Do yer think it would upset yer, lass, if I were to tell yer?'

'Well, I don't know till you've told me, do I? But if it'll make you feel any better then I can put up with a bit of upset. Come on now, out with it.'

'I killed him, lass.'

'Killed who?' Ruth's face drained of colour.

267

'Arthur Dolan, our Jack's father. It weren't an accident. I killed him outright. It were't best day's work I've ever done.'

Ruth couldn't conceal her shock. 'Why? Why did you do it? How?'

''E was always mocking me, about 'ow 'e'd only married me for me money. Me father had worked his guts out to build up the farm, out in all weathers, out on the cart an' all. Then Arthur Dolan came along. To the lodging house over at Warrentickle, where I worked. Turned on all the fancy talk, about how lovely I was, and I admit I wasn't bad, although I'm not one to brag.'

'I know, I've seen your wedding photograph. It's all fadey brown, but I could tell you were lovely.'

'I thought I'd burned 'em all.'

'Your Jack saved one, I suppose so he could look at his father.'

'Aye well, it's only natural, I suppose, seeing as I could never bear to talk about him. Anyway, he twisted me mother and father round his little finger, as well as me. They thought butter wouldn't melt in his mouth, until he got me wed that is, and then ... eeh, lass, you don't know what he was like.'

'I think I do.'

'Always taunting me about the women 'e was meeting up yonder, Manchester way. Spending money on drink and coming home all violent. Then came the day 'e turned on me father, threatened to poison livestock if 'e didn't hand over some money to straighten out a gambling debt. I was in bed at the time after having our

Jack. I could hear him ranting so I got up.' Her voice faltered and Ruth squeezed her hand encouragingly.

'Go on love.'

'I came on to't landing, and shouted for him to leave me father alone. 'E staggered upstairs towards me. I were frightened and weak from childbirth. 'E put up an arm to hit me.'

'Go on.'

'I shoved him, with all me strength, backwards, down the stairs. 'E bashed his head on't wall at bottom. 'E were dead when we got to him.'

'And a good thing too, by the sound of it.'

'Eeh, lass, I didn't want to worry yer. Do yer wish I'd never told yer?'

'I don't. And do you know something? If I'd had the courage I'd have done the same to Walter. God knows, I thought about it often enough. Fortunately the good Lord did it for me.' Ruth giggled. 'I'm sounding like our Alice now.'

Suddenly Martha's face bore the semblance of a smile. 'Eeh, lass, I am glad I told you. I feel better already now I've got it off me chest.'

'I can tell. It's the first time I've ever seen you smile except at Christmas.'

'Eeh, I bet you thought I was a right owd misery. How do yer think our Jack'll take it, though?'

Ruth frowned. 'Oh, you're never going to tell him, are you? I mean, what good would it do? Why don't you just mention that he fell down the stairs? Say he'd been drinking to wet the baby's head. That he were in such a hurry to see Jack that he stumbled. I think he'd be pleased to know his father was eager to see him.'

'Aye, perhaps it would be best. Besides, that's what we told the doctor at the time. Eeh, I am glad our Jack married you, lass.'

Ruth grinned. 'So am I. It isn't every woman who can share secrets with her mother-in-law, either.'

'Aye well, I reckon it's time I was getting up. There's work to do and them hens to feed. Their bellies'll be thinking their throats have been cut. Then I might set to with me sewing. I've been thinking of making our Margaret a new frock with a bit of smocking on it.'

'That'll be lovely.'

'And another thing I'm thinking is I might go to't Sisterhood this afternoon.'

'That'll be a change. Our Alice'll be pleased to see you.'

'She'd be pleased to see you an' all, lass.'

'I couldn't. I've far too much to do. Besides, she'll only go getting ideas about the kids going to all those Bible classes and things.'

'Aye, yer can have too much of a good thing, lass. I reckon Sunday school once a week should be enough.'

'Yes. Mind you, the Lord certainly works in mysterious ways, the way the war's landed her with Jennifer and Brian. They've really brought about a change in our Alice. Oh, and there's another thing – that's if you can keep a secret.'

'I've kept one for nigh on forty years, lass.'

'Well, unless I'm mistaken – and I've never been before – you're going to be a grandma again.'

'Eeh, lass, I'm not surprised with the way them bedsprings have been going. Why, it's the best news I've had in years. Not that I don't love the others, but it'll be nice for our Jack to have one of his own flesh and blood.'

'Don't go telling him, though, not till I'm sure.'

'Do yer know, instead of going to't Sisterhood I might save me energy up and go to't show with you lot tonight. I haven't been to a show since I was a young lass. I reckon it's time I made up for lost time and enjoyed meself a bit. Besides, it's time I spent some money on me grandchildren; God knows they've transformed the old place. It used to be like a morgue, although I didn't think anything of it at the time.'

Ruth gathered up the dirty crockery. 'Your Jack'll wonder what's got into you.'

'Aye, he's a good man, Ruth. Takes after his grandfather.'

'And his mother.'

Martha blushed and looked embarrassed. 'Aye well, away with yer, let me get dressed and feed them hens.'

Suddenly a cry came from the next bedroom as Margaret called for her mama. Ruth hurried out to her little girl, calling as she went, 'And I'll get our Margaret dressed and fed, then I'll start on the ironing.

The change in Martha that day was beyond belief. She fed the fowls, polished the furniture until it gleamed and did the vegetables – not an easy task with two land girls and Sam as well as the family to feed.

It was late afternoon when Jack returned from a meeting in Sheffield. A representative from the ministry of agriculture had been giving a talk, which was mainly to urge the need to increase the yield per acre of ploughing land, to make the best scientific use of fertilisers and to ensure the maximum of grain went into the flour. As every available square yard of his land was already producing, Jack considered the day could have been better spent. Nevertheless he had met a number of farmers, exchanged ideas over a drink and a cheese sandwich and discovered that the main problem facing most of them was that the extensive ploughing had left them with a short-age of food for the animals, which was aggravated by a lack of imported feeding stuffs. Jack was not as seriously affected as most, thanks to Sam's foresight. Jack had taken the man's advice and let meadowland to the west remain grass, another example of how indispensable Sam had proved himself to be.

Frankie heard the van long before it drew into the yard and was outside waiting for Jack to still the engine. 'Dad,' he called. 'Come on, hurry up or we'll be late for the concert.'

'Nay, lad, let me get into't house before yer start nattering.' His eyes searched the room for his wife. 'Hello, love. By gum, you look smart.' He kissed her before washing his hands and sit-ting to the table.

'Well,' Ruth said, blushing, 'I thought I'd better doll myself up a bit, seeing as we're going out.'

'Yer should go out more often, love. It's nice for you to socialise a bit. It's like the back of beyond up here with no neighbours to have a gossip with.'

Ruth laughed. 'I've got quite enough company with this lot. Mind you, it's good to have the girls around. Some of their talk would make even you blush. There's never a dull moment since they arrived.'

'They're a grand pair though, not afraid of work or a bit of muck.'

Ruth paused by the window and looked out. 'I wouldn't swap this for all the neighbours in Cottenly,' she said. 'I love the peace and quiet and it's so beautiful at this time of year. Everything seems all golden somehow, the trees and the hills. It all seems so unreal. Even the rooftops down in town look lovely from up here.'

'Wait till we get a hard winter.'

Ruth laughed. 'We couldn't possibly have one worse than the last. Why, I've never seen so much snow in all my life, what with the stable roof collapsing under the weight of it and the milk taking all day to be delivered.'

'No, but last year we were still starry-eyed from our honeymoon.'

'I still am. I'll never regret coming up here.' She placed a plate of hash and dumplings before him. 'Get it down you before the dumplings spoil.'

'I don't want any. I want to go to the concert,' Frankie announced.

'If you don't eat your dinner we shan't go,' Jack said. 'If you want to grow up big and strong yer'll need to eat properly.'

Frankie tucked in sullenly before muttering, 'I am big and strong. I've picked two rows of taties after school, so I must be.'

Jack patted him on the back. 'That's a good lad. I can see I shall have to pay you a bit of a wage then.'

Frankie's face broke into smiles. 'Can I 'ave it today, then, for the concert?'

Ruth interrupted. 'You'll not be going if you don't clear your plate.' Then she added, 'Our Sadie's been a good help too. She's put all the clean washing up to air and sewn some buttons on for her grandma.'

Jack put his head in his hands, 'Oh, Lord. I shall be skint when I've done paying out. It's a good thing I've got a removal tomorrow. It's a pity there isn't a concert every week, though, if it's going to get all the family working.' His mouth suddenly dropped open as his mother entered the kitchen. 'By gum,' he quipped, 'I thought it were Queen Mary herself coming in.'

'Aye, well, it isn't often I go out so I thought I'd get dressed up a bit.' She went back upstairs, leaving Jack dumbfounded.

'Where's she going?'

'She's coming with us to the concert,' Ruth answered.

'Bloody 'ell, things are looking up. What's got into her?'

'Dad, you swore,' Sadie complained.

'Sorry, love.'

'Nothing's got into her, she's just decided she'd like to go with the kids to the concert. She says she's never been to a concert since she was a little girl. And there's no point in wasting our Billy's ticket. I'll go get Margaret changed.'

'Are you getting changed now, Dad?' Frankie asked.

'Aye, I might as well, or I'll never get any peace.'

'Our Billy doesn't want to come. He says

people will laugh at him going with his mother.'

'Aye well, perhaps they will, Sadie. He's growing up now, love.'

'He's going out with Joan Sanderson. I heard them arranging, down the hollow field.'

Jack rose to his feet. 'Maybe, but there's no need to tell tales. It's natural to fancy the lasses at his age.'

Ruth frowned as she entered the kitchen with Margaret looking a picture with her apple cheeks and blonde curls. 'You ought to have a talk to our Billy, Jack, make sure he isn't going to get in any kind of trouble.'

Jack threw back his head and laughed. 'Who, our Billy? Nay, lass, he's probably more knowledgeable than I am, especially now he's working alongside the land girls.'

Ruth looked shocked, 'Oh Jack, you don't think they've–'

'No I don't,' Jack interrupted. 'But I can imagine how they get a kick out of teasing a handsome young lad like Billy.'

'Did you fancy the lasses, Dad?' Sadie asked.

'Aye, I fancied 'em, but I never loved one until I met yer mam. Then I fell in love at first sight.'

Ruth blushed. 'Aye, and we know where I was at the time – scrubbing the step.' Jack slapped her on her well-rounded rear and disappeared upstairs grinning, passing Billy on his way down.

'Aye well, I'll be on my way then, Mam. I promised our Joseph I'd meet him at the pictures.'

'Ooh, Billy Wray, you liar.'

'Sadie, another word out of you and you'll stay home.'

Luckily Martha joined them at that moment, distracting everyone, dressed in a coat she'd never worn since her son's wedding. She looked round at the children, all newly scrubbed. 'Well, and don't you all look nice?' Jack joined them, sporting a dazzling white shirt and his best suit. 'Eeh, but you make a grand-looking couple,' his mother remarked. 'Eeh, Jack, yer look fair smart. Still, yer father allus kept himself smart.' She paused, then added, 'I can remember how smart he looked the night he died. So proud he was to have become a father, he had been out celebrating. The trouble was, he celebrated a bit too much. There he was, in such a hurry to come up and look at yer that 'e went and fell downstairs. Eeh, it was a crying shame the way it happened. Still, he'd 'ave been right proud of yer all tonight. Oh well, are we going or aren't we? I'm getting right excited.'

Jack was staring at his mother, a wondering look on his face, then he pulled himself together. 'Aye, we're going, Mother, and I'll tell you this: me father'd have been right proud of you as well. You're a grand-looking woman when you're dressed up.' He opened the door, allowing a flurry of feathers to enter the kitchen. Margaret screamed with delight, and Sadie shooed the old brown hen out into the yard. 'Aye,' Jack repeated as he ushered them all out, 'you're a grand-looking woman.'

Ruth grinned as the two women busied themselves strapping Margaret into her pushchair. 'Oh, you're a grand-looking woman right enough,' she said. 'And I'll tell you another thing.'

'What?' her mother-in-law enquired with a smile.

'You'd have made a bloody good actress too.'

Martha laughed. 'Aye, well, as long as I've made him happy. He's a good man is our Jack.'

'Yes,' Ruth agreed, 'he's a very good man.' Then she trundled the pushchair across the yard and through the gate, taking care to avoid the cow muck.

The concert had been organised in aid of the local war effort, and proceeds on this occasion would be donated to the Star War Fund. Olive was one of the main organisers and was on tenterhooks worrying that it might all turn into a catastrophe. Tom Baraclough had volunteered to do the scenery, mainly to please Olive, and the couple had become almost inseparable over the past few weeks of rehearsals. Emily had made costumes for the girls who were to perform a dance routine, little Mary amongst them. Alice had agreed to provide accompaniment on the battered old piano. The Cubs and Scouts were to do a marching routine and various local artists consisting of a tenor, a comedian and an accordionist were engaged to perform.

The concert was a sell-out and by the time the curtain went up a packed audience was sitting to attention on the hard, uncomfortable chapel chairs. The comedian cum compère opened the show with hilarious impersonations of a host of famous comedy artists. Then came the dancing, during which Lizzie shed a few tears of both pride and sadness that George couldn't be here to see his little daughter perform, especially as she was looking so much better. 'We're going to hang out the washing,' sang the childish voices as they danced in and out of a washing line. Little Margaret, who until then had perched mesmerised on her mother's knee, suddenly came alive. 'Mary,' she called, 'Mary,' to the amusement of the audience and the embarrassment of her performing cousin. Luckily the applause drowned the toddler's enthusiasm, and fortunately, before Ernest Edward took to the stage with the Cubs, Margaret settled down and went to sleep.

When the audience applauded wildly at the end of the evening's entertainment Olive was ecstatic, especially as the concert tickets and raffle had raised an amount far exceeding anyone's expectations. Lizzie was proud when her daughter took centre stage to present a cheque to the Star representative and to ask him to do the honours of drawing the raffle. Prizes had been donated by most business people in Cottenly, including a bottle of spirits from the Rag and a voucher from the Co-op. A Fair Isle jumper had been given by Katie Swann, who hoped the winner wouldn't notice that the front was slightly faded from when it had been left for too long as part of a window display. Jack had promised a fowl, to be collected on Christmas Eve, and he decided to make it two when Ruth pointed out that it had been won by one of the large families from the Twenty Row. The Star photographer had taken a picture of all the entertainers in the grand finale, and another of Olive handing over the cheque, looking so flushed and lovely that Tom Baraclough couldn't resist kissing her, right there in front of everyone. This brought the largest cheer of the evening from the audience, and a shout from her brother Jimmy, 'Ugh, he must be daft to want to kiss her.' Everyone left the hall with a smile on their face, declaring it the best night out for years.

The show was still in progress in fact only halfway through, when Hubert Hancock paused on his way home from a board meeting to light his cigar. It was a grand night, with a huge harvest moon, and he was in no hurry; after all, there would be no welcome from Sophie. He was lost in self-pity when the shout came, 'Hey, doesn't tha know there's a war on? Put that light out.' Hubert wasn't used to being told what to do and had no intention of taking notice, especially when he saw that his critic was Ruth Wray's father, Isaac having joined the ARP after Harry complained about a shortage of local volunteers. He drew level with the man. 'Didn't you hear me? I asked thee to put thi light out.'

'All right, all right, I was only lighting my cigar. Not that anyone's going to take any notice of a cigarette lighter.'

'Tha'll be laughing at the other side of thi face if tha gets a two-pound fine,' Isaac warned him, knowing that two pounds would mean nothing to a works manager.

'It's a grand night,' Hubert said, attempting to draw Isaac's attention from his burning tobacco. 'A grand night for the concert. I gave my donation earlier.'

Isaac ignored the last sentence. 'It's a sell-out, I hear. All my lot are there.'

'All of them? They'll have half filled the place,' Hubert joked.

'Aye, every single one of 'em, except me. Still, my effort's as important as theirs, I suppose.' But Hubert Hancock wasn't listening. He didn't like anyone remotely connected to Ruth Wray, and just the thought of her was inflaming him with desire, not only for her body, but with a desire to get even. He left Isaac and quickened his step, still puffing frantically at his fat cigar.

The farm was in complete darkness, not a single chink of light sneaking through the blacked-out windows. So the ARP warden had been right, the family were all out for the evening. He looked up at the windows, imagining the slim, desirable body of Ruth Wray, even the thought of her sharing a bed with that Dolan fellow filling him with longing. The lass had fallen on her feet, so he'd been told. He wondered if she would have been so eager to marry the man if he had been without a few bob. Perhaps if the farmer hadn't come on the scene the lass would have been a little more free with her favours. The anger seethed inside him as he peered through the darkness at the property. His eyes rested on the Dutch barn, looming eerily in the moonlight. He made his way crazily towards it. He would show that air-raid warden that if he wanted to light up the countryside he would do so. He would show Ruth Wray as well. The misery of the past year, his wife's indifference to his needs, and now that damned man all served to turn his mind to thoughts of revenge, to madness even. He moved towards the huge mound of stacked hay, flicked his cigarette lighter and held it to one of the bales.

Old Shep stirred and slunk to the door. Something was afoot. He barked, agitated, unused to being left alone. Sam prised himself out of his comfortable old chair and walked stiffly to the door of his cottage. Though he wouldn't move to the farmhouse, he had taken to staying in the two-roomed outbuilding more often, and though the place should have been condemned Sam liked it just the way it was, with the few pieces of furniture from the house, not needed, but too good to be got rid of. He went out to investigate, deciding to let the old dog out, just as the stocky figure hurried out of the barn and across the yard. He grabbed a rake and made after the man, and then the smell of burning reached his nostrils. He stopped, and turned to see the glow. He panicked, but only for a few seconds, then hurried as fast as his arthritis would allow him across the yard and grabbed a bucket. He ran towards the trough, filled the bucket and rushed to douse the fire. To and fro he went, almost stumbling over half a dozen rats, scurrying to escape the flames.

'O God,' Sam prayed, 'don't let it get hold.' He could imagine the whole barn, the stables and even the house going up in flames. The trough was almost empty when he remembered the thick canvas tarpaulin Jack used to cover the cart. He tugged the heavy sheet until it fell almost on top of him, sending a shower of rainwater into his face. Thank God for the heavy rain earlier in the week. He dragged the sheet with all his strength, his mind working continuously, telling him what to do next. He lifted the canvas with the outside towards the crackling hay, but wasn't tall enough to reach. He knew he must cover the whole of the burning area in order to stop the air flow. Looking about him he made out the shape of the ladder and lifted it on to the edge of the fire. He knew the tarpaulin would take some lifting and didn't think he could climb and lift at the same time. Twenty years ago he could have done a job like this blindfold.

He knelt on the ground, folded the sheet into four and edged it across his back, with the fold on top of his head, then straightened up beneath the weight and climbed laboriously up the ladder rung by rung. The smoke choked him, causing him to cough and splutter, but he climbed steadily. When he was high enough, he bent across the stacked hay, allowing the sodden sheet to slither over his head. He tugged it forward and his stomach lurched as the ladder slipped and steadied again. The sheet was flat over the hay; all he had to do now was unfold it. He climbed higher, until he could reach, and leaned over, lifting and throwing at the same time, smothering the burning hay. He crawled across the canvas, pressing, damping down the smouldering mass, ignoring the steam rising towards his face, scalding his cheeks and hands. He could do no more. He didn't know if the fire was out, and was too exhausted to find out. Then, suddenly, the bales beneath the sheet collapsed under him, and he fell. He could vaguely hear Shep barking desperately to be let out, but then a searing pain caused everything to fade as he lost consciousness and lay still on the ground.

Martha was uneasy, even before they reached the yard. She knew Sam would have released the dog from the confines of the house to silence his barking. 'I don't know what's up with Sam,' she said. 'Either he's going deaf in his old age or he's fallen asleep.'

'Perhaps he decided not to stay tonight after all,' Ruth suggested.

'No.' Jack hurriedly unlocked the kitchen door. 'He told me he'd keep an eye on the place. He'd never go back on his word.'

The dog almost knocked the children over, but instead of greeting them excitedly and wagging his tail he charged across the yard, yelping as he reached the almost lifeless body of his old friend. Jack followed at a run with the others behind him. 'Oh, my God.'

The smoke was still rising from the damp hay littering the floor. There amongst it all lay Sam, his leg twisted beneath him. Jack carried the man into the kitchen and upstairs, where Martha insisted on his being put to bed in her room. 'I'll manage in with our Sadie,' she stated as Jack hurried off to fetch the doctor, vowing as he went to have a phone installed. It was ridiculous not to have one, out here at the back of beyond. Why, someone could be dead by the time a doctor could be contacted. Aye, it was time he came up to date and arranged for electricity too. After all they could afford it, and Ruth deserved it – in fact nothing was too good for his wife and his new family.

Sam had regained consciousness by the time he was put to bed, but in great pain, from what Martha diagnosed as a broken leg. Driving off in the wagon, Jack tried to fathom out how the fire could possibly have started. Sam would probably be able to enlighten them after recovering from the shock, but Jack remained mystified. Fortunately the doctor was at home and followed Jack back to the farm, where he dressed the patient's scalded hands and face and disagreed with Martha's diagnosis.

'A badly sprained ankle and a torn muscle. I'll be damned if I can understand why a man of your age should be prancing about in a hayloft at this time of night.' Then he added with a chuckle, 'You didn't have a woman up there, did you, Sam?'

Sam glared at the doctor. 'The bloody place was on fire. That's what I wor doing up theer, putting the bloody thing out.' He glanced at Martha's worried face. 'I did manage to put it out, didn't I, lass?'

'Aye, you put it out, Sam, but how did it start, that's what we'd like to know.'

'Deliberately, that's how. And if I'd of been a minute sooner 'e'd 'ave 'ad the pichfork up 'is arse.'

Dr Swinbourne frowned. 'You mean someone torched the barn on purpose? You saw him?'

'Aye, well no, I didn't see 'im do it, but I saw 'im rushing out of 't yard. I expect 'e was surprised to find anybody 'ere.' The old man shivered. 'Eeh,

Martha, lass, I dread to think what'd 'ave 'appened if Shep 'adn't barked. The whole place could 'ave been up in flames.'

'Now, don't go disturbing yerself, Sam,' the doctor advised. 'You've had enough upset for one night. You did exceptionally well, especially for a man of your age. But it's a serious accusation. If someone did commit arson then I advise you to call the police.'

Ruth was standing, white and anxious, by the door. 'Why would someone want to do such a dreadful thing? Children I could understand, but a grown man! Didn't you notice anything about him, Sam? I mean, was he fat or thin? How old would you say he was?'

'Fat, and definitely not young. Waddling, rather than running. I'd 'ave caught 'im if I 'adn't 'ad the fire to deal with.'

'Well, I'm glad you did, deal with the fire I mean. Many a person would have panicked.'

The doctor was packing his bag. 'I'll leave you a letter. Just in case, I'd like you to have an X-ray. To be on the safe side. Will someone be able to take him?' He glanced at Ruth.

'Yes. Oh, yes, we'll see to it.'

'In the meantime, a couple of aspirins won't go amiss.'

'Aye.' Martha was already fussing with the bedclothes. 'Don't you worry, doctor, I'll take good care of 'im.'

Jack saw the doctor out into the yard. 'I should keep an eye on him, Mr Dolan, for the shock. It could be a day or two before it affects him. Call me if you're worried.'

'Aye, thanks, I will. And thanks for coming so prompt like.'

'The least I could do, considering the man's never called me out before. In all my years in Cottenly I've never had to treat Sam Robins.' He chuckled. 'Must be a healthy occupation, farming.'

'I hope so.' Jack frowned. 'It's a rum job though, doctor. The fire, I mean. Why would anyone do such a thing?'

'God only knows. Spite? Jealousy? I've come across some queer folk in my time, liable to do anything. Still, I'd keep my wits about me, if I were you. There's a lot at stake with the farm.'

'It's the family I'm worried about,' Jack said. 'They mean more to me than any farm.'

The doctor started up the car, with a great crashing of the gears and a few curses. He remembered the place Ruth Wray had lived in before the death of that brute of a husband and was thankful that the lass had found herself a good man like Jack Dolan. 'Yes, I'm sure they do.' Then he bade Jack good-night.

'Goodnight to you too, doctor.' Jack walked slowly to the Dutch barn. 'Oh, God.' He could see the whole place burning away in his mind's eye, and old Sam lying dead amongst the carnage. He would call the police first thing in the morning.

Sophie Hancock looked at the shoes her husband had thrown on the hearthrug the previous night. She took them to the kitchen, got out the shoe polish and brushes and attempted to clean them.

Then she realised the mud would have to be scraped off before the blacking could be applied. Where the devil had the man been to get them in such a state? Never at a board meeting. Nor did she think he had been to his club. More than a couple of drinks and his snores could be heard through the wall and even downstairs. No, he definitely hadn't been to his club. She brushed at the soft black leather, wondering why on earth she kept on doing his dirty work. Pride, probably. Though there was no semblance of love left in their marriage, she wouldn't give him the satisfaction of being able to fault her housekeeping. Instead, she kept his wardrobe in perfect order. Immaculate white shirts, pressed trousers and clean undergarments daily. In fact, to the eyes of the world, Sophie was the perfect housekeeper, and indeed the perfect wife. And so she would have been had it not been for the man's infidelity. And now it had begun again, despite his pleadings and denials of the past year.

She dumped the toast on the table, poured the tea just as he entered the room and walked out without saying one word. If he was up to his philanderings again she would no doubt hear about it sooner or later, and this time he would lose not only his bedmate but his housekeeper too. Sophie Hancock had suffered enough humiliation and had made up her mind that next time she would leave him. To hell with keeping up appearances; she had had enough.

Had Sophie but known it, her husband had gained no satisfaction from his previous evening's activities. In fact he was regretting approaching

287

the Dolans' place at all, particularly as he was worried that the old man had caught a glimpse of his face. Not that the man knew him personally, but the problem was that being a public figure Hubert Hancock was frequently photographed for the press, especially the local *Express,* which almost everybody in the area read at some time. What the devil had the man been doing anyway, hiding away in the outbuildings in the dark? He might have given him a heart attack. He held his head between his hands. He hadn't slept at all, listening for a sign that the fire brigade had been called out. Now he had the devil of a headache and would no doubt spend all day waiting for the police to turn up. He smiled wryly. All he had to do was to deny any knowledge of a fire. No one would argue with the departmental manager, not if they had any sense. He was a powerful man and almost every family in Cottenly had someone in his employ. Well, perhaps not so much now with the war on, but even the men away fighting would need jobs to return to after the war.

He cheered up, ate the deliberately burned toast and prepared for another day. He was disappointed that taking revenge on Ruth Wray had brought him so little satisfaction, but there was always another time. He set off for the office, without a word from his wife, and wondered how long she would be prepared to keep up this Sent to Coventry business. She would stall of it soon, he was certain of it.

Thanks to Sam, the damage to the barn turned out to be less than at first thought. It was the old man who had suffered the most and every step was agonising. The X-rays proved the doctor's diagnosis correct: no broken bones but a lot of internal bruising as well as a torn muscle and sprained ankle. Sam was warned to expect a lot of pain. 'Keep the ankle moving and rest the thigh,' he was told.

'Bloody silly fool,' Sam commented as Jack helped him into the taxi to bring him home. 'What am I supposed to do? Leave me leg at 'ome and tek me ankle wi' me?'

Jack laughed, despite his anxiety. 'Just keep turning yer ankle, Sam. It's back to bed for you when we get home, for a day or two at least, until the bruises come out.' Jack was thinking about the shock more than the injuries, but Sam seemed to have taken things in his stride.

Martha was ready with the comfrey when they got back. 'Nothing better than comfrey for sprains, according to young Olive.' She then bound a wet crêpe bandage round the swollen ankle.

'She's turning out to be worse than Old Mother with her concoctions,' Ruth answered, but her mind was far away. If someone was out to destroy the property, she wondered if her children were safe. She had made up her mind to fetch the twins home from school rather than let them make the journey through the wood on their own. Frankie had protested and made her promise not to wait outside the playground. 'People'll think we're sissies, won't they, Sadie?'

'Yes,' Sadie agreed, 'and they'll laugh at us.'

'Like they laugh at Michael Dandridge,'

Frankie grumbled. 'He's a sissy.'

'That's not fair. You shouldn't call people names. Besides, there's no such thing as a sissy.'

'Yes, there is. It's the same as a lass-lad.'

'Well, don't you call him names, he can't help the way he is and you'll only upset him. You just be kind to him.' Ruth couldn't argue about Michael; he had drawn her attention with his immaculate appearance and the way he played in the girls' yard and shunned the boys. She had also noticed how happy he had seemed when dressed as Angel Gabriel in the nativity play. Ruth had wondered at the teacher's wisdom at casting the boy in a role that called for a girl's nightdress and a halo. Surely she must know how his classmates would tease him.

'Well,' Frankie compromised, 'just wait at the edge of the wood where nobody can see you.'

Ruth had agreed but she still couldn't help worrying, despite the fact that Sergeant Reynolds did not consider the incident to be of a serious nature.

'A tramp perhaps, resting in the warm barn, probably having a smoke and then dropping his cigarette end accidentally. An isolated incident in my opinion.' Sam had pointed out that the man hadn't looked like a tramp, and if he was one he was a very well-dressed one with plenty of meat on his bones.

The sergeant hadn't seemed unduly worried. After all, old Sam was knocking on in years and no doubt his eyes weren't all they should be. Jack had agreed, after the sergeant left, that there was very little evidence to prove it had been done deliberately and, in an effort to relieve his wife, said they should all try to forget about the fire.

'Forget?' Martha Dolan stared at her son. 'How can we forget, with poor Sam looking like he's been run over by a tramcar?'

'I know, I know, and if I could lay my hands on whoever did it, they would end up in exactly the same state as Sam. But I can't, and what I'm saying is, what can't be altered is best put behind us.'

'Jack's right, Ma,' Ruth conceded. 'All we can do is look after Sam and get him better.' But her words belied her feelings and she kept a watchful eye on Margaret, making sure she stayed within sight of the house, and that Shep was kept out in the yard as her bodyguard.

Billy was the only one for whom the upheaval had proved a blessing. He had stayed out longer than he was permitted, carried away by the banter and camaraderie of the young crowd. They had hung around eating a bag of chips and peas, with a liberal helping of fish bits on. But it was Joan Sanderson who had caused him to lose all track of time. He thought she was the prettiest thing he had ever set eyes on, apart from Olive, of course, and Olive didn't count any more. Besides, she seemed old all of a sudden, and serious. Not like Joan, who was always laughing and had a dimple on one side of her mouth, which he couldn't resist staring at. And she didn't mind him putting his arm round her waist, and last night outside the chip shop she had kissed him for the first time, on the lips too. Afterwards she had let him walk with her as far as the end of her street. That was why by the time he set off for home he had already been half an hour late. And although Billy knew every tree root, every protruding rock and every dip in the path where the stream trickled down to the river, it had still taken him a while to make his way home in the darkness of the wood, and even though his mother was lenient when it came to his freedom he was still expected to be in on time to prevent her worrying. So he had been prepared for at least a telling off when he arrived at the farm. Instead, no one had even noticed he was missing. He had been able to sidle in and upstairs unnoticed and into bed, where he could think and later dream about his first sweetheart, the delectable, blue-eyed Joan Sanderson. Billy was sorry for Sam, but couldn't help being thankful, all the same.

Chapter Nine

The night of the benefit concert had also proved an eventful one for Olive. It was the night Tom Baraclough had told her of his love for her. After the costumes had been packed away, the scenery dismantled and the chairs stacked in piles at one end of the hall, he had taken her in his arms and kissed her, with the pent-up emotion of many weeks. Olive had responded by pressing herself close and winding her arms round Tom's neck, overwhelmed by unfamiliar sensations and a warm glow of elation. Then it had all been spoiled when Tom had told her he would be leaving in a few days to join the army.

'Will you wait for me, Olive?' he had asked, gazing deeply into her large brown eyes, saddened to see the tears welling there.

'Oh, Tom! Of course I'll wait, but I'm going to miss you so much.'

'Me too, but it won't be for long. I'll be back.'

'You will write, won't you?' Olive pleaded.

'Don't be daft. I'll write every day.'

'Only' – Olive searched for the right words – 'only my dad wrote regularly at first, and now we haven't heard anything for going on three months.'

Tom frowned at her words, knowing something must be wrong but not wishing to worry her. 'Oh, the letters'll have been mislaid. I've heard how unreliable the mails are.'

'Really? You think he'll be safe then?'

'Safe as houses. You'd have heard otherwise.'

Olive smiled, her beautiful, radiant smile, then her face clouded again. 'Oh, Tom, I do love you. I don't know what I'll do without you.'

'Me too, but like I said, it won't be long before the war's over. Then we'll all be home again, your dad as well.'

'I'll be waiting.' Olive was silenced by Tom's lips on hers.

Tom wondered if he was being fair: she was so young and he might be gone a long time. But Olive had no doubts at all. No matter how long Tom was away, she would wait. She loved him, and that was that. She would carry on with her work for the war effort, and with Tom gone, she would experiment with her beauty products. The time would pass swiftly if she kept herself occupied. In no time at all, Tom would be back holding her close, but all the same she couldn't help worrying about what the war was doing to her world. First of all her father, and soon to go, Tom, and if it went on much longer, Harry would be next. Olive thought of how her mother had changed over the past few weeks. She had sunk into a despondency even worse than when her father first went away. Not only was she neglecting the house, but she was letting her appearance go too. She no longer seemed to care about her hair and wore the same cardigan and pinafore for days on end. Olive and Bessie were doing their utmost to lift her out of her depression, and even little Mary was rallying round and helping with the household chores. Lizzie, however, seemed to spend all her days slumped on a kitchen chair, gazing into the fire. Little Ernest Edward no longer tried to persuade his mother to take him to the pictures or up to the farm; he knew it would be a waste of time. Jimmy wasn't helping matters, either, by becoming involved in one escapade after the other. He was a constant worry to the family.

Olive's anxiety had continued long into the night after the concert, but it was mixed with another, unfamiliar, feeling, a feeling of belonging, and knowing Tom Baraclough felt the same. When Tom held her, it was as though their two bodies melded into one, fused together by a strange, warm longing, and even now, when they were apart, her body was still charged by it. Olive knew that even if he were sent to the other side of the world, the feeling of belonging to Tom Baraclough would stay with her until the day he returned.

Jimmy Crossman didn't go out looking for trouble, it just seemed to find him, and however hard he tried nothing seemed to turn out the way he intended it to. Besides, he wasn't expected to do anything right, and if he did nobody would notice. Harry had always been the clever one. Olive was known throughout Cottenly as the beauty of the family. Bessie was forever being praised by Grandma Stanford for the way she could turn her hand to the household chores. As for Mary, everyone made a fuss of her; even Jimmy loved and cosseted her as he would a lovable kitten. Ernest Edward was too independent to care what anyone thought, involved in the Cubs and the Joy Hour. But Jimmy cared. If only somebody, just once, would notice something good about him, but nobody noticed him at all, except when he was in trouble.

Nobody except Grandad Crossman, that is. Grandad Crossman actually enjoyed Jimmy's Saturday afternoon visits to Warrentickle. He would take him into the front room with the aspidistra in the window and the Margaret Tarrant pictures on the wall, one – called the Wind's Song – on which a boy was said by Grandma Crossman to look exactly like Jimmy. There, in the warm cosiness, Grandad Crossman would let Jimmy wind up the gramophone and put on the records. Grandad had the largest record collection in Warrentickle and had started providing music for local events such as carnivals, socials and weddings. His collection included everything from Gracie Fields and Kathleen Ferrier to the very latest dance music. Jimmy and his grandfather would sit enthralled and Jimmy would keep the gramophone wound and the needle compartment full. Grandad Crossman would always give Jimmy a bag of Jap Desserts and for a time he would feel noticed and important instead of the runt of the family. Between them they would sort out the records ready for Saturday evenings when most of the social events seemed to take place.

However, this was not Saturday afternoon but Saturday morning, and Jimmy had once again landed himself in trouble, and in his opinion very serious trouble. It had all begun when he called for Brian, whom Auntie Alice had said he could take for a walk. They had set off to the very top of Queen Victoria Street and out on to the moor. Brian had never been to this particular spot, which was a favourite playground for Cottenly's youngsters.

'I'll take you to Dragon's Cave,' Jimmy promised his newly acquired cousin.

'Is there a dragon in there, then?' asked Brian, uncertain if he had the courage to go inside or not. The vastness of the open countryside after the closed-in security of London's East End was somewhat unnerving to the small boy.

'There used to be,' Jimmy answered, 'but I expect it died long since.'

Brian decided he wouldn't take any chances and turned back from the entrance to the dark, damp hole, which was surrounded by masses of grey rocks. Instead he climbed up the steep crags until he was high above the cave and could look down over the valley and the main road winding alongside the river, connecting the city of Sheffield to Cottenly. Jimmy followed Brian and together they perched on the edge of a rock.

'There's a ghost up 'ere,' he said, determined to prove to the Londoner how brave he was.

'How do you know? Have yer seen it, then?'

'Oh, aye. Many a time.'

Brian looked around him uncomfortably. The silence seemed eerie and unnatural. The rock struck cold through his short grey trousers, and his legs were blood red in the cold, damp, November air. 'I'm cold,' he said. 'Let's be going.'

Jimmy picked up a stone and rolled it down the hillside, and it reached the river with a splash. 'I'm not cold. It's because you're from London, not used to the country.' He sent another piece of rock rolling down to the bottom.

'You missed that time.' Brian picked up a stone and copied Jimmy. Down the rocks clattered, some of them rolling off course and stopping short of the water, others losing themselves amongst the bracken.

Showing off, Jimmy rolled a small boulder to the edge. 'I bet this goes further than yours.' He pushed the boulder over the edge and watched it gather speed as it descended. Brian saw the Sheffield bus come round the corner just as the boulder hit a ledge of rock and bounced across the river, right into the window of the double decker.

'You've smashed the winder, Jimmy,' Brian informed him unnecessarily. Jimmy's face was a sickly white. 'I'll bet you've killed somebody. Now you're for it.'

''Ave I 'eck.' Jimmy cowered back so that he couldn't be seen by the driver of the now stationary vehicle.

'I fink we'd better get lost,' Brian said. 'If 'e comes up 'ere and finds us we might get 'ung for murder.'

'Shut up. Don't talk daft. The windows are covered with netting in case of being bombed, so I can't 'ave killed anybody.' Jimmy tried to sound brave but he was already hurrying along the path. 'Anyway, we'd better be off. I'm cold,' he said. Brian ran on in front. 'Not that way.' Jimmy cut through the bracken and over a dry stone wall. 'We'll take a short cut across the fields to Auntie Ruth's, then nobody'll see us. Nobody'll know we've been up 'ere at all. That's unless you tell 'em.'

'I won't tell, honest, Jimmy.' The small boy liked his new friend, who stuck up for him when the kids at school called him names such as Carrots, Vaccy and Townie.

They hurried on in silence until they came to the lane leading to Dolan's Farm. They climbed the stile and cut across the field. It was only as they reached the yard that Jimmy asked, 'Do you think it'll be in the papers?'

'Probably,' Brian comforted him. 'Especially if anyone's got veir 'ead bashed in.'

Ruth gave the youngsters a couple of slices of bread and dripping and a pot of tea. It was a surprise to see Jimmy, who didn't come very often. 'You look half frozen, the pair of you.' Jimmy's face was ashen, and his aunt wondered if he'd been up to something. He usually had. Ruth had a particularly soft spot for her nephew, who didn't seem to be able to keep out of mischief, but was in her opinion the most lovable of Lizzie's bunch. She always wanted to take him in her arms and give him a cuddle, something she guessed the family were short of these days. She frowned as she worried about Lizzie's condition. She would persuade her to see a doctor after the weekend. 'Well, what have you two rascals been up to then?'

Jimmy looked alarmed. 'Nothing, Auntie Ruth, honest, have we, Brian? We just came for a walk, to see you, that's all.' The look on his face confirmed Ruth's suspicions.

'Yes, well, sit up to the fire and have a warm.' No doubt she would hear about their adventures sooner or later. 'How's your mam today?' she asked.

'Don't know,' Jimmy answered. 'She doesn't say anything, just sits there all day, waiting for the postman. Miserable as sin, she is.'

'You must make allowances, love. She misses your dad.'

'I know, but she's not the only one, Auntie Ruth. I miss me dad an' all.' Jimmy looked down at the pegged rag rug he was sitting on, unwilling to betray the emotion and the tears which threatened.

'I know, love, but he'll be back soon, you'll see.' Ruth longed to take her nephew in her arms and hug him close, but knew he would be horrified with Brian there as a witness. She must talk to Lizzie, get her to pay more attention to her children, especially Jimmy, who really needed a father to keep him disciplined.

'I miss my dad as well,' said Brian. 'But I've got my Uncle Joe.'

Bessie Crossman hated Saturdays. She couldn't help comparing them with the Saturdays before her father had gone away. Then Saturday had been her favourite day. A walk with Grandad Stanford to Miss Fiddler's sweetshop in the morning. Playing out in the afternoon, either with the long skipping rope down on the green, or hopscotch in her best friend's backyard. And then the first house pictures after tea. Now it was the most miserable day of the week, especially as Olive had to work Saturday mornings and her mother didn't do anything except sit staring into space. Bessie took the pegged rug outside and shook it, ashamed of the dust which pothered out of it, a sign that it hadn't been taken up for a full week. She swept the lino and washed it before replacing the rug.

'Give me a lift with the table, Mam.' She stood waiting, hands poised under the edge of the large, heavy board, but Lizzie didn't respond. 'Mam, I can't lift it on my own.'

Lizzie seemed to come to life slightly. 'Oh, leave it for this week. It isn't dirty.'

'Yes it is. If you won't help me I'll get Mrs Palmer.' Bessie knew the mention of Mrs Palmer would rankle. It had long been a contest between her mam and the next door neighbour as to who could complete their household duties in the shortest time. Lizzie prised herself from the chair and took hold of the table at the other side. They lifted it on to the clean half of the floor and then Bessie set to work on the remainder of the room. After the table was replaced the young girl got out the mansion polish and started on the furniture. She hoped her grandparents wouldn't arrive until she'd finished, then she could go with Isaac when he took Mary and Ernest Edward for their Saturday sweets. She wondered where Jimmy had disappeared to. No doubt he would be back in time; he wasn't likely to miss his treat. 'What are we having for our dinners, Mam?'

'I'm not bothered. You'll find something,'

301

Lizzie said.

Bessie sighed and went to the cellar head to bring out the potato basket and a couple of onions. Thank goodness for Auntie Ruth, who kept the family supplied with fresh vegetables. Bessie decided on fried potatoes and onions, seeing as there wasn't much else, and was peeling the vegetables when her grandparents arrived.

'Now now, what's all this crying about?' Isaac pretended to be concerned.

'I'm not crying.' Bessie giggled. 'It's the onions.'

'And how's yer mam this morning?'

Bessie shrugged and filled the kettle. Emily frowned and removed her coat. 'Well, Lizzie, aren't you going to make us a cup of tea?'

Lizzie patted her escaping hair back into its pins. 'Our Bessie'll make it, won't you, love?'

Isaac guessed the agony his daughter was suffering, but knew it was time she pulled herself together. He had never been one to sympathise with self-pity. 'It seems to me that our Bessie's busy enough without having to make tea for the likes of us.'

'It's all right.' Bessie began to set out the cups and saucers.

'No, love, sit thiself down, have five minutes. Thi mam'll do it.'

'My mam's not well,' Bessie said.

'Oh?' Emily poured the boiling water into the pot. 'What's the matter, Lizzie? If you aren't well, we'd better send for Dr Swinbourne.'

Lizzie glanced sharply at her mother and flushed. 'No, I don't need the doctor.'

'Then why aren't tha seeing to the dinner, lass?' Isaac asked gently. 'It seems to me you're putting on our Bessie. She's only a child, Lizzie. I don't think thar being fair.'

Emily hated confrontations and attempted to change the subject. 'Where's your brothers and sisters, love?' she enquired of Bessie.

'Our Olive's working, our Harry's gone to a meeting and our Mary's over at Auntie Alice's. She's always over there now – her and Jennifer's as thick as thieves.'

'And where's our Jimmy and Ernest Edward?' Isaac asked. 'Don't tell me – I expect our Ernest's playing on the green and the Lord knows where our Jimmy's gotten to.' He grinned. 'I expect they'll come rushing in in time for their spending money.' He turned his attention back to his daughter. 'What are you doing today then, Lizzie?' Lizzie stared blankly back at her father.

'She never does anything,' Bessie stated matter-of-factly.

'Well, then it's time she started doing something,' Isaac said. 'Get thi coat on, Lizzie. Tha can come down to the shops with us.'

'Our Bessie'll do the shopping.'

'No, she won't. Our Bessie's done enough for today. She can go out to play, it'll do the lass good.'

Bessie's face lit up and then clouded again at the look of panic on her mother's face. 'I can't go out. I don't go out any more. I have to look after me mam.'

'Well, it's time you did go out, and thi mother too. Get thi mam's coat, love.'

'No, I can't.' Lizzie shrank back in the chair. 'George might come home. I've got to be here when he comes home.'

'When George comes home he'll wait if you're not here.' Emily looked perplexed as her daughter began to sob. 'It's all right, Lizzie, don't upset yerself. You needn't go if you don't wish to.'

Isaac glared at his wife. 'Damn it, Emily, you're not doing the lass any good at all. She needs pulling out of this' – he struggled for the right word – 'this melancholy.'

'But it won't do any good upsetting her further, Isaac.'

'No, and it won't do her any good sitting there feeling sorry for herself. Get thi coat on, Lizzie. We'll go visit our Alice.'

'I ought not to.'

'Rubbish,' Isaac stated firmly. 'When George comes home what do you think he's going to do? Go away again if you don't happen to be sitting here all idle, on thi backside? And another thing, tha looks a sight. What's George going to think of thee, getting into a rut like that?'

'Isaac!' Emily chided him, but he carried on.

'It's time tha considered others a bit, Lizzie. Why, I feel right ashamed of thee, lass, though I never thought I'd say so to my own daughter.' Lizzie's face turned a deep beetroot colour. 'It makes me wonder where the country would be if all our womenfolk sat on their backsides feeling sorry for themselves. Why, even thi mother, at her age, is doing her bit towards the war effort.'

'I've enough to do at home with six children.'

'Enough to do? Thar doing nowt so far as I can

see. Letting the lads wander off without knowing where they are. No, lass, I'll not listen to any of thi excuses. It's time tha showed willing.'

Bessie stood open-mouthed, eyes streaming from the onions. Never before had she heard Grandad Stanford raise his voice to anyone. Lizzie suddenly burst into tears again, deep, heart-rending sobs escaping her.

'Now look what you've done,' Emily snapped.

'Aye, I know. Exactly what I set out to do,' Isaac said. 'She's been wrapped up in hersen too long. I'll bet she's never let open the floodgates since the day George left. She'll come round now it's all let out.' He looked at his granddaughter. 'Put on thi coat, Bessie love, and go out to play.'

'I'll just put the taties and onions in the oven first.'

'Right, then thi mother'll see to 'em when we get back. Here, take yer spending money. Don't tell the others, but I've given thee a bit extra this week. I reckon tha's earned it.'

Bessie's eyes shone as she pocketed the money and hurried into her coat. Grandad Stanford placed piles of pennies on the dresser. He never failed to give them all a bit to spend, even the grandchildren who were working. Mostly it would go towards an evening at the pictures, or in Joseph's case into his motor bike fund. The evacuees were treated in exactly the same manner. Isaac realised the pair had brightened up Alice's life and reckoned they were worth the few coppers he doled out on Saturday mornings. Emily's thoughts were travelling on the same lines, except that she couldn't help comparing

Alice's exuberance to Lizzie's dejection. No one would have believed that over the years her daughters could have changed personalities so completely. Emily cursed the war that had robbed Lizzie of the husband she so idolised, then cursed herself for giving in to the fear that George Crossman was never to return. If she herself had lost faith no wonder Lizzie was at such a low ebb.

'Come on, lass.' Isaac's words broke into her thoughts. 'Comb thi hair and take off thi apron. If George comes marching up the road, we don't want him marching back down again at the sight of thee.' He handed Lizzie a comb and gently wiped the tears from his daughter's cheeks. She was still sobbing deep inside when he led her through the door, which Emily locked behind them, dropping the large, heavy key on its string through the letter box, in wait for the first one home.

The first one home was Jimmy, who was amazed but delighted to find the house deserted. Not that his mother would question him about his whereabouts, but their Bessie was a nosy parker and would probably notice how uncomfortable he seemed. He warmed his hands in front of the fire until he developed hot aches and had to shake them until the pain disappeared. Then he noticed the piles of pennies and cheered up as he considered what to spend Grandad Stanford's money on this week. He decided not to go to Miss Fiddler's today. If someone had been killed on the double decker he would rather keep away from the area near the bus terminus. Besides, he would be having his usual bag of Jap Desserts from

Grandad Crossman later, and somehow he didn't feel much like eating this morning.

Two days later a small article in the local paper reported an incident which had taken place on the previous Saturday on the Sheffield to Cottenly bus. It was only by a stroke of luck that the windows had been protected. Otherwise, with a bus full of Saturday morning passengers, someone was bound to have been seriously injured. As it was, only two people had suffered slight lacerations. The police were appealing for any witnesses to come forward. Jack read out the report to Ruth at the breakfast table. 'Probably loose rocks,' he said. 'Or the ghost chucking them down,' he added laughingly. Ruth laughed with him, but she couldn't quite dismiss Jimmy's scared, white face from her mind. She hoped it didn't mean extra worry for Lizzie. She doubted her sister could cope with much more.

On the following Monday the postwoman came to Lizzie Crossman's with the news that George was coming home. He was on his way to the Wharncliffe Emergency Hospital, one of two hundred sick and injured men to return from the front. The news brought Lizzie leaping from the pit of despair. The following day she caught the train to Sheffield and offered her services at the Victoria Station canteen which had been set up for the forces. She might not have been told the extent of George's injuries, but he was alive, when she had believed him dead. Her beloved George was coming home.

Both Warrentickle and Cottenly chapels were

filled to capacity on the following Sunday, as both the Crossmans and the Stanfords gave thanks for George's return. Jimmy decided to attend the service at Warrentickle, knowing that Sergeant Reynolds was bound to be amongst the congregation at Cottenly. Brian, who had no option but to attend with Auntie Alice, felt quite sick after being forced to stare at the back of the frightening man throughout the service, so sick that he had to stay home from school on the following day. Alice was glad of the excuse to spend the day mollycoddling him, much to Brian's disgust and Jennifer's envy.

Because of the excitement at the news of George's return, only Ruth noticed her nephew's absence from chapel and afterwards the change in Jimmy's behaviour, and as it seemed to have quietened him down somewhat she decided that whatever had happened it could only have been for the best. At least the little lad would soon have his father back, even if he wasn't the same healthy man who had gone away. Ruth said a special prayer as she looked around her at the congregation, a prayer that the end would come soon to the war which was robbing children of fathers and mothers of sons. She looked at Olive, parted from a young man she loved, uncertain if he would ever return. She prayed that the fighting would end before Harry and Joseph and her own Billy were old enough to join the evil wickedness of war. The Luftwaffe had blitzed Coventry only a few nights before. Ruth frowned and wondered where they would strike next. She reached out her hand and twined her fingers round those of her husband and thanked God that as a farmer he was safe. She opened her hymn book and joined the others in singing 'There is a happy land, far far away', and found her eyes brimming with tears so that the words formed a blur on the page and she wondered about a God who could allow men to begin wars, and innocent children to be slaughtered. Then she prayed to that same God for forgiveness.

Jimmy and his grandfather were enthralled by the music. The boy had been bored by some of it but the Hallelujah Chorus was another thing altogether. He found his foot tapping to the beat and couldn't help joining in with the choir's enthusiastic 'Hallelujah, hallelujah'. Grandfather Crossman's face was flushed with pleasure and pride that at least one of George's brood had inherited his appreciation of music, not only the music hall stuff, but real music. Then the atmosphere was suddenly shattered as the long wail of the air-raid warning filled the hall. Jimmy glanced round him with excitement. Coming into Sheffield at night was in itself an adventure, but an air raid on top of it, wow. The choir faltered slightly, but the conductor carried on to the end. Although tonight was just a rehearsal for the proper concert on Sunday, he was determined to finish and see how the performance went down with the invited audience. It was probably a false alarm anyway and there was no sense in causing a panic. Eventually, after much bowing and applauding, the hall slowly emptied.

'Can we still go for our pie and peas?' Jimmy

enquired, obviously expecting the promised treat to have been cancelled. Not wanting to let down his grandson by getting the first bus home, the old man looked around him. Nobody seemed to be in a hurry to clear the streets and it would probably turn out to be a non-event anyway.

'As long as we don't linger too long,' he said, 'I don't see why not.' He glanced at his gold retirement watch. 'Plenty of time before the last bus.' Then he led the lad, skipping beside him, to the pie and pea stall down by the market.

Unfortunately for the pair, they never boarded the last bus. Instead, they were caught up in what was to be the first and worst raid on Sheffield throughout the whole war. The bus station was in chaos, with buses either diverted or at a standstill. Trams were still running, intent upon getting as many people home as possible just in case this time turned out to be the real thing. As far as Walter Crossman could make out he had two choices: take to the shelter – as most people seemed to be doing after the second alert had sounded – or board a tram to the outskirts of the city and cover the last several miles on foot. He chose the latter, cramming into the crowded vehicle and standing the whole way until they reached the end of the line.

'Looks like the blighters are here at last,' the conductor called as the sound of planes droned overhead. 'Come on, you lot, shift yerselves. Let's get the next lot home.' Only a handful of passengers boarded the tram as the man made his way to the other end of the vehicle. By this time the bombing had begun and flames could already be seen rising above the city to the south. 'Daft lot. You'd be better off in the shelters if you ask me.'

'I'm going to work.' A young woman in a nurse's uniform glared at the man, who looked shamefaced.

'Aye, lass, so I notice now I've opened me peep-holes.' He waved away her proffered fare and gave her a ticket. 'Looks like yer'll be needed before the night's out.'

Jimmy set off by his grandfather's side, turning frequently to view the glow, orange against the darkness of the sky. 'It's a long way, Grandad, for you with a bad leg I mean.' The old man grinned and thought about the miles he'd tramped during his working life, out to the pit and then back again underground, almost bent double through waterlogged seams before reaching the required work place. An upright walk on dry ground would be a doddle, even with a rheumaticky leg.

'Don't worrit about me, lad,' he said. 'Worrit about the poor souls back there. Let's hope it's not a repetition of Coventry.'

Jimmy turned for another look, and at the same moment the drone of a plane drew his eyes upwards. Suddenly his grandfather grabbed him by the waist and pushed him across the footpath and down flat beneath the hedge overhanging the wall. 'Keep down.' He covered the boy with his body as the stray bomber shed its load, not on its obvious target of the industrial part of the city, but out here where nothing except stone houses and shops lined the main road. The plane had

311

gone, heading on towards the deep, red sky over the centre. The two figures untangled themselves and looked about them. The explosion happened just as Jimmy finished brushing the mud from his best Sunday trousers.

'Eeh, lad, some poor devil's copped it.' But Jimmy had already jumped the hedge and was running in the direction of the blast. Falling and tumbling, he descended the bank to where the flames and smoke rose thickly into the night. He stumbled over something – a kitchen chair – and now he could see the house, a small one, more like a cottage. The door had gone, disappeared with the blast, and the heat sent another window shattering towards him. Then he heard the scream, and the cry of a baby, or an animal. Jimmy could hear his grandfather calling him to come back. The old man, unsure of his feet in the darkness, had made his way the long way, along the path to the gate, and down the field.

Jimmy went towards the doorway, but the heat forced him back, singeing his fringe of hair. He ran round the building, stepping in a saucepan in his hurry, twisting his foot out of it and rushing to the back of the house. There was no door here. He went to the window, relieved to see the rooms on this side were in darkness. Still holding the heavy iron saucepan, he used it to break the glass pane and climbed in. The heat met him, even through the thickness of the inner stone wall. Fumbling in the dark he made his way to the door, frightened of what he would be met with when he opened it. Suddenly he remembered Olive's reading book, the one he had seen her studying from the first-aid class. He felt around on the floor and found a rag rug. Wrapping it round him, he covered as much of his body as he was able and pushed open the door.

Nothing but smoke met his eyes and he realised he was in a narrow passageway. He felt the heat through a second door and was just about to open it when the sound of screams filled his ears, coming from the other end of the passage. He ran blindly towards the cries, which led him onwards and up the stairs. On the landing he was faced with a wall of rubble and from behind it the screaming continued. Jimmy grappled with his hands, digging, shifting plaster and roof tiles. He tugged at a heavy beam of wood and heaved it down the staircase. Eventually, after what seemed an age he managed to make a way through the rubble and break into the room.

The woman crouching against the wall looked like a corpse in the darkness, her eyes staring and her screams so hideous that the baby in her arms was crying mainly from fear of its mother. Jimmy took the baby from her and heaved the woman to her feet. He pulled her roughly out of the bedroom, just as the flames burst through the downstairs door. 'Look sharp,' he said and pushed her towards the stairs. The smoke billowed upwards and filled their lungs. Jimmy found the rug amongst the rubble and covered the baby, still pushing the terrified woman, so that she fell halfway down the stairs, where she sat, fearful of entering the flames and agonised by pain from the leg trapped beneath her.

'Go on,' Jimmy shouted. 'Run through the

back.' But the woman sat trance-like, blocking the stairs. 'Bloody 'ell,' Jimmy cursed, and ran up towards the room they had just vacated. He could hear the sound of a fire engine somewhere. He went to the window, twisted the latch and heaved at the sash, managing to slide it upwards. He could see nobody. Where were they all? He called out, 'Help! Round the back.' Then, at last, somebody was coming, then the sound of footsteps was drowned as the woman started to scream again. Bloody stupid woman. Why wouldn't she move? He knew she had left it too late to go downwards but she couldn't stay there. Jimmy saw his grandfather now, his face ashen beneath the window.

'I'm going to drop the baby,' he called. 'You'll have to catch it.' He looked down; it wasn't too far. He wrapped the child tightly in the rag rug and leaned as far as he dared before dropping it gently from his arms.

'I've got it.' He heard the well-loved voice. 'Jimmy, there's help on the way. Stop where you are.' But Jimmy was gone, back to the woman. By now the wooden laths, the staircase and even the ceiling beams were alight. Jimmy dragged the woman to her feet, by the hair and her under-arms, any way he could to heave her back up the stairs. He beat out the flames from the hem of her nightie with his bare hands and dragged her into the room, managing to close the warped door as far as it would go. He pulled her feet first across the floor, wondering if she were dead.

Jimmy vaguely noticed the ladder and the face of the fireman at the open window before the smoke made breathing no longer possible and he sank into unconsciousness.

Lizzie looked at the clock. Jimmy should have been home hours ago and she had spent the last few hours pacing the house and mashing endless cups of tea. She had sent Harry to Warrentickle, in case his brother had decided to stay the night with his grandparents. Her panic had increased when Olive had announced on her arrival home that the fires in the city could be seen from the top of Queen Victoria Street. Bessie, in her usual blustery manner, had almost allayed her mother's fears – but not quite. 'It's just like our Jimmy to stay out and not let us know. I'll bet he's at Grandma Crossman's. It's a wonder he doesn't pack up and move in there altogether.'

Lizzie considered the possibility but then dismissed it. 'No, your grandma wouldn't keep him without letting us know. Something's happened, I know it has.' By this time the whole household was awake and gathered round the table. Olive, calm as ever, simply thought they had missed the last bus and set off walking. 'The bus has probably stopped running, what with the air raid,' she said. 'You go to bed, Mam, I'll wait up. Knowing our Jimmy, he'll have persuaded Grandad to loiter about, simply to watch the excitement.'

'Excitement!' Lizzie looked aghast at her daughter. 'How could anyone get excited about something as awful as war?'

'Our Jimmy could. Oh, come on, Mam, he's only a child. A high-spirited one, I admit, but still a child.'

'High-spirited! He's a little bugger.' Bessie let the word slip out without realising it.

'Bessie, what did you say?' Lizzie wondered what was happening to her family. Oh, she wouldn't half be glad when George came home.

'Sorry.' Bessie poured her mother a cup of tea. 'But he is, Mam, you know he is.'

Lizzie took a sip of the warm, stewed tea. 'Yes, well, don't let me hear that word in our house, ever again. Do you all hear?'

Young Ernest giggled and Lizzie glared. 'I know lots of swear words,' he said.

'Do you all hear?' Lizzie raised her voice.

'Yes, Mam.' They all knew when they had gone far enough, including Ernest Edward, who wasn't at all concerned about his brother. Jimmy could look after himself. He wished he dared do half the things his brother did. Not that he'd have wanted to sit through some boring old concert.

Mary was fast asleep on the couch. She had settled down quite happily, not thinking so much about Jimmy as about being allowed down every time there was an air raid. She didn't actually know what an air raid was, but it sounded exciting. The clock on the wall had just struck quarter past four when the knock came on the door. Olive ran to open it, praying it was Jimmy, or at least Harry, who hadn't yet returned from Warrentickle. She glanced from Grandad Crossman to the stranger accompanying him, her heart missing a beat as she realised her brother wasn't with them. 'Where's our Jimmy?'

'He's fine,' the firewatcher hastily reassured her. The two men followed Olive into the kitchen.

316

Walter Crossman looked round at the family, all white-faced and heavy-eyed, some from worry, others from sheer exhaustion at the effort of staying awake, rather than missing anything by going to bed.

Lizzie moved towards Walter. 'Where is he?'

'Now then, lass, don't start getting upset. Our lad's going to be fine in a day or two.'

The night's activities suddenly became too much for Lizzie and she began to sob. 'In a day or two? But where is he now? What's happened?'

'Oh, lass, don't take on so. I've told yer, he's fine, just a bit of smoke on his chest and burns on his hands, but nowt to worry about.'

'That's right, missus.' The firewatcher stood twisting his cap in his hands. 'The lad's going to be all right, and I'll tell you summat, missus, your lad's a hero, a right little hero. Saved a woman's life, he has, and her baby daughter's. Deserves a medal, your lad does. I should be right proud if he belonged to me.'

Lizzie sat down with a look of incredibility on her face. 'Who, our Jimmy?' Then she jumped up again. 'Suffering burns and smoke on his chest?' She hurried to the peg behind the door and lifted down her coat. 'Where is he? Take me to him.'

'Not now, lass. The lad'll be fast asleep by now, I shouldn't wonder, and as right as rain in the morning. We'll go first thing, don't you worry.' Walter led his daughter-in-law back to her chair.

'Is he in the infirmary?' Lizzie asked, still buttoning up her coat.

'No, Mrs Crossman, he's in the Salvation Army Citadel, but he's being nursed as well as in any

317

hospital. There's a doctor seeing to the injured. The infirmary's bursting at the seams, do yer see, what with the blitz. Nobody knows how many poor souls are still unaccounted for. Lost their homes and everything. Eeh, but the Jerries have a lot to answer for this night.'

Lizzie looked at her daughter. 'Make a fresh pot of tea, Olive, and pour one for your grandad and Mr, er, sorry, I don't know your name.'

'Turner. But I won't have any tea, thanks. I must get back. I ought not to be here, do yer see. But with Mr Crossman here so shocked I couldn't leave him to make his way home, not by himself, all that way. Thanks all the same.' He nodded to the door, 'If you're ready, I'll see yer back to Warrentickle. It won't take five minutes.'

'Aye, the wife'll be having a fit. I'll be grateful for the ride.' He sighed. 'Eeh, but it's been a long night. I hope I never see the likes of it again.' Lizzie opened the door. 'Goodnight then, lass. I'll be over in the morning, first thing.'

'Goodnight, Dad. Thanks for letting us know, and thank God you're all right. Thanks to you too, Mr Turner.'

The two men nodded and made their way across the pavement, and Lizzie closed the door to the sound of a motor bike being revved up. She clapped her hands. 'Come on, you lot, upstairs. School in the morning.' She took off her coat and gently covered Mary, tucking the knitted blanket round her. 'No point in waking her, she's fast on.' Then she turned out the gas and ushered her family upstairs.

'What a night,' Olive sighed. 'It's almost time to

get up again.'

'Have we got to go to school?' Ernest Edward moaned.

'Yes, you have.' Lizzie pushed her son playfully up the stairs by his bottom. 'And no arguments.'

'Fancy our Jimmy being a hero, though,' the little boy whispered. 'We ought to be given a holiday to go and see him, I think.'

'Well, you think wrong.' Lizzie laughed. 'Good-night, all.'

Long after the house was silent Bessie remained awake. She was proud of her brother and sorry he was hurt. But she was more content than she had been for ages, and the feeling was mainly caused by her mother. Tonight she had cried, and smiled, and been angry at the swear word. Her lovely mother was back to normal.

Ruth was on her way home from the doctor's. During her other pregnancies no doctor had been necessary; she had simply depended on Old Mother, knowing she would be present at her confinements. This time, however, she would need a midwife and would be expected to attend the clinic.

Doctor Swinbourne had been delighted. 'Yes, Mrs Dolan, there's a baby on the way, I'm happy to say. Just what Mr Dolan needs, a child of his own. I know for a fact what an excellent father he is.'

Ruth laughed. 'He would have to be, taking on my lot. But you're right, he's a marvellous dad to them all.'

'No more than you all deserve. He's been a

319

different man since he married you.'

'What's this?' Ruth scowled at the white piece of paper. 'I'm not ill. I don't need medicine.'

'Vitamins, that's all.'

'But I never had vitamins with the others, and I wasn't eating half as well as I am now.'

'No, but then you didn't come to me with the others.'

'I couldn't afford to when I was married to Walter.'

'But now you can. So you'll take the vitamins and you'll attend the clinic and I'll deliver you of a fine, healthy child. Let's see, round about midsummer's day I should think.'

Ruth thanked him and set off home, dubiously carrying the vitamin pills. Hubert Hancock watched her leave the main road and felt the familiar stirring in his groin. He watched the way her hips swayed as she hurried towards the edge of the wood. She had filled out since he last saw her, and her calves were more shapely. If it hadn't been for that Stedman woman being a friend of his wife he could have had her. That exquisite body could have been his. He couldn't understand how he had ever married a woman with such common friends. Hubert Hancock, member of the golf club and the bowling club, in fact almost every club in the district. Hubert Hancock, county councillor, in line for mayor if he made the appropriate donations and played his cards right. Hubert Hancock married to a woman who fraternised with the residents of Wire Mill Place. He spat on the pavement and turned to make his way home, his thoughts on Ruth Wray, as he still thought of her, and on the common farmer she had married. He was still picturing the pair of them together as he sat down to his dinner of soggy cabbage and dried up shepherd's pie. He took one mouthful and threw the rest, plate and all, into the fireplace. Sophie found the mess when she came home from her weekly visit to Wire Mill Place. Winnie and she were the best of friends these days. She cleared up the mess and wondered how much longer she could bear to live in the same house as that fat, repulsive pig.

The Thursday night's raid over Sheffield was followed by another on the Sunday. This time the east end bore the brunt of the bombing and though there were fewer fires on the whole, at least half a dozen air-raid wardens were killed when a parachute mine fell close to a warden's hut. More than a dozen steel works were damaged in the Sunday raid, but considering how many armament works were concentrated in the east end, damage to them was surprisingly light.

The steel works were not as seriously damaged as initially thought and production was soon back to normal. The city trams were a different matter, with tracks and overhead wiring needing to be replaced, and it was weeks before normal service would be resumed. However, any bus which could possibly run was immediately back in service and others were sent from as far afield as Hull, Leeds and even Newcastle, all to make up for the missing tram service. The residents of Cottenly fortunately escaped the attack but in the city itself nearly forty thousand people were left homeless.

Harry Crossman was in the thick of it all in the aftermath. As he pointed out to Grandad Stanford, organising repairs to the gas supplies was one of the main priorities and as water had got into the gas mains they all had to be pumped clear. In some places sewage and rubble had also to be cleared out of the pipes, and after that the pipes of course needed to be sterilised. Harry said all this was made more complicated by the telephone network's being out of order. Nevertheless, all repairs to the water supply were completed by the end of December. Harry seemed to thrive on the long hours he was required to work, but found time to call in and congratulate Jimmy the day after the young hero was injured. He found him propped up in bed looking rather pale, but although he was obviously in pain from the burns on his hands he was looking quite pleased with himself.

Harry perched himself on the bed. 'Well, what does it feel like being a lifesaver, then?' he asked, grinning at his brother.

Jimmy winced with pain. 'I did, didn't I? Save their lives, I mean.' He couldn't quite believe what he'd done yet. 'The man brought the baby to see me. She's lovely, and not a scratch on her either. He was at work on nights – the baby's dad, I mean. And the woman, she's going to be all right as well. He says she's got burns on her legs, and smoke on her chest and frizzled up hair and no eyebrows left, but she's OK.'

Harry couldn't help smiling. 'She doesn't sound OK to me, but if you say so.'

'The man said so. He said the baby would have died if I hadn't dropped her out and got her away from the smoke. He said the woman was too shocked to move. He said they'd both have died if it hadn't been for me.'

'No doubt they would. Anyway, we're all proud to have a hero in the family.'

Jimmy grinned. 'Really? Proud of me?'

'Yes you. Who else?'

Jimmy settled comfortably against the pillows. 'And I shan't have to go back to school, shall I?'

'Not until your hands are better. Well, there wouldn't be much point, would there? It'll be after Christmas I should think.'

'Will Dad be home by then? Do you think he'll be proud of me as well?'

Harry frowned. 'Well, I don't know if he'll be home in time for Christmas, but he should be at the hospital.' He noticed Jimmy's face cloud over. 'He'll certainly be proud of you, though. Just like we all are. In fact I shouldn't be surprised if he doesn't get better much quicker when he hears the news.' Jimmy's face lit up. 'Look, I'll have to go now. I'll pop in again.'

'I can come home tomorrow, the nurse said so.'

'Well, that's OK then. See you tomorrow.'

Jimmy couldn't believe how different his mother looked when she too visited him the day after the fire. Not only was her hair looking pretty but she was wearing lipstick.

Working at the canteen had made a new woman of Lizzie. The women were a grand lot and the work was satisfying, even though she couldn't help wondering what would happen when the school broke up for the holiday. The children, especially little Mary and Ernest Edward, were too small to be left with Bessie for long. However, Emily was so pleased at Lizzie's recovery from her bout of depression that she had volunteered to mind them for as long as was needed, but now there was the added difficulty of Jimmy's injuries. Grandma Crossman didn't see any problem and said Jimmy could stay with them for a while. Lizzie, however, back to her normal, motherly self, knew she would suffer guilt at the neglect of her son. She grinned widely as she approached the bed and Jimmy's face coloured deeply as she kissed him. He glanced round, hoping nobody had noticed, but was really quite pleased. He couldn't remember anyone kissing him before, except Jennifer Smith, the evacuee. She was forever following him around and Brian said she was telling everyone she was going to marry him when she grew up. Jimmy said she had another think coming, he would never marry anybody, he would be too busy supplying music for special occasions.

Lizzie gave her son a bar of chocolate. It had been hidden on top of the wardrobe in readiness for Christmas, but she considered this to be a far more important occasion. 'Here you are, son. Don't eat it all at once or you'll make yourself sick, and then they'll never let you come home.'

'Cor! Mam, where did you get this?'

'Ask no questions and get no lies. Just one thing, don't tell the others. It's a kind of a reward for being so brave.' Jimmy beamed. He had never been singled out before. Lizzie looked concerned at the thick dressings on her son's hands. 'Do they pain you a lot, love?'

Jimmy shrugged. 'I suppose so, but I'm not bothered.' It was worth it not to have to go to school. 'Besides, I saved a baby's life, and the woman's too, the ambulance man said. He said she was nearly not breathing, I heard him. But the baby didn't get hurt at all, thanks to Grandad Crossman. It was him who caught her.'

'But it was you who saved them and I'm so proud of you I could cry. Wait till your father hears about it.'

Jimmy grinned and tried to unwrap the bar of Bournville. 'Bloody 'ell,' he said, 'I can't even open my own chocolate. And what do you think? I had to ask the nurse if she'd help me to pee. I've never been so embarrassed in all my life.'

Lizzie frowned. 'We'll have less of the language. Just because you're a hero it doesn't give you the right to swear.' But Jimmy noticed she was trying not to smile. She broke off two squares of chocolate and popped them into his mouth, the smile getting the better of her.

'Well, I'm glad I'm not a nurse if that's the sort of thing they have to do.'

'What?'

She grinned. 'Having to help people to wee.' She wondered how Jimmy would cope once he got home.

Jimmy blushed. 'It's all right you laughing, but what about when I need to go to the lav properly? Who's going to wipe my bottom?'

Lizzie looked at her son's crestfallen face and it was just too much for her. She burst into laughter.

Jimmy's face slipped and suddenly they were both laughing so much the tears were rolling down Jimmy's face. 'Oh, love!' Lizzie managed. 'I don't know. Just one thing.'

'What?'

'Just, I hope you don't have prunes for dinner or somebody'll be in for a rough task.' She moved closer to her son and took him in her arms, hugging him tight. And Jimmy Crossman, for the first time in his life, felt loved, important and special.

Chapter Ten

The toys were piled up in the clothes closet at Alice's. Joe said to be careful not to spoil Brian and Jennifer. He also said she must remember they were someone else's children and not theirs. He worried at times about how Alice would cope when the war was over and the pair returned to London, but Alice seemed to ignore the fact that it would ever happen, especially as the children's mother didn't seem interested enough to even bother writing.

Joe had made a doll's house for Jennifer and a garage for Brian. A set of furniture for each of the four rooms had been added to the wooden house, which had been covered in red brick effect paper. A pair of petrol pumps and a set of toy cars had completed the garage. There were also fur gloves, a doll, and a white leather hymn and prayer book for the little girl, and a fort, jigsaw and set of soldiers for Brian. Joseph was still saving for a motor bike – much to Alice's consternation – and was hoping for money. Nevertheless, Alice had bought books, clothes and various other surprises for her son, aiming to make this one of the best Christmases ever. Joe was somewhat relieved that for the moment at least Alice's inability to produce another child was apparently forgotten. He was, however, concerned that Mrs Smith had not yet sent as much as a Christmas card for her children.

It was Christmas Eve when George arrived at the Wharncliffe. He seemed only half the man who had gone away and Lizzie had all on not to break down at the sight of his thin, haunted face and emaciated body. Instead she fixed a smile on her face and went towards the dear man, intending to throw her arms round him. She saw George stiffen and cringe as she came closer, and then he began to tremble. His whole body shook as though he was having a fit. Lizzie backed away in horror and called for a nurse.

'Shell shock,' the uniformed young woman whispered. 'Most of the new arrivals are suffering in the same way, worse in a way than the amputees. Still, time is on their side.'

Lizzie perched on the bed by the side of George's chair, not knowing what to say. 'The kids wanted to come,' she attempted, 'but I didn't know if you could put up with their chatter just yet. Besides, I sort of wanted you to myself, after all this time.' She touched his trembling hand gently. 'Oh, George, I've missed you so much,' she whispered.

He turned his head away and Lizzie saw a tear land on the arm of the chair, then another, as George began to sob. His whole body shook, but at least the tremor had ceased. The pretty little nurse came back from the desk in the middle of the room, smiling at Lizzie. 'Good,' she said. 'That's what he needed, a good cry.' Lizzie tried to smile back but her throat was completely blocked and tears forced themselves out of her eyes and nose, and then she at last placed her arms round her husband and they cried together, until Lizzie's hair was limp and wet and for the first time since his arrival back in England George spoke.

'You're wet, Lizzie,' he said. 'I'm sorry.'

It was Isaac who accompanied Harry to the station. Lizzie, who was already there, had managed time off from the canteen to see her son on to the train. Her heart felt like clay but she knew she mustn't cry.

'Here, love,' she said, in a voice sounding strange and false, 'I've made you a cake. Ginger, your favourite.'

'Oh, Mam.' Harry took the brown paper parcel and with his other hand pulled Lizzie towards him, nestling her head into his overcoat. He found it difficult to swallow for the lump in his throat. 'Take care of Dad, won't you, and the kids.'

'I will. Your dad's much better already.'

'Yes.' They both knew there was very little improvement in George's condition. The train was already filling and doors were being slammed. 'I must get aboard,' Harry said. He heaved his bag up into the carriage and slid down the window so that he could lean out.

'Take care,' Lizzie called. 'Come home safe.' Isaac shook his grandson's hand, clinging hold as the tram set off with a chug. The whistle cut off his goodbye. Not that words were necessary: the love and respect the two men held for each other would carry them through the days ahead until Harry was back home again with his family. They waved until the train rounded the curve and only the spiral of smoke could be seen. Then Lizzie and her father made their way to the station exit amongst other families heavy-hearted at the departure of sons, fathers and husbands leaving Sheffield to fight for their country.

'Please, God,' Lizzie prayed, 'keep my boy safe.' Isaac knew that not even prayer would give protection against the ravages of war. He had been there himself, and would willingly have taken the place of his grandson this time if it had been possible. All the same there was no prouder man in Sheffield, indeed the whole of Britain, than Isaac Stanford.

'It was the bestest Christmas I ever had,' Jennifer told Alice as she arranged furniture in the doll's house.

'I'm glad.' Alice smiled. She sharpened a pencil in readiness to begin on the accounts book for the collections in connection with the war effort.

'We never had a Christmas tree in London,' Brian remarked.

'And no holly eiver,' Jennifer added.

'Well, I don't suppose there were any holly trees in the East End,' Alice said. 'I expect that was why.'

'No, it wasn't. Our mam never bovered wiv Christmas.'

'But our dad always bought us a present.' Brian tried to be fair.

'But Father Christmas never came to our house, not ever.'

Alice decided to change the subject. 'Would you like to go to the pantomime?'

'What's a pantomime?'

'It's a kind of play, based on a fairy story. This year it's *Cinderella*.'

'Is it at the chapel?' Brian asked. Most of Auntie Alice's activities were in the chapel.

'Yes,' Alice answered, 'but it's nothing to do with Sunday school. It's only taking place in the chapel hall. All the money will go towards the war effort fund.' She smiled as she totted up the column of figures. The amount was increasing steadily week by week.

'Will Uncle Joe be going to the pantomime?' Jennifer enquired.

'I expect so. Why?'

'Because our mam never wanted our dad to go anywhere wiv us.'

'That was because our mam never took us anywhere anyway.'

Poor little mites. Alice couldn't bear the thought of them going back to parents who didn't seem to care about them at all. She wondered if the lack of love could be classed as cruelty. Perhaps if she reported the Smiths she would be allowed to keep the children, adopt them eventually. But even as the thought entered her head she knew the idea was ridiculous. All she could do was make them happy and enjoy them whilst she had the chance.

'Right, then, let's have the toys put away, then it's time for bed. I'll put the milk on for the cocoa.'

'Can we have biscuits as well?'

'And a story?'

'Depends on how long it takes to tidy up.' Alice was rapidly learning the subtle art of bribery. By the time cocoa was made the toys were cleared away and the kids upstairs undressing. This was the time Alice enjoyed best of all. The bedtime story, the kisses and cuddles and the two ginger heads against the whiteness of the pillows. Sometimes she worried about whether it was Joseph who had not cared about cuddling, or she who had been restrained in her showing him affection. Somehow he had seemed more independent than these two little ones. She consoled herself by telling herself that the reason was that Joseph had been sure of her love, whereas the evacuees didn't seem to have had any. She supervised the saying of prayers, adding a silent one of her own that God would let them stay. Alice had long since ceased to pray for another child of her own. The evacuees were the next best thing.

Jimmy Crossman received a letter, an official-looking one with a picture of the town hall on the envelope, and on the letter itself. It was beautifully written in green ink. Jimmy had never had a letter before, except for school reports, and they weren't actually his but were addressed to his father or mother. This was addressed to Master James Crossman. He flattened it out on the table, and read:

Dear Master James Crossman, I reported your brave deed at our meeting the other night. I am writing on behalf of the Committee to thank you for your successful effort in rescuing a woman and baby from a blazing house. I know it must have given you enormous pleasure to perform this heroic deed.

It is also heartening to know that your parents encourage you to be a kind and courageous citizen.

I sincerely hope you will not grow up to see another war but that you will remember this heroic act. There is no kinder work than helping those less fortunate than ourselves.

I trust your injuries are now healed and that you may enjoy a happy, healthy and pleasant life and that you may live in peace.

Kindly accept our many thanks.
Yours most respectfully,
Councillor RS Knowles

Jimmy read the letter at least three times before giving it to his mother. Lizzie read the words through a wall of tears, whilst Jimmy, silent for once, just stood there.

'Oh, Jimmy,' Lizzie sobbed, 'I'm so proud of you, love. I want to run out in the street and show it to everyone.'

'Oh, it weren't owt,' Jimmy mumbled. 'It were me grandad who caught the baby.' But Lizzie noticed his face had reddened and his eyes were sparkling with excitement. 'Can I go and show me grandad?' he said, grabbing his coat from the hook behind the door.

'Don't you think you ought to show it to your father first?'

Jimmy's excitement seemed to diminish as he mumbled, 'You won't let us, though. You won't take us to see me dad and I want to show somebody now.'

Lizzie smiled. 'I think the time has come to take you,' she said. 'Only one at a time, mind. But something as important as your letter must entitle you to a visit. Only if you're quiet, though,' she added.

Jimmy's face was a picture. 'I won't say anything, not even one word,' he promised. 'I'll just show him my letter.'

So the visit was arranged for the following Saturday, with special permission from the hospital matron.

George was gazing into space when Lizzie and Jimmy entered the ward, one of a number of long, low buildings set in the grounds of the mental hospital. Lizzie was glad of Jimmy's company. She always felt uneasy coming up the long, gloomy drive on her own. George wasn't sure at first which of his children it was. Then, as they approached his chair, he recognised the impish grin, even though Jimmy was trying to curb his excitement and appear serious, as he thought the occasion warranted.

'Jimmy! Lizzie, you didn't tell me I was having an extra visitor.' For a fleeting moment Lizzie thought George was about to smile, but the tension was visible again almost immediately.

'Hello, Dad,' Jimmy said, and then all his good intentions were thrown aside as his normal spontaneousness rose to the fore. 'I've come to show you my letter. Mam said I could if I were quiet. When are yer coming home, Dad? You won't have to go back in the rotten army, will yer? We don't like it without a dad. My mam's been all miserable and our Bessie's had to do all the work and Grandad shouted at our mam and–'

'Jimmy!' Lizzie interrupted. 'You've forgotten your promise. And what about your letter? I'll bet your father can't wait to read it.'

George didn't look impatient to see anything, Jimmy thought, in fact he didn't look like his dad at all. Nevertheless, he handed over the precious envelope to George.

With trembling hands and Lizzie's help, George Crossman opened the folded sheet of paper. As he read, his shoulders seemed to lift and his back straighten and then Jimmy was horrified to see a tear roll down his cheek. Then, as though a veil had been lifted, George Crossman smiled and then began to laugh, which reminded Lizzie of the happy days before the war. Jimmy looked uncertainly at Lizzie and then they began to laugh too, and Lizzie took her son in her arms, hugging him close. Then George held out his arm to his son. 'Oh, Jimmy,' he managed through the laughter, 'this is the proudest day of my entire life.' He placed his good arm round his son, then reached out for his hand. 'You've proved yourself a man,' he said. 'So let me shake the hand of a man.' Then for the first time George realised how fortunate he was that his right arm had escaped injury; then he wondered if perhaps he might regain the use of his left arm, in time. Jimmy's lip trembled as he gulped down the lump in his throat. George read the letter again. 'Now,' he said, 'are you going to tell me exactly what happened, and what are those injuries mentioned in the letter? You never told me our Jimmy had hurt himself, Lizzie.'

'Oh, it wasn't owt, Dad, just burns on me

hands, that's all. That was because the woman wouldn't move, so I had to put out the flames on her nightgown. And I couldn't go to the lav on my own. Oh, it was so embarrassing.'

Lizzie and George tried hard to appear serious. 'I'm sure it must have been,' George sympathised. 'And what about the baby?'

'Oh, she's lovely. I had to drop her through the window and Grandad caught her and she wasn't hurt at all. Do yer think he'll have got a letter as well?'

'I don't know, son. I only know you did a very brave thing. Many a man would have panicked.'

'I didn't have time. To think about panicking, I mean.'

At that moment Matron came striding towards them, the dark navy uniform covered by an even darker cape. Jimmy didn't like the look of her and wondered if he had been making too much noise. Cowering at George's side he looked up at her frowning face and thought he had never seen anyone with a nose quite as big or as red. Or a bosom as big either, come to that. 'Time's up!' she snapped. 'Half an hour only.'

Lizzie kissed George tenderly and Jimmy didn't know whether to do the same. He had always thought it was sissy to kiss, but he thought his dad might like it so he went up to George and gave him a quick peck on the cheek, blushing furiously as he did so. 'Can I come again, Dad?'

'I hope so, that's if Matron will allow it.' George looked questioningly at the lurking woman. Matron hadn't failed to notice the change in her patient: a remarkable change, in her opinion. In fact for the first time George Crossman was smiling and his hands were relaxed upon the arms of his chair.

'I'll tell Sister I've given my permission,' she snapped. 'Only one child per visit to start with.'

Lizzie thanked her as they set off towards the door of the ward. They had reached the exit when Jimmy remembered. 'Here,' he cried, setting off back to George. 'I've forgotten my letter.' He folded it carefully and placed it safely in the pocket of his Sunday jacket. Then he marched proudly outside to where Lizzie stood, silently thanking God that at last George resembled his old self.

On 6 January Sheffield was given a huge boost in morale when the King and Queen turned up to view the devastation and talk to some of the air-raid victims. 'We shall get him down,' one woman told the King, referring to Hitler.

'Yes,' said the King, 'I believe we shall.'

Tom Baraclough was home on leave. Burlington Cottage was waiting for him, welcoming, warm and scented with lavender, amongst a host of other herbs, and the unmistakable smell of Mansion Polish. The furniture shone like ripe chestnuts, and a vase of dried grasses brightened the room. Olive had saved hard and had found some crêpe de Chine in her favourite green and Grandma Stanford had run her up a dress in no time at all. Her glossy dark hair was tied back with a ribbon of the same shade. The dress showed off her legs to perfection and Emily had had doubts as to whether she should have made it quite so short. The legs in question were coloured an attractive tan and Bessie had drawn a line up the back of each. Now all Olive had to do was apply her make-up, a cream she had concocted herself, and dab perfume behind her ears. She thought the time had come to give samples to the girls at work, but was nervous as to what their verdict would be. Anyway, it would be well tested by Tom's reaction. Grandma Burlington used to say that men's noses didn't work half as well as a woman's, but tonight she would see.

Olive locked the door of the cottage and went towards the cinema. She was to meet Tom at seven. Her heart palpitated as she thought about her decision as to what would happen later.

The perfume must be satisfactory, Olive thought. Tom's nose had nuzzled her neck all through the film, and being in a double seat she hadn't failed to notice how aroused he had become. It hadn't occurred to Olive that she was so desirable that Tom would have become aroused even if she'd smelled of fried onions. Not knowing what the film was about, and not being the slightest bit interested, Olive whispered halfway through the performance that she thought they should go. Tom was surprised but eagerly agreed, and, feeling guilty, Olive fumbled along the row, hoping nobody recognised her and guessed what she was up to.

'I thought we might go to the cottage.' Olive blushed and was glad of the darkness covering her embarrassment. 'We could have a drink.

There's a bottle of elderberry wine that Grandma Burlington made.'

Tom grinned in the darkness. 'Should we?' he asked. 'It must be mighty potent after all these years.'

'Why not?' Olive clutched his hand more tightly. 'After all, we might not get chance again for a long time.' Knowing she had said the wrong thing she tried to cover up. 'I mean, you might not get another leave for a few months.'

'No.' Tom hadn't wanted to tell Olive, not tonight anyway, but she was intelligent enough to know. 'I won't be home as often when I go back; in fact, I don't rightly know where I shall be this time next week.'

Olive unlocked the cottage door and drew down the blind at the tiny window, before putting a match to the gas mantle. She broddled the fire until it blazed, reflecting on the polished brasses in the hearth. She didn't refer to what he had just said. Instead she told him to take off his coat. Tom undid the brass buttons and took off his greatcoat. Olive came to take it but he let it fall on to the couch and pulled her towards him, gathering her close and covering her lips with his own. 'Oh, Olive,' he muttered between the kisses, 'you shouldn't have brought me here. You're too much of a temptation.' She felt him hard against her and a tingling ache began deep within her. He felt her nipples erect through his shirt and he began to undo the tiny pearl buttons down the front of her dress. Impatient, she began to help him and let the dress slide on to the pegged mat.

'Oh, God.' Tom's fingers caressed her breasts

through the satin bra and moved down to the French knickers, seeking and finding the moist softness beneath the silky triangle of dark hair. Probing, opening, until she could wait no longer and drew him down on to the brightly patterned rug. She struggled with his webbing belt, and Tom, too impatient to wait, undid the buttons on his trousers, freeing his pulsing erection.

Olive reached out, touching, feeling the warm hardness for the first time. 'I want you, Tom,' she whispered. Suddenly Tom drew away.

'We shouldn't be doing this, Olive. I love you.'

'Don't you want me?'

'Course I bloody want you, what do you think this is, Scotch mist?' Olive giggled, but Tom wasn't amused. 'Isn't this proof how much I want you? But I don't want you regretting it afterwards. You might meet someone else.'

Olive kissed him, pulled him towards her until he could no longer resist her. 'I want you, Tom, nobody else, and I never will. I won't regret tonight; I've waited too long already. I want you now.'

There was no going back. They were each lost in the other's body. Olive gasped when he entered her and then the pain turned to pleasure, a more wonderful, powerful pleasure than she could ever have imagined. Afterwards they cried and laughed and fell asleep, still entangled together.

It was almost light when they left the cottage and went home, Olive to sneak in, remembering to stride over the fourth step on the stairs, the creaking one. Love was making her devious, but she didn't care.

Jenny and Brian were ready, dressed in their best clothes for the visit to the pantomime. Brian had asked for the fourth time how long they were going to be before leaving, and Jennifer had had her ribbon tied at least three times because her fine, silky hair kept slipping out. Alice was at last putting on her hat when the knock came on the door.

'See who that is,' Alice said.

Jenny ran to the door. 'I bet it's Mary. She said she'd call for me.'

'Well, who is it?' Alice called, but there was no reply. She went to the door, curious to see who could be visiting and standing on the step.

Jennifer's face was pale, and she clung to Alice's skirt. 'It's my mam.'

The woman stood with arms folded across her faded coat. Her hair was hidden by a turban and her thin face daubed with rouge and bright red lipstick. She held a cigarette between her fingers and a crocodile skin handbag over her arm.

'I've come for my kids,' she said. 'I'm grateful for yer having 'em, but now I want 'em back.'

Alice gasped. 'Won't you come in, Mrs Smith? I'll make some tea.'

'Aye, I could do with a cuppa. I've come a long way.' She stared round the room, saw the piano they'd made so much of. Then she looked at her children. 'Well, you've grown, I'll say that for you.'

Alice wondered how a mother could act so rationally after being parted for so long from her children. Why didn't she hug them, kiss them?

Then she realised with a shock that she would have acted exactly the same in the old days. She began to shake, feeling her heart thudding and the blood pounding in her head. She was filled with panic as she realised the woman had come to take her children away.

Jenny and Brian were sitting as far away from the table as possible, silently watching their mother sip the tea that Auntie Alice had poured into the pretty, rose-patterned cups. Jenny thought of the thick, chipped, brown-stained mugs she would be drinking out of tomorrow if they were taken back to London.

'...so yer see, I thought if Sheffield is being bombed they might as well be back wiv me. After all, there's no place like yer own home, is there?' Doris Smith's eyes were everywhere. 'Must say it's a nice place you've got, though. 'Fraid my house isn't as posh as yours.'

Alice's hand trembled as she picked up her cup and the tea spilled into the saucer. She wished Joe was here to make the conversation she found herself incapable of. 'We're quite safe here,' she managed. 'No problem at all here in Cottenly.'

'We haven't seen any bombs at all,' Brian said, 'not even one.'

'That's good,' his mother said. 'But yer see I miss yer both. Now yer dad's gone overseas I want yer at home with me.'

'But they're so happy here,' Alice burst out.

'Aye, yes, but that's the trouble, yer see. They're too happy. I could tell from the letters. I said to my friend, I said that woman is taking over my kids, I said. They'll not want to come home at all if they stay any longer. Her wiv the posh pianner lessons and fancy house. I'm their muvver, I said to my friend. So if you'll just pack up their fings we'll be on our way. Don't fink I'm not grateful cos I am, but I fought my kids have been away long enough.'

Doris Smith stood up and Alice thought her stomach was about to turn a somersault. 'Please wait, at least until my husband comes home.'

'I want to see Uncle Joe.' Jenny began to cry and ran to cling on to Alice's dress.

'Sorry, we've waited long enough. Uncle Frank'll be leaving us. It was good of him to bring me all this way in his car.'

'We haven't got an Uncle Frank,' Brian muttered.

Doris Smith pursed her lips in annoyance. 'Yes you have,' she said. 'And you should be grateful for the lift. Especially wiv petrol so scarce.'

'I don't want a lift. I want to stay here.' Jenny was sobbing uncontrollably by this time. 'I want Uncle Joe and Joseph.'

Doris Smith grabbed hold of Brian's hand and glared at Alice. 'Are yer going to get their belongings or not?' she asked. Alice tore away from Jennifer's hold and made for the stairs. Jenny began to scream.

'I don't want to go home if my dad isn't there. Who'll look after us when you go out? Auntie Alice never leaves us on our own.'

Alice could hear the exchange as she found the battered case and opened the closet where Jennifer's little dresses hung on satin-covered hangers. She opened drawers and almost collapsed as she

343

took out the lovingly ironed pants and vests and socks. Then she did the same with Brian's things. She found a holdall and filled it with toys, books, models and soft toys accumulated over the weeks. Oh, God! Why wasn't Joe here? Then she realised Joe could do nothing. The woman was simply reclaiming her children. She brought the bags downstairs and collected the warm, new coats from behind the door. She forced Jennifer's reluctant arms into the sleeves and buttoned the coat, her eyes unseeing and swimming with tears. Don't cry, you mustn't cry, she told herself. Don't upset them any more than they are now. Then they were being pushed out of the room and into the cold, dark night.

'What about the pantomime? Mary'll be coming soon.' Jennifer's eyes were appealing to Alice to be rescued. Brian carried the case, dragging it along behind him. He never once looked back. He knew if he did, his little heart would break in two.

The car doors slammed behind them and they were gone.

As Emily hurried down St George's Road she wondered what was happening to her world. There was Harry giving up his perfectly useful job and going off to fight in God knows where, George coming home with all the fight knocked out of him and Jimmy still scarred from his burns. Now, on top of it all, Joe had sent a message with Joseph to say that Alice was ill. She hoped it might be that Alice was pregnant at last. They had all prayed that the operation would help but the prayers didn't seem to have done any good. Oh, well, Alice should be thankful for a strong, healthy son like Joseph. Many a woman would be grateful for even one child.

Alice was on the bed staring at the ceiling. Joseph had explained what had happened. 'She just turned up and took them,' he had said. Emily had expected something like this. She had warned Alice not to become too involved, but Alice hadn't seemed to realise the little ones were only here temporarily. It was all due to Alice's upbringing, and Emily's heart was heavy as she acknowledged the part she had played in the past. Oh, everyone thought Alice had done well out of being the old lady's companion, what with all the money in the bank. Now she had a fine house and a loving, attentive husband. Only Emily seemed to understand that nothing could compensate for a lost childhood, a childhood Alice was trying to make up for now through other children. She had had Joseph for a while, but Joseph was an independent lad, just like his father, not the type to be mollycoddled. Besides, Alice had been newly wed when Joseph came along; she had had Joe on whom to lavish the affection she had been unable to give or receive whilst living with Grandmother Stanford. Now that the evacuees had gone Alice was bereft. If Emily had been the type of woman to curse and swear now was the time she would have let fly, at herself for agreeing to Isaac's suggestion and letting Alice go to the miserable old woman who had scarred her so deeply. Emily sat on the bed beside her eldest daughter, who was still beautiful despite the dark smudges beneath her eyes, and the taut tenseness of her mouth.

'Alice! Come on, lass, let's get you up and undressed. You can't sleep in that lovely dress, it'll be spoiled.'

Alice turned towards her mother. 'They've gone. She came and took them away. She was awful, not fit to be a mother.'

'But she is their mother. Nothing can change that. You knew they would go home one day.'

'But not yet. What about the bombs? And she doesn't look after them. Brian said she would leave them on their own, I heard him. I can't bear it, Mam.'

Emily took her daughter in her arms. Alice rarely called her Mam these days. 'Alice, there's nothing you can do. Anyway, if she's the sort of woman you think she is, she'll probably send them back again. Maybe it was just spite and jealousy that made her take them home. Come on, love, you must get on with your life, for our Joseph's sake. He's not much more than a child himself. He needs you.'

'Who, our Joseph?' Alice smiled, but it was a cold, cynical smile. 'He doesn't need me, or anyone.'

'Of course he does. Oh, I'll admit he's an independent lad, which is a good thing what with the war and everything, but he still needs your love and affection. So does Joe. I dare say they've been feeling a bit left out since Jenny and Brian came on the scene.' Alice let out a long, keening cry at the mention of the children, which was what Emily had intended. 'That's right, let it all

346

out. No use bottling it up. It's not as if they're dead – they've gone home a damn sight healthier than when they came. So have a good cry and then we'll get you in your dressing gown and see about some supper.'

Alice tried to swallow the soup Emily had warmed but it wouldn't go down. She put down her spoon. 'I can't,' she said. Emily held another spoonful to her daughter's lips. Alice took a sip but her throat seemed to be constricted, and she shook her head. Emily sighed.

'Oh, Alice, please don't go to pieces. You saw what our Lizzie was like.'

Alice didn't answer. She felt as though a vice was tightening across her chest as she fought for breath. Her pulse was pounding in her ears. She prayed to the God she worshipped so faithfully but He didn't answer and she saw the floor rising up to meet her as she fainted at her mother's feet.

It was Joseph who lifted his mother into bed and tucked the eiderdown snugly round her. It was Joseph who telephoned for Dr Swinbourne. It was Joseph whose eyes filled with tears at the state of the mum he loved so much. He did all that needed to be done because his father seemed to be in shock, but Alice was oblivious of it all, of everything except the picture of Grandfather Stanford laid to rest in his coffin, and the voice of her grandmother quoting the scriptures to the little girl Alice had once again become, deep in her subconscious mind.

Jennifer Smith couldn't eat either. She couldn't remember the food being so bad before she went away, but that was because she had been spoiled by Auntie Alice's cooking. 'I don't like these chips,' she said. 'They're all greasy.'

'Well you'll just 'ave to go wivout then,' her mother said.

'Eat them up, Jenny.' Her brother forced the soggy mess into his mouth and wondered how they would bear it back in this place. The table was covered in newspapers instead of a cloth and the house smelled of all kinds of horrible things. Brian realised that it had only been his dad who had done any cleaning in the house and now he had gone the place was disgusting. Uncle Frank seemed to have taken his dad's place and Brian resented the man, hating his mother more with every passing day. He had written a letter to Auntie Alice but had no money to buy a stamp, so it remained under the mattress he and Jenny slept on every night whilst his mother and Uncle Frank went to the public house on the corner. It was a yellow-stained, filthy mattress and he knew his mother would never find the letter as she never cleaned underneath or changed the bed. Jenny talked of running away and going back to Cottenly but Brian knew that even if it was possible to get there, *she* would only fetch them back. Brian wondered why, when it was obvious that she didn't want them here. Neither did Uncle Frank, who sent them out to play so that he could lie down on the rug with *her* and take off her clothes. He didn't think of *her* as their mother any more. Auntie Alice was their real mum and Uncle Joe was their dad until their real dad came home.

'I wonder what Mary is having for dinner,'

Jenny said.

'Something better than this.' Brian sighed, and wished Jimmy was here to cheer him up.

'By, but I've never seen weather like it,' Jack remarked as he dug his way out of the door and across the yard. The snow hadn't stopped for a month and according to the wireless thirty inches had fallen. The farm would have been completely cut off from civilisation had it not been for the tractor's managing to make a way through to the town.

'You should see the snowdrifts,' Billy said. 'There's one on the edge of the wood, I'll swear it's twenty feet deep.'

'And the Don's frozen over in places,' Sam grumbled.

'Well, at least we're warm and snug,' Ruth consoled him. 'I dread to think what the poor things in the city are going through, some of them without a roof over their heads.'

'Or a thing to call their own,' Martha added, as she kneaded a batch of dough on the kitchen table. 'And here are we, still eating like royalty. All I can say is that we're very fortunate.'

'Can we go out, mam?' Frankie was itching to try out the sledge Jack had made the twins, but the conditions had been too treacherous even for tobogganing.

'Come on.' Billy pulled on his wellingtons. 'I'll take yer to the moor edge where the slope is. We'll be safe enough if we stick to the lane. Besides, it's stopped snowing at last.'

'You'll not even find the lane,' Ruth said.

'We will. It's sheltered by the trees just there, and not too deep. They'll be safe enough with me.'

'And they'll be back in five minutes.' Martha grinned. 'As soon as they get hot aches.'

Ruth watched the excited youngsters pass the snowman old Sam had made and which had grown another five inches during the night. She frowned as she thought of Alice, wondering if there was any improvement. Dr Swinbourne had reluctantly had her admitted to the mental hospital. The place was a stark, red brick prison, not at all the setting for one of the Stanford lasses, but it had the means to treat the kind of illness Alice Jackson was suffering and some forward-thinking doctors. The modern approach seemed to be to talk out the problems with the patient, rather than filling them full of drugs so that they resembled zombies. Dr Swinbourne guessed it was Alice's infertility that was at the root of it all, brought to a head no doubt by the removal of the evacuees. Oh, but this war had a lot to answer for, and he doubted it was anywhere near over yet.

Joe was an extremely worried man. He visited the hospital whenever he was allowed and could see no improvement in his wife. His spirits dropped even further as he ambled along the never-ending corridor. There was nothing cheerful about the place. Even the pictures on the walls depressed him, in one of which a lady in long, flowing garments stood on a rock looking out on to a stormy sea. Joe thought she looked about to throw herself into the lashing waves, not the type of subject designed to uplift one's spirits. And some of the poor patients he passed were enough to chill the blood.

Alice was sitting in the communal room staring at the wall. A girl was stroking her hair, admiring the dark tresses. Others were walking unceasingly round the room, one tall, thin woman counting her steps, one – two – three – four – turn, there and back, there and back. Joe wondered how long she had been doing that and why someone didn't sit her down.

'Alice!' Her gaze never wavered. Joe sat beside her and the girl's concentration shifted from Alice's hair to Joe's. She began stroking her fingers across his head and he shook her away, not unkindly but firmly.

'Alice, how are you, love?'

Alice suddenly realised she had a visitor. 'Hello, Daddy,' she said. 'Have you come to take me home?'

'Not yet.' Joe shivered. Oh, God, Alice didn't even recognise him. 'But soon.'

'I want to go home. I want to play with our Lizzie.'

'Alice, it's Joe. Our Joseph sends his love.'

'Where's my skipping rope? Take me home. I don't like it here. Grandmother won't take down the picture, and it scares me.'

'What picture? Alice, what picture?'

'The one of Grandfather. He's dead. I don't like pictures of dead people.'

Joe felt sick. 'I'm going now, Alice. I'll be back soon. I love you, lass.' He wrapped his arms round his wife, holding her close. Then he hurried away before she saw his tears. He could hear her calling after him.

'Don't leave me here, Daddy. I want to play. I don't like it here. I want our Lizzie and Ruth.'

Joe stood in the corridor to compose himself, then went in search of a doctor. He needed to know what was happening, what was being done, and when the horror would end.

An horrific raid on London was said to have killed fourteen thousand people, but by the time Ruth's baby was born at least a bit of good news had come with the sinking of the *Bismarck* in the Atlantic.

Isaac and Emily came to see their new grand-daughter, who proved to be just as beautiful as little Margaret. Emily offered to take Margaret and keep her until Ruth was on her feet again. It would be a great help; Mrs Dolan had enough to do without an active toddler to keep under control. Besides, Emily would enjoy the chance to spoil the little girl. She picked up the new baby and as usual was reminded of the births of her own three. If only Alice had conceived again, perhaps her eldest daughter wouldn't be in the state she was in now. Still, Joe said the psychologist had made a breakthrough and Alice had shown a slight improvement. Emily hoped so, then maybe the guilt would go away, the awful feeling that she and Isaac were the ones to blame for Alice's suffering.

'What are we going to do, Brian?'

'I don't know, Jenny. I'm still thinking.'

'I'm hungry.'

'I know. Me too.' There was nothing edible in

the house, the windows had been blown out and the door was hanging on one hinge.

'And I'm cold,' Jenny added.

'I know. I told yer, I'm thinking what Jimmy would have done.'

'Jimmy would have gone to Auntie Alice's, or Auntie Ruth's.'

'Well, we haven't got an auntie, and now we haven't got a mum eiver.'

'Or a dad. I want my dad.' Jenny started crying again.

'Our dad's dead, Jenny. I told yer. The telegram came last week. Uncle Frank told us it came from the War Office.'

'I didn't believe him.' Jenny sobbed.

'Neiver did I, but he showed it to me. It's true, Jenny. He was killed in action. He was brave, our dad.'

'Well, why didn't our mam cry then?'

'Because she was a hard-hearted bitch.'

'Mrs Bradwell called her a dirty bugger as well. And she didn't love him,' Jenny said. 'She didn't love anybody. I'm glad she's dead, but not our dad. He loved us.' Jenny wiped tears and a stream of snot on her sleeve. 'How do we know she's dead? She might come back.'

'Mrs Bradwell told us. You were there, you should 'ave listened. Our mam and Uncle Frank were in the pub. You've seen the pub, Jenny. Nobody could have survived in there, it was a direct hit. We're lucky we live at this end of the street or we'd have been dead as well.'

'Why didn't Mrs Bradwell tell us what to do?'

'She will. She said she'd come back for us but

she'll have had others to see to. People wiv legs blown off and arms, and babies wiv no mams.'

'Will we be orphans, Brian?'

'We are orphans.'

'Will we have to go to an orphanage?' Jenny asked fearfully.

'No. Well, I don't know. We'll ask Mrs Bradwell for a stamp. I'll write anuvver letter to Auntie Alice. She'll know what to do. But don't tell Mrs Bradwell she's not our real auntie. Tell her she's our dad's sister, if she asks.' Brian found a fountain pen in one of Uncle Frank's jacket pockets and a sheet of paper, then he wrote in his best handwriting with their address at the top.

Dear Auntie Alice and Uncle Joe and Josef, we want to know if we can come back. Our dad as been killed in action and our mam as been killed in the pub in the air rade. There were hundreds and hundreds of bombers but Jenny and me were under the table and none of them killed us if we can come back will you send us some money becorse we avent got any for a ticket we ave looked in uncle franks pockets and there is no money. There is a nice fountin pen though. I dont expect they will need any mony to bury them wiv as they are already buryd under the pub. Please let us know before they put us in an orfanige we are orfans now you see.

Love from Brian and Jenny

PS I ave writen before but it is still under the bed becorse we avent got a stamp.

PS again I am going to sell the fountain pen and buy some food and a stamp.

'There,' Brian said. 'We'll post it tomorrow when I sell the pen down the market. Somebody'll buy it – it's a Swan. Then I'll buy us some chips or something for our dinner.'

Jennifer began to cry. 'I'm hungry now, and I'm cold.'

'I know, but we'll be warmer if we go to bed. Come on, I'll get all the bedding and coats and we'll soon get warm.'

Jennifer cried all the harder.

'Come on, if you stop crying I'll tell you the password for Jimmy's gang.' At the mention of Jimmy, Jennifer's crying miraculously ceased.

'Right,' Brian said. 'Scab and matter custard, scab and matter pie. Dead dog's giblets, cat's green eye. Hospital phlem so green and thick. Swallow it down with a cup of cold sick.'

'Oh! That's horrible,' Jennifer cried.

'I know, but we say it every day when we're in the gang. Jimmy made me learn it, but don't tell anybody I told yer when we go back.' He suddenly looked a bit wary. 'Especially not Auntie Lizzie.'

'I won't, nor Auntie Alice.'

Brian giggled. 'Especially not Auntie Alice,' he said.

Oh, dear God, what do I do? Joe's mind was in a turmoil as he watched his son read the letter. Would Alice benefit from having the children back, or would her recovery be hampered by the worry of it all? Joseph was smiling for the first time in months as he read the words. He hadn't

355

appreciated how much he missed Brian and Jenny until now. He hadn't had a breathing space to even think about them because of all the worry about his mother. But now, at last, Alice was almost herself again. Well, at least her body wasn't occupied by the mind of a tragic little girl.

The psychologist had worked miracles, brought all the fear and loneliness of the wasted years as Grandmother Stanford's companion to the surface. Alice had talked it all out, in many long and painful ordeals, and gradually a calm, relaxed and affectionate woman had emerged. Yet not once had she mentioned Brian or Jennifer; it was as though they had never existed. The psychologist had suggested leaving that episode in the past, unless Alice herself mentioned it.

Now Joe was troubled. The little ones had meant a lot to him, as well as to Alice. He couldn't turn his back on them now, not when they had no relatives, or so they said. He must find out; if there was the slightest chance of anyone turning up later and demanding the kids back, then he mustn't become involved.

'I need to go to London, Joseph,' he said. Joseph grinned.

'Are yer fetching them back, Dad?' he asked eagerly.

'No. But at least I need to make some enquiries, about any relatives they might have. They seem to have just been abandoned by the authorities and everyone.'

'And then?'

'I don't know. I don't see how I can bring them back with yer mother still in hospital.'

'But don't you see, Dad, if they were back for good, I think it would be the makings of Mam. In fact I'm sure of it.'

'Well, it might. After all, she was fine whilst they were here, and she might be again. I'll see what the doctors think. We can't risk undoing all the work they've done with her. I don't think we could face a nightmare like that again. But I still need to go to London. I can't leave them on their own without money. God knows what the authorities are thinking about.'

'Well, they've more than they can cope with, I dare say. We don't know we're born up here, Dad. When will you go?'

'As soon as I can arrange with Mr Hancock.'

'Him? How you can take orders from him I don't know. He's dead ignorant, he doesn't even say good morning, or kiss me arse.'

Joe stifled a grin. 'No need for that, but you're right, he turns his back on me an' all, lately. Don't know why.'

'The girls hate him, he's always touching 'em.'

Joe didn't know about that. He'd keep an eye on him from now on. If there was any indecent behaviour the directors must be made aware of it.

The doctors discussed Joe's suggestion and reported back, agreeing that the children's return could be just the boost Alice needed to complete her recovery. Just one point was emphasised: it would be disastrous for them to be taken away a second time. Joe already knew that, and would make certain of the situation before revealing anything to Alice. He decided to talk to Emily

357

and Isaac before going to London. After all, he would need their help and co-operation until Alice came home.

'What shall I do, Isaac?' he asked. 'If I don't get the kids now it might be too late. On the other hand, Alice can't look after them whilst she's in hospital.'

Isaac hummed and ahhed. 'I'm sure I don't know what's best, Joe, lad. For our Alice, I mean.'

'Isaac Stanford, you know damned well what's best for our Alice. The sooner those evacuees are back in Cottenly, the sooner she'll be well again.'

'But look what they did to her before? Put her in the lunatic asylum, they did.'

Joe flinched. 'No, Isaac.' He considered carefully whether to tell the couple where the blame really lay. 'The children being taken away wasn't the reason for Alice's breakdown. That was just the final straw. Alice's illness had been on its way for years. Since she was a little girl, actually.'

Isaac's mouth dropped open. Joe continued, 'It were the years at Grandmother Stanford's. Alice was terrified during her time there. All the horror has finally been released. Can you imagine all the Bible bashing continuing night and day? While all the time her sisters were enjoying a normal life. Can you imagine the atmosphere?'

'Aye, I lived there. It never did me any harm.' Isaac faltered.

Joe continued, 'Did you spend most of your time with the picture of a dead man in a coffin on the wall? That alone was enough to turn a child's mind.'

'Well, no. My father wasn't dead when I lived at

home. But she never said. Why didn't she tell us? About her fear, I mean.'

'Because she was a dutiful, obedient child. She thought it was what you wanted.'

'Well, we did, but not to make her unhappy. Why, tha should know that, Joe. We loved our Alice – we loved all our lasses.'

'Aye, she knew that, and she loved you. So she did as she was instructed, without any protest, unfortunately.'

'But Ma promised her everything, all the money, the lot. I thought it was a good thing, would set her up for life.'

'Oh aye, she got the money all right, but lost her peace of mind and almost her sanity in the bargain.'

'Oh, Joe lad, why didn't she say? To think it's me who's caused all this upset to my lass. And to thee and our Joseph.' Isaac put his head in his hands. 'Oh, Joe lad, I'm so sorry.'

Emily knelt in front of Isaac and gathered him in his arms. 'Nay, Isaac, it wasn't just you. It was me too. We didn't know but that it wasn't for our Alice's best interests – we were both as guilty.'

Joe stood uncomfortable at the sadness he had caused. 'It was nobody's fault. You were both the most loving of parents. Nobody could possibly have foreseen the outcome. Most kids would have been hardy enough to bluster their way through.' He grinned. 'No doubt your Ruth would have got the better of the old girl. But Alice – well, Alice would have been more sensitive.' He clapped his hands. 'Anyway, what do you suggest we do now?'

Emily threw back her shoulders and drew

herself tall. 'Fetch the pair back, Joe. Now, before they themselves are victims of this awful war. We can't leave them there, right in the thick of it all.'

'That's easier said than done, Emily. I have to work. I can't be responsible for two youngsters during the day, and with Alice to visit as well.'

'Fetch them home, and bring them here. We'll keep them until Alice is well again. God knows, if it's a way to relieve our consciences then it'll do us both good. What do you say, Isaac?'

Isaac relaxed a little. 'Aye. Oh, aye. It'll be a pleasure to 'ave 'em, a real pleasure.' He even managed a smile, and Joe grinned. It was what he had hoped for.

'Well, then, I'd best get off. I've a journey to plan and our Joseph to organise.'

'Send him up here, we'll look after him,' Isaac suggested eagerly.

'Who, our Joseph? Nay, he'll be up at the farm before I've got me bag packed. Taking the flaming tractor to bits or summat. Though I think your Ruth has enough on with her lot.'

'Our Ruth's like the other two, never happier than when she's a family around her.'

'But you can have enough of a good thing, surely?'

'Not the Stanford lasses,' Isaac said proudly. 'They take after their mother.' And he was right. Emily couldn't wait to get the spare room ready for Brian and Jennifer.

Olive could hardly contain her excitement. Not only was Harry home on leave, but Tom Baraclough was due home too. And to complete her happiness her dad was home for good. Uncle Joe had arranged a job for George. Sadly the doctors had decided his left arm would remain almost useless, but Joe said there was a desk job vacant and George was to be interviewed the following Monday. Olive hoped his shattered nerves would hold out – he still had bouts when he could hardly control the sweats and tremors. The sight of Harry, smart in his air force blue, always put new life into Isaac, and Lizzie seemed to have shed the careworn look she had had when George first came home. So all in all Olive was a happy and even more beautiful young woman.

Tom was to arrive early evening so Olive had taken her best dress to work and a new pair of high-heeled shoes. The dress had used up eleven of her precious clothing coupons but she didn't care. She changed after her shift and set off for the station, looking for all the world like a film star with her flushed face and new hairstyle.

It was this glamorous vision that Hubert Hancock caught sight of as he left the works to go home. It was only when he realised she was the daughter of one of the Stanford lasses that the smile on his fat face changed to a scowl. By, but she was a looker if ever there was one, almost more so than Ruth Wray, if that was possible. He removed a cigar from its carton and prepared to light it in an effort to control his excitement. Then he found his matchbox was empty. What the devil was he doing with matches anyway? He threw the box into the road and cursed Sophie for the umpteenth time for the absence of his lighter. Well, she needn't think she had won that battle. He would go now and purchase a new one. After all, he was a man of importance, a manager and a councillor. He adjusted his short, fat erection, brought on by the sight of Olive Crossman.

Olive and Tom walked from the station still entwined in each other's arms. They wanted to be alone and Olive had prepared the cottage for Tom's homecoming. Of course, they would have to wait until Tom's parents had greeted their son. 'I'll see you later, then,' Olive told him as they reached the end of Tom's street, reluctant to leave him after so short a reunion.

'Oh no you don't.' Tom grabbed her wrist and pulled her with him along the street. 'I'm only here for a week; you're not escaping that easily. You're coming with me to meet the family.'

Olive thought it was a mistake. 'They'll want you to themselves for a bit,' she said.

'Then they'll just have to want.' He grinned. 'The girl I'm going to marry comes first from now on.'

Olive stopped in her tracks. She loved Tom, she wanted to be with him all the time, but if this was a proposal it was a bit premature, she thought. 'Tom,' she whispered. 'Don't let's rush things. We've both got a job to do. I wasn't going to tell you but I've applied to be a nurse at the Royal. Let's just enjoy being together, and I mean together, at the cottage. Please don't say anything to your parents yet. There are so many things happening and everything's so uncertain.'

Tom's face had paled and she could sense his disappointment as his body tensed. 'But I

362

thought you loved me, Olive. If I were wrong, I apologise. I should have known someone like you wouldn't be serious about somebody like me.' His voice trailed off and Olive wanted to gather him into her arms, right there in the street.

'Tom, you've got it wrong. I love you, I want to be with you the whole time, but we can't. You'll be going away again in a few days. And I'll be starting my training for a whole new life. That's going to be a hell of a shock for the family, without a wedding announcement on top of it. Let's wait, Tom, please, until we can be together properly, all the time.'

Tom saw the pleading in her large, almond-shaped eyes. He saw her lips tremble and pulled her into his arms. Then the atmosphere changed and he laughed. 'You're a witch, do you know that? And I don't mean with your herbs and cures and God knows what else you concoct. I mean a real witch, who can bewitch a man just by looking at him. OK, we'll wait, but I'm warning you, I won't stay at the cottage, not at night anyway. I respect you too much. You're too precious to have your reputation ruined.'

'OK.' Olive grinned.

But they both reckoned without the witchcraft the cottage was capable of, and the sexual attraction of a couple in love.

George was trembling and his face was deathly white when he returned from his interview. He had known almost immediately that his job application had been unsuccessful. Hubert Hancock had not even turned him down gently, simply told him he couldn't be expected to set on every lame dog that limped home from the war.

George, still not recovered from his injuries, had felt an urge to smash his good fist into the fat, pug face. Managing to resist the impulse he had simply pointed out that all the lame dogs had been fighting for the likes of Hubert Hancock. Then the shock had set in. If he couldn't get a job what would Lizzie and the children do? Oh, God. If only Joe hadn't gone to London. Surely he would have stood up for him? Surely Joe's recommendation would have been enough? But Joe wasn't here.

After George left the office Hubert leaned back comfortably in his chair, put his feet up on the desk and lit a cigar. He had vowed revenge on the Stanford lasses, and the payback had begun, and by God he hadn't finished yet, not by a mile.

Both Tom and Harry were unwilling to discuss anything to do with the war and George wondered if Harry would have spoken much at all had it not been for Jimmy and Ernest Edward wanting to know all the gory details, such as how many dead Germans had Harry seen and had he seen a Blenheim bomber and how fast could they fly. Harry seemed so preoccupied with his thoughts that George wondered to what horrors his son would be returning at the end of his leave. He prayed Harry would be spared the terror George had already experienced.

Tom, on the other hand, wanted nothing to mar the time he had with Olive. Despite his reluctance to stay the night, once he found himself at the cottage with Olive it was impossible to tear himself away and it was early morning before they locked up each time and went their separate ways. Fortunately Tom's concern for his lover meant he was sensible enough to take precautions and make sure Olive didn't become pregnant. This was a relief to Olive, who intended throwing herself wholeheartedly into her nurse's training. But first she had to tell her parents and give up her present job. However, until Tom Baraclough left she was determined nothing was going to spoil their time together. Olive had a feeling it would be a long time before she saw her wonderful man again.

Chapter Eleven

Elizabeth Dolan, adorned in an Irish lace christening gown worn by her father and grandmother before her, was baptised at Cottenly chapel on a crisp, bright autumn day. Alice and Lizzie were her doting godmothers. Though Alice was still pale and slimmer than she had ever been, the protective cage she had built round herself so many years ago had vanished, leaving a softer, still beautiful woman, one capable, at last, of giving and receiving affection, without the fear of its being withdrawn. She was wearing a smart two-piece in a soft shade of powder blue, instead of the black she had favoured for so long. She smiled serenely down on the sleeping child and glanced at Joseph, a son to be proud of who had proved his love for her during her illness. She smiled at her mother and her father and vowed to tell them how much she cared for them, something she had never said to either of them even though nobody could possibly have had more loving parents. Then she thought of Joe with a rush of emotion she would until recently have been incapable of.

Where was Joe? He had promised to be here in time. It wasn't like him not to keep his word.

Alice handed her baby niece into the preacher's arms and Elizabeth began to cry, drowning the sound of the chapel door opening and closing gently. She felt a hand tuck itself into hers and looked down into a freckled, smiling face. Alice's heart missed a beat and she looked round wildly for Joe, wondering if the madness was returning, but Joe was smiling and nodding reassuringly. By his side stood Brian, grinning like the Cheshire cat in Wonderland.

The preacher was oblivious of the miracle taking place at the font. The miracle of Alice and Joe's family coming home.

Hubert Hancock knew about Olive's cottage. He had stalked her like a cat after its prey. He had watched her remove the key from its hiding place and let herself in on most nights. He didn't know what she did in there but he knew what he'd like to do to her. In fact it was becoming an obsession, transferred from the unobtainable Ruth Wray to the delectable young girl. He knew the soldier had gone and was planning carefully how to achieve his goal. He knew where she went each night and the time she arrived at the cottage before going home. All he had to do now was await his opportunity.

'What's up with our Billy?' Jack asked. 'He's quiet lately.'

'Love's young dream,' Ruth answered. 'Joan Sanderson.'

'Oh, that's all reight then. I thought it was something wrong.'

Billy was quiet, and it was true, he was pretty serious about Joan. But that wasn't the reason for his silence. The truth was he was wondering what his mother would say about the fact that he intended to join the army. He didn't need to go, in fact Jack would say he couldn't be spared, but Billy knew the land girls were every bit as competent as himself. Besides, Frankie was proving to be a boon to Jack. It wasn't that he wanted to go, and if the truth were told he didn't know if he could bring himself to kill a man, even if he was a German. He just couldn't hide away on the farm whilst Harry and other Cottenly lads were away fighting his war. Besides, Joseph said he was going, even though Uncle Joe said he was in a reserved occupation and didn't have to. Joseph had made his decision and was just waiting. There was time yet before Billy was of the age to go, but go he would, even though it would break his heart to leave the farm and everybody in it. In the meantime he had Joan to think about. He was meeting her tonight and if he was lucky he might get a feel inside her blouse. He didn't expect more; Joan was a good girl and he intended keeping her that way.

The key turned in the lock and he replaced it in its hiding place, went in and closed the door. It was pitch black with the blinds still closed from last night. He felt the excitement mounting as he knew she would just about be leaving the first-aid class. The herbs hung pungent in the air and another scent, musky and sweet, disturbed his senses. He waited, poised to take her when she came through the door, from behind so that she couldn't see his face. On the off chance of her recognising him he would threaten her with dismissal. Anyway, no one would believe her. They wouldn't dare. Hubert Hancock was too important in the town and even the ones who didn't work under him themselves had somebody close who did.

Olive wondered why the key didn't turn. She must have forgotten to lock up last night. She must be more careful in future; Grandma Burlington's things were too precious to lose. She closed the door and picked up a box of matches to light the gas. The arm came round her body, fingers clasping her breast. Olive screamed, loud enough to waken the dead in Cottenly churchyard, before a palm stifled the sound. She bit as hard as she could, knocking her teeth against a ring. He tore his hand away and fumbled with her dress, lifting her skirt, his fat, podgy fingers feeling her bare thighs above her stockings, then ascending to the soft mound between her legs. She knew he was unbuttoning his trousers and made a sudden, violent attempt to escape, grabbing the door latch and yanking it open, screaming the whole time. Thank God, somebody was coming.

'Olive, is that you?' Billy heard footsteps slithering on the earth but he was too concerned about Olive to give chase. Followed by Joan, he sprinted across the garden towards the cottage. Olive was trying to strike a match but her hands were trembling so violently the contents of the box spilled out on to the floor.

'What's up, Olive?' Billy couldn't bear the idea of anything happening to his precious cousin. 'What happened?'

'Did – did you see him?' Olive stammered.

'Who?'

'I don't know. Oh, he was horrible. He tried to rape me.'

'Oh, no.' Joan held Olive in her arms while Billy turned on the gas. 'Did he ... did he...' Joan couldn't voice her question.

'No. Oh, no.' Olive started to cry uncontrollably. 'He touched me, though. Oh, Billy, he was awful, repulsive. He smelt of cigar smoke and he was fat.'

'Did you see him?' Billy led Olive to the couch. Joan looked round and filled the kettle, placing it on the gas ring.

'No, he was waiting for me. He grabbed me from behind. Oh, Billy, it makes me sick just thinking about it.'

'I'm going for the police. Stay with Olive, love.'

'OK. I'll make some tea,' Joan said.

'I've only camomile or peppermint.'

'It doesn't matter, if that's what you like.'

Olive sipped at the hot camomile. It seemed to soothe her and she gradually stopped shaking. Joan pulled a face at the taste, but drank it all the same.

'Who would want to do such a thing?' Olive cried.

'Anybody, I should think. I mean, any man would fancy you, Olive. All the lads remark on how gorgeous you are.' Joan tried to lighten the mood and cheer Olive up a bit.

'But he wasn't a lad, I'm sure he wasn't. He was old. And who do we know who wears a ring?'

That was a question the constable was to ask himself. Cigars? Rings? Not many men in Cottenly. Well, that should narrow down the search. Without any evidence, though, there wasn't much could be done, and as far as he could see there was none, except the key and the door sneck. If any fingerprints could be detected, they might just possibly find their man.

Olive wasn't much the worse for her ordeal. The family seemed to be more upset by the incident than Olive herself. But then, Olive didn't have time to feel sorry for herself. She had a new job to think about. Billy was relieved that she wouldn't be at the cottage so much when she began at the hospital. He would never have had peace of mind otherwise. He did wonder, though, if she might let him keep his eye on the place for her. He and Joan, of course. It was cold in winter, standing out on the river bank for a goodnight kiss. There was a nice, comfortable couch in there, and even a bed. But no, Joan was a nice girl and he loved her so he wouldn't think about beds. He would offer to look after the cottage anyway, and the first thing Olive must do was stop leaving the key handy for the likes of rapists and thieves.

For Alice, Christmas really was the best one ever. The adoption of Brian and Jennifer had been straightforward and the children would soon legally belong to the Jacksons. Alice might have been less exuberant had she known of Joseph's plans for the new year. Joseph was a good worker and at the turnover of the department to the manufacture of Bren guns he was certainly in an essential occupation. However, rather than inspecting them, Joseph wanted to be firing them. He knew that he could safely break the news to Alice now she had the little ones to take his place. A new brother and sister had their uses, after all.

The family gathering was to take place at Alice's this year and though Emily protested she was actually relieved not to have to do the organising. After all, she and Isaac were not getting any younger, though they were both loath to admit it. The poultry, as usual, was supplied by Martha, and though the Christmas pudding was more carrot than fruit it was doubtful if any other family in Cottenly enjoyed better fare. Afterwards Jenny asked if she could play the piano. Alice said she was a born pianist.

'Shall I play some carols?' Jennifer asked.

'No.' said Alice. 'Play something more cheerful.' Joe spluttered in his drink and Alice wondered why everyone was laughing, then she joined in the laughter, happier than she had ever thought it possible to be.

On Christmas morning the farm as usual was like a madhouse. Presents were opened and admired and Jack was surprised when Frankie and Sadie gave him a present, something tiny wrapped up in brown paper.

'That's for you, for being such a nice dad.' Sadie blushed as she handed it over.

'We didn't buy it, though,' Frankie added. 'We found it.'

Jack opened the roughly wrapped package to find a cigarette lighter.

'I've polished it up,' said Sadie. 'And it's got a pattern on.'

'Well, you've certainly made it shine,' Jack said. And no wonder, he thought. The lighter was solid gold, and the pattern was a pair of initials, HH. 'Where did you find it, love?'

'In the Dutch barn,' Frankie said proudly.

'Hmm. Well, it's lovely. Thank you very much.' Jack gave each of the twins a hug, his mind in a turmoil. As far as he knew, nobody at the farm smoked except old Sam, and he had never bothered with a lighter. He would never have smoked in the barn anyway. He would discuss it with Ruth later, but perhaps he should pay another visit to the police station. Of course there were the land girls, he would ask Billy about them, but neither of them had names beginning with H, and he doubted if they would own a gold lighter anyway.

It was almost midnight before he had the chance to mention his suspicion to Ruth. Ruth pondered on the subject for a while, sure in her mind that the lighter and the fire were connected. It was when she awoke in the early hours that the initials began to register and the puzzle was solved. She began to shake. Sam had described the man as fat, well dressed and not young. She shook Jack awake.

'Jack,' she whispered, 'I know who fired the barn.'

'What?' Jack was instantly awake. 'Who?'

'Hubert Hancock.'

'Who's Hubert Hancock?'

'Councillor Hancock, manager of the wire mill.'

'A manager? Why would a manager want to do

such a thing?'

Ruth couldn't control the tremor. All the terror of the days after Walter's death returned, the house in Wire Mill Place, the sight of Hubert Hancock sitting in the chair, his eyes undressing her as she fought to avoid his hands. Oh, why hadn't she confided in Jack at the time? It was so much worse now, to try to explain. 'Because he fancied me and I spurned him. Ask Winnie Armitage, she'll tell you.' Ruth told the whole story, right from the day she went to his office. Jack reached out and took her hand and she wondered again why she hadn't told him at the time. It could have saved the barn from being fired.

'Aye, well, it seems you might be reight,' Jack said. 'We'll go see Reynolds first thing.'

'But it's Boxing Day.'

'Oh, aye. We'll give the man a break. We'll go the day after.'

Ruth suddenly jumped up in bed. 'Oh, God,' she whispered. 'Our Olive. It was him who broke into the cottage, who laid his filthy hands on her.'

'Here, hold on, we don't know that.'

'We do. I do – it's just the way he is. I'll bet my life on its being him.'

'Well, we can't do anything about it just now. Try to get a couple of hours' sleep.' They both knew they wouldn't sleep until Hubert Hancock was behind bars, but Ruth snuggled down into her husband's warm embrace. Here at least she knew she was safe.

Sergeant Reynolds experienced immense satisfaction on arresting Hubert Hancock on suspicion of arson and attempted rape. The thought of little Olive – as he always thought of her – being mauled by that jumped-up, pompous prick made his blood boil. Especially as it took place in Old Mother Buttercup's place. Sergeant Reynolds had always had the greatest respect for Old Mother and little Olive had been like a daughter to her. On the other hand Hancock had been a thorn in his side ever since he married Sophie. If the truth were known Reynolds had fancied Sophie himself and had heard of the life she endured at the hands of that vain, arrogant creature.

On the day Sergeant Reynolds arrested her husband Sophie packed her bags. She would always have a home with her unmarried sister in their late parents' house. In fact she could just hear her now, saying, 'We all told you so.'

Hubert was in the office when they came for him. He wasn't too worried when his secretary showed them in. Nobody had any evidence and even if the girl suspected, who would believe a mill girl against a public figure? However, his fat, flabby mouth dropped open when Reynolds spoke. 'Hubert Hancock, I am arresting you on suspicion of arson, breaking and entering and attempted rape.'

Reynolds knew the man was guilty even before the fingerprints proved to be those of the charged. His face gave him away the moment the lighter was produced. Reynolds stared at the man with distaste. For one thing, he was a Conservative and Reynolds had leanings to the left. Well, he wouldn't be anything for much longer, neither councillor, public figure nor manager of the

works. Nobody would give a position of importance to a man who had done time.

George Crossman began work in Joe's office the
following Monday, and proved to be as competent
as the next man, and though he mentioned it to no
one he thought he noticed pins and needles in his
wounded arm, surely a sign of better things to
come.

Joseph was the next member of the family to go
to war. By this time Alice – though still on
medication – seemed to be almost recovered and
surprised her son by holding him close and
planting a warm kiss on his cheek as they waited
for the train. 'Come home safely, son,' she
whispered, 'and remember we love you.'
   There was no embarrassment between mother
and son. Both had decided during Alice's illness
that feelings must be expressed, particularly in
wartime when boys going away never knew if
they would return. Joseph did return, along with
Billy, who had followed his cousin into the army
as soon as he could. Fortunately, the war was
almost over by that time, and both came back
unscathed: Joseph to return to the mill, this time
to a position in the motor room, and eventually
to become the proud owner of a gleaming BSA
motor bike.
   Billy had always loved the farm, but never
realised quite how much until he went away. The
day he returned for good he walked across the
field and stood by the stile. He breathed in the
odours of the land and cast his eyes down towards

Cottenly and over in the direction of Warren-tickle. His eyes followed the river towards the town and over the rooftops of Wire Mill Place. For the first time since it happened he allowed himself to think back to the night of his father's death. Always before he had closed his mind to the nightmare incident; now he found he could recall it in perfect detail. The beating of his mother and brother. The fear on his little sister's face. The hatred he had felt for his father as he plunged the knife into the flesh of his arm. He acknowledged the guilt he had been aware of deep down inside. Guilt that he had never mourned the drowning of his father, never felt grief at his passing. Now he could remember without regret. It was the men who would never come home at all, good men, brave men, who were the ones to be mourned. Billy put the thought of Walter Wray out of his mind once and for all. He couldn't think of him as a father, just a cowardly bully, not worthy of a lost night's sleep.

Billy jumped the stile and went towards the house, to his mother, to Frankie and his sisters and the man who was in every sense his father. The old dog sensed his approach and lolloped towards him. Billy hurried across the land he loved and was to work on for the rest of his days. By his side would be Joan Sanderson, who had remained a good girl for the duration of the war.

He heard the commotion in the kitchen as Grandma Dolan shooed a huge red rooster from off the table. Oh, it was good to be home.

Everyone in Cottenly turned out to celebrate VE

Day. Even the poor souls whose loved ones had failed to return from the war decided that an end to the atrocities called for some kind of celebration, if only for the sake of the children. Jack had delivered a cartload of tree branches to the Twenty Row so that a bonfire could be erected, adding to the string of fires which were to light up the countryside for the first time in years. He had thrown in a sack of potatoes so that the little ones could have potatoes roasted in their jackets: God knows little else was available for the large, impoverished families. Jack, however, had underestimated the residents of the Twenty Row and the surrounding streets. A battered old piano was already in pride of place outside one of the houses, and bunting was hanging from each of the bedroom windows across to the outside lavatories. Tables were already covered with white – if threadbare – linen and whatever rations anyone could spare had been pooled to make some kind of party. The bonfire supplied by Jack would be the crowning glory for kiddies and grown-ups alike.

'You're a bloody angel, Jack Dolan. These 'ere taties'll go down a treat,' Jack was told. 'There'll be no livelier party this side of Sheffield, once we get a good owd-fashioned knees-up going.' Jack almost wished he was staying to join them but Isaac had already decided that this night would be something his grandchildren would remember long after he had shuffled off to the next world. A crate of Nut Brown had been delivered to the Stanfords', along with pop and crisps for the youngsters and port for the ladies.

'You're turning into a right old boozer,' Emily

chided Isaac good-naturedly.

'Nay, lass, if I can't celebrate all the lads coming home safely, I reckon it's a sad day.' Isaac smiled. 'I reckon we're fortunate, thee and me, lass.'

It was much later when Tom Baraclough returned, having spent time as a prisoner of war. He came back only half the man who had gone away, but Olive with her potions and witchcraft soon helped him back to his former state of health. Olive remained at the Royal Hospital until she and Tom were married and settled in Buttercup Cottage, where little David George was born. Lizzie was on cloud seven when she held her grandson in her arms for the first time. 'He's beautiful,' she said.

'I know.' Olive straightened her son's bib. 'He's going to be a clever one, this one, just mark my words.' Lizzie's face paled. 'What? What have I said?'

'The very words Old Mother said about Harry.'

'Well, she turned out to be right. Our Harry is a clever one.'

'I know. It was just uncanny, the way you quoted her very words.'

'It's always happening.' Olive frowned. 'It's as though her thoughts are here in my head, like she's thinking for me. In fact according to Grandma Burlington I'm ready to set up stall in Castle Market. She told me in a dream. Tom thinks I'm daft but it's true. Do you think I'm stupid, Mam?'

Lizzie cuddled little David closer. 'Who am I to say? I only know she had the gift when she was

379

alive; none of us can speak for the dead. I know one thing, though: if Old Mother's guiding you, it'll be in the right direction.'

'So you think I should take on the market stall?'

'Well, it was always your intention, but it'll be hard work. And what about David? I'll help out but he's going to need his mum. And what about Tom?'

'Tom's all for it, and I wouldn't be standing the market. I thought perhaps Bessie would run the stall for me. She's always shown an interest in my work and she's outgoing enough to enjoy serving the customers. I could prepare the stock at home and look after David. What do you think?'

Lizzie laughed. 'Don't ask me. If Old Mother says so, then go ahead.'

Olive did go ahead and eventually, guided by Grandma Burlington – or so she said – invested some of her inheritance in her own health and beauty store, not in the market but right in the heart of the shopping centre in the city, where she employed Bessie, Sadie and Mary – who had outgrown her frailty and was turning into another beauty. Olive's herbal creams and remedies became quite famous, especially the Blue Burlington perfume. Buttercup Cottage was eventually extended, but not until after daughter Rose came on the scene, just as beautiful and bewitching as her mother.

Wing Commander Harry Crossman suffered nothing worse than a burst eardrum. Beneath the surface, though, was another matter. The sight and sound of his friends and comrades flying to their destruction would live for ever in his memory. Harry told no one of the horrors but vowed to take his grandfather's advice and work towards a position where he would do all in his power to prevent another war.

Jennifer Smith remembered her promise and married Jimmy Crossman. Together they ran the Mobile Music business, entertaining at functions, weddings and parties, travelling the length and breadth of the county until Jimmy was offered a residential position in one of Sheffield's top night spots. With his quick wit and ready patter he was probably one of the city's most popular DJs. However, he never lost his love of classical music, inherited from his beloved Grandad Crossman.

Ernest Edward followed his father into the tyre mill, looking forward to promotion now that Uncle Joe had been given the job made vacant by Hubert Hancock, who would be seeking other employment in a few years' time.

Sergeant Reynolds knew that divorces were long, drawn-out affairs but he was a patient man. In the meantime Winnie Armitage was keeping him informed regarding Sophie's health.

Jack Dolan and Billy made a good team as they worked their beloved land. The farm continued to flourish and Frankie expanded the haulage side. According to Frankie, he had always wanted to be a rag and bone man, but then, he had his second dad as a prime example.

Brian Smith became a bus driver and cringed every time he did the Cottenly run, expecting at any moment a boulder to come tumbling down and in through the windscreen, or a ghost to put in an appearance on dark, moonless nights.

Isaac Stanford passed away peacefully in 1955, surrounded by Emily and his three lovely lasses. At the foot of the bed stood his eldest grandson, Harry Crossman, newly elected Labour MP for Cottenly and Warrentickle.

Isaac died a proud and contented man.

The publishers hope that this book has given you enjoyable reading. Large Print Books are especially designed to be as easy to see and hold as possible. If you wish a complete list of our books please ask at your local library or write directly to:

Magna Large Print Books
Magna House, Long Preston,
Skipton, North Yorkshire.
BD23 4ND

This Large Print Book for the partially sighted, who cannot read normal print, is published under the auspices of

THE ULVERSCROFT FOUNDATION